Patterns of

CELIA MICKLEFIELD

Patterns of Our Lives Celia Micklefield
PATTERNS OF OUR LIVES

Copyright © 2014 Celia Micklefield

Celia Micklefield hereby asserts the moral right to be identified as the author of this work of fiction

All rights reserved.

Second edition 2021

No part of this publication may be reproduced, stored in a retrieval system, or transmitted, in any form or by any means, electronic, mechanical, photocopying, recording or otherwise, without the prior permission of the author.

ISBN-10: 1499329393

ISBN-13: 978-1499329391

All characters in this publication are fictitious and any resemblance to real persons, living or dead is coincidental

PATTERNS OF OUR LIVES

This book is for my family. All of them. Where would any of us be without the people who went before us?

ACKNOWLEDGMENTS

I have borrowed very heavily on knowledge of my birthplace. I hope the good people of Keighley, West Yorkshire will forgive my free-handed messing with its geography and that of its neighbour, Bingley, in my creation of Kingsley.

I'm also guilty of a similar amount of messing with my Norfolk settings. I must ask their forgiveness too, but I think it will be all right. Norfolk folk may take their time in getting to know you, but once they call you friend, it's a title you keep forever.

I even pinched my best friend's surname. I know she'll forgive me.

Patterns of Our Lives Celia Micklefield

Photographs used in the cover design are the property of the author.

Patterns of Our Lives Celia Micklefield

PROLOGUE

NOVEMBER 2010

Cameras flash as I mount the steps to The Forum Exhibition Centre. A glittering crowd of city dignitaries and well-wishers waits to greet me and other celebrated Norfolk names. There's a buzz of conversation, a sea of excited fans, arms holding up cameras and mobile phones.

'Mrs Freeman,' someone calls above the clamour, 'how does it feel to be famous at your age?'

My agent hurries me along.

'There'll be an opportunity for questions after dinner,' she tells the press.

But the question has lodged in my thoughts. I've often searched for the answer to that one. It still amazes me that all these people want to talk to me. I never sought fame. How *does* that make me feel?

Unreal.

I take hold of my agent's arm and I'm still thinking about the journalist's question as we enter the dining hall. The room is very grand. High ceilings and lots of chrome and glass reflecting light from massive light fittings. I couldn't call them chandeliers; they're too modern for that with arms that go off at unusual angles. I rather like them. I appreciate a mix of old and new, a bit like this building and me.

There are waiters everywhere wearing livery and serious faces. But, I'm just Audrey Freeman. How did all this happen?

Who could have guessed the impact of my paintings and bronzes of a goose playing with a baby? Who could have foreseen the popularity of Walsingham Matilda? She's a household name today. She's why I'm here.

We're moving toward the top table where there's an ice sculpture of one of my own creations. It's very good. I tell my agent so. The artist has captured Matilda's expression, her way of tilting her head at you.

Matilda the goose is with her own kind now where she belongs. She was literally a flying visitor in my life who stayed for the briefest time and in that short episode changed everything. Her image will stay with me forever. I often look at the photographs I took of her.

We take our places at the top table. The waiter behind my chair looks like a schoolboy, very nervous. I smile at him and I can tell he doesn't know whether he's supposed to smile back. No matter. I can't worry about that just now. The room grows noisy; voices buzz. I want to laugh at the heavy seriousness of all this ceremony. I want to tell my mother about it.

How strange to think that now.

You want to tell your mother, Audrey? Good grief, woman, get a grip.

But, even elderly women like me have those thoughts from time to time. I don't think you ever stop thinking about your mother.

Everybody keeps old photograph albums, don't they? With all those little black and white snaps glued inside? Pictures of your parents or grandparents sitting on a picnic rug in the park with a huge *Silver Cross* pram in the background. Hundreds of little photographs taken with an old *box brownie* in the days before digital cameras and computers and all the rest?

I will always treasure all my old albums. Family pictures are important to me. I often take them out and look at them. But I know now those small, square prints are only illusions. They are veiled images of fleeting moments exactly like the ones taken outside just now. They are like covers on a novel; they don't tell you everything.

I have learned the truth behind the snapshots in my family album and it doesn't matter. It isn't a problem. When I think of my mother, it's still the face of a young Jean Thompson that I see. There she sits in the favourite photograph I have of her, proudly posing with the silver trophy she had won for her gymnastics. Jean Thompson, with her long legs sprawled in front of her and her thighs disappearing into a pair of woolly gym knickers. She was a remarkable woman. Her story couldn't happen today. Nor mine.

PART ONE

ONE

SNAPSHOTS 1935-1937

Jean Thompson raced along the street, the soles of her shoes ringing against the sandstone pavement. People stared and made way for the twelve year old as she flew past, her hair tousled and bouncing around her face, her arms pumping at her sides. Long legs stretching out, she crossed over the main road in six easy strides and continued on around the corner by the grocery store. Down the lane and past the Drill Hall, she darted around another corner and disappeared into a narrow alleyway between two rows of houses. She slowed at the end of the passageway where it opened into a large shared courtyard at the back of the houses. She came to rest on the doorstep of her sister's house. Catching her breath, she hammered on the door and bellowed.

'Hilda. Hilda! Let me in. It's me. Let me in. Quick.'

A man's bespectacled face appeared at the window, disappeared and then the door opened. Jean fell inside.

'George, I want Hilda,' she gasped, collapsing into a chair by the fire grate.

'She's not here, love. She's on late turn today. Won't be back for another couple hours.'

Jean leaned forward, rested her head on her knees, threw her arms over her head and sobbed loudly.

'Now then,' George said, his voice kind and soft, 'what's going on?'

George had a different way of speaking. He was the only foreigner Jean knew. His English pronunciation was a mixture of the sounds of his Polish roots and the Yorkshire accent he'd acquired since leaving his homeland as a small boy. Jean knew her parents disapproved of Hilda's choice of husband. He was five years younger than Hilda and Jean had heard her parents call him names. But it didn't matter to her that he was a foreigner. He was kind and she liked him. She admired his thick black hair and

Clark Gable moustache. When he took his glasses off he was quite good-looking.

'Come on, Jean,' he said. 'Tell me what has happened.'

'It's them, me mam and dad,' she said between sobs. 'They're at it again. She's got him pinned up against the mantelpiece with the sweeping brush against his neck.'

Jean heard George sigh. She'd lost count of the times George had done his best to intervene. It made no difference. Mary and Charlie, Jean and Hilda's parents, would never stop having a go at each other, whatever anybody said. George knelt beside her and stroked her hair out of her eyes.

'How did it start this time?' he asked.

'They came in from the Black Horse and me mam started to make us our tea. Me dad sat down at the table on a stool, and forgot he wasn't on a chair. He leaned back and fell right over backwards. I couldn't help laughing, George, honest I couldn't 'cos his legs went up in the air and he rolled over backwards. He just looked so stupid all in a heap on the floor. I couldn't stop laughing.'

George put his hand over his mouth. Then he said,

'What happened next?'

'He got mad. He got right mad with me. He got up and started unbuckling his belt. Me mam saw what he was going to do and grabbed the sweeping brush. I legged it. George, she'll kill 'im. He's so drunk he doesn't know where he is. She'll kill 'im!'

'No she won't, no she won't. She'll get him into bed to sleep it off, that's what she'll do. Now come here, and sit up at the table and I'll get you something to drink. We've got Dandelion and Burdock. You like that, don't you?'

Jean stopped her sobbing and wiped her eyes. She got up from the fireside chair and went to the table. George took the fizzy drink from the cupboard by the sink and handed it to her. She drained the glass and thanked him.

'George?'

'Yes?'

'Do you think I could come and live with you and our Hilda?'

'I think we'd better wait till she comes home before we start talking about that, love. Now don't start crying again. You'll give yourself headache. Just be patient a bit. We'll talk about it later. I promise. Right then, let's go to the park, and on the way back we'll get some fish and chips. How does that sound?'

'It sounds nice. But George?'

'What?'

'Do we have to go to the park? I'm too old for swings.'

'Don't be daft, lass. You're never too old for swings. Come on, Twinkletoes, I'll race you.'

◆

By the time George caught up with her and came puffing into the playground area of the public park, Jean was sitting waiting for him. She was trailing her toes in the dust below the swing, rocking gently to and fro, her arms wrapped around the chains.

'What kept you?' she said.

'Less of your cheek,' George said.

'Ha, ha,' she laughed. 'You'll have to do better than that if you want to catch me.'

'Jean Thompson, where did you learn to run like that?' George said as he took the swing next to her. 'You're the fastest thing I've ever seen on two legs.'

'I know. I don't know why. I just can, that's all. I can even beat all the boys.'

George smiled. It wouldn't be long before she learned different. The time wasn't too far away when she'd know to slow down and let the boys catch her. She had a pretty face underneath all that wild hair, a slim figure and long legs. She was at that age when girls needed guidance about growing up into nice, young ladies. She wouldn't get that from her parents. Hilda would be the best one to help Jean with all those women's problems.

'Miss Linford says I might be able to go in for some competitions when I'm a bit older.'

'That's good news. What does your mother say?'

He regretted the words as soon as he said them. Fool, he told himself. The child doesn't need reminding about that useless pair, propping up the bars till throwing out time, making a comedy of themselves in front of the whole town.

'She says I have to leave school and get a job.'

'Well that won't stop you going to your evening club, though, will it? You'll still be able to do your sports.'

Jean stopped rocking on the swing and her face clouded.

'It might stop me if I have to go down the mill. Hilda says working down there isn't good for you. It made her cough.'

'Yes, love that's why she left and went on the trolley buses.'

'She told me how being out in the fresh air, even if it's raining is better than breathing in all that fluff. Do you remember, she used to come home with fluffy bits all over her hair and clothes?'

'She did.'

George smiled at Jean's innocence. There was no doubt, she was a lovely girl and she didn't deserve to have Mary and Charlie for parents. He would like to take her in and help her grow and develop into a proper young woman. She didn't have Hilda's strength and determination. She couldn't stand up to her parents like Hilda had. She needed someone to look out for her. It would be an honour to step in and help the only family he had. As far as he was concerned, the time had come to put things right. Let Mary and Charlie continue their carry-on. Let them give all their money to the landlords, making a laughing stock of themselves. Let Jean come and live with them, where she'd have some security, some stability. He and Hilda would love her as their own daughter. And if ever they did have little ones of their own, why, it would be better still. He could hardly wait for Hilda to come home from work to tell her the news.

◆

They heard her coming. Jean recognised the rhythm of her sister's footsteps echoing through the narrow passageway as she strode up to the door.

'Hello,' she said, kissed her husband and kicked off her shoes. 'Have you come for tea, Jean? Everything all right, love?'

George pursed his lips and signalled to Jean not to say anything yet.

'Fish and chips keeping warm in the oven,' he said. 'Are you ready to eat, Hilda?'

'Just give me a minute.' She put her jacket on a coat hanger and hung it behind the back door. At the butler's sink in the corner of the room, she washed away the grimy evidence of all the coins she'd handled through her day's work.

Proudly, George regarded his wife. She was twenty six and beautiful. In her stockinged feet she cut a neat and tidy figure, more petite than her young sister with smaller features and paler colouring. She wore her fair hair in a short bob that stopped at the collar of her conductress's uniform, which she kept immaculately pressed.

'Look at these,' she said, holding out her hands. 'I'll never have nice nails in this job. I've broken two today, scrabbling for change in my money pouch.'

She pulled on a cotton wrap-around pinafore over her white shirt and rolled up her sleeves. 'Come on, then. Let's tuck in.'

George waited till after supper was finished and things cleared away. He winked at Jean.

'Hilda,' he said. 'Jean's got something to tell you. Haven't you, love?'

The story wasn't long in the telling. Jean raced through the events culminating in the sweeping brush, the mantelpiece and the unbuckling of Charlie's belt. Hilda dashed up from the table.

'Did he touch you, Jean? Did he? I tell you now, George, if he so much as laid a finger on our Jean, I'll do me mother a favour and kill him meself. I'm sick of him!'

'So can I stay with you then?' Jean pleaded.

'You can stay tonight. Tomorrow, we're going round there and sort him out once and for all.'

'I've got school tomorrow and I won't have any clean clothes to put on.'

'I'll lend you one of my nightdresses, love. Go and put it on now and bring me down your underwear and socks. I'll wash them in the sink. They'll dry in the oven and be ready for you in the morning. Now, you're not to worry about a thing, Jean. Leave it to me and George. We'll take care of it. Won't we, George?'

'Yes, love,' he said with a satisfied grin.

It warmed him to know his wife and young sister-in-law felt they could depend on him, trusted him to do the right thing. He drew himself up to his full height and smoothed his moustache in the mirror over the fireplace. He adjusted his spectacles. *Bottle bottoms*, the kids at school used to call them. *Speccy-four-eyes* they used to shout after him whenever he walked past a group of boys.

All that didn't matter now. He never felt more of a real man than he did at that moment, with his own small family around him, needing him. He sighed with contentment and began to plan how he would handle the Thompsons. A few well-chosen words would avoid further trouble, he believed. Carefully handled, without appearing condescending he would be able to encourage them to see the right thing to do. If he could get Mary Thompson on her own first, he'd point out the mutual benefits of the arrangement. The matter just needed a bit more careful thought.

Jean appeared at the bottom of the stairs holding out the things to be washed.

'Hilda?' she asked quietly.

'Yes, love?'

'Why are me mam and dad so horrible?'

'It's just how they are, Jean. Take no notice.'

'Have they always been like that? Was it the same when you were at home?'

Hilda put her arms around her little sister and drew her close.

'Jean, sweetheart, I couldn't wait to get away from them. They should never have had children, those two. But I'm glad they did or else we wouldn't have each other, would we?'

TWO

Kingsley Modern School lived up to its name. Designed at the height of the Art Deco period, in 1935, after the first few years' intake, it still looked brand new. Its iconic clean lines fanned out smartly behind a colonnaded foyer encompassing blocks of spacious, airy classrooms surrounded by grass playing fields that ran down the slope to the river. Tall windows on every side ensured that corridors and classrooms were always bathed in light. It was a far cry from the gloomy Victorian- era primary schools, where the windows could only be reached by a long pole, and where the dark brown and green tiled walls made the narrow corridors dark unwelcoming places.

The Modern School breathed; it breathed life and hope into the young minds attending classes. There were new subjects to study; there was new equipment and there was a brand new body of staff, pleased and proud to take their places in the first of a new generation of educational reform.

Sandra Logan cared nothing for these new opportunities. As she crept down the riverbank, out of sight of the staffroom and the caretaker's lodge, she chuckled to herself at the stupidity of the out of bounds rule the school had placed on her favourite hidey-hole.

'Come on, Jean,' she called. 'Be quick. Come on. Stop faffing. Nobody can see us.'

'Are you sure? I don't want to get into trouble,' Jean whispered, edging along the grassy bank on her backside.

'Course I'm sure. Look, sit down there behind that tree.' Sandra delved under the tea towel covering her domestic science basket and brought out a packet of Woodbines. 'Want one?' she offered.

'No thanks. Where did you get them?'

'Off our Ronnie. He gives me them sometimes.'

'The teachers will know you've been smoking, Sandra. They'll be able to smell it on you.'

'No they won't. They all smoke. They're in there smoking now. Haven't you ever been to the staffroom at dinnertime? When they open the door the smoke nearly knocks you out and you can't see to the other side of the room. Smokers can't smell smoke on somebody else. And anyway, we've got Mr Travis next and he stinks of smoke all the time.'

Jean leaned back against the trunk of the tree and gazed up through the branches, watching the sunlight flicker through the canopy as leaves twisted and shifted in the breeze.

Sandra took a long drag at her cigarette. 'Ronnie says he saw your mam and dad last night in The Cavendish.'

'Did he? Well I don't care who your brother sees and who he doesn't see.'

'I'm only saying . . .'

'Well don't. I don't want to know.'

Another puff of smoke. 'What's it like at your Hilda's?'

'I like it. They're both really good to me. They say I can stay on at school for another year, if I want to.'

'Stay on? Jean, you must be barmy. I can't wait to get a job, get some money, buy me own fags, get a fella. Don't you want to have some money of your own and a bloke to smooch?'

'I suppose it'd be nice to have money. But I don't know so much about fellas. I wouldn't want one that turned out like me dad. George is nice, though.'

'Have you seen a man's willy yet?'

'Sandra!'

'Well, have you? You still haven't, have you?'

Jean liked Sandra. She admired the older girl's couldn't-careless attitude, her flouting of authority. She enjoyed being in her company most of the time, but could never understand why Sandra often wanted to bring the conversation around to men's *things*. Why would anybody want to talk about what they wee out of?

'Give over, Sandra,' she said, pushing her on the shoulder. 'That's dirty talk.'

'Who says it's dirty? I don't think it's dirty. It's only natural. It's what everybody does. Our Ronnie's got a right big willy when he gets up in the morning. Sometimes I can see the shape of it pushing up the front of his pyjamas.'

'Sandra!'

'Well, it does. I asked him once about it.'

'You never.'

'I did. He calls it a piss-hard.'

'Sandra!'

'Yes. It does it by itself in the mornings. But Ronnie says that's not like the other times it does it.'

'What other times?'

'The other times when a man's willy gets hard.'

'What does it do that for?'

'Oh, Jean. Don't you know anything? It happens when a man wants a shag. You know what shagging is?'

'I think so. I've heard about it, but I'm not sure really.'

'Well, you know how babies are made?'

'They grow inside the mother's belly.'

'Yes, but I'm talking about how they get there in the first place. The man puts his willy up the woman's hole.'

'What hole?'

'We've all got a hole underneath. You can find it with your fingers dead easy. It's just behind your knobbly bit.'

'You don't mean where your business comes out of?'

'No. It's in front of that.' Sandra rolled her eyes. 'Jean, you've got a hole for your wee, a hole for your business, and in between you've got a hole where babies come out of.'

'I haven't. I haven't got anything that big.'

'Well, it's not that big now. It gets big to let the baby out. But before that, it's just the right size for a man to put his willy in and make a baby.'

'Ugh! I don't think I'll be doing that. It sounds disgusting.'

Sandra stubbed out the cigarette and hugged her knees.

''Course,' she continued, 'you can only make a baby after the woman has started her periods. I've got mine. Have you?'

'No, not yet. Hilda's told me about it, and we've got some pads and stuff ready for when it does. I'll be fourteen soon. Hilda says it won't be long before my monthly begins.'

'Well you'd be all right then if you wanted to have a go at shagging. You wouldn't have to worry about making a baby. Once you've started your periods you've got to use a rubber johnny. Ronnie told me.'

'Ronnie knows a lot about it, doesn't he?'

'All fellas do, Jean.'

Jean shook her head. 'I don't think George does. Our Hilda has never had a baby.'

THREE

Hilda pulled back the lace curtain and peered out at the weather. Sky the colour of cigarette ash hung low over the chimneys, dull and threatening.

'Shit,' she said, 'wouldn't you just know it? Weekend again. Jean!' she shouted up the stairs. 'Give us a hand, love. We'll have to go to the washhouse today. Quick as you can. I want to get it all done before my shift starts. And bring down a couple of clean towels from the chest. We'll have a slipper bath as well while we're there.'

'Can we take some of your bath crystals, Hilda?' Jean shouted back.

'If you like. I'll get them.'

Hilda opened the gate to the cellars and went down the stone stairs to the wash-cellar below, where she kept her gas boiler and the mangle and a wicker basket for her dirty laundry. Jean threw on her clothes and ran down to help her sister. She thought Hilda and George were lucky to have so much space in their house for themselves.

The back kitchen was a lovely big room with a shiny black fireplace and a brass fender that Hilda kept brightly polished. Two fireside chairs were arranged around a large tab rug that George had made himself to cover the stone-flagged floor. There was a big old white sink in the corner of the room with cupboards built in to the alcove and a gas heater so you could get hot water any time you wanted it. At the other side of the chimney breast Hilda had her gas cooker. There was an oven in the fireplace, too, where people used to cook their meals and even bake bread, but Hilda said those days were gone, and she wasn't going out to work in all weathers to put up with that old nonsense when she got home. George and Hilda used the fireplace oven for warming their clothes in the winter, or drying out the last few bits of washing.

The dining table was at the back of the room. It was real French-polished and Hilda kept it protected with a thick piece of felt under the tablecloth. The back door opened out into the shared courtyard, which was usually strung across with loaded washing lines, so you had to bob and weave to get into your house.

The front room was hardly ever used. It had a proper wooden floor and a beautiful white fireplace. There was a three piece suite in there that looked nice but was very hard to sit on. An old upright piano that George had picked up cheaply at the sale rooms stood against the back wall but nobody in the house could play it properly. George kept his gramophone and his record collection in the front room, and sometimes they would have a musical evening. George let Jean choose her own favourites, from time to time. He even showed her how to change the needles in the pick-up, and how careful you needed to be to place the arm of the pick-up onto the clear band at the outer rim of the records so the needle could find its way into the groove. He wouldn't ever let her do the winding, though. He said if the gramophone was wound up too much it would break.

A small vestibule connected the front room with the outer door to Larksholme Lane, and the cellar-head connected it with the back kitchen. Above these ground floor rooms were three bedrooms. Theirs was the only house on the street with three upstairs rooms and that was because one of them was directly over the passageway below. It was a much nicer rented house than the back-to-back basement flat where her parents lived with only one door to the outside.

But there was no bathroom and no inside toilet. Each house on the street had its own toilet in a block across the courtyard. Jean hated going across to it in the dark. She knew there were spiders in there and at night she couldn't see where they were.

She helped Hilda bundle the bedding into two large sacks. They carried one between them; George carried the other. He went with them as far as the washhouse entrance, but he wouldn't go inside.

'Not on your Nelly, love,' he said to Hilda as they reached the steps. 'I'll be in the library changing my books. Send Jean round when you're finished, and I'll help carry it back home.'

He slipped off, and with a smile and a wave turned the corner towards the library.

The washhouse was women's territory. It was hot and steamy and noisy. The massive drying cabinets creaked and rumbled as racks of sheets and clothes slid open and closed. The wheels of metal trolleys screeched across tiled floors as the women pushed their loads from the washing machines to the drying area. Copper boilers gurgled and spat as strong arms wielding large wooden tongs pummelled and lifted hot wet clothes, separated the twisted garments and pushed them back under the foam. The women shouted their conversations across the machines and between the aisles.

'How's your Francis?'

'Is your father any better?'

'Have you seen our Theresa's new boyfriend?'

'Just look at the size of these!'

And somebody would hold up their grandmother's brassiere to hoots and howls of good-natured laughter.

There was a separate entrance for the slipper baths but one pay kiosk, so people could pay for both and while the washing was in the drying cabinets take their towel and wash bag into one of the private cubicles where there was just enough room for a bath, a chair and a mirror. Toilets were along another corridor.

Hilda was anxious to get the laundry finished. She knew several of the women working at the machines alongside, but was reluctant to be drawn into their conversations. Chatting and gossip was all well and good, she explained to Jean later, in fact that was why most of the women enjoyed the communal washhouse so much. It was as much a social gathering as it was a workplace, but Hilda had a shift on the buses to do, and she needed the bedding quick sharp for the next lodger.

'Why have you started taking in lodgers?' Jean asked as they waited in the queue for two private bathing cubicles.

'Because one day, sweetheart, I'm going to get out of this shit-hole and live in a decent place.' Hilda looked up and down the queue of women in their well-worn clothes and down-at-heel shoes and lowered her voice. 'Look at them, Jean. I know it's not their fault they've got nowt but I don't want to end up like them. It's not enough for me. It's not enough for you either. That's why me and George want you to do well at school, get a good job and get yourself out of it as well.'

'Won't I be coming with you, Hilda, when you have your new place?'

'Jean love, you won't be with us forever, no. You'll grow up and want your own place.'

Jean fell silent. They took adjoining cubicles. The partition walls were so thin you could hear everything the person next door was doing. Jean heard Hilda's plug chain chinking and the swoosh of water from the taps. She heard Hilda taking off her shoes and dropping them on the floor. Then there was a squeaking noise like a chair dragging across the hard floor. Jean threw her clothes on her chair and climbed into her bath.

As she lay back in the warm water watching Hilda's purple bath crystals dissolve into the water Jean felt a shudder of fear. The future was frightening.

It meant having to have periods every month where blood came out of the baby-hole and she would have smelly blood-soaked pads to dispose of in the fireplace when there were no men to see what she was doing. It meant growing large bosoms and having to wear a brassiere; learning how to wear stockings and fasten them up with suspenders. It meant sitting with her legs pressed close together, and it meant finding out about men's *things*.

When you got married you had to get into bed with a man who had a *thing* and you had to let him put it in the baby-hole when he wanted to. And you had to do the washing and cleaning and cooking and go to work as well.

She didn't want to grow up; she was afraid to. She wanted to stay just as she was, forever. Underneath the bath water her hands slid between her legs, and her fingers probed for what was there. She hoped it was missing, that she didn't have all the bits Sandra had told her about, but there it was, the knobbly bit and the cleft between fleshy pouches. That must be where the hole is, she thought, but dare not investigate any further.

FOUR

Sandra Logan had the afternoon off. It was half-day closing every Tuesday in Kingsley and the pharmacy where she'd got her first job as an assistant closed at twelve-thirty along with all the other shops in the town centre.

She'd managed to secure the position on the strength of her lively personality, although Mr Hall, the chemist had instructed his wife and business partner to keep an eye on the youngster and make sure she didn't become too lively. It was one thing, he had pointed out to Mrs Hall, finding a young woman who could remain unembarrassed by the mention of bodily parts and the recommended medication thereof, but quite another to allow gossip about it. Many of the Halls' regulars had been with them for years and he wanted no one to be offended by sniggers over the haemorrhoid preparations or false teeth fixatives.

On the other hand, the lass had shown enthusiastic interest with regard to the range of accessories available to nursing mothers and had nodded her head sagely when he had explained the proper use of prophylactics. It was unlikely she would be called upon to take sales for this last, however, as most of the town's gentlemen preferred to purchase their items for the weekend upstairs at the barber's.

But Sandra Logan would be invaluable in helping to promote the new lines in cosmetics he had decided to make space for. It had become apparent that respectable ladies of all ages and status enhanced their features with a little colour here and there, and it had to be acknowledged that in that department Mrs Hall would struggle to inspire confidence in their customers. A fresh young face was needed and Sandra fitted the bill. He had offered her a trial to begin with and, so far, things were going well.

Sandra had arranged to call for Jean at Hilda's before leaving for the early evening showing at the Cosy Corner cinema. Mr Hall didn't want the complimentary tickets they were given each week in return for displaying posters in the window. He had no interest in the current crop of films produced by the American film industry. On the whole, they annoyed him. He found it repugnant that at a time when Europe appeared to be at the brink of warfare, Adolf Hitler re-arming and marching into the Rhineland going completely against the Treaty of Versailles, his fellow countrymen could sit in the dark slurping orange juice, chuckling at inane story lines written by people who had no idea what life was really like for the majority over here.

'But Cyril,' his wife would say to him,' that's why we need cheering up with these happy comedies. What's the point of worrying about what's threatening in Europe when it might never happen? Eh?'

'You don't understand, my dear,' he would reply. 'We're not prepared. After the last lot who'd have thought it would all build up again so soon? But, I'm telling you, mark my words, somebody is going to have to do something about that madman. And who do you think that will have to be? It'll fall to us, that's who. We'll end up sending another generation of our best young lads to get blown up.'

Sandra would listen to her employers, understanding little of it, not wanting to understand more. It made her afraid. Everybody seemed to be talking about the same thing, in the streets, on the buses, in the shops.

Older folk reminisced about the Great War, and whose uncle was lucky just to lose a leg; whose sons never came back or whose boys did manage to return home but were never the same again.

She stood, looking dismayed at her employer as he handed over the cinema tickets.

'Off you go, Sandra,' Mrs Hall said, smiling. 'You have a lovely time. Pay no attention to all these tales of gloom, my dear. You go and cheer yourself up. What are they showing this week?'

'I don't know, Mrs Hall. We haven't got an up to date poster yet. Anyway, me and Jean just like to watch whatever it is.'

'And is that some of the new Max Factor you're wearing? You've applied it very well.'

'Yes, Mrs Hall. I'm trying out the samples you gave me.'

'As long as you don't put too much on, dear. Cheerio then.'

'Ta-ra! See you tomorrow.'

Sandra collected her things from the small cloakroom at the back of the shop and stepped out of the rear door into the street. She crossed the town hall square where elderly folk whiled away sunny afternoons on the wooden benches, exchanging gossip, giving this open space in the middle of the town the nickname, Old Man's Park. A central stone plinth supported the Great War memorial statue, a lone bronze Tommy, his helmet already encrusted with droppings of the many pigeons that roosted there.

She crossed another road and made for Larksholme Lane, passed Hilda's front door and continued on, down the hill toward the railway line. By the bridge over the tracks a narrow, iron stairway descended steeply to the coal yards below where Ronnie worked and primping up her hair she stood at the top and shouted down to him.

'Are you on your dinner break, Ronnie? Is it alright if I come down?'

◆

Ronnie Logan watched his sister negotiate the steep steps and scowled at the way she came sashaying across the coal yard towards him. He stood with his hands on his hips looking her up and down.

'Bloody hell, Sandra,' he said through gritted teeth. 'Who do you think you are? Does me mam know you're out in the street wearing that muck on yer face?'

'It's not muck; it's Max Factor,' she said with her nose in the air. 'I'll have you know I'm now a representative of the company and must be seen at all times demonstrating the benefits of our products.'

'Jesus, Mary and Joseph,' Ronnie swore. 'Have you swallowed a dictionary an' all?'

Sandra pursed her lips and put her hand to her throat in an effort to exude glamorous indignation. 'Mr Hall, my employer, don't you know, approves of my determination to improve myself, thank you very much. I shall be attending the cinema with my friend this evening, and, may I inform you, that the stars on the screen will be wearing the same make-up as myself. That is why it is called the make-up of the stars.'

'Well, you look like a tart,' Ronnie said. 'You look like you've had yer mouth round the jam pot.'

Sandra pouted and rolled her eyes.

'Ah, of course such an uneducated lout as yourself would be surprised by my glossy Cherry Kiss,' she said, batting her mascara'd eyelashes at him. 'But I have it on good authority that Garbo herself prefers this particular shade. Naturally, as you always associate with tarts and loose women you may be forgiven for not recognising a lady when you see one.'

Ronnie broke into a smile.

'Hell's bloody bells,' he said. 'You win our kid. That's enough. I know when I'm beat.' He put his arm around his sister and led her to the wooden shack at the back of the coal yard where the men took their mugs of tea and sandwiches.

✦

Ronnie Logan knew he could have any woman he wanted and he frequently did. With his matinee idol looks and a physique honed through the physical nature of his work, humping sacks of coal on to the backs of delivery trucks, he didn't even have to try. The young women of Kingsley considered him a catch. They adored him and competed with each other to be the next one he favoured with his disarming smile and smouldering, dark eyes. He had only to look in a girl's direction and she would tremble and blush under his gaze, and if he were to approach her and actually speak, she would become the envy of all her friends. Sometimes, when he was out for a drink with the lads he would play the game, just to see the reaction he could engineer. He would feign interest in some virginal type while his mates watched and waited for the usual outcome, but he was growing tired of the charade.

One day his father had taken him on one side.

'Ronnie, you'll be choosing a wife in the not too distant future. Remember, lad, she'll need to be a good Catholic girl. Your mother will stand for nothing less.'

Ronnie knew immediately his father was not only reminding him of what was expected of him, but was referring to rumours that linked him with females his father would consider entirely inappropriate.

It's a bloody good job he doesn't know the half of it, Ronnie thought. *It's a bloody good job nobody does.*

But Ronnie was careful. He knew the pitfalls of getting involved with lasses who wanted to snag him. With young single women he never went further than a smile and a few words, so that when he went to confession there was little real harm to confess. He didn't count adultery as a sin he needed to mention. To his way of thinking it wasn't him committing the act: it was the married women who took him to their beds who were sinning, not him. His conscience was clear. So far, it had been a mutually convenient arrangement. The wives he pleasured needed to keep their little dalliances secret.

He was even more careful about which wives he bedded. He never wanted to find himself in the position of one of them declaring undying love for him and threatening to walk out on her husband, so he deliberately selected women who would have too much to lose. They were classy women, some of them, out of his league in the normal sense, but he knew how to spot a female who was gagging for it whatever her background. When the affair was over, it was over, as simple as that. There were no ties, no commitments. It was easy. He moved on to his next selection without a backward glance or a single regret.

His latest, Gloria, the landlady at The Black Horse kept him busy two or three times a week. In no way was she a classy piece like some of the business wives he'd had, but she was hot. She had an appetite for sex to match her appetite for gin. It was unbelievably simple to get together with Gloria. Her alcoholic husband would collapse early into his bed most nights, sleeping soundly like a baby right through until morning. Gloria would leave the back door unlocked so he could slide along the rear alleyway and let himself in without being seen.

There was little foreplay needed with Gloria; she loved sex and would take it any way he wanted to give it to her. She kept a stash of dirty French postcards in a box under her bed and encouraged Ronnie to copy the positions, yelping like a bitch and crying out for more cock, more cock. It had occurred to him on more than the odd occasion, as she obligingly leaned over the bar counter in the *select* with the velvet curtains drawn tight, spreading her ample thighs widely so he could penetrate her from behind whilst at the same time watching their own reflections in the mirror behind the bar, that she had worn out her husband, Denis, and that was the reason he had turned to the booze: to escape her conjugal demands.

◆

'I don't want to get my clothes all dirty,' Sandra was saying as they stepped inside the workmen's shack. 'I won't sit down, Ronnie. I only came to say hello.'

'Wheeeew,' one of the lads whistled as he caught sight of her. 'Who's this jail-bait?'

'Put your eyes back where they belong, Sid. This is my sister Sandra, and she's only just gone sixteen. You'll watch what you say or else you'll have me to answer to.'

'Fair enough, Ronnie. How-de-do Sandra,' Sid replied, giving her a wink, anyway. 'Can't stop. I've already had me snap. Gotta get back to it, eh?' He went back out into the coal yard.

'So, what are you up to? Got the afternoon off today?' Ronnie asked.

'Yes. If you spent a bit more time at home you'd know more about what your sister's doing these days. Where do you get to, anyway?'

'Just around, that's all. Doss down at a mate's house, sometimes.'

'What, a mate with a C cup? I'm not daft, Ronnie.'

Ronnie shrugged and looked at the ceiling.

'I'm going to the cinema tonight with Jean,' she told him. 'I get free tickets every week.'

'Nice, luv. Look, when you see mam, tell her I won't be home for tea tonight, will you?'

'I won't see her till later. I'm having my tea at Jean's sister's.'

'What? Her that's married to the DP?'

'Don't call him that, Ronnie. It's not nice. He's not a displaced person. George is from Poland. What's wrong with that?' she flashed back at him.

'He's a bloody Jew, Sandra.'

'So? Anyway, he isn't any more. He doesn't go to their church, whatever they call it.'

'Only because there isn't one in Kingsley. If you want to get a bad name for yourself you're going the right way about it, Sandra.'

'Ronnie,' she sighed. 'You are so old-fashioned.'

'Well, just be careful,' he called after her as she turned to leave. 'You can't trust them foreigners.'

'See you later then,' she said, hurrying back across the coal yard and up the steps onto the bridge. Jean would be on her way home now and with a bit of luck she'd be able to catch her before they went to Hilda's.

FIVE

Jean was at the top of the lane when Sandra spotted her.

'Jean,' she shouted. 'Hang on a minute!' She ran to link arms with her friend.

'Look,' she said, 'Come over to Old Man's Park for a minute with me, will you?'

'What for?'

'I want to wipe off some of this make-up. I don't want your Hilda getting the wrong idea about me.'

'Well what have you got it on for in the first place?'

'It's part of my job. I have to model Max Factor, but I'm not used to using it, and I think I've put too much on.'

'I didn't want to say anything, Sandra, but your face does look, well, a bit orange. Your eyes are good, though. What have you got on them?'

'Mascara and eye shadow. Do you really like it?'

'Oh, yes,' Jean agreed. 'That colour on your eyelids is lovely, and your eyelashes look really long.'

'It's in my bag. I've brought it with me so you can have a go as well.'

'No, I can't do that. Our Hilda'll kill me.'

'She won't know will she? Listen, I'll wipe all this off now, and then when we get to the cinema we can go in the toilets. They've got big mirrors in there, and we can do each other.'

'I don't know how to do that eye stuff. Hilda only uses lipstick.'

'I'll show you. It's dead easy. Go on!'

'Alright, then, but I'll have to take it off before I go back home. What do you get it off with?'

'Spit on your hanky. You can rub it off then.'

Jean helped Sandra to rid herself of the tan coloured coating and they returned to the house on the lane where Hilda was waiting, having finished her early shift for the day. The girls ran along the passageway between the houses and Jean let them in.

Sandra hung back, waiting to be invited.

'Come on in, love,' Hilda called from the back of the room where she was busy at the gas cooker. 'I shan't bite you.'

'Hello Mrs Pozyzcka. Thank you for having me to tea. Oh, something smells good.'

Sandra knew when to be polite.

'We're having a big meat and potato pie tonight, Sandra. I hope you like it.'

'How did you know it's my favourite? I love meat and potato pie.'

'We'll wait for George to come home from work. He won't be long. You'll still have plenty of time to get to the pictures. What's on this week?'

'We don't know yet,' Jean replied. 'But we don't care, anyway, do we Sandra? They're all good. We haven't seen a bad one yet.'

'Do you like going to the cinema, Mrs Pozyzcka?' Sandra asked.

'Yes, love. But we don't get there often, what with my late shifts and everything. Jean, love, why don't you show Sandra those film magazines George got for you while I get on here? You can both go upstairs if you like.'

They disappeared in a flurry of skirts and legs and shoes. George came in while the girls were still occupied with their film idols and Hilda whispered quickly to him.

'She's got that Sandra upstairs. I don't know whether I should be allowing this friendship between them to go on like this. What do you think?'

'What do I think?' he repeated. 'Why shouldn't they be friends?'

'Well you know what the bloody holier than thou Logans are like. Bloody Catholics. They're all top show, thinking they're better than everybody else.'

'I'm surprised at you, Hilda. I thought we knew better than to let other people's faith get in the way of friendship. You of all people should know that.'

Hilda stopped what she was doing and went to sit at the table.

'George Pozyzcka,' she smiled up at him. 'You're right again, aren't you my love? I won't ever go far wrong with you looking after me.'

'Come here,' he said, and planted a kiss on her mouth. 'I will always love you, my Hilda. I am proud that you are my wife.' He kissed her again.

'Now stop that,' she said. 'The girls will be down in a minute.'

'So we can set them good example of how a man and his wife show their love for each other. Come, kiss me with passion,' he teased.

'George! Enough.'

But the girls were already standing at the bottom of the stairs watching and grinning.

'Hello, you two,' said George, 'Is this how they do it at the pictures?' and he grabbed his wife around the waist and drew her in towards him in a tight clinch.

♦

'Sandra has got to model the new Max Factor make-up for her job at Hall's chemist, haven't you, Sandra?' Jean said later, while they were eating.

'Do you? Aren't you a bit young for that?' Hilda wanted to know.

'It's alright to wear a bit of make-up now, Mrs Pozyzcka, and Mr Hall wants to me learn how to use it properly so I can give customers advice about it.'

'Oh,' Hilda replied, not knowing quite what to say next.

'Yes,' Jean added. 'It's called the make-up of the stars because all the film stars wear it.'

'Oh,' Hilda said again, 'I didn't know that.'

'Max Factor is Polish man like me,' George said, taking command of the conversation. 'That's something else you didn't know, isn't it?'

'Is he really?' Sandra asked, surprise lighting her eyes.

'Oh yes. His family took him to America when he was little boy, like my family brought me to England when I was little boy.

'When people who go to America first arrive they have to go to a place where they must sort out their passports and papers, you know what I mean?'

The girls nodded in wide-eyed silence. George continued. 'Yes, it is a place called Ellis Island just off the shore at New York and all the Poles and the Irish and all the other people who are looking for a new life have to make a queue and wait in line to be processed. There are so many people that the queue is miles and miles long and there is nothing to eat and nothing to drink while they are waiting, and the babies are crying and the women are fainting because they have been travelling on the sea for so long and the men can do nothing to help. All they can do is wait.'

George stopped speaking, his eyes fixed in a hard cold stare. Hilda gently touched the back of his hand. Sandra was the first one of them to speak again.

'Why do they do it then? It sounds awful. Why do they let it happen?'

George took a deep breath and gathered himself. 'Because it means so much to them to get away from where they have been.

'And when they arrived at the front of the queue the authorities there could not understand what one Polish family was saying. They were just giving their name, but the Americans could not say the name and so they made up a name for them, and it was Factor, so the little boy became Max Factor on his papers. Now he is grown up like me and he is making this make-up for the stars.'

They were all staring at him. He cleared his throat, forced a smile and began polishing his spectacles with his handkerchief.

'That is the end of the story,' he said.

Hilda and Jean glanced at one another, each knowing what the other was thinking, sharing a sense of empathy with George, feeling his torment over things he'd experienced but would never tell them. Sandra was still wide-eyed.

'So it's a happy ending,' she cried out. 'Hurray! A happy ending.'

There was no further happy ending that night. When Jean and Sandra arrived at the Cosy Corner Cinema, they were delighted, at first, to discover that the star of the silver screen for the night's performance was to be the one and only Greta Garbo. They handed in their tickets and rushed straight to the ladies' toilets where Sandra showed Jean how to spit on the block of mascara and rub the little brush included in the compact over it, picking up the black substance and stroking it onto her eyelashes. They used their fingers to apply the smoky blue eye shadow, drew on the Cherry Kiss, just like Garbo, and blew kisses at themselves in the mirror before taking their seats in the auditorium. The lights dimmed and they waited in excitement as the curtains drew back and the screen flickered into life.

It was 1936 and the film was Camille. By the time Garbo had gasped her last breath their tears had overflowed and, cascading down both their cheeks, turned their faces into streaky rivulets of black and smoky blue.

SIX

Jean hung back while Hilda parcelled up sanitary towels in newspaper and threw them on the fire.

'I'm really sorry about last night,' Jean apologised. 'It's not supposed to be till next week.'

Hilda poked at the fire to make sure everything was burning away.

'Don't worry about it,' she said. 'It's not important.'

'But I made such a mess in the bed. I feel stupid.'

'You weren't to know it was going to happen, so there's no need to feel stupid.'

'I just don't know where I am with it. Sometimes it's early. Sometimes it's late. I can't work it out.'

'Well, you're not on your own. I used to be like that. It'll settle down eventually. There's nothing to worry about.'

'What about the sheets?'

'I've put them in some bleach in the cellar.'

'George won't know about it, will he? You won't tell him?'

'Of course I won't tell him, Jean. Stop worrying. We'll get the sheets out on the line to dry and nobody will ever know.'

Hilda seemed impatient. Jean watched as her sister kept on poking the fire with sharp, jagged movements as if her hands were angry. There was something else bothering Hilda but Jean didn't know what it was.

'I'll have to tell Miss Linford I can't train tonight,' she said.

'You can still go, though, can't you? See your friends?' Hilda said, still jabbing at the fire.

'I suppose so. But I won't be able to try out on the beam.'

'The what?'

'The beam. Miss Linford says I should be good at gymnastics. She wants me to give it a go.'

Hilda straightened up and replaced the poker in its stand. 'What do you have to do?'

'It's all about keeping your balance. The beam is four inches wide and you have to go through a programme of set exercises on it.'

'It sounds difficult. I bet it takes plenty of practice. Never mind, you'll be able to try it out next week.'

Hilda rubbed her hands on her apron and sat heavily in one of the fireside chairs. She gazed into the flames, rubbing at her back and front as if she had something the matter with her own belly. When she looked up she had a worried face. She smiled with her mouth but her eyes still looked troubled.

'Hilda, are you all right?'

'Yes, love. Why?'

'You don't sound yourself. That's all.'

'Don't I? I'm probably a bit tired. I've had extra shifts lately.'

'You don't have to do them, do you? Can't you say you don't want to work overtime?'

'But I do want to work them. I want the extra money. Now, Jean, don't get me wrong. It's got nothing to do with you living with us. You know that. Blimey, what do you cost? You don't cost us anything extra at all. You don't eat enough to fill a sparrow. You know why I want the extra money.'

It was a puzzle to Jean why Hilda wanted so desperately to get away from Kingsley when George had been so desperate to get away from somewhere else and was very happy to be here. She couldn't work it out.

'What's so wrong with Kingsley?' she said. 'George likes it well enough.' There, it was said. She waited for Hilda to answer.

'I'll tell you when you're older,' was all the answer she was going to get.

There was no point in pressing for more. Jean knew very well you could never get anything out of Hilda if she didn't want to tell you. But Hilda's worried expression bothered her. She couldn't get it out of her mind. Hilda had said the problem wasn't anything to do with the cost of having her with them, but what if that wasn't true? It *must* cost more to feed three, not to mention the extras needed for Jean's clothes. Hilda's hand-me-downs weren't always suitable.

She lay in bed that night on her clean, bleached sheets thinking about it. She was a burden on them. Whatever the cause for Hilda being so keen to move away from Kingsley, she, Jean, was the reason it would take longer to afford it.

When Jean saw an advertisement in the window of Mancini Modes she knew what she was going to do. She hurried through the town centre on her way home from school and stopped outside Hall's chemist. She could see through the glass panel in the door. There was only one customer being served. She couldn't see either of the Halls. When Sandra noticed her peering through the glass and waved her in, Jean waited until the customer had left the shop.

'I'm going to give up school and get a job,' she whispered over the counter.

'Are you? Where?'

'Mancini Modes, but I need your help.'

'Mancini Modes? Have you told your Hilda?'

'No. Not yet. Don't say anything to anybody, will you?'

'You know I won't.'

'So, will you help me?'

'What do you want me to do?'

'I want you to lend me some of your makeup and I want you to show me how to put it on properly. Not too much, mind. I want to look older when I go in and ask for the job. But I don't want to look orange.'

'You're not chatting to friends while we've customers waiting, I hope,' came a voice from the back room.

'No, Mr Hall,' Sandra said, winking at Jean. 'This is a friend here, that's true, but she would like some advice on our latest eye makeup. She has an important event coming up and wants to look her best.'

'That's the ticket. Carry on.'

'I'd better go,' Jean whispered. 'I don't want to get you in trouble.'

Sandra leaned forward and whispered back. 'He's in there with a pot of tea and his newspaper. He won't come out for another half hour. Do you want to meet up tonight?'

'Yes, but it'll have to be at your house.'

'Right then. See you later.'

Jean hugged her secret all through teatime and told Hilda she was planning to pop in on Miss Linford at the athletics club. There was only Sandra at home when she arrived at the Logans'. Sandra's parents were at a church social and nobody knew where Ronnie was.

'Do you think I should cut my hair short?' Jean asked, holding up a hand mirror and trying to see round the back of her head.

'No. Pin it up.'

'Urghh! Not in a bun. I don't want to look that old.'

'I don't mean in a bun. I mean like this. Look.' She handed over the latest *Picturegoer* magazine showing Jeanette Macdonald in *Rose Marie.*

'Sandra! I don't want to look like an Indian squaw either.'

'Not that picture. This one.'

Sandra set to work, curling locks of Jean's hair around her fingers, clipping them in place in a swept back style either side of a central parting.

'We won't use any foundation at all, Jean,' she said. 'You've got a good colour in your complexion anyway. It must be all the exercising you do. I'm not going to use bright colour on your eyes either. I think a hardly-there grey will be best. More sophisticated for Mancini Modes. 'Course, we'll use loads of mascara, just remember not to get upset about anything. First though, I'm going to pluck your eyebrows.'

'What? Will it hurt?'

'Yes. Sorry, but it will. First time you do 'em, it hurts. Look, I'll show you how to do it.'

By the time they'd finished, Jean looked every inch the Hollywood starlet. She had taken off her short white socks and Sandra had applied some leg makeup. Jean stood and admired herself in Mrs Logan's living room mirror. She twirled in the dress borrowed from Sandra, showing off her new self, feeling thrilled and excited and very grown up.

'Well, if they don't give you the job, they're stupid and don't deserve you,' Sandra said. 'Just remember. Stand tall with one leg slightly in front of the other and when you sit down keep your knees together.'

'Like this?' Jean said, settling into one of the Logans' armchairs and taking up a pose she'd seen in *Picturegoer*.

A door slammed. Footsteps crossed the hall. The door to the living room opened and Ronnie Logan walked in. He had a face like thunder.

SEVEN

Ronnie Logan had had a day to remember. Not that he particularly wanted to remember it. He was glad it was over. It had been nauseating. He swore never to have anything to do with that slut, Gloria ever again. On the train back to Kingsley from Leeds he cursed himself for ever getting involved with her in the first place. He rested his head against the window as the train steamed past industrial estates on the outskirts of the city. He didn't want to think. He wanted to empty his head.

The route travelled into open country alongside the canal and then the river Aire, but he watched none of it. He closed his eyes and tried to forget what he'd done. He prayed to God to forgive him for his debauchery.

When he finally reached home, he was glad his parents were out. He wouldn't have been able to face them. His mother would know there was something the matter. He was still sweating. He needed a bath. He probably smelled.

On their last encounter Gloria had presented Ronnie with a French postcard from another of her secret collections.

'You know how I like to do everything they do in the photos?' she'd said to him. 'Well, I want to do this next.' She handed him a picture. 'Can you arrange it, Ronnie? Have you a friend who can be as discreet as you are?'

He should have thrown it back in her face there and then. As soon as he saw the entangled bodies and the close up photographs of female genitalia stuffed to the hilt, he should have finished it, walked away, straightened himself out. Sex with a woman was one thing. That was what everybody did. It was normal, but sex in a group was filth. One woman and how many blokes? All poking and licking each other?

But it was like a drug. He was crazed. The pornographic images Gloria showed him set him on fire with lust. He wanted to know how it would feel to do things like that. He hadn't been able to resist the temptation.

God forgive him, he'd shown the postcard to Sid at work.

'Fuckin' hell,' Sid said at first glance of it. 'Where the hell did you get this from?'

'I can't tell you just yet. I need to know first if I can trust you.'

'Trust me? What with?'

'If I told you I know a woman who likes this sort of thing and wants me to bring another bloke with me next time, what would you say?'

'When do we go?' Sid had answered.

Gloria had made the arrangements. She wanted Ronnie and Sid to meet her at an address in the city and promised they'd make enough money out of it to more than compensate them for taking an afternoon off work. What excuse they used to get the time off was up to them.

She met them at the appointed time and greeted them politely as if they were going for tea and cakes together instead of getting their kit off and shagging her senseless. She led them down a street and through an arcade. They went into a building by the side entrance. They climbed to the second floor.

A brightly lit room was furnished with all the accoutrements of a photographer's studio. There was a one-armed couch spread with a cloth and fancy cushions like in the French postcards. Lamps all around the room were trained on the sofa bed.

'Here we are,' Gloria said. 'This is going to be fun. Where's Robert? Oh, there you are. Have you got everything ready for us?'

Robert shambled across the room and kissed her on the cheek as if they'd just met in the park. He was ancient. His face was so lined there was no smooth skin left. He looked as if he was a sixty a day man. And a bottle of whisky. He positioned himself behind a tripod.

Gloria reached behind her and rubbed at the front of Sid's trousers. 'Well, *he's* ready, at least,' she said and unbuttoned him. She knelt and licked his erection.

'Fuckin' hell,' Ronnie said with a gasp.

'Come on, Ronnie, love,' Gloria said, still licking between Sid's legs. 'Show me what you've got for me.'

He'd felt silly, standing there with his cock in his hand, letting Sid have first go at Gloria while the old bloke, Robert took pictures of them, Gloria on her back on the couch with her legs in the air, Sid pumping away for all he was worth. He'd come too soon and Gloria was crying out for more.

Ronnie took over. Gloria flipped over onto her hands and knees and presented herself.

'Jesus, fuckin' Christ,' Sid yelled and started wanking himself.

Ronnie shoved into her from behind.

'That's right,' she shouted. 'Right up, love. Get it right up. I want to feel full.'

Sid was ready again.

'Oh, you lovely boy,' Gloria said. 'We can't waste that, love, can we? Lovely stiff cock like that? Ronnie lie on your back. I'll get on top.'

She slid onto him and rode him while Sid watched and kept rubbing himself.

'Up the arse, love,' Gloria said to Sid. 'Come on. Don't hold back. I told you I want to feel full. Really full. I want cock coming out me ears.'

She was insatiable. She couldn't get enough. She wanted everything all at once. The two of them couldn't satisfy her craving. She would have gone on all night. If the photographer, Robert hadn't been so past it she would have had him too at the same time as Sid and himself. They'd had her between them thrusting into her front and rear and the bitch was *still* crying out for more cock. Ronnie wished Robert hadn't been so decrepit. He could have shoved his in her mouth just to shut her up.

Afterwards, Ronnie knew Gloria was going to want to go that next step. Then three cocks wouldn't be enough. She'd carry on wanting more and more. He looked at her reapplying her lipstick and what he saw was no longer his bit on the side, his entertainment for an easy, no strings attached shag. He saw a blousy ageing tart. She was ugly. Inside *and* out. He turned to Sid.

'What do you think?' he said.

'Bloody fantastic. I can't believe it. Me knob's gonna be famous. When are we doing it again, Gloria?' he asked and squeezed her breasts.

'Soon, I hope,' she said. 'As long as you keep quiet about it. Robert's bringing in a movie camera next time, aren't you, love? And maybe some more boys?'

'Not me,' Ronnie said, shaking his head. 'Over to you, Sid.'

He turned away and left them discussing arrangements for their next appointment. He couldn't get down the stairs fast enough, out into the fresh air. But, even the city streets looked tarnished. The air was stifling, too sour to breathe. He ran along the arcade and raced toward the station and his train home.

He thought he'd have the house to himself but there were voices in the living room. Sandra had her friend in there. All dolled up they were, with too much lipstick and fancy hair.

'Ronnie! What's up?' Sandra said.

How could he tell his sister what he'd been doing?

'Nowt,' he said. 'What are you two doing?'

'I'm just practising on Jean,' Sandra said. 'I've got to keep up with all the latest trends. Doesn't she look lovely?'

Ronnie looked. He saw a fresh-faced innocent kid wearing his sister's dress trying to look older than her years. He felt sick and dirty by comparison. He tried to smile but his mouth was dry and his lips caught on his teeth.

'What's the matter, Ronnie?' Sandra asked again.

He shrugged and shook his head. He couldn't think of a good thing to say.

'Well, go on, then,' Sandra urged. 'Tell Jean what you think.'

He looked again. The kid was obviously embarrassed, as if she wished a hole would open in the carpet and swallow her. He saw her cheeks blush and the redness spread to her neck.

'You're pretty enough as you are,' he said quietly. 'You don't need all that muck on yer face.

EIGHT

AUGUST 2009

As the huge jet hurtles through the skies, I close my eyes and think about my mother. Whenever I think of her I find it so easy to remember her face. She was beautiful when she was young, with large, dark eyes and a full mouth. She had an athletic build and natural poise. My favourite photograph of her is the one where she is sitting on a wall holding up a silver cup which she'd won for her gymnastics, with those long legs stretched out in front of her and the top of her thighs disappearing into thick woollen gym knickers. I can remember her broad cheekbones, the ready smile and, in later years, the Queen Elizabeth hairdo. I remember the way her hair waved at the front and how it would always lighten in the sun when she'd been on holiday.

She loved her holidays. They were what she lived and worked for all year long, putting away as much as she could afford in preparation for the big day. Holidays always fell during the last week in July and the first week in August when I was a child. These were the *feast* weeks as they were known in our town, when all the mills and factories closed down and our bit of the Pennines emptied onto buses and trains whisking the workers away for their annual break. Not many people had cars then. I knew only one family with a car and one other family with a television set. I wonder what she'd think of all the possessions people expect to have today?

Like so many other things, I never asked her and now it's too late. Her generation struggled to put their lives back together after the war. They worked hard to furnish their homes and put food on the table.

'Waste not, want not,' she'd say, saving bits of string and left over gravy. 'You never know when you might need that.'

They aspired to the American style of fitted kitchen as seen at the cinema where films from Hollywood showed us Mr and Mrs Average in their large detached houses with two cars in the garage and enough space in their living rooms for three families to share. At that time their counterparts in Britain were experiencing for the first time the convenience of owning a refrigerator or a washing machine of their own. Pleasures were simple. Luxuries were rare and greatly appreciated. My mother's generation handed down to mine the importance of earning your place in the world.

As children we learned to respect our elders, empty our plates and take care of our toys and possessions. There was no such thing as a fussy eater. If you didn't eat what you were given, you stayed hungry. If you were cheeky to your parents, there were consequences. We took great care of our books and toys because we didn't have so many of them. Children learned they were part of the family, not the centre of everyone's universe. Adults were in charge and children felt safe that way. And we always knew that we were loved because we felt secure in the knowledge that mum and dad were taking care of us. No meant *no* because there was a good reason for it.

But my thoughts are racing ahead. I'm losing my focus. I find I tend to do that rather a lot lately. My son, Malcolm points out I keep drifting off into my own world and I can tell by the expression on his face he has very little desire to find out why that might be. He shows little interest in me or how I'm doing.

After his father died he started visiting me a bit more, but it didn't last long. Now I hardly ever see him. When I telephone it's really obvious he can't wait to get off the phone. But then, I suppose it has to be partly my fault he turned out so selfish. I tried to be the kind of mother to him mine was to me. I had an excellent role model in her, but somewhere along the way I failed.

I adored Malcolm from the very first moment I laid eyes on him. He was born clean and pink with golden hair. I held him close to me and felt such a surge of love for this new being that it was like pain. I'd never experienced anything quite like that. It was a new kind of love. It obliterated the memories of continuous nausea, aching legs and the searing spasms of childbirth immediately I saw his pink tiny fingernails and his beautiful features. My heart leapt with joy at this brand new creation, this miracle, this perfect little person who was made from me and Jim. I couldn't stop looking at him.

Even from that moment of his birth he had the power to hurt me. I turned myself over to him absolutely, adoring him, loving him so completely I felt here was my reason for living. This is what my fate was to be: mother of Malcolm. I was so proud. He was an adorable baby. People used to stop in the street to stare at him, he was so cute.

'Excuse me, Madam. Would you like some refreshment?'

It's the cabin steward. It takes me a moment to gather myself. I look around and see most passengers are having a pre-dinner glass of something. The steward senses my momentary bewilderment and smiles at me.

'We have complimentary champagne on ice for all our first class passengers, Madam. Would you like me to pour one for you?'

I steal a quick glance at the woman who is sitting next to me and notice she's already sipping from hers. I smile back at the steward and nod my assent. The woman looks at me and raises her glass.

'Cheers,' she says and takes another sip. 'I'm Deborah. We're going to be sitting next to one another for a long time. It's too long to sit in silence. Don't you think?'

'Hello,' I reply. 'I'm Audrey.'

She looks very nice. Quite a bit younger than me. Late forties? She's wearing the kind of travelling clothes that stay smart but look comfortable at the same time. Her hair is cut in a short, modern style and her jewellery is of the chunky ethnic variety I admire but which never looks right on me. She slips the book she has been reading into the pocket by her seat and turns toward me.

'I've never flown first class before,' I tell her. 'I didn't know they gave you champagne.'

'Neither have I' she says and laughs. 'Isn't it great?'

Sometimes you know you are going to get on with a person you've just met. There's an immediate rapport which has nothing to do with shared values or common interests because you don't know enough about one another to be aware of those things.

'Are you going on holiday?' I ask.

'No. I'm going home. I've been visiting family. You?'

'My mother died. I'm going to . . . you know . . . sort things out.'

'Ah. I'm sorry. How long is it since you've seen her?'

'Just over three years. At my husband's funeral.'

'Oh, God. How awful. I'm so sorry. I feel terrible now for asking. You must wish I'd never opened my mouth.'

'Not at all,' I reassure her. 'I asked you first.'

There is a pause. She bites her lip. She takes another sip of her champagne and it seems she feels she must offer a corresponding revelation about herself. Shifting in her seat, she lowers her voice.

'I don't really want to go home,' she tells me.

I wait. I don't know what to say. Here we are, two strangers on a long-haul flight to the UK sharing personal details as if we were long lost friends.

That's how it happens, sometimes. Sometimes it *is* easier to talk to a stranger. Maybe it's because some of us bottle up these feelings for so long that at the first show of kindness from someone the emotions bubble up to the surface and come rushing out in a torrent of release. It doesn't matter that you don't know this person to whom you are unburdening yourself. You're not going to meet them again. They're not going to become part of your life. You can let it all out and not be judged for it. Perhaps you'll get an objective response with suggestions of solutions you'd never thought of. Maybe you don't want answers anyway; you just want to get it off your chest. Deborah wants to talk. I give her an encouraging smile.

'It's true,' she continues. 'I'm not looking forward to going home. I feel as though there's nothing there for me any more. It's a terrible thing to say, I know, but I'm bored with my life. I'm bored with my husband. I don't want to be selfish, but I thought when your children left home to make their own lives, you got your own life back. Do I sound ridiculous?'

It doesn't sound ridiculous to me. I've been there. I know what it feels like to wonder who you've turned into and what you're supposed to be doing with the rest of your life. I try to offer her some consolation.

'No, I don't think you're being ridiculous. But, you know, I think it might be a *woman* thing. Lots of us go through that stage of losing our way. You can't go back to the person you were before you had your children. You and your husband are different people now. Wouldn't you say so?'

'Oh, yes. That's the trouble. We're different from who we were, but the changes are not complementary. We want different things, whereas at one time we were *so* together.'

She sighs and runs her hand through her hair. Her expression tells of longing for that desirable something which is out of her reach.

Dinner arrives. It's a much more comfortable affair than eating in tourist class. We comment on how much space we have for our elbows. We take delight in the proper cutlery rather than bendy plastic. The food itself is very good. Between munching with contentment and sipping our fresh glasses of wine, we are becoming friends.

I'm in first class because of a dogged determination to award myself some special treatment at the start of a journey into my past. I have left behind a selfish son whose only comment about my returning to England to sort out grandma's affairs was to enquire whether it was really necessary to spend so much in the process.

Deborah is in the seat next to me because she got lucky and was upgraded for free.

NINE

We eat our first class dinner and chat. I learn more about Deborah's husband, Philip. She tells me he's become obsessed with his hobby and ignores her much of the time. I'm conscious that, of course, I'm hearing only one side of the story, but I'm willing to give her the benefit of any doubt.

'Do you know,' she says, 'I don't think he notices I'm there half the time. Sometimes he starts to tell me about something that's been on television and I'll tell him, *I know. I was there. I was watching it with you.* And then he just grunts and says he couldn't remember whether I'd seen it or not. Honestly. What is the point of my being there if he can't tell the difference?'

'You don't think it might be real short term memory problems?' I suggest.

'No. He can remember everything he wants to remember.'

She laughs, but it's an uncomfortable sound. It jars like a cracked bell. I'm reminded of complaints I've read in the agony aunt columns. I guess it works the other way around as well, when a man feels unloved and left out. I'm no expert on relationships, but having had troubles of my own I know this at least: you shouldn't leave the responsibility of your own happiness to someone else. It's simply not fair to put that responsibility onto your partner. It's not their job to see to it you're happy. It's yours.

I don't want to talk about Jim and me so I let her go on. Eventually the conversation moves to her children. Her son, Stephen is with an IT company at their Asian headquarters in Singapore, which is where I had my stopover on my way from Sydney. Deborah has spent an enjoyable week with her son and his partner.

'Philip couldn't stand it when Stephen told us he's gay,' she says. 'Looking back, I think that's when Philip started immersing himself in his model planes. If he's not in his workshop fixing and mending, he's on the computer emailing who knows how many enthusiasts. Answering their queries. I was amazed to learn how many grown men get obsessed by what seems to me a rather childish interest. They write to him. They ring him up. Now he's even set up his own blog thing. It takes up all his time. I mean, he's even got himself qualified to teach beginners how to handle the different models. It's like he's reliving his childhood.'

'It sounds to me as though he's filling his time because he can't face the truth about his son.'

Why is it you can see through other people's problems but you get stuck in a rut with your own? I can't sort the difficulties between Malcolm and me but feel I can offer advice to someone else.

Fathers and sons: one problem after another. I wonder if anybody manages to lead the ideal family life? We all know how it's supposed to be. We see it in adverts and in magazines, happy couples raising their children with just the right amount of encouragement, using humour to see them through bad times, buying this or that product to make their lives complete. Then when the kids have flown, the same couples are still in love, leaning over the rail of an ocean-going liner as they celebrate their ruby wedding on a world cruise. It sounds wonderful, but I don't know anyone it's happened to.

It's not an easy thing for any woman to admit she doesn't like her only child. Malcolm's selfishness disappoints me. I wanted to hang onto those early days when he was the golden-haired child with the cute smile. I wanted to keep those same feelings inside me when I couldn't bear to be apart from him. I wanted him to love his old mum the way I thought sons should. Why didn't he offer to take me out for the occasional jolly or a pub lunch? That he never wanted to spend any time with me gnawed at me. I tried to push the thought away and I made excuses for him. But you can't go on like that forever.

He hasn't grown up. He must have things his way. His father and I are to blame, I suppose. He was an only child and we put him first. He always got what he wanted so he never learned to cope with disappointment or having to wait for things. We taught him to put himself first.

A light brush on the back of my hand: Deborah. She leans forward.

'I knew about Stephen long before he told us. When he was quite small I suspected he was different from other boys his age. By the time he was about twelve, I knew for sure.'

Hastily I banish thoughts about my own son and concentrate on what Deborah is telling me.

'How did you know? What was it made him different?'

'To begin with it was hard to put your finger on. I mean, he liked his computer games but he played in a different way. He really didn't like joining groups. He became very solitary for a while as he was growing up and it was a worry. His body language was quite effeminate. He didn't walk like his father, for instance. He walked like me. Oh, I don't know, Audrey. There were hundreds of clues, all small things in themselves, but added up together . . .'

'Did you talk about it with him?'

'No, and I wish I had. I think I could have made his life more tolerable if I had let him know it didn't matter to me. He's my son and I love him. I should have let him know. Neither of us imagined what Philip's reaction would be, how cold and unfeeling. I'm glad Stephen got the chance to work abroad. It means he can live his life quite separate from his father's constant disapproval. Philip doesn't have to deal with it either. It's better for both of them.'

'It isn't better for you, though. Is it?'

'No.' Her shoulders droop. 'What can I do?'

'You can't sort it out for them. They have to do it themselves.'

After dinner, there's a film presentation. I'm glad Deborah wants to watch it. I take the earpiece and settle back as if I'm going to watch, too, but I can't concentrate on the film. My head is full of thoughts banging against each other, making no sense, clamouring to be analysed, compartmentalised, filed, put away. Malcolm. Jim. My mother.

I try to focus on one thing. It's too much to think about all at once. I should stay on track. Deal with first things first. My mother has died alone in England and I must come to terms with that. She had reached a good age and we all know it's going to happen sometime, but I have to deal with the guilt I have because she was alone, the hurt I feel because she never told me she was ill and I have to get my head around all this before I can begin to grieve.

Grief takes you by surprise. After Jim died I went through all the stages. I've done the denial thing. I've done the anger, *the how could you leave me on my own* scenario. I've wept for the lost dreams and lost hopes. I've blamed myself for not being kinder, more understanding, more loving. And I've blamed him for not being kinder, more understanding, more loving. I've read the bereavement websites and ordered self-help books. I've poured myself a larger nightcap than might be good for me and fallen asleep in front of the television. Watched weepy films and deliberately played music I knew would set me off again.

And then, just when I thought I'd accepted and learned to cope with the reality of losing my husband, when I could say his name without a lump forming in my throat, when I could recall an event, an outing, a place we'd both enjoyed with a smile for the happy memory rather than a tear for the loss, when I thought I'd got it under control, something came out of the blue and slapped me in the face so hard it stung.

The thing that hit me hard, knocked me almost senseless and had me reeling was the wonderful feeling of freedom that began to well up inside. Suddenly I could go where I wanted to go. I could get on and do things I fancied. I felt guilty at first for finding anything pleasurable at all, as if somehow I was betraying Jim. Then, I began to enjoy my new found freedom. I began to enjoy my life.

'Are you staying in London?'

Deborah's question nudges me back into the present. I peer through the cabin's tiny windows. It's still dark. Are we still in today or have we flown into yesterday?

'No. I have to get to Norfolk.'

'What? Straight away? Audrey, you'll be exhausted. Don't even think about travelling on until you're properly rested. You haven't booked tickets have you?'

'No. Not yet. Is there still a direct train?'

'I expect so. I'll help you find out. But look, don't dash off. Come with me. Come and stay for at least one night. Please say you will.'

TEN

Deborah pats my hand.

'Come on,' she says. 'Please say you'll stay. It's no trouble. In fact, I'd love your company for a little while longer.'

'I don't know.'

She pats my hand again. 'Say yes. There's nobody expecting you at the other end straight away is there?'

'No. I have a telephone number to call, but I'm not expected on any particular date.'

'What about your mother's funeral? Isn't there a date set for that?'

'I missed it.'

More unanswered questions to crash into all the others bouncing about in my head. Why wasn't I informed until afterwards? Is that what my mother wanted? If so, why? My head's in a spin. Deborah's offer begins to sound attractive.

'I *am* tired,' I tell her. 'Thank you for your kind offer.'

It takes an hour after landing to collect baggage and clear customs. A new day has begun and people are at the beginning of their day's work. The airport is crowded and noisy and I'm grateful when Deborah calls out,

'Philip, over here. We're over here.'

Philip is charming. He greets me warmly and is not in the least put out that his wife has invited me to stay in their home. He passes on his news to Deborah, tells her not to worry about food shopping as he's taken care of it and makes every effort to make me feel comfortable.

'The guest room is made up,' he says. 'I expect you'll both need to get your heads down.'

We make our way to their car, stow the cases and get rid of our trolleys, all the while chatting about travel and crowds and traffic and jet lag, but there's not a word spoken about his son. Not once does he ask his wife about her trip or how Stephen is.

I doze on and off in the car during the journey to their home. I have no idea where I'm going. I've turned myself over completely to generous strangers and it's an odd feeling, like an adventure. Two hours pass and I'm woken by the car coming to a halt.

'Here we are,' Deborah says. 'This is it. Home.'

I'm looking up at a lovely pre-war detached house with bay windows and a very pleasant outlook along a leafy lane and across sunny meadows. It's just the kind of house my mother used to dream about.

'Leave the cases, ladies,' Philip offers. 'I'll see to them. You two go in and put the kettle on. I expect you're dying for a good cup of English tea.'

I can't reconcile the image of Philip I had conjured up from Deborah's description of him with this attentive and thoroughly charming man. Deborah must be reading my thoughts.

'He's happy you're here,' she says. 'It means I've got company and he won't have to feel guilty about leaving me on my own. You'll see what I mean later on.'

I think she's being uncharitable, but I hold my tongue. I'm too tired for discussions about anything. Even though the seats on the flight were more comfortable than usual, I still ache from head to toe. My neck has disappeared and my head is sitting right on top of my shoulders. It's heavy.

We drink tea and eat a few biscuits then Deborah shows me where to find the bathroom and takes me to their guest room where my suitcase sits by the window. I thank her and say,

'You are both so kind. I think I shall feel more sociable after some better sleep.'

'Don't worry about a thing,' Deborah says. 'I feel exactly the same. It's like wading through syrup, isn't it? Everything is in slow motion. Each movement or word is such an effort.'

I thank her again.

'Sleep as long as you need to, Audrey,' she says. 'Just come down when you're ready. There's no need to stick to set times. I expect we'll both wake when we're hungry.'

I find my bathroom bag and take a quick shower in the pretty en suite. I look in the mirror. When did I get to look so jaded? I feel a little refreshed, however, and stand for a moment by the window overlooking Deborah's garden. It's well-tended with a lovely lawn and flower beds. The sight of lush, green grass always awakens old memories. It's one of the things about England we expats miss most. There is nothing to beat the smell of newly mown grass or the sensation of its cool softness between bare toes.

At the bottom of their garden in one corner stands an ancient oak with half its branches overhanging the garden and the other half leaning into open fields beyond the fence. There's a rope swing still hanging from one of the sturdier branches. You'd have to be quite an athletic type to reach the wooden seat; it's so high from the ground. I wonder whether Deborah's son had been able to reach it when he was a child. Or was it one of the things in Stephen's early life that disappointed his father?

I hear a door bang below me and there is Philip crossing the lawn, making his way to the shed in the other corner of their garden. He disappears inside and closes the door behind him.

I am exhausted. I throw off my towel and slip between the sheets. It's heavenly to stretch my back and legs. I'm feeling my age and try to remember the first time I noticed aching in my hips, but I can't pinpoint when it began. It seems as if they always ached, but that isn't true. I used to be sporty. Now, I don't even run. *And* I've developed a fear of falling, but I'm not ready to be old. There's so much I want to do, so much of life still undiscovered. I don't want to stop. In any case, there are too many things in the here and now which I have to put right.

Malcolm doesn't know yet that I've sold the family home and set out to the other side of the world without an idea of what I'm going to do next. He hasn't a clue his mother is not planning to return any time soon. He won't like it.

It's too risky a venture for minds like his where everything has to be planned to the *nth* degree. His whole life is organised with precision. He always knows what he's going to do next and after that, too. He is so precise and punctual. If he says something has to happen at ten twenty-six, he really means ten twenty-*six*. Even the way he speaks sounds contrived to me. He doesn't leave, he *departs*. He doesn't begin, he *commences*. I didn't teach him to speak like that, nor did Jim. Malcolm chooses to be so precise in his speech as well as with everything else. He runs his life like a transport timetable, making *windows* to fit in anything unexpected.

I don't think he'll be too worried the family home has gone. He didn't like the area and could never understand why his father hadn't moved us out once the business had taken off.

What? Not reinvested the money, Ma? I can imagine him saying. *You're not planning to spend all of it, are you?*

There'd be a lecture on interest rates and house prices. He would become like the parent; me the child.

Malcolm thinks your home and possessions reflect your true self and you should live according to your status. It's one of his *rules*. That's the black or white sort of way he thinks. He believes a man's true worth is shown even in details such as what his wife is wearing, which associations she belongs to. It's so important to them *who* they know.

He'll be very annoyed I let the house go to another property developer and not let him have the opportunity to make another tidy profit. In fact, I think he'll be beside himself that I could actually go ahead and do it. He'll chew it all over with his wife. Angela.

Angela. It isn't a good name for her. There's nothing angelic about her at all. She's hard and cold and selfish as he is.

I guess they're a good match for one another. I suppose their life together must be how they like it. No children. No other reason than they're too involved with themselves and their networking and their contacts. It's probably the right decision. There would be no time for a child in their lives.

I wonder what made Malcolm choose a girl like Angela. Perhaps that's my fault as well.

ELEVEN

I hear a radio somewhere and realise where I am. I look at my watch. I have slept for six hours. There's a wonderful smell of baking wafting upstairs from the kitchen below and my mouth begins to water. I lie still for a moment, taking stock, preparing myself for meeting Deborah and Philip once more. I feel a little prickle of embarrassment. What if we're uncomfortable with each other?

I get up and find clean clothes. The shower is good and hot. I tidy my hair before going downstairs.

'Audrey. There you are. Come into the kitchen and I'll make us a drink. Hot or cold?'

Deborah immediately makes me feel less self conscious. She's preparing dinner. Briefly, I wonder whether she might have regretted her impetuous invitation to have me in her home, but she looks relaxed. If she regretted some of what she told me, there's no sign of it. She's happily humming along to the tune on the radio. Philip is nowhere to be seen. In his shed, I guess.

I think they are both lonely. Lonely and locked into their separate pain. They are both suffering, but suffering apart. I take the cup of coffee Deborah offers and follow her out of the kitchen into a conservatory where there are large comfortable chairs facing the garden and fields beyond.

'It's a lovely view,' I say. 'How nice it must be to sit here and watch the seasons change.'

'Yes. We're lucky to have that. We get the best of autumn here as the leaves change. And in winter, when there's a deep frost? Oh, it's lovely.'

'I'm used to winter in the sun,' I remind her. 'Summer in December. Christmas barbecue.'

'I don't think I could ever get used to that,' she says.

'No. I never did, no matter how I tried. I still hanker after a traditional white Christmas.'

There's a framed photograph standing beside a lamp on one of the coffee tables. I ask Deborah about it and she launches into the story of a holiday in the United States and how Philip felt out of place with the wealthy family they met. Eventually,

'Audrey, what a bore I'm being prattling on about things that don't matter. Tell me. You're not from Australia originally, are you?'

'No. I'm from Yorkshire.'

'But you're travelling on to Norfolk?'

'Yes. My mother went to live there after my father died. It was where they'd spent many of their summers. They loved the place.'

'And you've been there before?'

'Yes. When I was a girl. Then later, just before I left England. A couple of times since. Mother usually came out to us.'

'I can't imagine how you must feel not knowing about your mother's funeral.'

'Yes. It's very odd. I'll find out when I get there, I suppose. Right now, I don't know any details.'

'So, how *did* you find out?'

'I had a letter from the nursing home where she spent her last days.'

I don't want to say much more. I have so many unanswered questions of my own, I can't cope with Deborah's. I'm thankful when she excuses herself to check on supper. I put my head back against the soft cushions and close my eyes.

Why would my mother do what she did? Why would she want to hide things from me? Why had she gone into a home without telling me?

Immediately, I feel the enormity of this great backup of disappointment, hurt and frustration. There's a hard, choking sensation at the back of my throat that makes me want to weep or scream. I have no loving husband. I have no *loving* son. I don't want to be lonely.

'Hello, there. I hope I'm not disturbing you. Only, Deb says dinner's about ready. I hope you're hungry. She's made enough for the whole village.'

I look up at Philip. He looks freshly showered. His hair is still damp around his ears. He wears a clean pressed shirt open at the neck and he has put on some aftershave. He is smiling kindly at me and I notice for the first time the soft benevolence in his expression, the slight tilt of his head, the openness in his eyes. He's like a child's favourite primary school teacher, solid, reliable, dependable. Yet he has turned his back on his own son and now distances himself from his wife out of the guilt of it.

Deborah appears at the door.

'Ready, Audrey? We're eating in the kitchen tonight.'

'Something smells delicious,' I say.

The food is wonderful. Our conversation covers cooking, favourite dishes, gardening, travel, wine, but I notice both Deborah and Philip direct their comments at me. They don't look at one another. The warm ease of their meeting at the airport earlier has cooled. I sense the cold discomfort between them. There are no signs of togetherness from either of them, no brief glances, no shared jokes. The unspoken questions about their son and Deborah's trip to see him sour the atmosphere. They are more like strangers to one another than I am.

After coffee Philip disappears into his study to attend to his emails, he says. I ask if he would be so kind as to look up comparison train and coach times for my onward journey. As soon as leaves the room, Deborah begins,

'You see?' she says. 'He can't wait to get away from me.'

'He hasn't asked you about your trip, has he?'

'No. He can't without Stephen coming into it. He refuses to talk about him, Audrey. What would you do?'

I take my time. The truth is, I'm not sure where to start. I know how it feels to be hurt by your own son so I can begin to understand what Philip might be going through. He has a son who hasn't turned out the way he wanted. *I* have a son who disappoints me. Is there much difference? My son has a cold, uncaring personality. There is shame in such an admission.

This is the same shame Philip feels. I can't agree with his reasons but I understand his pain.

'I can't give you a ready answer,' I say. 'I don't know what I would do in your shoes, but I think I can help you understand how Philip is feeling.'

'How *he* is feeling? What about how all this is making me feel?'

'You see, that's where I think you're coming undone. You're both locked into your own feelings. I don't think you can afford to wait for your husband and son to sort it out themselves. I'm sorry. I've said too much. I have no right to do that.'

She looks straight into my eyes and I can see she's holding back tears.

'No. You're right. I have to face up to it. It's not going to go away or get better. I can't let it go on. We're growing further and further apart. I think we're both afraid of the next step, Audrey. Oh dear. I tried so hard.'

The rest of the evening is difficult and strained. We watch a little television and comment on the news. Philip has found some timetables for me. He offers to run me to the station. He says it's no trouble; he's going into town in the morning anyway.

Before I take my leave next morning I write down their address and contact numbers. Deborah gives me her email address as well in case I get myself online at some point. Also, I call the telephone contact at the rest home in Norfolk.

Philip deposits me at a convenient rail station and as he leaves I wonder what Deborah will decide to do. I tell myself to stop thinking about them. Good heavens, I've known them for what, thirty six hours? Deborah will most likely forget all about me and our brief friendship in no time at all. I'll probably send them a Christmas card and that will be it, like a holiday romance, okay while it lasted.

◆

My journey is pleasant. I am enthralled by the sights. It's been almost twenty years since I was in England and now, at the height of an English summer, everything looks clean and green. As we approach the capital I spot some of the familiar skyline in the distance and then we are slipping into a tunnel which will take us underground and into the heart of the city.

A short taxi ride to Liverpool Street and once more I'm seated by the window of a train carriage. The train moves out from the station and soon we're passing through glorious countryside, patchwork fields of green and gold rolling off into the distance toward a hazy horizon. And now I'm staring out of the window, looking but not seeing this time, rather drifting in and out of thoughts about yesterday and all the yesterdays before that.

TWELVE

I remember other fields, other horizons, other journeys. When I was a child in Yorkshire we'd have coach trips into the country and then when I was older, train rides to Norfolk for our summer holidays.

We were living in a council house then, I recall, although I have memories of an older house, a stone built terrace on one of the cobbled streets in the centre of town. Mother would have loved a house of her own, but it was not to be. My father was ill and there wasn't much money coming in.

On the day we went to see the new council estate, the bus took us as far as the pre-fabs, *tin houses* we used to call them. They were prefabricated square boxes, hurriedly thrown up after the war to help meet rising demand for family housing. They were supposed to be temporary. The last one came down in the 1980s, I believe. Demolition had to be very careful: the flimsy buildings were insulated with asbestos.

We left the bus at the terminus and continued on foot. It was impossible to walk much further. There was no road, no footpath. The whole of the hillside was being scraped away in front of us and reshaped before our eyes. Huge earth shifting machines lumbered heavily; smaller lorries darted from site to site. As far as you could see there were the first foundations of a group of houses here, another group over there. The project was enormous to my child's eyes. It might have been a moonscape. It was all alien to me. And that was where our new house was going to be. My excitement lasted for months.

We moved into the house the same week we learned I'd passed the eleven plus exam. Mother was so proud and took photographs of me standing on the front doorstep of our new semi wearing my new school blazer. I went to the Girls' Grammar school. It was two bus rides across town and I had a bus pass.

Mother got over her disappointment at living in a council house and began to enjoy the benefits of having a reasonably equipped kitchen and tiled bathroom. There were small gardens back and front but I don't remember either being beautiful.

The Girls' Grammar school was a whole new world to me. Teachers wore cap and gown on Founders' Day. I was mixing with the daughters of people who had ponies, large houses and swish motor cars. Some of the mothers would wait in the drive at the end of the school day and I'd watch as my contemporaries hopped into the back seat, laughing and chatting as they drove away as if it was the most natural thing in the world to be chauffeured around like nobility.

I wasn't the only girl from the estate, though. There was Rita, God bless her. We had some fun together. Rita used to get on the bus to school in the morning two stops after me, by the tin houses. We'd sit and giggle together and make plans for meeting up after school. We knew who was going out with who, who had done what to who and we shared our most intimate secrets. I lost touch with her years ago.

◆

This inner *need* to put my thoughts in order must be something to do with growing older. For most of our lives we don't have time to wonder about it. We're too busy getting on with life, career and raising a family to care whether there is some cosmic destiny at work shaping our journey through this world. Maybe there is no such thing as destiny. Maybe we are all sailing along, reacting to chance, tragedy and opportunity as they randomly present themselves.

I ponder these things but always come down on the side of common sense. I look at the passengers around me on this train to Norfolk, all busily going about their own lives. What are their reasons for being here? What is it that makes their paths cross with mine today? Is any of it important?

We can't live with that level of consciousness all the time. We couldn't cope with that intense degree of awareness. We would wear ourselves out. So, I settle for common sense.

I glance through the carriage window. There's a farmer hard at work in a cornfield, turning over the land after harvest, getting ready for seeding of his new winter crop. We're like that farmer.

We simply get on and do things that have to be done. Sometimes it might be as a direct result of what has recently happened. Sometimes, it's in preparation for what we know will come along next. It isn't precision planning like Malcolm's. It's less aware. It's an automatic sort of thing like when you drive a certain route every day and one day you can't remember passing a certain landmark.

We drift through our lives at times. We find ourselves a comfortable furrow to plough along and we take little notice of gathering storm clouds until it begins to rain. Then something has to change. We have to make a decision to alter some of our comfortable routines and step out into a wider field.

The first time I became aware of this way of looking at the patterns of our lives was when I was standing with my parents gazing at that hillside where our new council house was going to be built. I remember being suddenly and vividly touched by a sense of altered reality. Our lives were going to change forever. I was going to stop being a child. This was going to be the beginning of my growing up.

I did my growing up in the early sixties. It was a wonderful time of music and dance clubs. I had my own record player and my first transistor radio. I was always playing one of them and my mother could never understand how I could complete my homework with what she called *all that noise* going on in the background.

She was working in one of the textile mills in the valley. She often looked tired. In my mind's eye I have an image of her coming home from work, getting off the bus loaded with shopping she'd done in her lunch hour. Her hair would be wrapped in a woollen scarf to cover the greasy fibres which clung to it. Dad and I would help her up the steps to the house, but my father wasn't strong and the effort would always make him cough.

Then it was meal time. We always called it *tea* in our house. Dinner was what you had at lunchtime. Meals were good old-fashioned tasty dinners, usually with plenty of fresh vegetables and the best gravy in the world. Mother always used to say it wasn't a proper dinner unless it had gravy on it and she was the gravy queen. You could have a dish of it on its own with some bread to dip in it and you'd be satisfied.

On Sundays there was always a roast dinner with Yorkshire puddings. Dad would make an apple pie or egg custard for *afters*. He had a magic touch with pastry and it pleased him to contribute to the family this way. They were meals for working class families: good plain, honest ingredients with nothing foreign or fancy in sight.

One year for our domestic science exam, which was called *Housewifery* at the Girls' Grammar School, I had to prepare a meal suitable for an office executive. The class of girls had to imagine they were housewives preparing an evening meal for a husband returning home from work. We drew cards from a box: there were different scenarios so we all picked out something different from each other.

I might have managed much better if I'd drawn *a meal for a coal miner* or *a meal for a bricklayer*. I didn't know where to begin. We didn't know any office executives.

I gave my husband Shepherd's Pie with carrots and cabbage followed by a baked rice pudding. It wouldn't have looked so bad if the rice pudding had browned a little more, but the bell went for the end of the lesson and we had to display our offerings for grading whether we were ready or not.

I didn't pick up any points for appearance. It was a very pale ensemble, the few rings of carrot being the only dash of colour in the whole menu.

'You have to remember, Audrey,' Miss Rawson reminded me, 'that part of the appeal of the food you put on the table is how attractive it is. It is the mouth watering appearance of the food that makes us want to taste it.'

'Yes, Miss Rawson,' I replied, staring despondently at my white tablecloth, white plate, white mashed potato, pale cabbage and white rice pudding.

She tentatively dipped her fork into the Shepherd's Pie and tasted. Then she took another taste. I got top marks for taste and a commendation for the gravy in my Shepherd's Pie. My final grade was B double plus and that's the highest grade I ever achieved for anything in Housewifery.

I was much better at Sports. I enjoyed Art, too and our teacher, Miss Tyler was a joy. She was proud of us and always encouraged us to think of ourselves as special and talented. She lived her work. She was always on the lookout for the unusual and found beauty in the strangest things. I loved how she dressed. She would cobble together the weirdest outfits, mixing colours and textures so she resembled a walking artist's palette.

We girls wore pleated skirts. In school, in sight of teaching staff, all skirts must cover knees. Outside, it was a different story. My friend Rita wore her skirt like a lampshade. She was the one who introduced me to American Tan tights. She showed me how to backcomb my hair and we experimented with her mother's Yardley cosmetics.

Rita and I both fancied Barry who was a friend of Rita's brother. The highlight of our week was when Barry called for Paul on his motorbike. Barry had a face straight out of *Valentine*, and with his perfect hair, sensuous mouth and strong jaw, he made our hearts flutter. One fleeting glance from him and the shiver would run down my spine and curl my toes. He wore tight blue jeans and a black tee shirt with a slashed neck which made the muscles of his chest and arms ripple and tease. His long legs straddling that shiny bike of his inspired complete abandonment of all our girlish inhibitions, so that afterwards Rita and I would admit to all the things we would like to do to him and what we would let him do to us. Barry was beautiful. Rita and I swore we would love him forever.

I got myself a Saturday job round about this time at the hairdresser where mother used to go for her weekly wash and set and regular perm. Suddenly I could afford tickets for the concerts which had been out of my reach. I never lost my interest in Sports though, and Rita and I would go and watch the local Rugby League team, especially if Paul had been selected to play that day, as there was a chance that Barry might be there.

I didn't step inside a pub until I was seventeen years old. There was plenty of choice of ale-houses in our town but I thought they were really quite smelly places, with the reek of stale beer and too much tobacco smoke. However, I still wasn't quite old enough at seventeen to be in a pub, but with my make-up on and the latest high-heels nobody would have been able to tell. I ordered the *Cherry B's* and Rita and I sat in a corner, by the window looking out across the bus station so we could see when our concert coach arrived. It was a Friday and we had tickets to see the Everly Brothers and, naturally, we both liked the same one.

A group of men came in and clamoured around the bar. They didn't look like local talent; for one thing they all had suntans and they spoke in an unusual accent. Neither Rita nor I had ever seen Australians before and it was the next day before we learned who they were.

It was November 1962 and we were disappointed that only one of the brothers was performing. We didn't know it at the time but Don had collapsed on stage and Phil had to continue the tour alone. It was almost symbolic, the irony of it. It was like an omen heralding the huge changes that were about to explode onto the music scene. Their career was beginning to fall away just as the friendship between Rita and I was also moving into another phase. There was a shift in the closeness we'd had; we didn't see each other every day now Rita was at work; we didn't have the shared experience of what had happened in school and we didn't tell each other all our secrets any more.

The day after our trip to see the Everly brother we'd arranged to watch Paul in a Saturday late afternoon fixture. There was to be a dance afterwards in the Rugby Club and Paul had invited us along. The weather was typical for November in Yorkshire: grey skies that threatened rain but with enough wind to hold it at bay. We pondered for some time, Rita and I, how we should dress for this occasion as we didn't want to freeze on the sideline, but we still wanted to look as glamorous as possible for the dance. In the end we decided on full length coats with scarves and gloves. We could have extra layers on underneath if we needed them, on top of our flimsy party dresses. We could change our shoes in the Ladies' toilets and leave the muddy ones in a bag till later.

That was the day I first met Jim. He was one of the group who had come into the pub the night before, and now here he was again, all kitted out in his team strip ready for the match against our local boys.

'Why do they bother to come all the way from Australia just to play league rugby?' I asked Paul on his way out of the pavilion.

'Hey, don't knock it,' he replied. 'It's great experience for all of us. We can't afford to go there; they enjoy spending their summers getting stuck in over here. They're good lads.'

'Is Barry coming along today?' Rita wanted to know.

'Tough luck, Sis. He's out with his girlfriend.' He winked at me with a shrug of his shoulders.

Rita grimaced and turned to me as Paul ran on to the pitch.

'Well,' she huffed, pulling her coat collar up around her neck. 'I don't mind standing out here in the cold if there's something worth looking at, but if Barry's not coming either I'm going into the clubhouse to get warm or . .' her voice tailed away.

'Or what?' I asked.

'Or else I'll just have to find something else to look at. I know,' she went on. 'Let's have a *best legs* competition.'

I don't remember the outcome of the match but I do remember who won the best legs competition: Jim Freeman. He had great legs and afterwards, at the disco, Rita couldn't wait to tell him.

I always remembered that night and the reason we first noticed each other, Jim and I, but in later years Jim had forgotten all about the best legs competition. It was as if it had never happened as far as he was concerned and if ever I brought it up he was dismissive. He didn't like to hear he'd once been the object of youthful female passion; he wouldn't have a joke about it try as I might to get him to loosen up and share a happy reminiscence. He didn't do that; as we grew older together he didn't ever want to be reminded he was once young and fit and desirable. He was still a handsome man well into his sixties, but he wasn't the same light-hearted individual he had been, with a lust for life and a joke for the journey.

◆

There's a rattling noise followed by a gush of air as the connecting doors between carriages open and a drinks trolley is pushed through by a pleasant looking young woman. I watch her serving passengers nearest the door first. I can see what's on offer and order a coffee and a small pack of chocolate biscuits.

The train hurtles through a station and I watch as gradually the conglomeration of town buildings dwindles into the last few groups of houses, and then we are in countryside once more. With half an hour to go before we reach Norwich I begin to check my bag: mobile phone, notebook, cash. I pull out the folded letter from the rest home on which there's a hand-drawn map showing its location.

Walsingham. According to the map it doesn't appear to be on the coast of Norfolk where I expected it to be, close to the familiar beach resorts where we'd spent holidays in the past. I think back to my last letters to my mother. All of them had been posted to her usual address in Wells-next-Sea. I dismiss the discrepancy. There's probably nothing in it, I tell myself. She simply chose to spend her last days somewhere else, that's all. Why look for mysteries when I already have plenty of questions? I refold the letter, replace it in my bag and pick up my coffee. Not far to go now. Soon be at journey's end.

THIRTEEN

Jim Freeman. I can't say it was love at first sight because it wasn't. That first time I met him I didn't have the confidence to know how to talk to an older man. Jim was twelve years older than me and at twenty nine was in his sporting prime, strong, big and rugged. He was a man's man. Physically, he was everything my former idol, Barry was not. Where Barry was snake-hipped, Jim was broad and firm. Barry had the build of a tango dancer, lithe and supple. Jim was built like a concrete bunker.

That night at the club house the Australians gathered with the local boys, buying rounds of drinks and swapping rugby stories. Rita and I were sitting at a table near the edge of the small parquet dance floor. Nobody was dancing yet. It was an unwritten rule that you didn't get up to dance until the evening was well under way and the lads had had enough Dutch courage to come across and ask the girls. My mother had taught me *never* to refuse a dance and I agreed with the sentiment that it would be churlish to do so. If you didn't fancy the poor guy at all it was much kinder to thank him at the end of the dance and say that you were now going back to your seat, or back to your friends. If your unwelcome admirer became too persistent you could always use a little white lie and tell him you were not looking for a boyfriend, that you already had one who couldn't be there tonight. That way nobody was really hurt.

Rita was going on about the Australians, and I knew she was building up to making an approach. I tried to keep her in conversation; I didn't want to draw attention to us, but as soon as she caught sight of her brother joining the crowd at the bar, she had her excuse. She was up out of her seat and crossing the room before I could stop her. I saw her reach up and say something in Paul's ear and then all the guys turned around and looked over at me.

I was mortified. I felt the blush rise up through my body and burn into my face. I watched, horrified, as Rita ran her hands over Jim's thighs and I knew she'd told them all about our best legs competition. I was on the point of fleeing to the toilets but they all turned away and started ordering more drinks from the barman. Rita gestured for me to join them at the bar, but I couldn't move; I was too embarrassed. She gestured again but I shook my head. She decided to stay where she was and I could see she was flirting for England, tossing her hair and laughing too loud. I didn't know what to do so I just sat there trying to look as if I was enjoying myself. I tried to find something to concentrate on, anything away from the direction of the crowd at the bar. Then Rita's empty chair was being pulled back and Jim Freeman was sitting down next to me.

'Hello,' he said, 'You're Audrey, I'm Jim, and this drink is for you. Your friend said it's what you like.'

I glanced over towards the bar and saw Rita glowering at me.

'Don't worry about your friend,' Jim told me, nodding in her direction. 'She's in good company. She'll come to no harm with my mates. Well are you going to speak to me? No worries if you're not. I can go back the way I came.'

'Thank you for the juice,' I uttered like a fool, taking in the size of him, the size of his hands, the breadth of his shoulders. I was overwhelmed. This was a real man. He made me feel weak.

'That's better,' he smiled. 'Now, what about this best legs business? I think it's only right you let me have a good look at yours. That'd be fair wouldn't it? No, wait a minute,' he continued. 'See, what you've got to do now, to make it fair, is to give me a dance. I can give them a quick once over while we're up there, and if I don't like your legs I can run like hell. You've seen me in action on the pitch, so you know I can run pretty fast for a big fella. What'd'ya say?'

He leaned back against the chair and folded his arms across his massive chest. He was so confident, so at ease, so *masculine*. I wanted to impress him with my answer. I wanted to come back at him with the witty repartee of a sophisticated woman, but my mind was a blank and I responded like the schoolgirl I still was.

'I can run too,' I mumbled.

'Ah, Jeez,' he laughed. 'You think you'd be able to catch me?'

'If I wanted to I could,' I said, smiling now. 'You haven't seen *me* in action. Do you dare risk it?'

He clapped his huge hand on the table and roared with laughter. I went along with the momentum of my new-found force, this energy that was reverberating between us now I felt I could match him. I could handle him, after all.

'Yes,' I went on, 'my mother was an Olympic champion before I was born,' I lied, 'and I'm currently in training for Tokyo. That's why I'm only on soft drinks.'

I took a sip of my juice and, copying his own body language, I leaned back in my chair, folded my own arms across my chest and waited for his response with a smile on my face and a warm sensation inside me.

I liked him. He didn't treat me like a schoolgirl. He seemed to be genuinely interested in what I had to say, and asked my opinion about things. I had no idea I was sitting across the table looking at my future husband.

FOURTEEN

SNAPSHOTS 1937-1938

Richard Mansfield, the proprietor of Mancini Modes had been interested in ladies' dresses for as long as he could remember. As a child he played with his mother's silk scarves, stroking the fabric and enjoying its sensual softness, holding its slickness against his face and taking in the aroma of his mother's perfume.

Childhood had been difficult for him, boarding school a nightmare. He created his own imaginary world as he lay in his dormitory bed, terrified of what the boys would find to do to him next day. They always found something, some new trick to play on him, some other means of shaming him and calling him names. In his imaginary world he was safe from their taunts and teasing and he began to plan his future: he would surround himself with all the things he loved best and be admired for it.

He set up his first ladies' fashion outlet on the south coast where he was delighted to find others like himself and soon had a circle of friends. He'd borrowed the name *Mancini*. It sounded exotic.

He left the south of England under a cloud. Nobody would have been able to detail exactly what the threatened scandal entailed, nor would they have been able to give any names of the people involved, but the outcome was that Richard had shut up shop and removed himself from the area to protect the reputation of some unknown person or persons. His most loyal friend moved with him. Godfrey wouldn't let him go away by himself.

'Just exactly how far north are we thinking of travelling?' Godfrey asked once the decision to leave had been made. 'Isn't it a bit dirty up there? Are you sure it's the right move?'

'Godfrey,' Richard replied, 'There are women who need my talents *everywhere.*'

Richard had chosen Kingsley. The town was strategically placed at the hub of a wide circle of larger cities. He reckoned professional people working in the cities would be more likely to live in the pleasant market town rather than in the city suburbs, and he was right. Kingsley provided an abundance of bankers' and business men's wives, as well as women whose husbands owned mills and factories down in the valley.

He found an ideal location for Mancini Modes at the entrance to a wide, sweeping arcade. The huge curved glass frontage thrilled him to the core as he imagined the wonderful window displays he could create there, and as the property had its own apartment above the shop it was as if it was meant to be.

'There you are Godfrey,' he said as they took possession of the keys. 'Let's do it!'

In public, he reined himself in; he acted the successful business man. But in the shop, with his ladies, his cherished clients, he had learned the level of outrageous effeminacy that would be tolerated in this northern town by each of them. Most of the wealthy women who patronised his establishment tolerated more than their husbands might have imagined. They enjoyed his chatter; they loved his bitchy comments about politicians' wives. Some sought his advice on style and colour, so that he had become a respected personal stylist for the very wealthiest and influential women on the social circuit.

When Jean Thompson walked in to enquire about the position of sales assistant he was impressed. It was obvious the child had made real effort with her appearance, not all of it successful, but he could see past the gaucheness of her youth as he appraised her immaculate deportment. She had natural grace, like a dancer. She held her head up, kept her back straight and knew what to do with her hands and feet. He could do something with her. He gave her the job, but there were conditions.

He sat her on a chair in front of one of the full length mirrors and explained.

'Jean, I want you to take off all your make-up. We'll put some of it back on again after we've finished, but for now we don't need it.' He handed her some cotton wool and an enormous pot of cold cream.

'This is what you should use to remove cosmetics,' he told her, 'You'll find it's better for your skin. Now then, we're going to do your colours.'

The child obviously hadn't a clue what he was talking about, but she sat waiting, trusting. He selected some scarves and evening wraps from the display racks and held them, one at a time, in front of her face.

'Look,' he said. 'Notice how some colours suit you better than others. What do you think of this one?' He draped a midnight blue chiffon across her chest. 'Go on,' he repeated, 'What do you think?'

'Not much,' she replied. 'It doesn't look right on me.'

'Good. Now this one. See what this colour does to your eyes and face. What differences do you see?'

The girl looked closely at herself in the mirror. The antique gold colour made her skin look completely different. Whereas the blue had drained her face and dulled her eyes, the golden shade had brightened her skin tone and brought out the flecks of hazel in her eyes.

'I can't believe it. Who'd have thought that the colour of your clothes could make that much difference,' she said.

'That's just the beginning,' he said. 'We'll work through the rest after you start work next Monday. Don't wear this dress you've come in today.'

'I can't,' she admitted. 'It's not mine. I borrowed it from a friend.'

'Well there you are, then,' he said with a smile. 'That dress was never meant for you, was it? Wait a minute. Stand up, please. Turn around. I've got just the thing.'

He disappeared into the stockroom and came back with a dark caramel knitted jersey skirt and jacket.

'Try this, please,' he told her. 'I believe you'll find the size is perfect for you. You'll need some shoes with a small heel and a different shade of lipstick. We can sort that out later.'

'But, Mr Mancini, I haven't got enough to pay for this,' she said, shaking her head.

'I know that. Jean, it's your first working outfit. A gift from me.'

He stood waiting for her to come out of the changing room, and she appeared like an angel framed by the brocade hangings of the cubicle.

She was glowing; her hair shone; her eyes sparkled and when she smiled at him he dismissed all the information she had so honestly given him about her working class background. He saw instead his *ingénue*, his new delightful muse and he clasped his hands in front of his chest.

'Perfect,' he beamed. 'Godfrey!' he shouted up the stairs. 'Bring down my vanity case, will you?'

◆

It never occurred to Jean to wonder why Mr Mancini would have his own vanity case of cosmetics, powders and creams. She simply accepted it was his job and he knew what he was talking about. Why shouldn't he know about those things? Max Factor invented most of them, after all, and he was a man.

When Jean looked at herself again in the mirror, after he'd redone her eyebrows and shaped them into a more natural arch, she could see he definitely knew what he was talking about. She smiled and congratulated herself on getting her first job with the most fascinating people she'd ever met.

'See you on Monday,' she called, on her way out with her new suit carefully wrapped in tissue and carried in an exclusive Mancini Modes carrier bag.

'Nine o' clock sharp Miss Thompson,' Richard called after her, and closing the door he swivelled on his heel and held out his hands in a balletic pose.

'Godfrey,' he exclaimed in a stage whisper, 'I am ahead of my time.'

◆

Breaking the news to Hilda wasn't as bad as Jean thought it was going to be.

'Well, I'm a bit disappointed, Jean,' she said, 'because you know George and I wanted you to stay on at school a bit longer. But if you're happy . . .'

'Yes, I am, Hilda. I'm really looking forward to working there. It'll be good to learn the trade from someone like Mr Mancini. He knows such a lot about fashions and everything.'

'Yes, love,' she agreed. 'I'm sure he does.'

'And it's better than going down the mill, isn't it?' Jean asked, looking for more enthusiasm from her sister.

'You're right,' she said. 'Tell you what. Why don't you put on your new outfit and we'll surprise George with your news when he gets home from work.'

George wasn't so easy to persuade. His face fell. He took it personally that Jean had made the decision without talking to him about it first. He was the man of the house and he had a right to know about everything that happened in it, *before* it happened. He thought he was doing the right thing, he pointed out to his wife, providing the means and the opportunity for Jean to stay at school and make something of herself.

'Why have you let me down, my Jean?' he asked her.

'Oh, George,' she said. 'Please don't be upset. I'm sorry I didn't talk to you about it first.'

'It makes me feel you don't care what I think when you forget to let me know your plans.'

'But I didn't really make any plans, George. It all just happened so quickly.'

'And your gymnastics and your running? Are you going to give them up too?'

'No. I'm still going to Miss Linford's, and when I have half-day closing off work I'll be able to do my training every Tuesday afternoon.'

'Well, that's one good thing, then,' he said, and his expression softened. 'You don't think I am stupid Polish bloke?'

Jean threw her arms around him and hugged him. There were tears in his eyes when they drew back from one another.

'You look like film star,' he told her. 'All grown up. Look at you. Like film star.'

FIFTEEN

There were so many new things to learn during Jean's first week at work the time raced by. Mr Mancini took her through an examination of the rest of the colours in the palette. He coached her on the correct ways to address customers when they came into the shop, and the polite ways to behave during their time there. He kept a list of his regular clientele and told Jean that she must do her best to memorise the names so she could greet each one personally. He explained that using *Good afternoon, Mrs Wilson* instead of Good afternoon, Madam demonstrated that the patron was highly valued. It also showed the level of personal care he wished to devote to his ladies.

There was also the telephone to learn. She was thrilled about being able to take telephone messages; she felt she was in a scene from a film.

Mr Mancini taught her about the social seasons and how he usually pre-selected several outfits from which his patrons would make their choice.

'You see, darling,' he explained. 'The poor dears would make all the wrong choices if I give them the run of the stock. They trust me to hand-select for them, and when you've been here longer I'll go through the check-list with you.'

Mr Mancini only ever called her darling when there were no customers in the shop. He called Godfrey darling too, and sometimes when he was in one of his flamboyant moods with a regular client, he would call her darling as well. They didn't seem to mind. They would put on an expression as if they thought he was being cheeky, but Jean could tell by their tight little smiles and their wagging of a gloved finger that they loved the attention he gave them.

She was to call Godfrey, Mr Jardeen. He was always on hand to make any alterations that were necessary; sometimes an evening gown was too long or a blouse might need the buttons moving. And each night she couldn't wait to tell George and Hilda all about her day, or pass on to Sandra the gospel according to Mr Mancini about style, texture and colour. Everything was perfect; there was not a cloud on the horizon.

One Tuesday afternoon when Jean had finished her training session at Miss Linford's and was in the house on Larksholme Lane by herself, there was a knock at the back door. When she opened it her stomach sank.

'Mam!' she exclaimed. 'Dad! What are you doing here?'

'Oh, you remember who we are then?' Mary Thompson said with a snarl. 'Three years and hardly a sight nor sound of us own daughter. Never see her at all these days, do we Charlie? She's too good for the likes of us now.'

Charlie said nothing, just pushed past Jean and stood in the kitchen, looking around. Mary followed him in and helped herself to a seat at Hilda's table.

'Well, close the door, stupid. We don't want the whole yard to hear our business,' she snapped at Jean.

Jean did as she was told. There was fear in her heart and she could feel her legs beginning to tremble. The blood drained from her face and her skin went cold. She managed to find her voice.

'What do you want?'

'What do we want, she says. What do we want? What do we want, Charlie?' her mother teased.

'Some of this,' her father grunted, looking around at Hilda and George's possessions, running his tobacco-stained fingers over the French polished table, and handling the little glass candlestick George had bought from a salesman at work one day.

Mary got up from her seat and walked across the room to Hilda's gas cooker, looked inside it, then turned her attention to the gas water heater next to the sink.

'Some of this'd be nice an' all,' she added, her face twisted in a menacing sneer. They were like prowling crocodiles, Jean thought. They were scale-covered ugly creatures.

'Stop it!' Jean cried out. 'You've no right to come barging in here causing trouble.'

'Oh, there'll be no trouble,' Charlie said quietly, his voice threatening and eerily controlled. 'Not if you do the right thing, my girl.'

Jean stood in front of her father and found the courage to face him.

'What are you talking about?' she said.

Her father sneered down at her. His eyes were cold.

'A little bird tells me you're working now. At that dress shop belonging to the two Nancy boys. Pay well, do they?'

'I haven't been paid yet. Why?'

'Why?' he repeated. 'She wants to know why, Mary. Nobody's been teaching you your manners, little miss high and mighty. If you'd learned good manners you'd know what you should be doing now. Don't you know you owe it to us to pay us back for all we've done for you? Listen to me, Lady. I'll be waiting for you every Friday, and every Friday when you come out of that pansy's shop, you'll hand over your wage packet.'

He took a step towards her and grabbed her arm.

'Leave her alone!'

Hilda was standing in the doorway. Jean had never seen her sister look so angry. Hilda slammed the door closed behind her, rushed into the room and grabbed her mother's wrist.

'Make him let go of her,' she screamed.

'Now, Hilda, we only want what's right,' Mary whined.

'You wouldn't know what's right if it jumped up and smacked you in the face. Let go of her, Dad.'

Jean felt Charlie release her arm. She ran to the back of the room. Charlie skulked by the cellar-head. Hilda relaxed her grip on her mother's wrist.

'We should get something,' Mary wheedled. 'We looked after her first.'

'No you didn't. That's what good parents are supposed to do. You two were useless.'

Jean watched as Hilda turned toward their father.

'*I* looked after her. All you could ever look after is your beer gut. Now get out of my house.'

'You can't do this to your own flesh and blood,' Mary simpered. 'We'll go to the police. We'll tell 'em you've kidnapped her and we want her to come home. Or we can always tell the real truth. All of it.'

Hilda threw back her head and laughed.

'Go to the police then,' she snorted at them. 'I dare you. You both know what I'll tell 'em if you do.'

Charlie pulled at the collar around his neck. His face reddened and his neck looked thick and hot. 'You haven't heard the last of this, Hilda, my girl,' he threatened.

'I'm not your girl. Don't ever call me that,' she hissed.

'I should have taught you more respect for your own father,' he said, making for the door.

'Well, on your way out have a good look at what you taught me instead.' Her eyes flashed as she spat out the words.

Jean was astonished at the venom her sister could produce. Her own heart was pounding and she was struggling to fight back tears. Her sister was amazing. She was fearless. Jean watched her as she closed the door behind the intruders and turned the key in the lock.

'I'm sorry you had to witness all that,' Hilda said.

'What did you mean, Hilda, when you said they'd both know what you would tell the police?'

'I can't tell you.'

'Yes you can.'

'No, I can't. I'll tell you when you're older.'

'Don't keep putting me off with that, Hilda. I *am* older. Tell me now. Please.'

Hilda sighed. 'Put the kettle on then, and when we've both calmed down properly I'll tell you.'

Jean made tea and waited for her sister to begin. Hilda looked at the clock and went to unlock the door.

'This is going to have to be quick, Jean,' she said. 'I don't want to be talking about this when George comes in. Do you understand what I'm saying?'

Jean nodded, but wondered what George had to do with it. Whatever it was had happened long before Hilda had met George.

'You know how we've all got private places on our bodies?'

Jean nodded.

'We share those places with our husbands, and it's a lovely thing to do.'

'Is it?' Jean questioned, thinking back to her early fumblings when she wasn't quite sure exactly what she did have *down there.*

'Yes, it can be. With the right person. A girl's father is *not* the right person.'

'You mean, me dad? He did that to you?'

'He tried, Jean. I suppose he was drunk at the time, but that's no excuse. He tried touching me where he shouldn't.'

'What did you do? Didn't you tell Mam?'

'You know what she's like, Jean. Do you think she would have taken any notice?'

'So what did you do?'

'I hit him. The first time he tried it on.'

'You mean he did it more than once?'

'Yes, but I always managed to fend him off. You know me, I've always had a gob on me. I've always kept an eye on him, Jean. For you, I mean. He didn't start on me till I was about thirteen, so I kept a lookout for you, in case he started on you as well. He didn't, did he?'

'No.' Jean tried to make a joke. 'They were too busy bashing each other.'

'Well, I always knew that one day you'd come to live with me. I always hoped so.'

At last Jean had her answer to the question bothering her. Now she knew the real reason why Hilda wanted to move away from Kingsley. She wanted to be free of *him*, of their father. She wanted to remove herself so far away from the memories of his drunken advances that they couldn't bother her any more. Suddenly, she was struck by a flash of realisation.

'George doesn't know about it, does he? You haven't told him. Have you?'

Hilda did not reply.

'He doesn't know, does he?' Jean took hold of her sister's hand. 'Oh, Hilda,' she said softly. 'I won't breathe a word. You can trust me. I won't ever tell a soul.'

'You've got to promise me, Jean. It'll spoil everything if you tell.'

Jean held on to her sister and stroked her hair as Hilda wept silently on her little sister's shoulder, and Jean vowed to herself that from that moment on she would do everything she could to learn from Hilda, to become as strong and as brave.

What better could she do than to grow into a woman like her sister? She would find the courage from somewhere. One day there might be a chance for her to repay Hilda and show her how much she loved her.

SIXTEEN

In 1937 there were only two hundred thousand soldiers in the British army. It seemed nobody was doing anything about the rise of the Nazi political party in Germany. England had no stomach for re-armourment to counteract any threat: the Great War was too recent a memory. Peace-loving citizens relied on the Treaty of Versailles to keep them safe. The sabre rattling Winston Churchill was considered a war-mongerer and dismissed as a political has-been. On May 12th the coronation of King George V1 took place and in the northern market town of Kingsley life went on as normal.

News of the Spanish civil war and the involvement of Nazi troops headlined in the national newspapers, but, more importantly for George Pozyzcka, Jean Thompson had her photograph in the latest edition of the Kingsley News.

'Look at this. Look at this,' George blurted to his work colleagues during lunch break in the office. He jumped to his feet, slapped the paper with the back of his hand and shook it under their noses. 'That's my Jean. That's my Jean.' He couldn't stop repeating himself.

She was pictured, sitting on a wall, wearing her gym outfit and holding up the silver trophy she had just been awarded for first place in the Northern Open Gymnastics championships for her outstanding performance on the balance beam.

'Listen to this,' George read from the column alongside the photo.

'Miss Elaine Linford, former Olympic athlete and British team coach has great hopes for the local girl. Jean, who works as a fashion stylist with Mancini Modes of Kingsley is modest about her achievement. *'I've always been good at sports',* she informed our reporter. *'I was just born that way, I think.'*

'Yes,' George said, 'she was always good, always good. She was beating me when she was only twelve years old. Ha!'

He sat back down in his swivel chair and twirled himself round and around.

'I think he's pleased,' said another Gas Board employee, and got up to give George a good-natured slap on the back.

'It's hard for me to tell you just how pleased I am,' George attempted to say, but his voice cracked with emotion and the last two words were inaudible. He took a handkerchief from his pocket and wiped his eyes. 'They are my only family, you know. You understand me? My only family.'

Hilda had some more good news. She'd been letting the spare bedroom to visiting acts from the Hippodrome theatre of late. They were never the stars of touring variety shows or repertory companies who came to stay with the Pozyzckas. Big names were usually put up at the Station Hotel or the Cavendish, but if there was a large ensemble the company would need lodgings for the supporting performers. Hilda had received a booking for two musicians from the orchestra of the touring production of *The Desert Song*. Musicians were the best lodgers to have. They always had their instruments with them and a musical party evening would often be arranged at the end of the run. Romberg's *Desert Song* was one of George's favourite musical shows. He had a recording of a famous Italian tenor singing selections which he guarded fiercely.

Over dinner that night Hilda made an announcement.

'Let's make it a real party,' she said. 'Let's invite the neighbours, some friends and other people from the production company who would like to join us.'

'Especially more musicians,' George added.

'Could I invite some people, Hilda?' Jean asked, her eyes burning with excitement.

'Yes, love. Who have you got in mind?'

'Well, Sandra, because she's still my best friend and there are two other people.'

'Who's that?'

'I'd like to invite Mr Mancini and Mr Jardeen. I think they would really enjoy that kind of party, and they have both been so good to me, letting me have time off work for my training and competitions.'

Hilda threw George a quick glance. He smiled back at her.

'Right you are, then, Jean,' he said. 'We'll make it a proper celebration. We have plenty to celebrate so we should mark the occasion in style.'

'We could make it fancy dress,' Hilda suggested.

'Oh, yes,' Jean agreed. 'That would be wonderful. Oh, I can't wait. What a good idea!'

Godfrey thought it was a stupendous idea too, when Jean mentioned it next day at work. He rushed straight upstairs to his workroom and brought down his sketch book to show her.

'It's been too long,' he gasped, out of breath from tackling the stairs two at a time. 'We really need to do this, Richard, for us. We haven't let our hair down in an age.'

He began flipping through pages of his designs. Richard peered over his shoulder.

'I'd forgotten,' he said. 'I'd forgotten all about this.' He indicated Godfrey's drawings and turned to Jean.

'We used to have such fun, darling,' he smiled. He gazed wistfully at the ceiling as though he could see the ghosts of parties past and with his eyes half closed he waved his hand in an exaggerated arc as if he were introducing a prima ballerina onto the stage.

'You're quite right, Godfrey, darling,' he said, suddenly. 'Of course we accept your invitation, Jean. Tell your sister we would be delighted to attend. Would she be offended, do you think, if we brought along some champagne?'

'I shouldn't think so, Mr Mancini,' Jean replied. 'Champagne? I don't think any of us has ever had any of that.'

'Ah, then we shall bring glasses too. You must have the correct glasses for champagne. They shall be a gift for the household.' He was in full flow now, and paced around the shop floor making plans and reminiscing about costumes he and Godfrey had concocted before.

'Mr Mancini,' Jean interrupted. 'We live in an ordinary house in the middle of the town. It isn't . . .'

'Don't apologise for where you live, Jean. We don't judge people by the houses they live in, do we Godfrey?' He didn't give Godfrey chance to answer but carried straight on. 'No, indeed.

That simply wouldn't do. Look at us, darling. We live over the shop with hardly space to swing a cat, but we don't consider ourselves to be pitied for it. No, we are honoured to be your sister's invited guests.'

He stopped pacing about and lowered his voice. 'Jean, dear,' he cleared his throat. 'Your people are aware aren't they that Godfrey and I are, shall we say, different?'

'We're all different Mr Mancini.'

'God Bless this child!' he cried. 'Jean, my darling, you are wise beyond your years. Now then, to work. We must decide on costumes. Godfrey, what have we got in the stock room?'

Jean met Sandra from work at lunchtime and gave her the news. Sandra was just as excited as everybody else.

'Oh, Jean, how fantastic. I've never been to a fancy dress party before. I'll ask my mam to help me. What are you wearing?' she asked.

'It's a secret. Mr Mancini is taking charge of my costume and won't let me tell anybody. Mr Jardeen is going to make it for me.'

'You lucky thing,' Sandra congratulated her. 'Imagine. Having your costume fashioned by a real designer. Why don't you come round tonight and tell my mam all about it?'

✦

The Logans lived away from the centre of town. It was a good fifteen minutes walk across Old Man's Park, up past the library and wash house and on, up again, climbing the hillside towards a row of elegant Edwardian houses whose bay windows commanded a panoramic view over the valley below. The front gate opened onto the path leading through a shrubbery up to the front door which stood at the top of two wide steps. Mrs Sylvia Logan kept two matching green glazed urns on the top step, either side of the door, in which she arranged garden plants according to the season. As secretary of the ladies' section of the Catholic Social Association she hosted the regular monthly meetings and felt that the first impressions of her home were as important as the décor inside.

Her husband, Thomas Logan, general manager at the Endura Iron and Steel works traced his roots back to the Emerald Isle, as he fondly referred to the home of his ancestors, but his grandfather, the first of the line to cross the Irish Sea had cannily changed the spelling of the family name into the more anglicised format.

Thomas and Sylvia believed themselves pillars of their society, not better than others, but certainly bearing the responsibility of setting a good example. It had been a disappointment that their son had chosen not to follow in his father's footsteps to learn the foundry trade, but there was still time for that. He was a headstrong lad, their Ronnie; it would do him the power of good to get most of it out of his system down at the coal yard. A few years working outside in cold winters would help him see sense. Their daughter was doing well at the pharmacy, it seemed. Cyril Hall spoke highly of her and they'd discussed the possibility of her training to become a fully qualified pharmacist's assistant.

Thomas sat in his favourite armchair with his newspaper. The news from Spain was not good: the bombing of Guernica by the German Condor Legion had been followed by a breakout of street fighting in Barcelona, and now, Republican Spain had formed the Servicio Investigacion Militar, controlled by communists and with numerous Russian so-called advisers. He folded up his newspaper and threw it to the floor.

'Madness,' he shouted at the empty room. The whole damned situation in Europe was escalating. It brought a shiver to the back of his neck. The possible outcomes were unthinkable.

'Sylvia,' he called out to his wife who was preparing supper. 'Put mine to keep warm in the oven, please. I'm going out.'

'Going out?' She hurried through to the sitting room from the kitchen. 'Whatever's the matter, dear?'

'I need a drink,' he said.

'Let me pour one for you, Thomas. What would you like?'

'I want a pint of strong draught Yorkshire Bitter. Nothing else will do, Sylvia. I won't be long.'

He walked past her into the hall, took his overcoat from the rack by the door and went out, leaving her looking perplexed by the suddenness of his decision.

The August night was chilly. Wind from moorlands above Kingsley hammered at his back as he hurried down the avenue towards town, where he hoped to find some solace in the companionship of the tap room at the Cavendish. He pushed through the revolving doors, crossed the lounge bar and swept straight on into the bar at the back: the working men's retreat from everything outside. He downed the first pint in a succession of rapid thirsty gulps and ordered the second.

'Dad.'

He looked around. Ronnie came up to join him at the bar.

'I thought your usual haunt was The Black Horse?'

'Ah, not any more, Dad. Time for a change. I come in here now for the craic after work.'

It was the first time ever that father and son had stood at the bar in a public house. It was the first time they'd met each other as equals, had talked to each other as one man to another instead of as parent and child. They fell into conversation as easily as falling off a log. The years peeled away from Thomas. He relaxed in his son's company and found he actually enjoyed the lad's way of looking at life. He took a quick look around the tap room and recognised a couple of men seated at a table, playing dominoes.

'Evening Mr Logan,' one of them called across to him. 'Fancy a game?'

He'd promised Sylvia he wouldn't be long. But what the hell? He was out with his son and he was enjoying himself.

'Thanks, Bob. Yes, me and our Ronnie will make up a four with you.'

They drew up another two chairs and settled in for a session.

◆

As she made her way up the hill, Jean saw Sandra watching for her through the living room window. She disappeared from behind the curtain. The front door opened. Jean stepped inside.

'Hello, Jean,' Sandra said. 'Look, I'm sorry about this, but I don't think it's a good time right now to tell Mam about your party.'

'Why? Has something happened?'

'No, not yet, but I think it might before long. Come in anyway. We'll go in the kitchen out of the way.'

Sandra's mother was pacing in the sitting room, watching the clock. They could see her through the partly open door as they made their way through to the back of the house.

'Has somebody died?' Jean whispered.

'Not yet,' Sandra laughed, 'but when Dad gets in she just might kill him.'

Sandra took a tin of biscuits from the larder and the girls sat whispering around the kitchen table.

'Dad hardly ever goes out without her, you see, Jean. She's furious. She's scraped his dinner into the dustbin.'

'I don't think I should stay, Sandra.' Jean hated the thought of drunken arguments. The very thought of Sandra's father coming into the house and causing trouble made her insides lurch.

'Don't go just yet,' Sandra pleaded. 'It might be funny.'

They stayed in the kitchen till ten. Sandra made her mother a cup of tea, but Mrs Logan wouldn't come out of the sitting room. Sandra thought she'd been weeping and didn't want to show her face.

On her way home Jean saw the hunched shapes of two men coming up the hill on the other side of the road. She passed below them and then turned to watch as they staggered across the road, tripped and lurched on to the opposite pavement. She recognised Ronnie and his father, arms around one another, keeping the other upright, but it didn't look funny to her. It made her feel sick.

SEVENTEEN

A few days later, Jean was dusting behind the counter when Sylvia Logan came into Mancini Modes.

'Good afternoon, Mrs Logan,' Jean said as she'd been taught. 'What can I do for you?'

She laid down her duster and rested her hands in front of her waist, one hand on top of the other in the accepted fashion.

'I'd like to speak to Mr Mancini.'

'He's engaged on the telephone at the moment, Mrs Logan, but I'll let him know you're here.'

'Thank you,' Sandra's mother said. She looked uncomfortable. Her eyes were darting about as if she didn't know where to look. She sat on one of the Queen Anne style chairs to wait.

Jean ran upstairs. Richard was taking a private call on the extension line.

'Tell her I'll be with her shortly, Jean,' he said. 'You know how to say it.'

'Mr Mancini sends his apologies, Mrs Logan,' Jean said. 'He'll be with you just as soon as he can. He is unavoidably detained at present.'

Sandra's mother nodded, but still looked the other way.

'Is there anything I could help you with for the moment?' Jean asked.

'I don't think so. Thank you. I have an enquiry regarding the laundering of a certain fabric.'

When Mr Mancini came down, Jean went to the small kitchen area at the back of the shop. Mrs Logan was speaking quietly, but Jean could hear everything she said. She threw her hand over her mouth to stop herself from laughing. She heard the door bell tinkle and, certain that Sandra's mother had gone, she could hold back no longer. She fell into fits of loud laughter.

'I don't suppose that pompous woman is used to being vomited on. How did you know about it, Jean?'

'I was there, Mr Mancini. I saw Mr Logan and their Ronnie going home in a right state. They'd been on the pop. They could hardly stand up.'

Richard Mancini rolled his eyes. Then, he said,

'How are the mighty fallen.'

He flicked back his hair and glided around the shop, rubbing his hands together. 'I have news,' he said.

He'd spent the last half an hour on the telephone attempting to discover the rearrangements for the production of the Desert Song. The leading man had developed laryngitis and if a replacement couldn't be found the show would have to be either postponed or cancelled outright.

'I've just heard it from the management at the Hippodrome,' he informed them. 'They've been able to reorganise their programme, so we shan't be disappointed. The show will still go ahead with the lovely David in the leading role, but it's to take place later in the year to give him time to recover from his illness.'

'Thank goodness,' Godfrey sighed. 'We'll still be able to wear our *Desert Song* costumes. I didn't want to have to start on another set.'

'How will that work with your sister, Jean?'

'Oh, it'll be all right, Mr Mancini. It won't make any difference to Hilda, unless she's got other lodgers booked in. What dates have they given?'

'Early December,' he replied. 'It'll be like an early Christmas present.'

◆

The residents of Larksholme Lane talked about the party for years afterwards. It had been the best time the neighbours had seen for as long as they could remember, and whenever a group of women gathered around the washing lines in the courtyard during the ensuing summers when there was little of cheer to gossip about, the conversation would turn to the exciting night they'd had, and they would drape themselves in the bedsheets before hanging them out to dry, as if they were fashioning their fancy dress costumes once again.

George and some of the other men from the street had set up a system of lighting the way to the outside privvies. It didn't present too much of a problem for the neighbours who were used to crossing the yard in the dark and negotiating their way down the narrow corridor of the toilet block, but they didn't want visitors tripping up over gratings or uneven flagstones. George had borrowed some workmen's paraffin lamps from the Gas Board and these created a pathway, lighting the route. Jean said she thought it worked well and added to the party atmosphere.

Elsie, the widow lady whose house backed onto the courtyard opposite George and Hilda dressed herself as a highwayman for the party at the Pozyzckas. She was a diminutive figure; her spine had grown into a curve so that she walked with a stoop, but because she'd stopped growing at an early age she was the size of a ten year old child with tiny feet. She could still wear children's clothing and the costume was one she'd had for many years. She was the first to arrive that night. In their Roman togas, Hilda and George met her at the door and she rushed to the table to reserve herself a chair.

'Pardon me Hilda,' she explained. 'Only, I'm so thrilled about all this. I don't want to miss a thing. I want to see all the people in their costumes as they come in. I can stand on the chair, do you see? I can get up on the chair so I don't miss anything. You don't mind, do you?'

The front room had been put to use that night. George had rearranged the furniture to make more standing room and there was a roaring fire in the hearth. Hilda and Jean had made some early Christmas decorations from crepe paper: plaited strips crossed from corner to corner on the ceiling; concertina style box chains draped the mirror and the wall lights. Interlocking coat hangers, covered in paper and tinsel, hung from the doorways. There was a real Christmas tree in front of the window, decorated with glass baubles and tiny candles held by peg-like clips pinned onto the branches.

There was another coal and log fire in the back kitchen and the table groaned under the weight of food Hilda had set out. Neighbours had donated more food, plates, glasses, and George had a barrel delivered from Timothy Taylor's brewery. It had stood settling its contents on a sturdy table borrowed from Lillian next door, and Lillian's husband, Frank who worked at the brewery in the centre of Kingsley, had helped George set it up. The two men had dealt with the bung and the tap during the morning and had taken the first tastes of foaming brew.

'By Gow,' Frank had exclaimed. 'That's proper stuff. You're a right proper Yorkshireman now George, lad.'

Sandra and Jean dressed together upstairs in Jean's bedroom so they could check one another's make-up and help with hair-dressing. Sylvia Logan had made a tinsel covered halo for her daughter so when she put on the Victorian nightdress and the wings fashioned from cardboard and cotton wool she became the Angel Gabriel. It was almost Christmas, after all. Ronnie had offered to cut short his own evening, to collect his sister from the party and bring her home safely.

Mr Mancini came as Rudolph Valentino and had kohled his eyes and tanned his face. He wore a red bandana around his head, holding the black hooded cloak in place and he had tucked his matching black trousers into riding boots. Godfrey was a Chinese Emperor bedecked in silks and satins and masses of jewellery. He had put on a false beard and moustache and carried a real Chinese fan.

Jean's costume was stunning. Following the theme of the *Desert Song*, Godfrey had turned her into an Arabian princess with sequins and beads sewn on to the bodice of her outfit that dangled over her bare midriff and jingled as she moved. The house buzzed with excitement; neighbours and friends greeted each other happily as they came in, comparing outfits and what they'd used to make them. There was much shaking of hands and slapping of backs as the door opened and closed admitting the next group of revellers.

The two musicians who were lodging at Hilda's that night had brought along three other members of the orchestra and they had all brought their instruments with them. George was beside himself in anticipation of the chance of hearing them play.

The little house was almost full to bursting when the front door opened at a time pre- arranged by Mr Mancini, and David Delaney, the leading man of the show, in full dinner suit with bow tie and with tails on his jacket made his entrance. On his arm was the leading lady, the soprano Miss Yvonne Armitage in white mink over a black satin gown with diamanté straps. The musicians quickly arranged themselves, one of them taking the old upright piano, and struck up with part of the show's overture and the gathered party-goers stopped in their tracks and murmuring, stood stock-still to watch events unfold.

Richard Mancini manoeuvred his way through the crowd towards the celebrated singing pair and greeted them.

'I can't thank you enough, David,' he said quietly. 'And you too Miss Armitage. It means so much to us. So much.'

Miss Armitage smiled and raised her hand in greeting to the stunned onlookers.

'Anything for an old friend, Dicky,' David whispered back. 'But look here, we can't stay long. We open in Edinburgh the day after tomorrow. Got to get along, you know.'

Miss Armitage removed her fur coat and a gasp went around the room as people caught sight of the fabulous diamond necklace at her throat. It was a stage prop made of paste, but in the lights of the candles and the glow from the fire it flashed and glittered and threw spangled rainbows on to her skin. Mr Mancini took her fur and placed it over his arm; Godfrey appeared with a tray of champagne and she took one and delicately sipped, then handing the glass to David Delaney, she began to sing as the five piece orchestra played her in with the cue to one of her solos in the show. David sang his most famous piece next and they finished with one of their duets.

George cheered and cheered. He cheered himself hoarse. The gathered guests clapped their appreciation and Elsie jumped up and down from her vantage point on one of the dining chairs, waving her wooden highwayman's pistols above her head.

Miss Armitage took back her glass of champagne but David Delaney declined the offer of one for himself, preferring a large glass of the local brew. Mr Mancini brought him over to George, who drew a pint glassful from the barrel and handed it over.

'Mr Delaney,' he said. 'I don't know how to thank you. Who would have thought that here in my own house there would be such a night?'

'It's been my pleasure,' the musical star replied graciously. 'But I'm afraid we can't stay on. We have to leave soon.'

George said afterwards that there never was such a gentleman as David Delaney, the famous operetta star who he had entertained in his own home that night. Nor had there ever been a more gracious lady whose voice had soared to a top 'C' in his own front room and who had dazzled the guests with her diamonds. She was a goddess. He would collect their recordings and defend their reputations for the rest of his life.

After the illustrious guests had left, the party continued. The band began playing their own interpretation of popular songs interspersed with some jazz and blues. The old piano had never sounded so good. They played for an hour then took a break for some food and drinks which Hilda had set on one side for them.

'Jean,' Sandra said, 'This is the best party ever. Shall we try some champagne?'

'I'll have to ask Hilda.'

'She's busy with the musicians. We can help ourselves can't we? Just a little taste. I'm dying to try some, aren't you?'

Jean had to admit she was curious. Miss Yvonne Armitage had looked like such a lady holding the beautiful stemmed glass in her delicate fingers with their rose pink fingernails. They took two glasses from the tray and had their first taste of champagne.

'What do you think?' Sandra asked.

'It's like fizzy pop,' Jean replied. 'It's a bit like American Cream Soda only not as sweet.' She emptied her glass. 'Shall we have some more?'

At half past eleven Ronnie was standing outside the Pozyzcka's house looking through the window at the festivities inside. The door opened and one of the guests crossed the yard on his way to the privy leaving the back door slightly ajar. Ronnie could hear his sister and Jean as they slurped further glasses of champagne. He moved onto the doorstep.

'Ronnie,' Sandra said. 'Oh, it's not time yet, is it? Can't I stay a bit longer? Listen, the music has just started up again. Oh, I'm having such a good time. Please don't spoil it. Please don't say I have to go home now.'

Ronnie relented. 'No, it's not time yet,' he said. 'I'll wait here for you.'

'Don't stand outside, Ronnie,' Jean offered. 'Come inside properly and try some champagne. It's lovely.'

'You need to be careful with that stuff you two,' he said. 'It's stronger than you think.'

Both girls dissolved into fits of giggles and he knew they were already under the influence.

'Jean,' Sandra whispered. 'I have to go to the toilet. Come with me, will you?'

'Somebody's just gone in there,' Ronnie told them. 'You'd better wait a bit.'

He watched as the girls drained their glasses. He couldn't take his eyes away from Jean and the enticing costume she was wearing. With the light from the kitchen behind her he could see through the delicate material of her harem pants; her legs were long and young and shapely. As she stood next to the open door the cold breeze from outside ruffled her hair and chilled her skin so that her nipples stood erect underneath the silky bodice. He felt the familiar stirring in his loins. He tried to ignore it, but the abstinence he'd imposed upon himself since the debacle with Gloria and Sid only served to heighten his need.

The guest came back from across the yard and the two girls set off together. Ronnie watched the way Jean moved. She walked with the easy grace of a cat, her limbs sleek and sensual. She had no idea how alluring she was and that very fact made her even more attractive to him. He wanted her. He wanted to be the first to have her. Sandra came back shivering.

'We've got to go soon,' he said, trying to shake off his thoughts about Jean.

'You don't think I'm walking home wearing this, do you? I've got to get changed first. Jean's in the toilet. Tell her I've gone upstairs to change my clothes.' She made her way unsteadily through the room, bumping into people and giggling all the way.

Ronnie slipped away from the house and waited in the shadows by the end of the row of outside privvies. He could hear the rustling of Jean's clothes and his breath came fast and shallow as he imagined her naked form. He thought about the sensation of her soft skin, the taste of her. She was young and fresh and sweet. He could bear it no longer. He unbuttoned his pants. He intended only to relieve himself but Jean came out and saw what he was doing.

All Jean could remember afterwards was there'd been a lot of giggling. She knew Ronnie had kissed her, but the cold air and the champagne had made her feel dizzy and disoriented.

She thought she'd stumbled outside in the yard. She recollected steadying herself with her back against the wall of the toilet block. She had no idea how it was that her costume had been torn. It was fortunate Ronnie had been there to assist and she hoped she'd thanked him for helping her back into the house.

EIGHTEEN

Miss Elaine Linford continued to have high hopes for Jean Thompson. Often, the youngsters who passed through her Academy as she chose to call her athletic and gymnastic club, would fall prey to the temptations of Kingsley once they'd reached their early adulthood. She could have written a pamphlet on the sorts of excuses they made. It was almost always a gradual thing: they would miss a training session here and there, then there would be a return for a few weeks and eventually they'd be able to come out with the truth and tell her they didn't want to attend any more. It was pointless trying to dissuade them. You had to want to be the best and put all your heart and soul into achieving your ambition. Half-hearted efforts did not win medals.

Jean wasn't like that. She loved her training sessions and was the ideal student, picking up on new ideas immediately and anxious to please. She was a joy to work with.

March saw the beginning of the spring programme each year when Elaine spent time with each of her students recording improvements, weaknesses and strengths, and planning the year ahead. With Jean, it was a long term programme with eyes set firmly on competing on an international level with a view to preparing for the next Olympic Games.

They'd been through the planned activities together and Jean's work on the beam continued improving steadily. She was a natural: her handstands and cartwheels were timed to perfection all executed with the utmost grace. Flips came easily to her and the transition from floor mat to balance beam had caused little problem; she was so sure in her sense of balance. Moreover, she was an intelligent athlete who could add just that little extra something during the routine to achieve a higher standard of presentation.

By April they had been working for a month on the floor practising forward and backward somersaults and both Elaine and Jean were looking forward to her first attempt on the beam. Elaine waited, with bated breath as Jean worked through the first few disciplines in the build-up of her new routine. She saw Jean prepare, arch and push off.

Jean mistimed. She stumbled badly and landed awkwardly, straddling the beam and crying out in pain. She fell to the floor and lay in a curled position, holding her abdomen and gasping. There was blood on the inside of her thighs.

◆

Hilda waited with Elaine Linford in the office of Dr Dawson for news of Jean. George had still been at work when Elaine arrived with the news of Jean's accident and Hilda had left him a note before they drove to St John's hospital. They comforted each other with assurances that Jean was going to be alright, that she was in good hands, but inwardly they could not forget the bloodstains on the towel in the back seat of Elaine's car.

When Dr Dawson entered the room they shifted in their seats in anticipation, hoping for good news, dreading the worst. He took his seat behind his desk.

'Which one of you is Miss Thompson's mother?'

'I'm her sister,' Hilda replied. 'Her mother can't be here.'

'I really need to speak to her mother, I'm afraid.'

'Jean lives with me, Dr Dawson. It's not possible for our mother to be here.'

'I see,' he continued. 'And this lady is?' indicating Elaine.

'I'm Elaine Linford her gym teacher, Dr Dawson. Jean was training at my Academy when she fell.'

'What I have to say is really for next of kin Miss Linford. I'm afraid I shall have to ask you to wait outside.'

'No,' Hilda said. 'I'd like her to stay, please.' Elaine grabbed Hilda's hand in both hers and sat firmly on her seat, both women refusing to budge.

'Very well then, as you wish.' The doctor cleared his throat. Hilda couldn't bear the pause.

'She's going to be all right isn't she?' she pleaded.

'Yes, she's going to be all right. We're going to keep her with us. We'll do all we can but there's no guarantee that we'll be able to save the baby.'

'The baby!' Hilda sat up, her back rigid. 'What baby?'

'Yes. I thought perhaps you didn't know. It seems that Miss Thompson herself was not aware of her condition, three to four months I should say, and that brings me to the next thing. How old is she?'

'Fifteen.'

'Ah.' He cleared his throat again. 'Then it would appear there are some questions to be answered. You will know who the father is?'

'No. How could I? I had no idea. She never even said she had a boyfriend. Do you know anything about it?'

Elaine shook her head. 'No,' she said. 'She's never mentioned a boyfriend to me.'

Dr Dawson got up from his chair. 'You'll have to excuse me, ladies. I have my rounds to complete. We are keeping your sister on full bed rest at present. Visiting hours begin at seven this evening.'

◆

Elaine stayed with Hilda in the back kitchen waiting until George came home from work.

'I don't know how I'm going to tell him,' Hilda said. 'I don't know how he's going to take it.'

'Calm down dear. Getting upset is not going to help.'

'And what must Jean be thinking now? How must she feel? How can she be having a baby? She's only a child herself. Why didn't I notice anything? How could this have happened without me knowing?'

'Please try to calm yourself Mrs Pozyzcka.'

'There's something not right here. There's something I'm missing.'

Hilda held her head in her hands analysing everything Dr Dawson had told them.

'The doctor said she didn't know herself. That's what doesn't sound right. How is that possible? What am I missing here?'

'I don't know if this helps,' Elaine said, 'but I remember Jean told me some time ago that her periods were uncertain. We need to look into those things, you know, so we can plan our competitions. We try to avoid competing at those times of the month for obvious reasons.'

'Yes,' Hilda agreed. 'She's always been like that. So was I.'

'Well,' Elaine continued. 'Earlier this year she came to me and told me the delay between her periods was longer than usual.'

'And she didn't seem different? Not embarrassed or anything?'

'No. Not at all. She was more concerned about her training schedule.'

'There you are, you see. That's what I mean. That's what I mean about something being missing here. She didn't know. She really didn't know she'd had relations with a man.'

'But, you'll excuse me for saying, Mrs Pozyzcka, she does know about the facts of life, I take it?'

'Oh, yes. I started to tell her one day and she just laughed and told me her friend Sandra had explained it to her years ago at school.'

Elaine touched Hilda's hand. 'It is possible,' she said, 'that she didn't quite understand. You know what young girls are like. They think they know everything but quite often there are important gaps in their understanding.'

'I suppose so. I reckon we'll get to the bottom of it when I speak to her tonight.'

Elaine stood up. 'I really do have to be going now, Mrs Pozyzcka. I wish you well. Please let me know if there's anything I can do for you, and of course, I shall say nothing about today, only that Jean has had a fall.'

'Thank you, Miss Linford. I appreciate that. And thank you for driving me to the hospital.'

'It was no trouble, my dear. Goodbye.'

◆

George was beside himself with rage. He couldn't eat the food Hilda had prepared for him. He banged his fist on the table.

'I'll kill the bugger who has done this to my Jean,' he shouted. 'When? When could this have happened?'

Hilda racked her brains. 'I don't know when, George. I just don't know.'

'Work it back. What did doctor say? Three months?'

'Three to four months.'

'Somebody must know something. Who would know? Her best friend. Sandra. She would know something.'

'I don't want to go spreading this round, George. I don't want anybody to know yet until we've spoken to Jean. Please wait. I think you're right about Sandra. We should speak to her, but not yet, George, please. Not yet.'

'Tonight. We will go to the house tonight, after we have seen Jean. It is decided.'

◆

Jean looked pale and tired as she lay propped against her hospital pillows. George's fury dissipated as he saw her wan face, her sad eyes and the dark circles underneath.

'My Jean,' he sobbed. 'My poor little Jean.'

Hilda took charge of the situation as George dissolved, overcome by his emotions.

'Jean,' she said quietly. 'We want you to know we're not angry with you. We're here to help and let you know we'll always stand by you, whatever happens. Do you understand?'

Jean nodded, her eyes brimming with tears, her face the picture of misery.

'We need you to help us though. We have to ask you some questions.'

Jean wiped her eyes with the back of her hand. 'I don't know how it happened,' she whispered.

'Sweetheart,' Hilda pressed gently. 'To make a baby you know you must have been with a man. Who was it?'

'I haven't been with a man,' Jean insisted.

'Oh, Jean. That can't be true. Now, please don't cry. Remember we're not angry with you. I want you to think back to, say, last December.'

'I haven't ever been with anybody. I haven't.' Jean sobbed. 'I'd know, wouldn't I? I'd know if . . .'

Her voice faded and her expression altered. She bit her lip.

'What?' Hilda pressed again. 'What have you just remembered?'

Jean sniffed and wiped her eyes again. 'It was at the party, I think.'

'Yes? Go on, Jean,' Hilda encouraged.

'I had some champagne. I went to the toilet and fell over, and then Ronnie was there. He helped me back into the house.'

Hilda put her hand on George's shoulder to stop him from getting up from his chair or saying the wrong thing.

'All right Jean. Let's go back to that night of the party. How much champagne do you think you had?'

Jean tried to remember. 'I don't know,' she said. 'More than one or two glasses.'

'And you felt a bit drunk did you, when you went out to the toilet?'

'Yes, I think so. I've never been drunk so I don't know what it feels like. I was dizzy and wobbly. Sandra was too. She came with me.'

George was struggling to keep calm; he looked as if he was ready to burst out of the hospital ward and go looking for Ronnie Logan. Hilda flashed her eyes at him.

'Did Sandra know her brother was there?' Hilda asked.

'Yes. We were both talking to him. He'd come to take Sandra home. Then she went upstairs to get changed. I was in the toilet. I came out and Ronnie was there and he kissed me.'

'What else did he do, Jean?' Hilda asked gently.

She wanted to remind Jean of the talk they'd had after Mary and Charlie had come to the house to try causing trouble for them. She wanted to let Jean know she understood how it felt to be touched intimately when you didn't want it. She had felt the shame herself and knew that if Jean was experiencing those same feelings now, she'd need the gentlest coaxing. But they were secrets between the two of them now. In front of George, Hilda could mention none of it.

Jean was adamant she couldn't remember anything more. Ronnie had kissed her that's all. Hilda battled with her thoughts to find another way of phrasing her questions to help Jean remember more.

'How did you fall over, Jean?' she tried.

'I can't remember exactly. I think I sort of fell asleep. I remember it was cold, and my head was dizzy. I was sitting on the ground, I think, up against the toilets. My costume got torn. I was in a muddle, but Ronnie helped me to get up.'

George could not hold back any longer. 'And that's not all he helped himself to either. The dirty swine. Taking advantage of helpless girl like that.' He leapt from his seat and made for the ward exit.

'George!' Hilda called after him, but he was gone.

'Hilda, what is he going to do?' Jean begged.

'I think he's just gone to stand outside and cool off a bit. He'll be all right. You know he cares about you very much and so he's angry you've been used like this. There's no other way of saying this, but it looks like Ronnie Logan took advantage while you were not aware. You're not used to drinking alcohol, Jean. I don't understand why you would suddenly have so much it made you pass out.'

'It was the champagne. It tasted like fizzy pop. I didn't know it was going to do that to me.'

Hilda sighed. 'It's not your fault, sweetheart. I should have been more careful. I should have kept an eye on what was happening.'

'Oh, Hilda, it was a lovely party, and now I've gone and spoiled it all.' She pushed herself up against the pillows.

'Hilda?' she asked. 'I don't want to be with Ronnie. I don't think of him in that way. He's just my friend's brother. I won't have to be with him now, will I?'

'No, Jean. Nobody is going to make you do things you don't want to do ever again, and that's a promise. Now you get some rest and I'll be back to see you again tomorrow.'

◆

The atmosphere in the Logan household was tense as George and Hilda, Thomas and Sylvia Logan sat looking at the clock, waiting for Ronnie to come home. Sandra had been sent to her room. They'd questioned her about the night of the party but she had little more to tell them. She'd confirmed what they already knew from Jean's description of events. In any case, Hilda knew

Jean didn't fabricate tales. She had always been honest; even so, it was good to hear the same version of what had happened that night.

Sandra couldn't understand what all the fuss was about. They'd only had a little champagne. Nobody had told them they couldn't. Nobody had said they were not allowed. The glasses were sitting there on a tray for anyone to help themselves. Why was it such a crime to have a little taste? It was a celebration night. Everybody was having a good time. Shouldn't Jean and she have a good time too? She agreed they probably should have stopped after the first glass, not being used to strong drink, but they had no idea just how strong it was, or what the effects of it would be. She didn't remember whether it had affected Jean in the same way as herself because she'd gone upstairs to change back into her ordinary clothes, and then Ronnie had brought her home and she'd gone straight to bed.

Was Jean ill or something? Why wait till now to bring all this up and complain about it? She decided to stand out of sight on the landing above the hall when Ronnie came in to find out what was really going on.

The colour drained from his face when Ronnie saw George and Hilda with his parents in their own sitting room. There was only one reason they would all be waiting for him, and when he looked at his father's expression and the pained look on his mother's face, he knew there would be no way out.

He'd cursed himself for his actions. He had prayed to God for forgiveness. He'd confessed and paid penance, and as time had passed he had begun to believe he'd escaped the consequences of his foolishness, that God had forgiven him and given him another chance. But God had not forgiven him. He was going to have to pay for the rest of his life for that one brief moment of madness.

His father spoke first.

'Ronnie, don't lie to me. I know what you've done. I can see it in your face.'

'I'm sorry,' Ronnie said, hanging his head. 'What's going to happen now?'

'You're going to be a father, you stupid boy,' his mother said. 'How could you do this to us?' She sniffed into her handkerchief.

'I expect you to do the right thing, lad,' his father said. 'Nothing less. You make your bed, you lie in it.'

He turned to George and Hilda. 'I'll give them a start, Mr Pozyzcka,' he said. 'I'll see that they have somewhere to stay. Ronnie will leave his job at the coal yard and come in with me at the foundry. He'll earn good money and they won't go short.'

Sylvia Logan turned her crumpled face away from the company and sobbed quietly into her handkerchief.

'No,' Hilda said. 'That is not what will happen, Mr Logan. You do with your son as you please. But he will never live with my sister. Jean doesn't want him. We came here only to get at the truth. We want nothing from you. Nothing at all.'

Thomas Logan straightened his back. His lips were stretched thin, in his eyes a steely glare.

'You say that now,' he said. 'But that child is my son's child and I will personally see to it that he provides for it, as all fathers should. You are speaking to a good Catholic family here, Mrs Pozyzcka. We stand by our responsibilities.'

Sylvia Logan rushed from the room in tears and her husband made as if to show the Pozyzckas to the door. 'We will keep in contact with you both,' he said.

George remained in his seat. 'It is not finished,' he said.

Thomas Logan turned to look at him.

'It is not finished,' George repeated. 'Please sit down again, Mr Logan. You too, young man. There is something I think you have forgotten.'

Perplexed, Thomas complied. Ronnie also sat down, his eyes already hollow and dark with fear.

'You forget my Jean is not same age as your daughter. Your son has committed crime, Mr Logan. My Jean cannot agree to have sex with nobody, because she is minor. You understand what I am saying? She is below age of consent.'

Thomas Logan sank back into his armchair. He could not look at his son; he addressed his words to the wall.

'And you knew this Ronnie.'

Ronnie gulped. He couldn't lie. He knew, and he couldn't reply to his father.

George stood. 'Yes. We *will* keep in contact with you. Make sure of this; you will be hearing from us again.'

They let themselves out.

'Get out of my sight,' Thomas Logan bellowed at his son. 'Now!'

Sandra watched Ronnie slowly climb the stairs towards her, up to his room. If he had hoped for the slightest morsel of sympathy from his sister he was to be disappointed. She looked at him like he was filth.

'You fucking idiot,' she hissed as he passed her on the landing, and as he opened his bedroom door and went inside she shouted after him.

'You dirty bastard, Ronnie. I'll never forgive you. Jean's my best friend. I'll never forgive you!'

PART TWO

NINETEEN

NOVEMBER 2009

It's hard to believe how the time has flown since I've been here and now it's only a few weeks to Christmas. My first Christmas in England for so long and I can't wait! I watch the weather forecast every night and keep hoping for snow.

I have made more friends here in this Norfolk village and I have a new name. Let me explain.

There's a woman in the post office who is such a gossip. She knows everybody and their business. I'm sure you know the type I mean. She wanted to get to know all about me straight away.

I went in to buy some stamps and she said, 'Here comes Waltzing Matilda.' She started singing the song and everybody in the little post office joined in. Everybody knows the tune to that song, don't they?

Anyway, next thing she's saying, 'No, no, that had better be Walsingham Matilda.'

And it's stuck. That's my new nickname. I don't mind really. It's like a new name for a new life. I feel very positive.

I hope this letter finds you well and I look forward to hearing from you again.

Have a very Merry Christmas,
Your friend,
Audrey.
P.S. I've treated myself to an early Christmas present - a laptop. As soon as I learn how to use it, I'll let you know.

I put down my pen and search in the kitchen drawer for stamps for my letter and Christmas card to Deborah. Although we telephone one another from time to time, I always think it's nice to receive a good old-fashioned letter.

I put the kettle on. I am feeling content. I love this old place; I loved it from the first moment I saw it. I rent the cottage from the dear gentleman who has contacts at the rest home and who met me at the station in Norwich when I first arrived. In these last months I have begun to feel as though I really do belong here.

That feeling first hit me when I stood outside looking at the cottage from the small front garden. It was like stepping back in time. It's a little bare out front at the moment, but last August there were flowering climbers everywhere. Out at the back there is a bigger garden, with roses and lavender and at one time there must have been a vegetable patch contained within a miniature box hedge and criss-crossed by narrow brick paths. There's a lovely pond and, beyond the hedge, the Norfolk sky goes rolling along for ever, big and wide, unencumbered by high rise buildings or street lights.

When I stepped inside the cottage my first thought was that Hobbits should live here. I was entranced immediately by the feel of the place. Although the windows are tiny it doesn't make the rooms dark, somehow. Instead it gives it character, and when the sun shines through the thick, bevelled diamond panes, pools of shimmering light go dancing around the walls. It's hypnotic.

The cottage was let to me furnished and the beautiful old sideboard and dining table carry the patina that comes only with years of care. The sitting and dining rooms lead off from each side of the hallway which carries through to the kitchen and the back of the house. The kitchen itself is large enough to house another table and there is a lovely old dresser displaying a beautiful collection of china. Upstairs, there are more delights: soft feather beds and pretty fabrics at the windows. It was such a wonderful welcome, as if the little house had been waiting for me and was saying *come and enjoy.* A foolish fancy, maybe, but I was quite touched by its effect.

John Starling, the elderly gent who drove me here from the station owns the cottage, and he's been so helpful. He's pointed me in the right direction for all my daily needs as well as stores further afield. I got myself a compact car and started having little adventures.

I have written to Malcolm and explained what I'm planning but I haven't had a reply yet. I've left messages on his answer phone but the one brief conversation I did manage to have with him left me feeling downhearted and miserable. Now that I've got the laptop I can keep sending him emails and we'll take it from there.

I'm sitting enjoying my cup of tea in my comforting surroundings when the phone rings. It's Deborah.

'Deborah. Hello,' I say. 'You must be psychic. I was just writing a Christmas card for you and Philip.'

Her voice is muffled and she keeps blowing her nose.

'Have you got a cold?' I ask.

'No. I'm all right, thank you. Well, actually Audrey, no I'm not all right. Do you think you could stand having a visitor for a few days?'

'I'd love to see you again, Deborah,' I say. 'Is anything the matter?'

'Just the usual stuff, really. You know how it is. I'd just like a change of scenery for a while. Would that be okay with you?'

'Yes of course. When were you thinking?'

'Would next Friday week be convenient for you? I was thinking of a long weekend.'

'That sounds great. I'll meet you at the station. Call me when you know when you'll get in.'

We say our goodbyes. Poor Deborah, she's still carrying a heavy burden.

Many of my own troubles have lifted since I've been here. There are still unanswered questions about my mother's motives for some of the decisions she made, but I've accepted there are some things where I'll never get to the bottom.

When I visited the rest home I was shocked to discover it's really a religious retreat, an Anglican Religious Community. The Reverend Mother, Maria Theresa greeted me warmly and told me she'd held my mother in high regard, and that although they don't operate as a hospice, she'd been more than happy to care for her towards the end. She told me my mother had slipped away peacefully in her sleep and was in no pain.

I was grateful for that information. I had been with Jim when he died and I watched his struggle to stay, his desperate fight to keep breathing. I saw the fear in his eyes, his hand clawing at the pillows. I listened to the ghastly rattle in his throat, the frantic sucking in of his last few breaths. And I was glad for both of us when it was over. I was thankful to Maria Theresa for telling me that mum hadn't had to go through all that. She said she'd been in contact with John Starling who was holding some of mother's personal belongings. When I pressed her for more information she said very little.

'All in good time,' is all she would say.

I wanted her to tell me why mother hadn't contacted me sooner, why she had instructed they should wait until after the funeral had taken place. But she expected me to accept that things would fall into place, all in good time, and I believed her. I left her feeling uplifted, satisfied. It was as if a tap had been turned off in my head, and the stream of bothersome, niggling doubts and worries I'd been tormenting myself with ceased their flow. That was the simple answer. All I had to do was accept that mother had done what she thought best.

I collected mum's things from John Starling and he sat with me at the cottage while I looked at them.

'Did you know her?' I asked him.

'Yes,' he replied. 'She was a friend of my sister. I think you could say that they became very close.'

'I'd like to meet her, John. Would that be possible do you think?'

'I should think so Mrs Freeman. I don't see why not.'

'Call me Audrey, please John.'

'Audrey it is then.'

There was some jewellery, a collection of old photographs and various defunct bank and building society savings accounts books. John gave me the name of the solicitor who was dealing with mother's estate and got up to leave.

'I expect you'd like a bit of time by yourself now,' he said. 'Let me know if there's anything else you need to know. You've got my number.'

I couldn't look at the photographs straight away. I wasn't ready. Instead, something else caught my eye. From the bottom of the cardboard box I lifted out a rounded hard green lump of clay and set it on the kitchen table in front of me. Suddenly, I found myself laughing out loud. I remembered making this queer green thing.

When I was a child I was fascinated by *The Wizard of Oz* and spent hours drawing scenes from the film. My favourite part came toward the end of the story where Dorothy and her companions finally make it to the Emerald City to meet with the wizard himself. I was disappointed when the wizard is eventually revealed as an ordinary little man hiding behind a curtain from where he operates the illusion of a magical apparition. The face in the flames was much more interesting to me and I recreated that image of an eerie green smile surrounded by licking tongues of fire in coloured pencils, wax crayons, whatever I could get my hands on.

Then one day at primary school we were given some real clay to model. We put on our little rubber pinafores and delved into a metal trunk containing damp, luscious clay. I think we were supposed to recreate the head of the person sitting next to us, but I went ahead and made the head of the apparition, twisting and poking at the clay until I'd got what I wanted. Now here it was after all these years staring up at me out of its ghastly green paint, and it occurred to me that I had invented Shrek years before other generations of children came to love a green monster.

There must have been prettier things I took home from school. There must have been bonfire night pictures, pressed autumn leaves, nativity scenes, paper doilies cut like snowflakes and all the other things primary school children have been taking home from school since poster paint and sugar paper were invented.

My mother liked the Shrek head and I'll never know why she kept it all those years. It's always going to be a mystery, one of those things Maria Theresa has taught me I must accept. I have it standing on the kitchen window sill now where it watches me putting on the kettle, or standing at the hob.

There was little else to inherit and it didn't surprise me. Mum was a widow living on her state pension and whenever I had offered to help out financially, she'd always refused. She'd always said that dad had provided a good savings plan for her and that where money was concerned she was doing fine. That wasn't the reason I had come to England. I wanted the personal effects, naturally, but I had never had any interest in looking for money.

That night I dreamed about her. She was getting off the bus carrying two heavy bags of shopping. She was wearing her old green raincoat and had her favourite checked scarf tied around her head. I saw her struggling against the wind. The path was steep and she had to lean into the gusts to keep her footing. I wanted to run and help her but I couldn't: my legs wouldn't move. She wanted to tell me something but the wind blew her voice away and I didn't hear it.

I awoke in a sweat next morning, wishing I had heard the message but I couldn't remember any more of the dream. Yet the green clay Shrek head had inspired me to do something creative with my time and I decided to take up drawing again.

I'd had some limited success with my work in Sydney. One of the galleries near the Westfield Centre sold a few of my pastels, but I always felt a bit of a fraud when I realised how much they would sell for. I think the proprietors took me on because of Jim. Their families went back together a long way and Jim had worked on both the gallery and their house. I didn't have enough confidence in myself at that time. Jim had always encouraged me to keep on with my drawing, but because I wasn't a *name*, I was uncomfortable mixing in those arty circles. I didn't belong. I couldn't talk about Art in the way people can who have studied its history and know the names of the different movements. I just know what I like the look of. I would handle it differently if I had the chance again. I'm not so afraid to say what I think any more.

Over the period of my first few weeks in Norfolk I walked the streets of Walsingham every day. It's like walking through history here and because it's been a place of pilgrimage since medieval times it's sometimes called the Nazareth of England. Kings and Queens of England came here to visit the Shrine where visions of the Virgin Mary were visited upon a lady of the manor in 1061. I don't remember any more. I've always been more interested in the people I meet today. So, I stepped out into the streets not as a pilgrim looking for healing or reconciliation with my God, but as a tourist simply enjoying my new surroundings. I hadn't made my mind up at that point that I was going to stay indefinitely.

There are still timber framed jetted buildings; other buildings bear lovely Georgian facades. I slipped in and out of alleyways and discovered courtyards and quaint shops, located the post office and the bakery and generally found my way around.

I visited the Garden of Remembrance too, and began to think about a fitting memorial for my mother. I searched for an art supply shop, and on the advice of the women in the post office drove out to a lovely old market town where I found an Aladdin's cave of a place, brimming over with paints, pencils, canvases and brushes. I wasn't confident enough to begin with colour so I selected paper and drawing pencils in various grades of softness and a second set in sepia. At home, I set my purchases out on the table, handling them, getting used to the feel, anticipating my first attempts. I was beginning to feel like myself again.

I've found my favourite place to shop for food. My regular supermarket must be convenient, competitively priced and not too big. I don't like these massive hypermarkets where you can't find anything and it takes an age just to get around the place. I like to have it all done in an hour and be on my way out of the car park again. It surprises me that experts who study these things haven't worked that out yet. They build bigger and bigger stores so they can get everything under one roof and the sheer numbers of people milling around with their trolleys is a nightmare. It puts me off going there at all. I have found my ideal store and the biggest bonus of all is the lovely short drive through country lanes to reach it.

I was there one day towards the end of summer. The Norfolk fields looked as if they'd had melted butter poured over them and the sky was softly blue. I remarked to myself how I'd started noticing these differences in my surroundings now that I'd begun sketching again.

I was loading my bags into the boot of my little hedgehog, the pet name I've given my Citroën on account of its shape, when I saw John Starling. He was standing in the car park talking to a young couple. Maybe they were in their forties. I would have said hello but they were so engrossed in their conversation that I didn't like to interrupt by drawing attention to myself.

The younger man seemed agitated. The woman, possibly his wife, and John appeared to be attempting to console him in some way. I realised I was being nosy and turned away. As I drove out of the car park I admonished myself.

'You'll be turning into a gossip if you carry on like this, girl,' I said out loud to myself, imitating the Norfolk accent. I sounded like the nosey parker in the post office. Heaven forbid.

She is quite hard work, that woman. She insists on drawing you in to her tittle-tattle and loves to give you her superior knowledge on all manner of topics. She can't resist adding a touch of drama to the tales she tells, weaving little spells of her own to spice up the story. And before you know it, you find yourself listening to her and once she's got an audience you'll have problems getting away.

I drove a different way back that day just to look at the surrounding countryside. The darker greens of full summer cast deep shadows beneath the trees, over the hedgerows and across the fields.

There is a certain poignancy about the height of an English summer. Autumn brings its own sense of nostalgia, with its songs and poems of falling leaves and lost loves, but the blowsy days of high summer are so fleeting, so short-lived, that unless you mark them in some way, they have flown by and you have missed them.

I put my shopping away as soon as I got home and went into the rear garden with my sketch book and pencils. Thoughts of my mother came to me as I sat drawing the flowers in the borders; how she would have loved a place like this. Although it's many years since I drew a picture of anything I was pleased with my efforts.

I looked at mother's photographs that night. There were some of my mother's sister who died before I was born and her husband, standing by a wall with a picnic spread out in front of them. Others showed people from my mother's childhood, neighbours possibly, or friends. Many of them were taken on holiday and it made me smile to see the fashions of the time. There were snaps of the holiday camp we used to visit; lots of small square black and white pictures where I think I must have been about six or seven years old, standing with groups of children whose names I don't remember. There's a large crowd posing for a picture on the decks of their chalets with some of the camp staff in their immaculate blazers. Dad looked thin even then; his trousers flap around his lower legs.

More photographs reflecting the passing years; I could see myself growing older, changing from a gawky child with no front teeth to a teenager wearing stiletto heels. There was even a photograph of Rita and me sitting on deck chairs outside our council house, both of us wearing almost identical white kitten heel sling back shoes.

There were also some photographs of Dad, Jim and me on our last holiday together after Jim and I were married. Mum's not in most of them; she must have taken them. We didn't know as we posed for those photos how little time Dad had left to live. I don't remember him being ill on that holiday; as far as I recall he enjoyed meeting friends from previous years and having a few beers with them. He looks happy and relaxed in the pictures; I don't think he was in any pain at the time. I'm ashamed to say that I wouldn't have noticed if he was. I was just married and looking forward to our new life in Australia.

Mum and Dad were delighted for me when Jim and I first told them. I'd taken him home to meet my parents, and in the time-honoured way he'd stayed for Sunday tea a few times. He was living in England then and was taking time to get to know my family. Dad liked him straight away. They used to rib each other and send each other up. Whenever we went out in a family group Jim would sit drinking beer with Dad while Mum and I talked. Then Jim would make a point of doing something nice especially for Mum, bringing her flowers, or taking her somewhere she especially wanted to go. We would hire a car sometimes, and I remember being amazed that my mother could drive while Dad had never learned.

Mother loved it when Jim let her take the wheel and drive us out into the country. She turned into a different person when she was in control of a car, younger and more vibrant, somehow. It seemed the natural thing to delay our honeymoon and have that last holiday together.

'Don't hesitate, Audrey,' mother said when she first heard Jim's plans for us. 'What an opportunity!'

'But what about you and Dad? Australia's so far away.' I said.

'Audrey,' she told me, 'go and be a good wife to Jim. Live your life. That's what it's for, you know. You're supposed to enjoy it.'

Dad died three months after Jim and I left England. We couldn't afford the air fare for me to go back for his funeral.

TWENTY

The day I visited the house in Wells was a kind of ending for me. Today they call it closure, this finally coming to terms with what has passed and will no longer be.

John Starling said he'd drive me there and I was grateful for his kind offer. It wasn't that I was afraid to drive myself, but I knew I would feel emotional and having some company sounded like a good idea. As we drew near I began to feel nervous and I think John must have sensed it.

'Well now,' he said to me, 'you said you wanted to meet my sister, and so you shall.'

'She lives in Wells?' I asked.

'Not only that,' he replied. 'She's moved into the house we're going to visit.'

'Your sister lives in mother's old place?'

'That's right,' he said, and offered me no more information. I had to ask.

'I don't understand, John,' I told him. 'Why would she do that?'

I listened to him telling me what good friends they had been, how his sister Margaret had always liked the house and how, since she was a widow, the move into the Wells house would make life easier for her. The shops were closer and there was a better bus service than where she was before. He glanced at me as we were driving along and must have read my puzzled expression.

'It was easy to arrange,' he said. 'I own the house, you see.'

He kept his eyes on the road ahead, and although I looked closely at him I could detect nothing in his demeanour to suggest he thought there was anything unusual about it at all. I turned my head to gaze out of the car window, thinking that perhaps I was reading into the situation more than was actually there. It had been a simple, practical arrangement based on the needs of everyday life. It made sense, but it seemed such a hurried agreement, so cold in its pragmatism.

It turned out John Starling had a sizeable property portfolio and as well as houses he owned several petrol filling stations throughout the area. Jim would have been impressed by the old boy's astuteness. He always admired the background stories of the self-made man who'd started from scratch. I knew then there was much more to John Starling than I'd given him credit for but it wasn't the right time to question him further.

Margaret met us on the doorstep to the house I remembered from my visits to mother when Malcolm was little. She welcomed me warmly and offered us tea. I took a seat in the familiar kitchen and tried not to stare too obviously at the changes which had been made to the interior fittings.

I thanked her for the tea.

'Do you live alone Mrs . . .?'

'Margaret,' she said. 'I'm just Margaret. That's good enough for me. John, be you 'aving some tea? No? Sure?'

I had to listen carefully to catch everything she was saying. Her Norfolk vowel sounds confused me. Her *sure* sounded like *shirr*. John said he had to go into town to buy some DIY materials and would be back to collect me in about an hour. I smiled and hoped I was going to be able to cope without him.

Margaret gave me a guided tour of the house to show me the new decorations, all the while chatting about her neighbours and her friends in the area and how they all took care to call in on each other regularly to make shirr everybody was all right.

'Well I am seventy-seven, you see, my dear,' she said. 'You need good neighbours when you get to my age. That's no good you living out in the sticks with not a soul to bid you good day. See now, Mrs Ely didn't she go have herself a fall?

'All she do wuz knock on her wall with her stick and round come young Matt and he stayed with her till the amb'lance come. That's a lovely young man, she say to me. Well I know he is I say, didn't he help old Mr Arnold that time he wuz stuck in his garden shed.'

I could hardly get a word in edgeways, but I was thankful for her lively chatter. It stopped me from dwelling on the past. Listening to her I could see how right it was she should live there, how happy she was in the house where my mother had been happy.

'Course, you're still a youngster,' she went on. 'But that's something we all have to think about in the end. Make shirr you've got good neighbours if you're on your own.'

'Is John on his own?' I asked her.

She picked up the empty tea cups from the kitchen table and took them to the sink under the window.

'Yes,' she said, looking out of the window. 'He lost his wife not long since.'

She turned back around to face me. 'We're at that age, my dear. We all lose our loved ones. I lost my Lawrence a long time ago now.'

An image flashed into my mind of the man's coat I'd noticed hanging on one of the bedroom doors. I supposed it brought her comfort to cling onto something that her husband had worn and reminded her of him. I think removing a loved one's clothes from the wardrobes must be one of the most heart-breaking jobs you ever have to face. It took me a long time to remove Jim's old hat. I pushed the thoughts away.

'Do you have any family, Margaret?' I asked her.

'I have John's family,' she answered. 'His boy Alex and Alex's children. Look here, that's a picture of them all taken last year. That's the oldest girl, Christina. She's twenty. And that's Laura, eighteen. Oh, they're doing really well, both girls, university and everything.'

I took hold of the framed photograph and recognised the man and his wife who were with John in the supermarket car park.

'It's a lovely photograph,' I said.

'Yes, it is. And they are a lovely family. It's a blessing.'

'Your brother tells me you and my mother grew very close to each other,' I ventured.

'That's right,' she said. 'We did. I shall miss her company. It's a good thing for a woman to have a close woman friend. Well,' she continued, 'there's things you can't talk about with a man. See, they don't think like we do, so they don't understand the things that bother us to bits. You might as well talk to the wall as talk to a man about woman things, I always say. My Lawrence, God rest him, would say to me,

Blust, woman, I haven't got the foggiest what that is you're talking about.

Like I say, you might as well talk to the wall. Well now, here he come, look. I expect you'll be needing to get away.'

John let himself in through the kitchen door and playfully slapped his sister on the back.

'You been talking this poor lady's ears off, Margaret? She could talk the hind legs off a donkey, this one, but I expect you've already found that out by now. Well then, I won't stop for tea, Margaret. I promised Alex I'd run these few bits of wood over to his this afternoon. So if that's all right with you Mrs . . . Audrey. Are you ready to go?'

I gathered up my things and stood up to leave. I had the sensation that I'd been railroaded by the pair of them. For a couple of septuagenarians they could certainly teach me a thing or two about how to control a situation.

Margaret had controlled the conversation by doing most of the talking and I came away feeling that I hadn't asked all the questions I wanted to. I'd wanted to hear personal reminiscences about Margaret's and mother's times together. I'd wanted to sit and listen all afternoon to tales of outings and shared events. But I was a passenger in John's car and he needed to leave.

He dropped me off at the cottage in Walsingham and waved a cheery goodbye as he set off again with his boot loaded with wood for his son. On the return trip from Wells he'd never mentioned to me who Alex was. Perhaps he assumed his sister had already explained. Anyway, I told myself, it was really none of my business. Why should he need to explain to me who Alex was? They had nothing to do with me and my visit to the house.

I decided to take a walk through the main street, buy something different for my evening meal, and pop into the paper shop for something new to read. I wandered around for a while before taking my purchases home and bought an ice cream from the van parked by the little children's play area.

Sitting there on the park bench eating my ice cream, I felt disappointed the visit to mother's house hadn't brought me what I'd wanted. I'd expected to experience some sense of being closer to her, as if the house itself had kept her essence there, that somehow I would have felt her in the bricks and mortar of the place. But she was gone. Another woman's things furnished the place. Another woman's family photographs decorated the wall. Another set of circumstances I must learn to accept.

There was a young woman and her toddler son playing by the swings and I watched them for a time. The little chap was chuckling so heartily as his mother pushed him gently to and fro, that I broke into a smile. It would be wonderful to have grandchildren, I thought. Who wouldn't love to have a beautiful child like that call you grandma and climb on your knee for sweets?

Malcolm didn't like being cuddled and as far as I can remember never sat on anyone's knee. When he was little if you picked him up for a cuddle he would wriggle and struggle to get down; when he was a little older he would turn his face to the side if you wanted to give him a kiss.

It hurt me when he did that but Jim would laugh and say he was a real boy and didn't like sloppy shows of affection. To me, it felt like my own child didn't love me. It was irrational to think that way because Malcolm was the same with everybody.

I remember Jim's mother remarking one day she thought Malcolm was unusual and didn't behave like most children at his age. Jim wouldn't have it, though. He would always point out how bright Malcolm was in other ways. He wouldn't allow anything he thought a negative comment about his son's development.

As time went by Malcolm's differences became more obvious to me. The way he learned to speak was strange. At times I couldn't understand what he was saying because he would substitute consonant sounds and sometimes say things the wrong way round. He liked making up his own words and got angry when people couldn't understand him, but at the same time he was accumulating such a wide vocabulary that it wasn't long before he began to sound like a little professor. Jim thought Malcolm was going to turn into a genius of some sort but I noticed Malcolm was memorising whole phrases and sentences and was repeating them word for word. He sounded like he knew what he was talking about but he didn't understand what the individual words meant.

Two tiny hands with little fat fingers appeared on my lap. I looked down and there was the happy little chap who had been playing on the swings. His chubby hands looked for all the world like two miniature bunches of bananas and his face was the picture of joy.

'Hello,' I said to him. 'And who are you?'

'Christopher!' his mother called out and came running up to me. 'I'm so sorry,' she apologised. 'I think he had his eye on your ice cream.'

'Is that so?' I said to her. 'That's easily fixed then. Look, Christopher, this ice cream is nearly finished. If mummy says it's okay we can go get a new one from the ice cream man.'

'Oh, no, really,' she began.

'Please,' I asked her. 'I'd like to buy him one. What a dear little boy. How old is he?'

We walked together, Christopher pushing his own stroller, leading the way. When we reached the van he climbed into the push chair and held out his podgy little arms waiting to be fastened in.

'He's eighteen months. Yes, all right Christopher. Good boy, that's it. We'll fasten you in and make you safe. Ice cream's coming.'

We ambled back to the bench and she was happy to stay chatting for a while.

'That's not a Norfolk accent, is it? Are you a stranger here like me?' I asked her.

'Yes, I'm from Wales. I'm Madeleine, by the way.'

'Hello, Madeleine,' I said. 'And I'm Audrey. I'm here visiting from Australia but I was originally from Yorkshire.'

She told me about her partner, Luke, who worked on the rigs and was away from home for much of the time. She missed her family and her friends and was finding it difficult to meet new people in this quiet corner of Norfolk. She must have been lonely, poor young thing.

'It'll be much better for you when little Christopher starts school. You'll meet other parents,' I suggested.

She smiled a strange little smile and I knew she was feeling unhappy.

'But I expect this lovely little one keeps you very busy anyway, doesn't he?'

'Oh, yes,' she replied. 'But it would be nice for him to mix with other children before then. Don't children need to be with their own kind too, sometimes?'

What a very sensible young lady, I thought. Being with your own kind: that's what we all need, however old we are.

'I'd better be going,' she said. 'It's been lovely talking to you. I hope we see you again.'

'Do you drive?' I asked as a thought materialised.

'No, I never passed my test,' she said. 'Luke keeps telling me I should do something about it.'

'How about we take little Christopher out in my car one day? We could visit the seaside or whatever you fancy.'

'Have you got a car seat for him?'

'Oh dear, no. I forgot about that.'

'Well, if you could call for me at our house, we could take the car seat out of the back of Luke's car and fix it in yours, if you don't mind.'

It was settled. We would definitely do that one day. We exchanged telephone numbers and addresses and I left the rest of the arrangements up to her. She said she'd telephone me one day, maybe come round for coffee, let Christopher get to know me better first.

'I'm so pleased we met, Madeleine,' I told her. 'I feel like an honorary grandma. You've both cheered me up so much.'

The Shrek head was grinning up at me from its place on the kitchen window sill as I began preparing my evening meal later.

'Ah, you wouldn't like what I'm cooking tonight,' I told it. 'Far too spicy for you.'

I heard a sigh and realised it was me sighing. It was an outward expression of letting something go.

I think that letting go is different from moving on. Moving on is what you do when you know you just have to get on with things. You get on with the everyday tasks of living, the automatic pilot jobs. Moving on from what has passed doesn't take much conscious thought, doesn't take much effort. Each day you find that you can move on with a little bit more, and a little bit more, until to all onlookers you seem to be back on track and fully functional. But you can move on without really letting go. To let go of what has passed means you have to confront it, you have to deal with it and not keep it bottled up inside because you are afraid of facing the pain.

At that moment I felt I was reaching the next stage. I'd moved on and let go of my life with Jim. Now I needed to let go of the mistakes I'd made with Malcolm, and forgive myself for not being with Mum at the end. This looking at yourself from a different perspective is powerful stuff, and I think it was at that moment that I first seriously began to think of staying in Norfolk.

I picked up my sketch pad before I went to bed and began by letting my pencil doodle across the paper. Curves and rounded shapes appeared in a pleasing arrangement. I went with the feeling, let my imagination wander. Shapes made themselves. A figure materialised out of the lines and curves. I gave him a face and curly hair. Suddenly there was a little fat cherub-like figure sitting on the page looking up at me. I adjusted the proportions, added sepia shading and there he was, little Christopher with his adorable smile, looking all round and juicy with his apple cheeks and his banana fingers. He looked good enough to eat.

TWENTY ONE

I didn't hear from Madeleine for a while and when I saw her again, by chance in the village, I noticed her bruised cheek and fading black eye. I couldn't pass by and do nothing. On the pretext of needing some company I persuaded her to come back to the cottage with me.

I bided my time with her. I didn't want to rush in and scare her away. We had a drink and I brought out some biscuits. Christopher was happy playing on the floor with my pencils, scratching wobbly designs on some paper and dribbling biscuit crumbs. I was careful to guide the conversation along neutral lines.

We talked about the recent spate of cloudy weather. She told me about Christopher's latest developments. I asked about her family in Wales, and finally, as Christopher began to get tired, she relaxed and began to open up to me. She settled the little boy in his stroller with his favourite blanket, and he fell asleep with his right thumb in his mouth and his left thumb and forefinger clasping the top of his left ear.

'He always falls asleep like that,' she told me. 'It's funny isn't it? When you have your baby you don't realise at first that they'll have a personality all of their own. They'll have their own little habits and likes and dislikes. But he looks just like his daddy.'

She stopped talking and I knew she was almost ready to tell me about Luke, Christopher's daddy. I asked her how they met and she talked for nearly half an hour before the real issues started to come out.

'He can be so demanding,' she said. 'Honestly, sometimes I think he needs more attention than the baby. I can't do anything right, he's always picking me up on something. He criticises all the time.'

'What does he say?' I asked.

'Well, sometimes he doesn't seem to understand that I get tired. If Christopher has needed me through the night, I'm already tired when I wake up. Sometimes I start the day feeling more tired than I did when I went to bed.'

'And you've told Luke how you feel?'

'He just laughs. He says I should try doing his twelve hour shift on the rig and then I'd really know what tired is.'

'So you're both tired?'

'I suppose so, yes. But I don't go on at him if there are things at home he's too tired to do.'

'Go on,' I encouraged her.

'He likes the house to be clean and tidy. He likes everything to be all tidied away when he comes home from offshore. I try to keep on top of everything, but babies make a mess. They have a lot of stuff and you have to keep it somewhere. You can't have everything out of sight so the house looks perfect when he comes home. I know he works hard when he's offshore and he likes to come home to peace and quiet. I'm just not very good at it.'

Her shoulders collapsed and she looked thoroughly miserable. Her confidence was very low. Luke was making her feel like a failure.

'Has something else happened?' I asked, hoping to get her to talk about the bruising on her face.

'He came home last Thursday,' she said. 'One minute we were all right and the next he started having a go at me. He said he wanted plain old beans on toast for his dinner. We didn't have any beans. I said I'd cook him a steak or some fish. He started shouting and losing his temper. He said he could have steak four times a day on the rig if he wanted to and all he wanted was something that should be in the cupboard all the time if I was doing my job properly. He got louder and started shoving things off the draining board onto the floor. I asked him to stop in case he woke Christopher, but he said I was being unreasonable. He said it wasn't too much to ask, to have beans on toast when he came home.'

I decided to say it. 'And that's why he hit you?'

The question hung in the air, unanswered but I waited and hoped she'd be ready to face what she must do.

'Does it still show?' she responded.

She began to make excuses for him. She began to blame herself and I could see she wasn't yet ready to face the truth. She thought that somehow things would get better, that Luke would grow to love his baby son and want to be the father the child needed. She didn't know that men like Luke had some deep hurt inside them that prevented them from truly loving anybody, including themselves. Luke had his own demons to face, and until he did he wouldn't be able to change his behaviour.

I offered her my support and told her she was welcome to come visit at any time. I asked her to promise she'd telephone me if she needed help and I would go to fetch her and the baby. I didn't like to leave it like that; I felt afraid for her, but I knew she had to make the decision herself. I told myself if I didn't hear from her I would go to call at her house anyway.

◆

The weather began to turn and I needed a fleece around me when I ventured outside to sketch. I watched colours in the hedgerows change, felt the wind strengthening and saw flocks of geese flying in V formations overhead.

I telephoned John Starling. I knew for certain then that I wanted to stay indefinitely and needed to arrange a long-term rental with him. He accepted my invitation to come to tea.

I saw him as he came up the path to the front door with that bouncy way of walking he has. Someone across the street called out to him and he turned and went back across the road for a word with a man who'd been out walking a dog.

Some people say they wouldn't like living in a small village because of exactly this aspect: everybody knows everybody else. I think it's charming. I think it brightens your day to know there will be somebody out on the street you can stop and have a chat with. I'm sure this is the reason why elderly folk who live by themselves make a point of buying small quantities of food and other household supplies. I don't think it's only a matter of spreading expenses. Popping out to the shop on a regular basis allows for just this kind of social contact. Without it we would shrivel and fade.

I know the simple pleasure of another human being calling out *good morning* to you as you pass by. It really doesn't matter that there are gossips like the woman in the post office. They don't mean any harm. It's all part of life's rich tapestry.

'There's something I want to talk to you about,' I told John as we walked through the hallway into the kitchen.

'Is there?' he said. 'There's something I need to say to you as well. But first, look I brought along some of my favourite cakes. I hope you don't mind. Can't have tea without my favourite cakes.'

He grinned at me boyishly. Even at his age he could do that little boy face. His eyes lit up underneath raised eyebrows. He pursed his lips and then his mouth stretched into a wide smile like the boy's expressions on the back of the *Fry's* chocolate bars I used to buy with my spending money.

'Did you teach Alex when to use that face?' I asked him.

He stiffened immediately. It was so sudden it shocked me. I thought I'd said something wrong. For a moment his bright grey eyes darkened and the corners of his mouth turned downwards. Then he recovered.

'Alex?' he queried. 'Why do you say that?'

'I didn't mean to offend you John. I was only referring to that boyish look you gave me just now. I meant to make a joke about teaching it to your son.'

'You've met Alex?' he asked, surprised.

'No, I haven't met him. I've seen him.'

'Where?' His question was too rapid, too strident. I couldn't understand what I'd done that was upsetting him.

'Your sister Margaret showed me a family photograph the day we went to Wells, and I recognised your son from when I'd seen you with him in the supermarket car park, some weeks ago. Why?'

He went to one of the kitchen cupboards and opened it.

'You've moved the plates,' he said, and then suddenly realised what he was doing. 'Oh, Audrey, I do beg your pardon. What am I doing?'

'Looking for plates, I think,' I joked.

He occupied himself untying the ribbon on the box of cakes. I put out plates for him and waited for him to answer my question but he chose to ignore it. It was obvious he didn't want to talk about his son. Maybe there had been a bit of a family rift. I let it go.

I made the tea and we took it through to the sitting room. He settled himself in one of the armchairs and allowed me first choice of the cream cakes.

'I expect you'll be making your arrangements for going home now, will you? Now that everything is settled here. Is that what you wanted to say?'

'Well,' I began, 'I did want to talk to you about arrangements, John, yes. But not about going home. On the contrary, I've decided I'd like to stay.'

He didn't say anything.

'I was hoping,' I went on, 'that you would consider a long term let on the cottage. Of course, if that's not possible, I'd be grateful if you could help me find other accommodation. I love it here in this village. I feel I can settle here.'

He chewed slowly on his cake and I tried to read his expression. I fully expected him to tell me it wasn't going to be possible for me to stay on in the cottage.

'No. That's not a problem,' he said eventually. 'We can sort that out.'

'So what was it you wanted to say to me?' I asked.

He coughed and mumbled for a second.

'That?' he said. 'Oh, that was nothing, really. It doesn't matter now.'

He caught sight of my sketch pad and went to pick it up. He flicked through the pages.

'Is this your work?' he asked me.

'Yes. I always liked artwork when I was younger. I'm enjoying myself recording whatever takes my fancy. There's so much that takes my eye here.'

'Blust, girl. This is good. No, this is very good.' He sat back down in the armchair and looked at my drawings more closely.

'Jean liked sewing, you know,' he told me.

'Yes, I know,' I replied. 'She could always run up a skirt or a dress for herself. She made my clothes too when I was a girl. John, how did you know she liked sewing?'

'What?' he said. 'Margaret must have told me. Yes, that's right because Margaret still has some of Jean's cross stitch work. Didn't she show it to you?'

'No she didn't,' I said.

'I'll bring some for you to look at, then. Maybe you'd like to choose one to keep. I should have thought about that before, Audrey. I'm sorry, it never occurred to me.'

He looked very uncomfortable and I began to feel on edge myself but didn't understand why I should. He picked up his empty plate and teacup and carried them through into the kitchen to put them in the sink.

'Hello, what's this?' he called out.

I followed him and saw what he was looking at.

'That is the magical green head of a very powerful wizard,' I told him. 'I made it at school when I was about seven, I think. Mother kept it all these years. It was in the box of her things you brought for me. Now he lives on the kitchen window sill to bring me luck.'

'Best you get some clay then, Audrey, and make him a friend. Then they could sit together on the window sill and stare at each other, for I don't like the way he's looking at me.'

We both laughed, but then I thought about what he'd just said.

'John, that's a really good idea. Where can I buy clay?'

♦

A few days later he came back to see me with a few framed samplers of cross-stitch. I'd already been up to Blakeney on the north coast and bought clay from the pottery supply shop there. I'd placed an order for a small hobby kiln as well and the assistant had helped me choose accessories and books to help me on my way as a beginner.

I was in the process of turning the outhouse adjoining the back of the cottage into a studio. There was water, light and power already and the small kiln I'd chosen would run on the regular thirteen amp supply so I wouldn't have to bring in an electrician.

I was working on my fifth clay model of little Christopher when John arrived. I didn't hear him; I had the radio on and was engrossed in my sculpting.

'You don't waste any time do you?' John was standing behind me.

'Be with you in a minute,' I said. 'I just want to tweak this bit here.'

'Tea or coffee?' he asked.

'Oh, I'd love a strong black coffee, please John.'

He went into the kitchen and I thought about what I'd recently learned about him. It was a shockingly sneaky thing to do, but I'd needed to find out more about this man. He was a mystery to me. He always evaded my questions. His sister was the same. He knew everybody in the village and beyond and yet would tell me nothing. It was obvious he'd known my mother quite well for some time but didn't seem to realise I would want to know more about her life here in Norfolk. During my visits to her in the past we had never got around to those everyday things. You tend not to talk about what you usually do when there is so much family news to catch up with.

Every now and then those little things would slip out, like the cross-stitching John knew Mum enjoyed doing, but I wasn't satisfied. I needed to find out more. Who better to quiz about what goes on in the village than Grandmother Gossip in the post office? I went in with the deliberate intention of drawing out of her all I wanted to know. It was manipulative and downright dishonest, but that's what I did. It was the easiest thing in the world to get her started. She couldn't wait to tell me.

TWENTY TWO

John Starling, I learned, was a well-loved character throughout the area. He'd helped countless people over the years. There wasn't a single bad word anybody would be able to say about him.

He'd started, just after World War Two, as a lad with a handcart delivering petrol in cans long before there was a garage or a filling station within miles. His only clients to begin with were wealthy people who owned cars, and farmers who at the time also qualified for the first category of customer. Before long he'd graduated through bicycle and trailer and then horse and cart, until he'd earned enough to buy his own small flat back delivery truck. He was on his way and still only a teenager. In 1951 he was seventeen years old when his older brother joined up to fight in Korea. John joined up too.

'They'd always done things together, see you?' Grandmother Gossip told me. 'During the War, when they wuz both just lads, they gone and joined the Broads flotilla. The pair of them, just kids, patrolling up and down the waterways in a little motor boat in case the Germans tried to land any seaplanes carrying spies and all that.

'That was a sight, they say, in them days. All the pleasure cruisers lined up across the Broads making barriers, like, to stop any planes from landing. They had an old machine gun left over from the Great War fitted on their souped-up little boat, been trained by the Home Guard, and everything. 'Course they never needed to use it; spent a lot of their time ferrying pilots from RAF Coltishall backwards and forwards to the pub at Horning.

'And they heard some tales! Two of them pilots told John about the queer things they'd seen from the sky. Strange piles of white lime all lined up pointing to the way to secret airstrips. Oh yes, turned out some Dutch company who owned the land was in league with the Germans, planning to help out in an invasion. They wuz a lot of queer tales told about them days in the War and the most secret one of all wuz the day they set the sea on fire to stop some German E-boats landing further down the coast in Suffolk. They say as lots of local people knew about it. Some of 'em had seen hundreds of burned bodies on the beach, but they wuz all told to keep it a secret. Government didn't want nobody to know about it. It's still a secret to this day.'

'But about John,' I interrupted her. 'You were telling me how he joined up to go to Korea.'

'Ah, yes, well, he lied about his age, do you see, Matilda?' she told me. 'What he did wuz clever. What he did wuz, he waited till his brother had gone off to the training camp, then he took his brother's birth certificate to the enlisting sergeant and pretended they wuz twins. And when the sergeant asked him why they had the same name he said *that's right, sergeant. We're both John James. I use the first name and my brother uses the second. That's common practice,* he say, *here in Norfolk. Yes sir,* he say, *that's what we do in these parts.* And he kept right on talking till the sergeant just handed over the papers for him to sign.'

'I didn't know John had a brother,' I said.

'Well that's it, you see, Matilda. John Starling thought he would meet up with his brother at the training camp but he never did. See, his brother never knew John had gone and joined up right behind him because they went into different regiments. They had both been in Korea for two years so that must have been about 1953 and never heard from each other in all that time. Then one day, right out of the blue, they wuz both walking down a street to a bar to spend some well-earned leave, and bumped right into each other. Fancy! Can you imagine? They had a picture took and sent home and it was in the newspaper. I seen it myself.'

'What happened next?' I asked.

'John Starling came home the year after. We never saw his brother again. No. His brother didn't come home. When they had their picture took that time on the pavement outside that soldiers' bar in Korea, that's the last time they saw each other.'

Even though I knew the woman loved to embroider her stories, I realised this was no fabrication. I began to feel ashamed of my deviousness.

'But when he come home,' she continued, 'he jest got stuck right in again. He worked all hours, they say, and after they'd cleared away all the mines and the barbed wire from the beaches and they opened up the holiday camps round the coast, he worked through the summers to build up his savings. He had got ambitions, do you see?'

'Which holiday camp?' I asked.

'That's enough gossip, Barbara,' the postmistress called across the counter. 'I should think Matilda has plenty of other things to be getting on with.'

'No, no, it's all right,' I began.

'No, that's enough. Isn't it Barbara?'

She closed up like a clam and I thought I saw a blush rise in her cheeks. I bought a few manila envelopes and left.

◆

I stirred some sugar in my coffee and watched John Starling as he unwrapped the things he'd brought to show me. He had been a handsome man, I thought. He still carried himself well and took care of his appearance. His silver hair was neat and shining and his shoes were always polished to a bright gleam.

He handed me the cross-stitch samplers. He reminded me I was to choose one to keep for myself and I selected one showing a typical Norfolk landscape complete with windmill and in the far distance a wherry sailing along an invisible waterway as if it were cutting across the fields.

'It's a very popular hobby, I understand. I never could handle a needle and thread properly. I'm not neat enough,' I said.

'But you've got other talents, Audrey. Your drawings are special, and I think your clay sculptures will be too.'

'Thank you, John,' I said. 'That's very kind of you to say so. What are these?' I asked him, referring to some plans and miniature paintings on squared paper tucked inside the bag which held the finished needlework.

'Now then,' he said. 'I remember those. Those are my designs, would you believe it.'

'Your designs?' I asked in surprise.

'Yes, that's right. When I found out that needlework was Jean's hobby I made up some designs for her to do. That's a long time ago now, Audrey. Nobody else knew it, but when I was young I used to do it myself.'

I looked closely at the designs and the paintings; they were charming: seasonal images of trees and country byways, picturesque corners of gardens ablaze with colours and scenes of Walsingham itself.

'How long have you been doing this?' I asked.

'It's not something a man of my generation was free to admit to,' he replied. 'At least, not in these parts. I always had an interest in creative things but it wasn't an option for me in those days. My father would never have approved of what he would consider a sissy thing to spend your time doing. But I used to run errands for an old granny in the village. She was all by herself and used to enjoy passing the time of day with me. She taught me how to do all kinds of needlecrafts. I enjoyed the working out of the plan, you know. It was like solving a puzzle to me as a lad. It pleased her to have somebody to teach and we kept it our secret to save me from a walloping.'

'And you've kept it up ever since?'

'No. After I came back from the war in Korea there were other things to sort out. I was in a bit of a mess and didn't have much heart for hobbies, you know. The old granny had passed away, and, well, it's a long story.'

It was the most he had ever revealed to me. I soaked it all in like a sponge feeling that, at last, he trusted me enough to talk to me properly but even though I wanted him to go on, I held my tongue about the past and concentrated instead on the present.

'John, I think your designs are fantastic. People would buy these. You could make a little business out of this. Haven't you ever thought of making them up into kits? People would love to stitch pictures from these designs. That's why they buy kits, isn't it? Because it's not as easy as it looks to work out designs from scratch?'

'I think I'm a bit long in the tooth for branching out into new businesses, Audrey.'

'Nonsense,' I said rather pompously. 'You'd be depriving a nation of hobbyists if you don't even look into it.'

'I'd like to be your friend, Audrey,' he said suddenly very seriously. 'But I'm afraid one day there'll be things come out about me that you won't like.'

It was a peculiar thing to say out of nowhere like that and I wondered what he could mean by it. I wanted to let him know I would be happy to support him as a friend.

'John Starling, what piffle. I already know more about you than you think. I don't think you've ever done a bad thing in your life.'

'Only one thing,' he said, 'and that wasn't so bad I suppose, because it was all right in the end, but even so . . .'

He began to say something else when there was an almighty crash outside at the back. Something had fallen from the sky with a clatter. We both dashed to the door and stopped in our tracks, staring at the unlikely sight before us.

There was a goose in the garden. The poor creature looked dazed and possibly injured and I could see an enormous dusty imprint of its body on the glass in the patio doors.

'That's only a young bird,' John said. 'It's a pink foot. Can you see the colour of its legs?'

'Yes,' I replied. 'What should we do, John?'

'Keep out of its way for now and wait to see what it does. I'll use the phone, Audrey, if that's okay with you. See if Alex is out and about.'

'Yes, of course. You know where it is. Why Alex?'

'Didn't I tell you?' he said. 'He works over at the bird sanctuary. He'll know what to do.'

He made the call and then we stood in the kitchen watching through the window to see what the goose would do. There was very little movement from it and I feared there'd be nothing anyone would be able to do. Eventually the poor thing tried to get up but fell over sideways and lay there looking very pathetic.

'I think it's hurt its leg, John,' I said.

'Yes, you may be right about that,' he replied. 'But Alex will know what to do. I think all we can do is wait.'

We waited for half an hour and then the phone rang. It was for John. Alex had been delayed and would be some time yet. He passed on some basic instructions for us to attempt to make the goose more comfortable.

We rigged up a kind of enclosure around the door to the outhouse. We left the door open so it could get inside if it wanted shelter. I made safe my modelling materials on a high shelf. We provided some fresh water and John dug up some weed roots and left them near the water, and when we'd done all that we both needed a cup of tea.

It was dark by the time Alex arrived. He brought some straw bedding and a list of suitable goose food. I thought he'd come to take the goose away with him and was somewhat dismayed by this news, but his advice was to leave well alone for a time. He made a quick inspection and said there were no broken legs or wings and that unless the young female died of the shock it had had, it should begin to recover gradually.

He thought as it was a youngster it had simply grown tired on the long journey from the Arctic regions to overwinter in Norfolk, had seen the pond in the back garden and then been confused by the reflection in the patio windows. She'd had a bumpy landing and was probably more stunned than anything more serious than that. Once the urgency had been dealt with John made the introductions between us.

Alex wasn't like his father. I found him to be rather a puzzle. I wouldn't say he was cold exactly, but he was slightly offhand with me. He made me feel like an intruder. Yet there was something about him that drew me to him. I made another pot of tea and as Alex was drinking and talking to his father I couldn't stop looking at him. I couldn't say whether it was his facial expressions or his mannerisms. I found him fascinating. I wasn't offended by his aloofness. It was as if I could see beyond his clipped words when he spoke to me, that somehow I knew there was another Alex he was shielding from me and that it was all right. I felt like I'd known him for years. He said he'd come back the next day to check on the bird and that I was not to worry. We had done all we could and now it was up to the goose herself.

'We must give her a name,' I exclaimed and both men looked at me as if I had lost the plot. Alex didn't wait to hear the rest of the conversation. He said goodbye and he was gone.

'John,' I said. 'I'm going to have a drink. Will you join me?'

We had very large brandies and by the time we had finished the second one I decided to hand over my Norfolk nickname to the goose. It suited her better than me.

TWENTY THREE

Matilda the goose was still with me the next time Madeleine called in to see me. Alex had popped in a couple of times to make his perfunctory check on the bird and had told me all was well. I could expect her to leave of her own accord. I was to remove the enclosure so she could have the run of the garden and she'd have enough space to get herself airborne and on her way to the wintering grounds at a short distance from the cottage.

But it seemed Matilda wasn't ready to go and I was getting used to having her around. She would come and stand by the kitchen door when she wanted fresh water or more food and seemed very happy with her unusual winter quarters. She was also a perfect subject for drawing and I made many sketches of my strange house mate.

Little Christopher was delighted by her. He showed no fear of the bird and Matilda allowed him to approach her and eventually touch her gently. Madeleine and I were both surprised. Matilda didn't allow me similar contact.

I grabbed my camera and quickly snapped the pair of them. I'd done some reading up on geese and the pink-footed variety in particular, and knew this was a wild creature I was dealing with. There was no possibility Matilda could ever become like a pet goose so I wasn't sure how much human contact I ought to allow. But then, Alex was an expert and if he'd felt she ought to be removed from her temporary domesticity surely he would have taken her and released her back into the flock. So it seemed that Matilda was to be allowed her own say in the matter.

I'd been mulling over John Starling's needlework designs and wondering what I could do to help him get started. It seemed such a shame he still felt embarrassed by his creative interest and I hoped to encourage him to take it more seriously. It was probably presumptuous of me but I wanted to present him with a plan so he could see for himself there was a real opportunity. Then if he was still uninterested I'd have to back off, but at least I would have tried.

As a favour to me Madeleine had been researching the feasibility of producing cross stitch and embroidery kits from home as she had her own computer and knew how to use a wide variety of programs. She told me it ought to be a simple matter to put together a basic package using desk top publishing software but suggested we buy some samples of professionally produced kits before we went any further. She proposed a visit to a nearby craft centre, a converted farmhouse with individual units housed in a refurbished stable block. We set off with Christopher in my newly installed child car seat.

It was a pleasant drive to The Craft Barns and I enjoyed having my little adopted family with me. We chatted about things in the news and we were very comfortable with each other despite the wide gap in our ages. Madeleine is a very intelligent young woman and I found it hard to understand why she tolerated Luke's bullying behaviour. She said very little about him that day. He was working offshore and she was enjoying helping me investigate this new business idea for John.

'What did you do Audrey before you retired?' she asked me as we drove along the country lanes.

'Do you mean in Australia?'

'Yes.'

'My husband Jim and I had an air conditioning and plumbing business. Jim worked very hard for a long time to build up the business and in the early years we didn't have a lot of money. But his work was good and eventually word began to get around, you know, and work began to come in through personal recommendations. Our son, Malcolm went in with him when he was old enough, and then branched out into property development.'

'Have you heard from him yet, Audrey?' she asked.

I told her Malcolm hadn't replied to my letters but I had managed to get hold of him on the phone for just one brief conversation. It had been as I'd expected: Malcolm showed no interest in my decision to stay in England. He only wanted to talk about how he would have made a better job of renovating the old family home than the company I'd sold to. He started listing all the things he would have done differently and I found myself resenting the tone of his voice.

The old longing crept back into my thinking. My stomach began to churn and ache for the son he wasn't, for the mother and son relationship we'd never had. I gave Madeleine a shortened version. I glossed over much of it, but she was interested and wanted to know more.

'What was he like when he was a little boy?' she asked me.

How could I begin to tell her? How could I expect this young woman to understand the disappointment I felt in my own child? I was ashamed of myself.

'Malcolm was always different from other children his own age,' I told her finally.

'In what ways?' she asked.

'Madeleine,' I said, 'how long have you got? I could talk for a long time about all the ways Malcolm was different. Do you really want me to go on?'

'Yes,' she answered. 'Why not?'

I went right back to the beginning. I told her how he was difficult to feed as a baby and would throw up all his formula. Sometimes it fountained out of him as if it was being pumped. I outlined the strange way of talking he developed and his dislike of showing affection. I told her about the odd way he played with his toys, lining them all up on the floor and not wanting anything moved. I gave her a summary of his physical awkwardness, how he walked on his toes at times, holding his hands in a strange position and his head on one side like a prancing pony and as I spoke I remembered more and more.

He never thought of himself as being a child. He always behaved as though he was on a par with the adults he was with. He saw himself as an equal, didn't recognise that other people may have authority over him. Yet he was so rigid about the way he liked things to be that he'd tremble and cry in frustration when events moved out of his control.

Years after all the other boys his age had learned to control themselves Malcolm could throw himself into a paddy without any embarrassment at all. The only people who were embarrassed by his outbursts were me and Jim. So it was difficult for us, his parents, to reconcile the little professor who thought he was entitled to equal rights in the household with the over-emotional sensitive boy who acted much younger than he was.

I told Madeleine about Malcolm's eleventh birthday party.

'We suggested an adventure park near to where we lived with rope swings in trees, zip-lines, all that sort of thing lads enjoy. Malcolm was adamant he must have a party in the house. I tried explaining to him the most important thing at a party is to see that your guests are having a good time. I thought he'd taken that in. I thought he understood. He told me he wanted to plan the party himself. He wanted to do all the organising, but when I questioned him about the games he'd arranged he listed all the things that were his own favourite subjects. I said to him *Malcolm, you can't expect the other boys to be happy sitting around in your room while you tell them about your collections.*

'I organised some games myself. I hid toy cars in the garden for them to find. I arranged a mini Grand Prix course, using Malcolm's remote-controlled cars.

He hated that I was taking control of his party away from him and he insisted on doing a demonstration lap with the radio car around the pool. He steered it straight into the water, broke the car and stopped the game. The boys began to get frustrated and bored and Malcolm burst into tears in front of them because they didn't want to do what he wanted them to do. Jim and I took over and sorted it out but in total Malcolm cried five times over two and a half hours that afternoon.'

I recalled other occasions when we had children around to the house to play in the pool. Jim was good with groups of kids. He could always make up new games on the spot and all the other kids would accept the rules, accept that Jim was the figure in authority, and he could say who was in and who was out. He always made it fair and easy to understand and it was obvious the kids loved every minute of Jim's pool-games.

Not Malcolm. He always wanted to change something to suit himself, never wanted to play by the rules, and would sulk and pout until Jim lost patience with him. Then we'd have tears again.

Eventually, the kids stopped accepting our invitations to come and play. They'd had enough of Malcolm's babyish behaviour and didn't want to join in with him any more. Naturally, this made Malcolm worse. He knew he was being left out of their arrangements, but could never accept it was his own fault.

Nothing was ever his own fault. It was odd; he felt no embarrassment about having a tantrum in front of his peers yet could not accept he'd ever made a mistake. He always wanted to be perfect, wanted to be right.

Night fears developed when he was about nine years old. He was afraid to be the last one awake in the house. He'd come downstairs every half an hour to check we were still there, and then he wanted us to go up to check on him at regular intervals in between. I knew his anxieties were getting the better of him and wanted to consult a child specialist. Jim wouldn't hear of it.

Events I'd forgotten came flooding back, things Malcolm had said and done, some that made me upset and worried, some that caused problems between Jim and me because Jim couldn't face up to accepting that his son was so different and may need professional help.

Madeleine listened intently to everything. 'What happened when he went to school?' she wanted to know.

'School was difficult for Malcolm,' I said. 'He found it very hard to make friends. To begin with he had to be first through the door in the mornings or he'd get agitated. He said he didn't like the noise and pushing of the other kids when they were hanging up their bags and jackets.

'His teachers said he didn't have much confidence but Jim couldn't understand that at all. He pointed out how comfortable Malcolm was in mixed company, asking questions, gathering knowledge. That was true, of course, when Malcolm was with adults but when he was with children his own age he didn't seem to know how to have a conversation. He would talk *at* them rather than with them and steer the subject round to his latest favourite.

'Academically he was very bright, and had a fantastic memory so he could always do well in exams. But he was teased and left out of group games and sports. That was one of the hardest things for Jim to accept, Madeleine. Jim had dreams of teaching his boy all about rugby. He'd hoped to watch him in the school team and all that sort of thing, but it wasn't to be.

'As he grew older Malcolm continued making up his own rules. I don't think he ever understood other people's ways. I don't think he ever understood the rules of society. But, it hasn't got in the way of him making a success of his life. He's doing very nicely, managing by his own rules.'

We arrived at the entrance to The Barns and parked the little French hedgehog. An enormous hand-painted sign pointed the way to the country shopping experience and after Madeleine had settled Christopher in his stroller we made our way into the courtyard in front of the craft units.

It was an attractive layout with a variety of handcrafted goods on display. I bought some fruit preserves from the food outlet and Christopher had a small bar of chocolate.

There was an artist in residence, a wood turner, a potter and a stained glass craftworker occupying units around the courtyard. We went inside the main store which at one time had been the farmhouse and found what we were looking for. The range of needlecraft kits on display wasn't large but there was a variety of embroideries, cross stitch canvases and tapestry designs to work with wool.

'Which ones should we buy?' Madeleine asked.

'Not embroidery I think,' I said. 'Look, they're simply drawings printed onto the support and then a plan to fill in the shapes. No, John enjoys the challenge of working out the stitch count on more open weave material.'

I selected a cross stitch kit and a tapestry design for a cushion cover.

'This is more like it,' I said, 'John will love looking at these.'

I paid for the purchases and we left the store. I have to admit I was feeling pleased with myself and a bit excited that we'd taken the first step, and had to remind myself that John Starling knew nothing about this yet. He might reject the whole idea out of hand but I hoped he'd understand I'd acted out of a genuine desire to do something nice for him. I wanted to let him know I was happy for him to consider me as a friend, even if those bad things he'd referred to ever came to light. How bad could they be? He was a dear old gentleman who'd done nothing but extend kindness and consideration to the people of his community.

He was an astute business man too, ambitious and hardworking throughout his youth but that hadn't prevented him from helping others where he could. Here was a chance for him to exercise another talent and I don't believe we're ever too old to take pleasure from that.

We took Christopher into the petting zoo before we left, then I dropped them off at home before returning to the cottage. Shrek head watched me making dinner and Matilda honked through the patio doors. I went out and gave her some more sugar beet greens.

'You're supposed to fly away,' I told her, but she just honked again and stamped her webbed feet. I checked her water trough and fastened open the outhouse door so she could get inside at night if she wanted to settle on the straw.

'One morning I'll get up and you'll be gone, Matilda,' I said.

I went back into the kitchen. The Shrek head was still staring at me and I picked it up and stared right back at it.

'One morning I'll get up and she'll be gone,' I told it.

◆

Madeleine telephoned next day.

'What do you think of the kits you bought yesterday, Audrey? Are they what you wanted?'

'More or less,' I said. 'I've had a good look at the way they put the packaging together. There's a printed header card with a hole for hanging display and it's stapled to the cellophane bag containing the materials. It looks quite simple really. So do you think we could really do this ourselves?'

'Easy,' she said. 'Why don't you come over with some of Mr Starling's designs and we'll make a mock up. I could scan his finished painting and use it as the design for the header card. We can use a clear plastic document wallet for now to staple to it and then if you get the go ahead we can Google suppliers of proper cellophane bags. You'd probably have to buy thousands of them to make it cost effective, though.'

'You're really getting into this aren't you?' I remarked.

'Yes, I am. I love a bit of a challenge,' she said.

I took the designs in the bag with mother's cross stitch work over to Madeleine's house that afternoon together with the kits from The Barns. She scanned the pictures and printed them out onto some stiff card. We carefully folded the card and stapled it to the rest of the home-made ensemble.

We were delighted with our two finished efforts: John Starling Designs, handmade needlework kits containing original patterns from the man himself. We used threads supplied with the kits I'd bought. The colours may not have been perfect, but that was another area for further research. We couldn't wait to show him what we'd done and wait for his reaction.

I arranged a little tea party at the cottage with John, Madeleine and Christopher and I set out our home-made kits on the kitchen table for John to inspect. At first he didn't realise we'd used his own designs but when he looked more closely he was thrilled.

'Well, I never!' he said. 'John Starling designs, eh?'

He turned the packaging over and over in his hands. There was a slight blush in his cheeks.

'You like them?' Madeleine asked him.

'I do indeed,' he replied. 'I'm a bit surprised how good they look. My old pictures, I mean. It makes me want to do some more.'

'Well, that's the idea, John,' I said. 'Look, your designs are far superior to the ones on offer in the shops. Wouldn't you like to pursue the idea? Madeleine and I are both interested in helping it along.'

He thought for a moment, and his grey eyes brightened with the light of enthusiasm. He inspected the packaging again.

'I think I'd like to do it,' he said eventually. 'But there's still a long way to go, finding suppliers and all.'

'How hard can that be?' I asked him. 'You know just about everybody in this part of the country. It wouldn't surprise me if you already knew exactly where to go to find a printer for the header card and the instruction leaflet to go inside the pack.'

'Yes, you're right about that, Audrey. I do,' he answered.

'How would you sell them, Mr Starling?' Madeleine asked. 'I don't know how you go about that.'

'Don't you worry about that, girl,' he replied. 'I know a thing or two about how to sell and who to sell to. I'll have a word with Gordon down at The Barns.'

'The Barns?' I asked. 'That's where we bought the packaged kits from.'

'Did you? Ah well, Gordon's been a friend of mine for years, you know. I sold him the farmhouse and stables thirty years ago or more. He's made quite a success out of the craft barn idea. I knew it was a winner as soon as he told me what he was planning to do with it.'

We parted company and agreed to meet again soon. I slept contentedly that night. We were an unusual group of people, to say the least: a man in his seventies, me in my sixties, a young mother and her toddler. Not to mention Matilda the goose in the back garden.

Our unusual circle of friendship filled me with pleasure and I looked forward to each day with renewed vigour. There was much to look forward to, after all. We had the challenge of bringing John Starling designs to the notice of the retail world and I had my own creative pursuits in clay to follow.

When Deborah arrives next Friday we'll have another pair of hands to help.

TWENTY FOUR

SNAPSHOTS 1938-1944

Ronnie Logan didn't know Jean Thompson had lost the baby she was expecting. Nobody could tell him what had happened because nobody knew where he was. He disappeared from the house in the early hours of the morning after the visit from George and Hilda and told no-one what he was planning to do. Even Sandra had no idea.

She hadn't heard him leave his room. She hadn't listened to him creaking down the stairs. She said she hadn't witnessed him creeping out of the front door with a bag of his clothes and quietly closing the door behind him. There was nothing she could tell her parents when they searched his room. He'd said nothing to her, not a word. She knew nothing that might help them track him down. He was gone and it was for the best.

Sandra hated Ronnie for what he'd done to her best friend but she loved him too. He was her brother; he was the one who called her *our kid* and had shown her how to look after herself. Her parents had never explained anything to her about growing up. It was Ronnie who'd described the things that happen in private between a man and a woman and how to protect herself from getting pregnant. It was ironic that now it was Ronnie who had fallen foul of his own advice.

She felt sorry for swearing at him and calling him names. When the house was quiet and her parents were sleeping, she'd slipped into his room. It was her turn to give advice to him.

'You've got to go away, Ronnie,' she whispered.

'Don't be daft,' he said. 'I've got to stay here and face up to what I've done.'

'You'll stand a better chance of putting things right in the end if you go away now.'

'I don't know what you mean.'

'Bad news is always worst at the beginning of it,' she said. 'If you went away for a bit it would give everybody chance to get used to it. You'd have to keep in touch with Jean to make sure everybody understood you had good intentions, but you'd miss all the shouting and the crying. You know it's only just started. There's going to be a right carry on. You must know it's going to go on for weeks. If you went away, you'd miss all the worst of it. Then when you came back they'd all be so glad to see you hadn't really run away and they would have sorted themselves out, you know, got used to the idea. You'd be able to talk to them properly.'

'What about my job, Sandra? I can't just leave my job.'

'Keep in touch with your boss, then. I bet he keeps your job open for you. You know there's nobody down at the coal yard can work as hard as you, Ronnie.'

She reached into the cupboard in the alcove and took out a small suitcase.

'Here,' she said. 'Take this. You won't need to pack much just for a few days. That's all I'm talking about, Ronnie. Just a few days.'

She turned to leave his room. 'I'm going to get some writing paper. You've got to let Jean know what you're doing and make it right with her. That is, if you want her.'

He stared dismally at the floor.

'I don't know what I want,' he admitted.

'There you are then,' she said. 'All the more reason to go away and give yourself some thinking space.'

It sounded reasonable to him. He didn't want to appear cowardly. He'd never run away from trouble in his life. He'd always cleared up his own messes, always been able to look after himself. Always stood his ground.

But that damned Pole had threatened him with the law. What was it called? Statutory rape. He was a rapist. Jesus, it was a horrible word. His mother would never survive such a scandal. She'd persecute him for the rest of her life for dragging her through the mud with him. She'd make his life a misery.

His mates down the Cavendish might slap him on the back, laugh and call him a randy bugger, but he'd seen the look on his mother's face. He couldn't bear to look at that pained expression every time he saw her for the rest of his life.

He'd heard rage in his father's voice. Ronnie knew he couldn't stand up to his father with the full weight of the Catholic church behind him. It was too much to bear. The fight was lost before he'd begun.

Did he want to be with Jean? He'd wanted her on the night of the fancy dress party. He hadn't been planning to touch her, though. He was just going to . . .

If she hadn't come out of the toilet block when she did, she wouldn't have seen him playing with himself. She wouldn't have got that round-eyed look on her face when she'd seen the size of him.

But she was just a kid. Being with her, living with her and a baby in some pokey flat down in the town centre, handing all his wage packet over at the end of the week, being a father, providing for a kid with a baby was not how he had imagined his future.

What Sandra was advising made sense. He needed to get away. Just for a while. A few days.

◆

Jean came home from hospital fifteen days after the surgery that saved her life. The stillborn child had been delivered by Caesarean section, a poor lifeless foetus, a tiny baby boy, perfect in all appearances, but pale and soundless, destined never to see the light of day, never to hear his mother's voice.

There'd been no formal naming ceremony of the unfortunate scrap of ravaged humanity, no Christian farewell nor resting place for him. He was removed from his mother and disposed of while she lay in a side ward, sick and fevered by poisons gathering in her abdomen.

Hilda had sat with her, hoping and praying for her recovery, refusing to leave her, cooling her forehead with cologne, talking to her and encouraging her to get well again and sleeping in a chair beside the bed. And when Jean's health improved enough for her to return to the house on Larksholme Lane the dead child was hardly mentioned.

Hilda told Jean it had all been for the best, that she mustn't grieve and worry herself, that now she had a chance to start over and get on with her life. She must treat the whole affair as if she'd had an illness, that's all. She'd had a horrible illness but she was going to get better and be as good as new.

Nobody was going to think any the worse of her for what had happened. In any case, very few people knew the truth. The Logans were hardly likely to go spreading gossip and Elaine Linford had already passed on the news that Jean had suffered an accident at gym class. There was nothing to worry about. Jean need never have any further contact with Ronnie Logan. He was out of her life now for good.

Jean, wearing her pyjamas and wrapped in a woollen blanket, sat in one of the fireside chairs in Hilda's back kitchen hardly able to concentrate on what her sister was saying. She felt exhausted and only wanted to be left alone to sleep. Besides, there was a searing pain in her belly whenever she moved and it was all she could do to prevent herself from crying out in anguish.

She felt no grief. It was difficult to imagine she'd ever been pregnant at all. It was all over before she'd really had time to come to terms with it. How could she grieve for a child she'd never wanted and never known she had created?

As well, she could feel no remorse for what she'd done with Ronnie because she couldn't remember any of it. She felt foolish that she'd underestimated the power of champagne and the effect it could have on her. She was ashamed that because of her the memory of that magical party night would be tarnished forever. And now, here she was, hardly able to stand let alone go back to work to help with the household. She felt more of a burden than ever.

When the letter arrived from Catterick military training camp, Hilda guessed who it must be from and told Jean to tear it up.

'Don't you go soft, Jean,' she said. 'Don't waste your time reading that. He's not worth a moment of your thoughts, even if he has gone and joined up.'

Jean sat quietly, listening to her sister. She knew Hilda meant well. She only had her best interests at heart and maybe she was right. Maybe she should tear up the letter or throw it on the fire. She was too exhausted to make the decision.

'Shall I get rid of it for you, Jean?' Hilda persevered.

'No,' Jean said. 'You open it, Hilda. There might be some news about him that his parents would be glad to know. When Sandra came to see me in the hospital she told me his mother is worried to death. They don't know what happened to him, Hilda. They don't know where he went. And anyway, it might not be from him at all.'

'Who else could it be from? We don't have anybody in the army.'

'There's only one way to find out. Please, Hilda. It's not for me. I don't care where he is and what he's doing, but Sandra does, and so do his parents.'

Hilda reluctantly tore open the envelope and pulled out the single piece of paper.

'Well?' Jean asked her.

'It's like I said. He's joined up. Good riddance, I say.'

'What else does he say?' Jean wanted to know.

Hilda read through the letter quickly, her face contorted by her hatred of the writer and her desire to keep him out of Jean's life.

'Well?' Jean repeated.

'It's rubbish. Take no notice.'

'What does he say, Hilda?'

'Jean, why do you need to know what he says?'

'Because he owes me something. He owes me an apology. An explanation. He owes me some kind words. Something!'

Hilda looked at her and softened. Jean was right. She deserved something from that bastard, Ronnie Logan, and she, Hilda, ought not to stand in the way of an opportunity for Jean to recover her self-esteem, the chance to mend herself.

Since the miscarriage George had dropped his determination to sue Ronnie in court for the crime he'd committed. There was no need to draw that kind of attention to her now. There'd be no useful purpose. Jean would fare better without public knowledge of it and have a better chance of remaking her life.

Hilda handed over Ronnie's letter.

'I'd like to lie down now,' Jean said. 'I'm so tired. I can't read it now. I'll read it later.'

Hilda helped Jean into the front room where George had set up her bed so she wouldn't have to negotiate the stairs. Each step was still painful for her and it would be weeks before she'd be able to stand up straight and walk normally. The scars across her abdomen were enormous, great red welts cut across her belly where her flesh was stretched and sore. It would be a miracle if she were able to take up her gymnastics ever again.

When Hilda left the room Jean took the letter from the pocket in her dressing gown.

Dear Jean,

I hope you can find it in your heart to forgive me for the terrible way I behaved. I have no excuses. I wanted you to be mine and I took you without your permission. It is unforgivable, but I ask you anyway.

As you'll see from the postmark I've left Kingsley to serve in His Majesty's armed forces. I don't know where I'm going to be sent, and you might think I deserve to be sent to Hell, but I mean to keep on writing to you from wherever I am in the hopes that one day you'll be able to think more kindly of me.

Ronnie

Jean folded up the letter and put it back in her pocket. She felt numb. She searched her mind for a thought. She searched within her being for some emotion. She sought some feeling that she could put a name to but there was nothing.

There were no tears in her eyes; there was no aching in her heart. She felt nothing: nothing for Ronnie Logan and nothing for his dead baby. It was as if all feeling had been drained out of her. There was no difference between good and bad. They were the same: they were nothing.

And in his letter Ronnie had never asked about the baby. He had never even asked how she was. The letter had all been about him and what *he* wanted. She surrendered to the emptiness and fell asleep.

TWENTY FIVE

In April 1939 the government introduced the Military Training Act. All men between the ages of twenty and twenty-one were required to register for six months' military training.

Thomas Logan sat in his office at Endura Iron and Steel Works reading his newspaper and visualising the photograph published the previous September of Prime Minister Neville Chamberlain pathetically waving his piece of paper which had promised *peace in our time*.

Thomas was suspicious then and he was even less trusting now. He knew there could be no guarantee of peace. He'd known it all along. The government obviously knew it too; why else would they bring in conscription? But would it be enough to hold off the threat? Could the country muster and train an army in time for the possible hostilities looming?

He scanned the published list of reserved occupations: dock workers, miners, farmers, scientists, merchant seamen, utility workers on the water, gas and electricity, railway workers. Foundry workers were not classified as exempt from conscription but with careful forward planning he should be able to avert a downturn in business. He'd called in the company accountant and together they'd drawn up several feasible alternatives based on experience during the Great War.

Then, there had been plenty of employment for the Kingsley works, making shells and fuel tanks for aircraft. For the first time women had been employed on the shop floor, making percussion caps and castings. War meant weapons. There would be sizeable contracts in the offing and he must be prepared. Where he lost young men to conscription he'd need to replace them with older workers or women. The problem would not be insurmountable.

At home, however, he had his wife, Sylvia to contend with. Nothing he might do could console her for what she deemed the loss of her son.

'If only he'd waited,' Sylvia said when first they received the news that Jean Thompson had lost the baby. 'If only he hadn't been so rash. I blame her, Thomas. I do. It's her fault our Ronnie took off like that, and now he's put himself in harm's way and all because of her.'

She paced about the room, alternately wringing her hands and patting her chest.

It wouldn't make any difference now, Thomas thought as he rescanned the newspaper headline. He would have been called up for his military training anyway, and the way things were going it wouldn't be just for six months either. The country needed an army if only to give the appearance it had the strength to oppose the Nazi party, that it wouldn't sit back and allow further occupation of European territories.

He had a sense of foreboding and he shivered involuntarily. A cold sweat rose up from his neck into his face and he wiped the beads of moisture from his top lip with the back of his hand. There was a sick feeling in the pit of his stomach and he knew it was fear. He wasn't afraid for himself. He was afraid for Ronnie and all the other lads like him. He was afraid for Kingsley, afraid for the country. He was afraid the politicians had made an enormous mistake in not mobilising earlier and that very soon they would all have to pay the price.

◆

Sandra Logan had visited her friend Jean several times both while she was in the hospital and after she came home. Sandra was always careful to keep the conversation cheerful. She took magazines for Jean to read and showed her photographs of their favourite film stars, pointing out each change of hairstyle and every desirable pair of shoes.

Sandra ignored what her mother was saying about Jean. Her mother could convince herself that Ronnie was somehow the injured party if she wanted to, but Sandra knew the truth about her brother. Ronnie had behaved like an animal. There was no other way to interpret his actions. He'd taken advantage of Jean while she was out of her senses and he only had himself to blame for the trouble he was in. He hadn't been *enticed* as Sylvia called it. He hadn't been tricked in any way. It was the other way around.

They didn't talk about Ronnie for a long time. It wasn't until Jean was well enough to return to work and they'd started going out together again as friends that his name was mentioned in their conversations. Even so, Sandra hadn't been able to tell Jean about her own part in Ronnie's escape. That would have to stay a secret from both her parents and her friend. She never meant for Ronnie to join the army. She'd suggested to him only that he stay out of the way for a short time so she couldn't be blamed for the decision he'd made himself. Besides, it had all turned out for the best anyway.

Jean had never wanted Ronnie. She wasn't like the rest of the silly girls in Kingsley who would have been only too willing to throw themselves at his feet. Now she wasn't tied to him. Now she could go back to being Jean Thompson again. They could be proper friends once more. They started going to the cinema again and once in a while there was a dance held at the Institute next to the Town Hall. Sandra used to say they scrubbed up well and there could have been plenty of boyfriends for Jean if she'd wanted but she wasn't interested in any of them.

Sandra knew it wasn't because Jean was pining for Ronnie. Jean behaved like she had completely lost interest in having a good time. It was as if she'd switched herself off from all male attention. The only men she was happy to discuss were George and the two queers at Mancini Modes. Sandra supposed it was because Jean felt safe with them. They could be trusted; they wouldn't treat her badly, but even though Sandra sympathised in the most part with her friend she was beginning to object to the way Jean's reluctance to be friendly with any of the young men who asked them to dance or who wanted to make arrangements to meet up again was affecting her own chances of having a good time.

Word was going around Kingsley that the pair of them were inseparable and there was no point in offering to walk either of them home. They went out together; they went home together.

'Haven't you heard what they're saying about us?' Sandra blurted out as they walked home together after their last outing to the Institute. 'They're calling us man-haters. You know, like girls who only like girls.'

'I don't care what people say,' Jean said. 'I'll live my own life the way I want to, and if they don't like it they can go to hell.'

'You've changed, Jean,' Sandra said, shaking her head.

'Of course I've bloody changed. What on earth did you expect? That I would just go back to being exactly like I was before as if nothing had happened?'

'Well nobody else knows what really happened except our families. Can't you just try to be a bit more, friendly like?'

The look that Jean threw her took Sandra by surprise. Maybe it had been a mistake to start going out so soon after Jean's *illness*. Sandra had thought it would do Jean good to get back out amongst friends and groups of people her own age, but perhaps she wasn't ready. Perhaps Jean needed longer to get over what had happened.

'I'm sorry,' she said. 'Look, do you think it would be better if we don't come out into town for a while? I can come round to your Hilda's instead, and we could still go to the pictures when there's something on we really want to see. What do you think?'

Jean sighed. She said she didn't know what she thought. Her head wouldn't let her think straight at all and there was always a great knot in her stomach which prevented her from relaxing and enjoying herself.

'Maybe you're right,' Jean said. 'I know I'm not much company for you.'

'Oh, Jean, I didn't mean that. I only want to do what's best for you. We're still friends, aren't we?'

'Yes of course we are. We always will be.'

They reached the corner by the library where they usually said goodnight to go their separate ways home.

'Have you had any more letters from Ronnie?' Sandra tentatively asked.

'Yes, he writes to me all the time. I never answer any of them but he still keeps writing. I wish he'd stop.'

'I asked him to stop, Jean. I wrote to him myself and told him you weren't interested. I said you were getting on with your life now and didn't want to hear from him.'

'They'll send him away soon. It'll stop then, I suppose.'

'Where will he go? Do you know?'

'No. I don't know if they're allowed to tell. You know he writes me these letters for his own good, don't you?'

'I don't know what you mean.'

'He doesn't ever want to know anything I'm doing. He doesn't want to make me feel better. He wants to make himself feel better. That's all it is. That's all he's concerned about. Making himself feel better. He knows he did wrong and he's still feeling guilty about it. He wants me to forgive him.'

'And can you?' Sandra asked. 'Forgive him?'

'Why should I? It's not important to me whether I forgive him or not.'

'But that's part of our religion, isn't it, Jean? It is important to us. It's the Christian thing to do, to forgive.'

Jean snorted and her voice was full of sarcasm as she responded.

'Religion? You want to talk to me about your religion? Don't make me laugh, Sandra. What kind of a way of life is it when all you have to do is confess and say a few Hail Marys and everything will be made all right for you? Does that make it all right for the people you've hurt as well? Does your confession and your penance make them feel better too, or is it just some handy system for getting rid of your own guilt?'

Sandra gasped. 'Jean, that's a terrible thing to say.'

They stood together in silence, neither of them knowing what to do or say next. Then Sandra found her voice.

'I think you would feel better if you could forgive him, Jean. I think it would help you to get rid of all that stuff you've got inside you that's making you different and angry all the time.'

They looked at each other but there was nothing more to be said.

'I'll see you,' Jean said as she turned away and crossed the road leading towards Larksholme Lane.

Sandra watched her go, wondering if this was really to be the end of their friendship. Then she turned and set off up the hillside to her own home.

◆

Hilda was worried about Jean and the length of time it was taking her to get back to normal. When Jean came home from work she no longer shared the day's events in the animated way she'd always done before. She used to have so much to say about Richard Mancini and Godfrey Jardeen, the places they'd seen, the people they knew. She could go on for hours.

Now, she would sit, silently eating her evening meal, hardly responding to anything she or George might say to her, then she would go to her room early every night. Sometimes they could hear her quietly sobbing before she fell asleep.

'What can we do for her, George?' Hilda asked one night. 'She's so unhappy. I wish there was something we could do.'

'We have to be patient,' George said. 'We can't expect her to mend just like that,' and he snapped his fingers.

'She doesn't even want to go back to her training. I saw Elaine Linford this afternoon and she told me Jean had been to see her to say she wasn't going back.'

'Yes, I can understand that,' George said.

'But you'd think she'd be glad to go back to it. She loved it, George. You know she loved her gymnastics.'

'I know she did. Now she doesn't. She does not want to be the old Jean. She wants to be a different Jean, I think, but she hasn't worked out yet how to do it. When she decides we must help her. Hilda, my love, our poor Jean has had to grow up so quickly, so suddenly. She was child before all this happened to her. Now she is woman. Her innocence is gone and she feels betrayed.'

'Betrayed?' Hilda said.

'Yes, I think so. Betrayed,' George repeated. 'It is hard thing to lose the innocence we have when we are children. Remember that Jean is not same character as you, Hilda. You have always been strong. You stood up to your parents didn't you when we first met? Jean could not be same like that. She has always looked to you to help her. So you must be patient.'

Hilda stroked her husband's face.

'You are a lovely, lovely man,' she said.

'Come to bed now,' he whispered.

'You go up,' she replied. 'I'm not ready yet, George. I'll be up in a minute.'

She knew she would have to hold back her own weeping. She would have to sob more quietly than Jean so George wouldn't hear her and come back downstairs. He had used that word *betrayal* and it had struck her so sharply she felt there was a dagger in her heart.

She had betrayed both of them. She'd held her secret close and lied to both of them and it was a lie that would have to be upheld for the rest of her life. Jean must never know the reality of her conception, must never experience the shame of her real mother.

It had been relatively simple to hide the truth in the beginning. Her parents, Mary and Charlie were always fighting and arguing so the neighbours were not unduly surprised by the sudden disappearance of Mary and her thirteen year old daughter Hilda.

Charlie had sent them to his aunt's house in Lancashire where nobody knew them and their terrible history, and when they returned with a new babe in arms the neighbours joked that Mary must not have realised she was pregnant when she left her husband but had had to return now there was another mouth to feed. Hilda was put to work at the mill to bring in another wage and the Thompson family took up their lives in Kingsley once more.

Hilda had lied to Jean when she'd told her about Charlie's attempts to seduce her. She hadn't always been able to fend him off. She had grown exhausted and afraid of the next beating and she'd stopped fighting him and swearing at him.

She'd given in to him. He had come, swaying and drunk on cheap whisky to her room and slipped into her bed beside her. Hilda choked back her tears as memories of his filthy touch flooded her thinking. She recoiled at the recollection of his awful wet mouth and his swollen manhood and what he wanted to do with her.

She forced herself to stop visualising those hateful nights but she couldn't rid herself of the sickening sensation in her stomach. And now her beloved daughter, her dearest Jean was cut down by the same sense of shame at what had happened to her at the hands of Ronnie bloody Logan. Now, when Jean needed her real mother more than ever, when only a mother's love could help her to heal, there was nothing Hilda could do or say to comfort her child.

It was unbearable to continue playing the role of sister but she tried to console herself with the affirmation that at least she had Jean with her. Her daughter was here, under her roof, under her care.

It was all she could have. It was all she could continue to hope for and George, in his infinite kindness would always say the right thing, always be at hand to give his support. She must count herself lucky, she told herself. She must stop regretting what she could not change and regain her strength and determination to carry on with their lives. And George must never know.

TWENTY SIX

Germany invaded Poland on the first of September. The ultimatum from Britain and France to withdraw their troops was ignored and so, on the third of September 1939, Britain and France declared war on Germany.

For the first few months of the war, apart from an enforced blackout and taped windows, daily life in Kingsley continued unaltered. People laughed and sang along with popular songs played on the radio making fun of Hitler and his generals. At first, everybody thought hostilities would soon be over but events around the world were escalating rapidly.

The merciless bombing of Warsaw by eleven hundred and fifty German aircraft led to the Polish surrender on the twenty-seventh of September, and although many men volunteered to join the armed forces, by the end of the month Britain could still raise only 875,000 men.

George wept at the news of the slaughter of his homeland and he wept again when his application for armed service was refused.

'George, I'm glad you're not going,' Hilda told him.

'I don't want you to go either,' Jean added. 'We need you here.'

'They need help more, my Jean,' he said, sobbing his sorrow on to his wife's shoulder. 'There must be something I would be able to do, but they tell me no. I am not fit for soldier. I say to them, *Let me do something else, then,* but they still say no. I have to do my job on the Gas, and also my eyes are no good for driving. *But I am no coward* I say to them, and they say *sorry, we can't use you.* And it makes me feel like bloody useless nobody. Useless bloody Polish.'

Jean threw her arms around him and kissed his cheek.

'Don't say that,' she said. 'You're the best thing that ever happened to me and our Hilda, isn't he Hilda?'

Hilda nodded with tears in her eyes.

In October the British government announced that all men aged between eighteen and forty-one who were not working in reserved occupations could be called to join the armed services if required. Conscription was to be by age group and the first group called to serve their country were men between twenty and twenty three.

Christmas was a strange affair in many of the Kingsley homes that year with spaces around the table where sons were absent or young husbands had been taken from their families. By the New Year there were other hardships to endure. The rationing of butter, bacon and sugar began on the eighth of January 1940, and in February plans were put in place to evacuate 400,000 children to rural areas away from the cities and the danger of bombing.

April saw the German invasion of Denmark and Norway and in May the Germans marched into Holland, Belgium and Luxembourg. The day after Churchill replaced Chamberlain as Prime Minister he gave the necessary permission to Bomber Command to bomb Berlin.

In that same month George joined the newly formed Local Defence Volunteers which later became the Home Guard and was eventually nicknamed Dad's Army, and by the time Belgium had surrendered, British and French troops were trapped at Dunkirk.

On the fourth of June the remarkable evacuation of the trapped men astonished the nation. As well as destroyers and large ships, around seven hundred small boats, fishing boats, paddle steamers, pleasure craft and lifeboats, crewed by civilians were employed to help evacuate the stricken troops.

The country breathed a sigh of relief, but only ten days later German troops entered Paris. The RAF retaliated by attacking Hamburg and Bremen. The leader of the Free French Forces, Charles de Gaulle, broadcast an appeal in support of the French Resistance to German occupation, but on the twenty second of June France surrendered and Hitler turned his attention to Britain. The Battle of Britain began on the fifth of August.

◆

Richard Mancini and Godfrey Jardeen comforted Jean and each other over a cup of lemon tea as they sat around the table in the kitchen area behind the shop.

'Make the most of this, darlings,' Richard advised. 'I shouldn't think our stocks of tea will last for long. Not to mention the lemon juice.'

'Really?' Jean asked.

'Yes, that's right, dear,' Godfrey added. 'Our merchant ships are doing a great job, but they shouldn't have to risk their lives just so we can put lemon in our tea, should they? And we can't very well grow our own in this climate either. So we shall have to learn to do without.'

'Godfrey?' Richard hesitated for a moment.

'What?' Godfrey asked.

'Godfrey,' he began again, 'You do know that I shall probably receive my call up papers quite soon, dear, don't you?'

'I don't want to talk about that,' Godfrey said.

'You'll have to think about it some time, darling,' Richard insisted.

'Well, not today,' Godfrey said and put up his hands as if he was stopping traffic on the highway.

'In any case we have to make plans for the business. Now Godfrey, and Jean, I want you to listen to what I've been thinking and then we'll discuss how we may implement my ideas.'

Jean put down her cup and saucer and settled into her seat to pay attention to her employer. She had much to thank these two men for. Unbeknown to Hilda and George she had confided in the pair of them about her trouble over the last year.

She'd told them all about Ronnie Logan and his treatment of her and how she'd found it nearly impossible to overcome her melancholy to get back her confidence and joy of living. They'd both been wonderfully understanding. They hadn't expected her to pull herself together or snap out of it in an instant as Sandra had expected of her. They'd listened and sympathised and simply told her she would get better, that she would conquer her fears and be able to deal with everyday life again. But she must be patient with herself. She must allow herself to feel awful at times.

It was easier for people with a broken leg or a bad case of measles to understand they were ill, Richard told her, because there was the physical evidence of the plaster of Paris or the spotty face. But when things get broken inside you, he said, you can't see the bit that needs mending. But it's just as real and it's just as painful.

He had touched the right spot with her. He'd spoken to her from a point of genuine understanding of how she felt, as if he too had been affected in a similar way in his life. But he didn't talk about himself. He gave her no indication of what it was that had happened to him. He kept his attention on her and her troubles. She felt she could tell Richard and Godfrey anything and they would be supportive of her.

Richard wanted to air his plans for the business.

'We'll have to be prepared,' he said, 'for a complete change in the nature of our business. There'll still be some special occasion ladies' wear I suppose, but on the whole I think we can expect that people will cut back on their spending. Luxury items are always the first to go when there are financial considerations.'

He wanted them to make a complete inventory of all their stock of ready made gowns, dresses and suits as well as a stocktaking of the bolts of material they had in store. In addition, Jean was given the task of telephoning all of their regular clients and offering to buy back their purchases.

'Whatever they want to part with,' he said. 'Offer them a third of what they paid; you'll need to pull out all our customer files to check. Oh, Jean, what am I saying? You know exactly how to do it, don't you dear? For the silks you can offer a little more, but only if you have to.'

'Yes, Mr Mancini,' Jean replied, getting up from the table.

'Just a minute,' Richard called her back. 'There's something else I want to say. Godfrey, I would like you to teach Jean some of your dressmaking skills. Jean, I'd like you to learn how to remodel garments.'

Richard Mancini couldn't have known how soon his business plans would prove to be incredibly astute.

◆

The people of Kingsley read with horror the stories of the Blitz of London which began in September, but although the night-time raids were designed to be so terrible they would lower the morale and fortitude of the British, they only served to strengthen the resolve of the people at home to redouble their labours for the war effort.

Posters appeared everywhere. Every gable end of every terrace of houses, every billboard space on station platforms, in every shop and post office and around the market halls, at the bus stops, in the library, in the foyer of the Cosy Corner cinema; wherever there was a space, the message to the people was pasted, encouraging everybody to play their part in the support of the nation.

Other catchy designs joined the by now familiar *Dig For Victory* posters, promoting the need to save and mend and recycle. Animal bones were to be saved for making fertiliser or glue or glycerine for explosives. Kitchen waste went to feed pigs and those with money were asked to buy government bonds as a means of lending money to the nation.

The message everywhere was economise, save and be careful what you say as you never know who might be listening. If you had to go out at night in the blackout another poster reminded you to be very careful by advising the shining of a torch onto a white-gloved hand to hail a bus.

On the eighth of November the RAF bombed Munich, the birthplace of the Nazi party and Herr Hitler was furious. He retaliated on the fourteenth of November by attacking the city of Coventry.

There was some controversy within the British camp over the intended target of *Moonlight Sonata*, the decrypted code sign for the raid which British intelligence knew to be imminent, but nobody could have guessed, least of all the citizens of Coventry itself, as to the intensity and the duration of the onslaught to which they were subjected.

Air raid sirens sounded at seven pm and it was a full eleven hours before the All-Clear was given. During that dreadful night, following incendiaries which German aircraft dropped to mark the target for their bombers and to start fires which were to engulf the city, the citizens of Coventry endured thirty thousand incendiary devices, five hundred tons of high explosives, fifty land mines and twenty oil mines which fed the fires and turned the streets into an inferno. It was a miracle that so many survived.

Production of munitions at Endura Iron and Steel Works was at full pelt. The nearby city of Leeds had also taken direct hits from bombing raids and although many shadow factories had been hastily constructed well away from the city centre and the railway line the Germans had nevertheless succeeded in interrupting the production of components for tanks and other armoured vehicles.

The location of the Endura Iron and Steel Works in Kingsley proved to be an unexpected bonus. Nestled as it was in the valley of the River Aire, and surrounded on all sides by the Pennines it presented a more difficult target for the enemy.

Thomas Logan had had to implement a twenty four hour shift-working rota, to help meet demand. He employed round the clock canteen facilities for his workers and kept them going with hot drinks and bowls of soup. The radio was turned up loud so it could be heard over the noise of the shop floor and he would, from time to time, join canteen staff to serve up hot refreshments, singing along with the silly songs and joining in with jokes about *Messershits* and *Pissfires*.

'Heard from your Ronnie?' Sid Carr asked him one lunchtime as Thomas ladled him a bowl of potato soup and a chunk of crusty bread.

'Yes, thank you, Sidecar,' Thomas replied using the nickname Ronnie had given his old mate from the coal yard. He couldn't resist adding, 'Got your papers yet, Sidecar?'

'Not yet,' Sid mumbled and shuffled away with his tray.

Everybody in Kingsley knew Sid had already received his papers, had dutifully turned up at the appointed time for his medical examination and promptly been turned away.

He'd been forced to quit his position at the coal yard as painful swellings in his groin had rendered him incapable of the heavy lifting the job entailed. When the first bout of sores and swellings had subsided he'd thought that whatever it was had gone away and he was better.

He started work at Endura but the sores began to burst out all over his body, including on his face and he was forced to visit the doctor. Thomas Logan had found him a less physical job at the foundry works. The doctor had started him on a course of treatment and Sid had to pay regular visits to a special clinic.

Sid had tried to keep the real reason for his incapacity under his hat but it was no use. He had boasted too loud and too often about his famous knob and the photographs of him putting it about. Now he'd got what he had wished for, but his famous knob and swollen testicles had kept him out of the Armed Forces and he'd be lucky if any female would ever touch him with a barge pole.

December came again and Londoners sheltered from the Christmas blitz. Church bells hung silently in their belfries: there was no message of *Peace on earth* to ring out.

The New Year of 1941 brought the next stage of rationing: clothes could no longer be bought as and when they were wanted. Each family was supplied with books of coupons allowing the bearers to purchase their clothes and shoes, but no coupons were necessary for second-hand clothes.

Godfrey Jardeen and Jean Thompson could hardly sew fast enough to keep up with demand for quality fashion at reasonable prices and children's coats and jackets. They unpicked and re-cut garments they'd bought back from Mancini Modes' wealthy clientele. They mixed and matched fabrics, incorporating some brand new materials from the store room, so that the finished garment couldn't be classified as new and their customers wouldn't have to use their precious coupons.

Godfrey designed a range of simple summer shifts made from the full skirts of evening gowns. Richard gave them prime position in the window display and made up tickets for them, giving each style the name of a famous film star. The young women of Kingsley could choose from the *Joan Crawford* with sweetheart neckline and belted pencil skirt, the *Bette Davis* with 'A' line skirt and short sleeves, and the popular gypsy style blouse with puffed sleeves and a scoop neckline, ticketed as *Barbara Stanwyck.*

Nothing was wasted. Left over swatches of fabric were sewn into hemmed strips of material which could then be stitched together to make little dirndl skirts, so during that summer a band of seven and eight year old girls played around the benches of Old Man's Park wearing almost identical rainbow striped skirts made from the finest natural silk but which had cost very little indeed.

Jean was still too young to be included in the conscription, that year, of single women aged between twenty and thirty to take up work in the reserved occupations and so continued her work at Mancini Modes, but when call-up papers arrived for Richard Mancini, Godfrey sank into a state of desperate gloom. He and Jean waved Richard off at the railway station then went back to the shop.

Godfrey was beside himself.

'I don't know how we're going to manage without him, Jean,' he sobbed.

Jean took hold of Godfrey's hands as they sat together in the kitchen.

'We've got to be brave, Mr Jardeen. As brave as Mr Mancini himself,' she told him.

'But he's not cut out for a soldier, Jean. Anybody can see that. I don't know why he was accepted. Being in the army will kill him, even if the German's don't,' and he collapsed into deeper racking sobs.

Jean tried a firmer tack.

'Mr Mancini left us in charge of the business. We have to pull ourselves together and get on with the job we've been trusted with. I don't want him to come back to financial ruin, do you? It's going to be hard enough as it is, keeping things going, and I'm depending on you to come up with some more ideas, Mr Jardeen.'

Godfrey blew his nose and stopped weeping. He looked across the table straight into Jean's eyes and she noticed, by the strands of grey around his temples, that he had begun to neglect his usual hair-colouring routine.

'Mustn't let standards slip,' she cajoled, emulating Richard's own way of speaking.

'You dear girl,' he sniffed. 'What a coward I am compared with you and all you've been through. Your horrible operation and how ill you were afterwards. What a weak useless old pooftah I am.'

'Now that's enough of that,' she said. 'You and Mr Mancini stood by me through all my troubles, and I wouldn't dream of doing any the less for you now. Come along, darling,' she teased. 'We've work to do.'

He sniffed again and braved a smile.

'Right then Jean,' he said, summoning up his will power. 'Time for some more designs. How about we do a *Katherine Hepburn*? Loose slacks with a tailored blouse, ready for the autumn, and we can use up some of that Harris Tweed. What do you think?'

◆

Sandra Logan was required to leave her job at Hall's Pharmacy and work in a reserved occupation as conscription rules dictated. Her father offered her a place in the offices at Endura.

'No thanks, Dad,' she said. 'It's not for me. I can do better than that.'

Sylvia looked up from her knitting.

'What have you got in mind, Sandra?' she asked. 'You know how much father needs the extra hands, and it's not as if there's much choice for you here in Kingsley.'

'I know,' Sandra replied. 'That's why I'm going away.'

'Where?' Thomas demanded.

'Wherever I'm sent. Sussex to begin with.'

'Sent?' Sylvia said, a tremor in her voice. 'Sent by who?'

'The Navy, Mum.'

'Oh no, you don't,' her father warned.

'Too late, dad. I've joined the Wrens.'

Sylvia's knitting dropped from her lap into a heap on the floor.

'Dear God in heaven, no. No, my God. No! No!' she cried and she grabbed hold of her husband's arm. 'Thomas, don't let her do it. Please, Thomas. Make her stop.'

'It's too late, Mum,' Sandra said calmly. She looked at her father. 'Dad, it's what I want to do. I think I'll be a good Wren. Actually it's the Fleet Air Arm. I want to learn other skills. I want to be useful. I want to make something of myself. This is my chance.'

Thomas Logan couldn't disguise the pride he felt. His mouth turned upward into a smile of satisfaction as he looked at his daughter.

'When do you leave?' he asked her.

'Not sure, yet. But soon, I think. My orders will come through in the post, they tell me, but I think I'll have time to catch up with a few friends before I leave.'

'You mean Jean Thompson,' Sylvia said flatly.

'Yes, Mother, I mean Jean. And you should really take that look off your face, Mum. Jean never did any wrong to this family, and you know it. She always . . .'

'I won't listen to any more,' Sylvia snapped, getting up from her chair and made to leave the room.

'Sylvia!' her husband shouted after her, but she hurried out of the sitting room and dashed upstairs to shut herself in her bedroom.

'You've got to put her right, Dad,' Jean said.

'It's hard for your mother, Sandra. Try to understand.'

'No, Dad. It's time she faced up to facts. It's hard for everybody now. What makes it so much worse for her? There are plenty of families a lot worse off than we are.'

'I know, Sandra. I know. But your mother's had all her dreams dashed. She finds it difficult to cope with the world as it is.'

'Well, I'm glad I'm not like her then. She should be out there volunteering to do something with her time instead of wishing things were different.'

Thomas nodded in agreement.

'You know, Sandra, I've just had an idea. That job in the office. It wasn't something I invented, you know. I really do need an extra hand. I'll ask her.'

'I think you'll have to insist, Dad,' Sandra suggested.

'I'll insist, then,' he replied with a smile.

◆

Two weeks before Christmas the Japanese attacked the American Pacific Fleet at Pearl Harbour and a few days after Britain and the United States declared war on Japan, Ronnie Logan received his new orders shipping him to Burma to help reinforce the overwhelmed British and Empire troops in their attempts to defend the vast Burmese frontier.

TWENTY SEVEN

Charlie Thompson would have drunk himself to death if Gloria and Denis Chapman had not been moved on from the Black Horse. The new incumbents were toffs according to Charlie, southerners who didn't know how to treat paying customers properly. They refused outright to run up a slate, would put nothing on the tab and had placed a notice behind the bar, proclaiming in large print: *Please do not ask for credit as a refusal may offend.*

Further, they'd refused to serve customers who, in their opinion, had already had enough, and wouldn't tolerate the merest hint of rowdiness or vulgarity. They'd already barred several of Denis and Gloria's old customers in the first few weeks of their tenancy.

'Who do they think they are?' Charlie shouted at his wife as they walked across the market place on their way home after a drinking session had been cut short by new landlord Tom Dixon. 'Bloody toffs, throwing their weight about. They won't last two minutes, silly buggers. They'll lose all their custom.'

He kicked at leaves in the gutter and glowered at Mary, his temper rising as they reached their basement flat. Mary opened the door and went to sit by the fire. She wanted to keep out of his way. She wanted to keep quiet; she knew how easily he could twist anything she said into a reason for taking his temper out on her and she was tired of arguing.

'I'm hungry,' he grumbled.

'I'll make you something,' she offered. 'What would you like?'

'I'd like a thick slice of beef with all the trimmings,' he answered with a smirk.

Mary rose slowly from the chair.

'You know we haven't got that, Charlie,' she said.

'Yeah, don't tell me. There's a war on,' he snarled.

Mary reached for her coat.

'And where do you think you're going?' he demanded.

'I'm going out of your way, Charlie Thompson.'

'You'll bloody well stay where you are,' he bellowed, but he wasn't quick enough to bar her way and she ran up the steps and out into a cold January afternoon.

She pulled her coat collar up around her neck as the biting wind cut into her, and she set out, back toward the town centre not knowing where she was heading.

Mary Thompson was fifty-two years old and felt like her life was over. She couldn't remember a time when she didn't feel like that. Everything she touched went wrong, she thought. Try as she might to keep things ticking over she was never going to be able to please that husband of hers.

Charlie was a bully. He'd always been a bully. He'd bullied and threatened her from the early days of their marriage when she'd expected him to continue being the same jovial Charlie who'd courted her and first won her affection. He was like two people in one body, she thought. His drinking mates thought he was the best, always a good laugh, always the first to buy in the rounds of ale and generous with his money. A plasterer by trade, a lot of his earnings went straight into his pocket to be spent in the pub, the rest he saved in a tin which he kept hidden. There was very little left in it since the war had begun and new building work had dried up.

Mary had learned never to question him about his own battle experiences of the Great War. When he'd been discharged from the Forces in 1916 when he was thirty-three, she had at first assumed it was because he'd been wounded and that his injuries made him unfit for active service. She could have understood how that might have made a man feel bad about himself. But in the tin where he kept his cash she'd once seen an official-looking document and the words *dishonourable discharge*. The first time she'd asked him about it was also the last. The beating he had given her was severe.

Her life could have been so different. If his best friend Jack Bolton had survived it would have been a different story. She would have left Charlie to be with Jack. They would have lived happily together and raised their family in a decent way.

She walked past the Black Horse and kept on, down the street and along Low Parade towards Victoria Park. Wind howled through elms' bare branches and scattered smoke rising from factory chimneys ahead of her. She'd spent years being afraid of Charlie Thompson. Those years had disappeared into the past just like the smoke in the sky, dissipated, spent, finished. Time had flown by in a fog of tap room smoke and beer-swilled weekends.

But it had been easier to handle Charlie when he was in drink. She could face up to him when he was hardly able to stand up straight. So she'd gone along with the carousing and the booze-soaked sessions. She'd put up with his unreasonable behaviour. Surely a lousy father for her daughter Hilda was better than no father at all?

She found herself standing in front of a notice on a factory gate.

NEEDED URGENTLY. ASSEMBLY WORKERS. APPLY WITHIN.

She went inside to the reception office and applied for a job assembling mortar barrels.

✦

Four of Asia's largest rivers flow among jungle covered mountain ranges which divide the country of Burma. Enormous zones of mangrove swamps surround deltas at the mouth of each of the rivers and the monsoon season between May and October turns the archaic roads into quagmires.

Ronnie Logan had never seen anything like it. After the fall of Rangoon and Mandalay his regiment began the long and labyrinthine withdrawal to India. They'd been overwhelmed by the rapid Japanese advance. They'd had no support from the RAF. There was little naval presence. Withdrawal had been the only option. Together with thousands of civilian refugees they faced the impenetrable jungle, the bogs underfoot and endless strafing from Japanese fighter planes. Sickness and disease were their constant enemies; it was a hell hole.

By the time Ronnie and his companions straggled over the last mountain range into India in May 1942, his body resembled a huge, weeping sore. Insects had laid their eggs under his skin. The hatched larvae had to eat their way out of him. Dysentery had reduced his once admirable physique to less than half his former body weight. And, unseen by human eye, other microscopic parasites which had entered his body were beginning their deadly journey to worm their way into his body and attack his lungs.

But he had made it; so far he had survived. He silently thanked his God for bringing him through and sparing him from the agonising deaths that had been the fate of the many who had been left behind, bloated and putrefying in the mud.

◆

Richard Mansfield of Mancini Modes, contrary to Godfrey's expectations, had found himself a niche in the Royal Army Ordnance Corps. Godfrey read aloud Richard's letter addressed to himself and Jean.

> *. . . . and the enlisting sergeant was quite right. They all seem to turn a blind eye to our little differences, darlings. Well, they knew as soon as I had to pick up a rifle that I would be a liability to anybody who was unfortunate enough to be near me. I would never be able to shoot straight to save my own life let alone anyone else's.*
>
> *So I'm to drive one of the supply trucks, and, would you believe it? I'm on the entertainments committee. We're trying to persuade dear David and Yvonne to come out and give us a concert next Christmas.*
>
> *So don't you worry about a thing, darlings. Apart from having to wear this damned scratchy uniform (oh, how I dream about our soft silk cushions), I'm actually quite enjoying myself!*
>
> *All my love,*
> *Ricardo*
>
> *PS I'm giving this letter to one of the hospital nurses who is going back to Blighty – just in case you were wondering about the postmark.*

'That's wonderful news, Mr Jardeen. Isn't it?' Jean said.

'Hmmph,' Godfrey replied. 'He'd better be behaving himself.'

The door to the shop crashed open and Elsie, the widow lady from across the courtyard rushed inside.

'Jean, come quick,' she panted. 'It's your Hilda. There's been an accident.'

Jean hurried to Elsie and grabbed her hands.

'Where is she?' she gasped.

'They're taking her to St James' in Leeds. George took a telephone call at work. He came home and asked me to come and get you. Then he went back to the office to wait by the phone for any more messages. He wants you to put some of Hilda's things together in case she has to stay in the hospital and he wants you to wait at home.'

'What happened?' Jean asked.

'I don't know all the details, love, only that Hilda was on the Leeds route and the bus had to swerve and ended up crashing. George knows the rest.'

Jean looked at Godfrey who was already fetching her coat.

'Go,' he said. 'Straight away. Off you go. Try not to worry. I hope everything's alright.'

The eleven-thirty Kingsley to Leeds bus had been held up that morning just outside Leeds, waiting for the All Clear.

The railway yards and nearby factories were taking another hammering. Hilda's driver, Bob, had joked that maybe the Luftwaffe had got wind of news that the people of Leeds had raised an astounding amount of money to build a new Ark Royal to replace the original adopted by the city and sunk by a German U-boat the previous November. The bus crews had done their bit, taking round the collection boxes during each bus journey to help raise funds. The final total amounted to a staggering nine million pounds. Even the much smaller market town of Kingsley had raised enough money to build a Spitfire and a Hurricane.

The All-Clear came and they continued their route but a lone fighter plane had circled back and coming in low over Kirkstall Road, opened fire. Hilda had seen the markings on its wings as the plane zoomed toward them. The factory wall on their right exploded. Splintered slivers of sharp brick blasted in all directions. The windows of the bus fell in, showering Hilda and her passengers with shards of glass.

Bob swerved to avoid a direct hit from the aircraft. The bus mounted the kerb and toppled sideways, crashing into railings surrounding one of the railway stock yards. It came to a halt balanced on its nearside with the offside wheels spinning crazily in the air. Some of the railings had punctured the side of the coachwork and penetrated through into the seats inside.

One week later and the railings would not have been there. They would have been taken down for smelting and used for armaments. Bob hadn't been able to save himself. He had saved his passengers but his own neck was impaled, pinning him at an obscene angle in his seat in the driver's cab. He died instantly.

Jean waited in the house for George to come home. She'd collected Hilda's nightgown, her robe and slippers and had put together a small wash bag containing essential toiletries. Elsie waited with her, neither of them knowing how serious Hilda's injuries were and both trying to keep their spirits up.

When George arrived they analysed his facial expression for clues. His face was relaxed. They saw in his eyes that all was well and they waited patiently for him to speak.

'Cuts and bruises. That's all. Cuts and bruises. Thank God. We can go and fetch her home.'

'I'll be off, then,' said Elsie. She blew out her cheeks in a huge sigh. 'Eee, I'm that glad, George. I am, really. Tell Hilda if there's anything she wants me to do . . .'

'I will,' he replied. 'Thank you, Elsie.'

The lump in Jean's throat erupted into loud racking sobs. She cried as if her heart would break and George understood. He let her cry it out. He knew she was weeping for more than Hilda's cuts and bruises, and he also knew she would feel better after it was done.

◆

Sylvia Logan accepted with good grace her husband's proposal that she should take a position in the offices at Endura. Many of her friends at the Catholic Social Association had volunteered to work for the war effort and she must not be seen to be willing to do any less.

On her first day of work she arrived on her husband's arm and immediately addressed the two other clerks at their desks.

'Good morning,' she said. 'I want you to know that I'm here to help. You must call me Sylvia. And you are?'

'This is Maureen nearest,' her husband informed her. 'And that old reprobate standing at the back is Mr Lilley.'

'But his Christian name, dear?' Sylvia enquired.

'It's a secret,' Maureen laughed. 'I've been here for seven years and I've never found out.'

Mr Lilley looked up from his ledgers, his cigarette clamped firmly between his lips, apparently unaware of the long string of ash ready to fall from the end onto the floor. In the manner of his training he stood at his station at a tall sloping desk that reached up to his waist. He would not sit at a desk. He said that it was bad for the circulation to sit down all day, and he occupied the back of the room so that the fumes from his constant chain-smoking could be sucked out of the window which he always kept ajar, whatever the weather.

He merely nodded at Sylvia with an inscrutable expression, his eyes like slits to avoid the stinging of his own smoke and a stretched smile on his thin lips.

'Well, good morning, Mr Lilley,' Sylvia added, trying to ignore the piles of ash around his feet.

'You'll share the partners' desk with Maureen, Sylvia. Here, you see? It's designed for two people to use facing each other. Maureen's been briefed on what your duties are, so I'll leave it to her to explain. Right then, I'll be in my office if you need me, dear. Maureen will show you where it is.'

Sylvia took up her position and smiled wanly at Maureen who suggested they begin the day with a tour of the works so that Sylvia could understand how everything was organised, and how the paper work it was their job to keep up to date fitted in with production on the shop floor. Mr Lilley raised his head and watched the two women leave the room. He reached into his tin of smuggled tobacco roll-ups and lit another before the one in his mouth went out.

◆

Mary Thompson didn't know who Sylvia Logan was when she saw the girl from the office showing her around. All she saw was the smart outfit the woman wore, the smooth hairstyle, red lipstick and polished fingernails. She turned her head away to concentrate on her work, but her thoughts were elsewhere.

Her purse was empty again and a whole week to wait for the next pay-day. Charlie had demanded she hand over her wage packets unopened. She'd refused. She stood her ground and threatened to tell the whole neighbourhood the lazy bastard wouldn't get off his backside to find work himself. Further, she'd promised to visit all his drinking haunts and tell his so-called mates the same. She knew she was on safe ground; he wouldn't attack her physically over this. He was a proud man and couldn't bear the thought of people knowing his wife was providing him with spending money.

Nevertheless, he went into her bag and helped himself. If she hadn't already hidden a ten bob note in her shoe there'd be nothing left for food. Well, she told herself, there would be no food for him. She'd have her hot soup and bread in the canteen and would buy something to eat on her way home after work, a Cornish pasty from the butcher maybe. Even though it would probably have never had a whiff of meat the butcher's recipe was tasty and filling.

She'd give Charlie nothing. She would sit and watch him and enjoy listening to his growling stomach. It was what he deserved. But she would need a new hiding place for her change. He'd be bound to go through her things looking for more beer money. Her cash would be safest left at work and she had already spotted just the right place.

'Come on, Mary,' the young woman next to her on the assembly line chirped. 'Got your head in the clouds? There's a war on, you know.'

Mary laughed and fixed her attention on her task. They were a good bunch of girls to work with and it was welcome relief to be alongside cheerful people who kept each other going with their jokes and gossip. The work was hard, mind. There was no doubt they were doing men's jobs and really should have been paid equally, especially when men like hers at home were bringing in next to nothing. But a good group of girls could talk at the same time as work and Mary had come to enjoy the lively banter. It helped her to forget the dismal grind of her own life.

It helped her forget the love she'd lost in the First War and put out of her mind the hardships she'd endured with Charlie Thompson. It helped her dismiss from her thoughts her own cruel neglect of her daughter and Hilda's child, Jean.

That had been a terrible time. But she'd been afraid of him then. All that had been before she'd learned how to handle him, how to avoid trouble. And anyway, she convinced herself, it had worked out all right for them. Hilda and Jean. They were together. They should think themselves lucky that they'd got out of it. They were all sitting pretty with three wages coming in. Why should she feel sorry?

◆

Godfrey had received a telegram he was afraid to open.

'You open it, Jean,' he begged. 'My hands are trembling too much.'

She carefully opened the thin envelope.

'Tell it to me slowly, please,' he added. 'Don't rush me with it. I won't be able to cope.'

Jean read through the message and looked up again into Godfrey's eyes. He interpreted the expression in her own eyes.

'No,' he cried. 'Please, no!'

He turned away from her and went to the window. He kept his gaze on the sweep of the arcade and added, 'Is it the worst?'

Jean went to him and touched him gently on the shoulder.

'No, it's not the worst, Mr Jardeen,' she said.

'Then what?'

'It would appear that Mr Mancini has been taken prisoner,' she said.

'By the Germans?' Godfrey asked.

'No. By the Japanese,' she replied.

'Is that better, then?'

'I don't know, Mr Jardeen. I suppose it depends how the enemy treats its prisoners.'

'You said it would *appear*. Does that mean there's some doubt about it?'

Jean handed over the paper to him. She couldn't answer his question. She didn't know enough about how this sort of thing worked.

◆

It was better that neither of them knew exactly what had befallen their friend. He'd been taken in the fall of Singapore along with over fifty thousand Allied Troops and held in Changi, on the outskirts of the city.

Changi was a 25 square kilometre peninsula, a suburb of Singapore which had formally been the British Army's principal base. With three major barracks it could house thousands of POWs separated each from the other by their nationalities.

Communication between different barracks was forbidden but within their own compounds prisoners were allowed to form their own regulations. There was water; there was power and although the rations were meagre, food was provided daily. To begin with.

In September of that year when large contingents of prisoners were taken from Changi and transported to Thailand to work on the railway, Richard had no reason to believe that conditions would be any different from those he'd already experienced at the hands of the Japanese. Some of the Japanese guards had joked with the prisoners in broken English, telling them it was going to be like a holiday, working out in the fresh air, good healthy work alongside their comrades. Richard felt optimistic.

He climbed into the back of the open truck, squeezed into a cramped space by the tail gate and by the end of the first day's journey, under the fierce glare of the sun with his back against red hot metal, he knew this was going to be no holiday.

◆

Jean touched Godfrey gently once more.

'We must hope for the best, Mr Jardeen,' she said.

'Yes, dear. You're right, of course,' he replied unconvinced.

'Shall we get on with the Katherine Hepburns?' she cajoled.

'Yes, dear,' he said again. 'Brown or grey?'

'Let's do some grey,' she suggested, trying to sound as enthusiastic as she could.

Godfrey attempted the same pragmatism.

'Is your sister better now, Jean?' he asked. 'After her fright?'

'Yes and no. I think so. There were no bones broken, or anything like that. Only, she always seems to be so tired. She's not like her old self.'

'It takes time, dear, doesn't it? We have to be patient. Has she gone back to work yet?'

'No, she hasn't. I think she should. She sits in the house just waiting for me and George to get home.'

'Oh dear,' he commented. 'That will never do. Can you think of anything that would help her?'

'I wish I could, Mr Jardeen. I'd love to see her smiling again.'

'What about a trip into the countryside. Would she like that, do you think?' Godfrey suggested.

◆

They couldn't manage to get out into the real countryside of the Yorkshire Dales where Godfrey had in mind. There was no transport to the east of town. Instead, they went to Kingsley Park, an open green space where there were walkways through pretty gardens and tree-lined avenues. It was a pleasant autumn Sunday afternoon and Godfrey snapped a photograph of George and Hilda posing near a wall where they'd laid out a picnic.

Jean held the memory of that day in a special place in her heart. She had succeeded in helping Hilda to smile again. That afternoon, in the autumn sunshine her sister had looked like Jean remembered. The fresh air had brought a bloom back to Hilda's cheeks, and she'd eaten as much as any of the rest of them.

Hilda was exhausted after the walk back to the house on the Lane and went to bed early, but Jean would always remember that day as one of the times when she'd been able to do something for Hilda instead of the other way around. When the photographs were developed, Jean kept the picture of George and Hilda safe in her collection.

TWENTY EIGHT

In January 1943 the remaining Jewish inhabitants of the Warsaw ghetto rose up against German occupation. Thousands of their people had already died due to disease and starvation in the densely packed central area of the city. Believing they were being taken to labour camps, they'd shown no resistance to the first wave of deportation and had gone along with SS directives. But by the end of 1942 word had spread that the deportations were part of an extermination process; the Jewish people were being rounded up in their thousands and sent to their deaths. Many of them decided to resist.

When the second phase of deportation began two resistance organisations took control of the ghetto. Almost a thousand men women and children armed with smuggled in weapons and Molotov cocktails were ready to fight. With limited supplies of ammunition against well-armed German battalions their efforts could not save them. They battled bravely until April when they were forced to take cover in shelters carefully disguised in the burned out ghetto ruins. Even then, many of them came out firing at the enemy, but by the middle of May it was all over.

Some thirteen thousand residents had been shot, burned alive or buried under the rubble of what remained of the ghetto. Nearly all of the remaining fifty thousand inhabitants were transported to Treblinka, for extermination. But a few, hiding in the sewers, would survive and live to tell the world.

George Pozyzcka was doing everything in his power to help the war effort. As a fire-watcher his duties were to locate and extinguish incendiary devices dropped by the Germans to light the path for their bombers.

Kingsley had escaped the worst of the bombing raids because of its position, tucked away in its narrow valley in the Pennines, and so, because he was rarely needed in this capacity George doubled up his duties and served as a warden, patrolling the streets and making sure houses were properly blacked out. He was out every night, patrolling the streets, and became well-known among Kingsley folk for his kindly personality.

George knew how to talk to people; he knew how not to rub them up the wrong way. He had a way of using his authority that made others feel good about their own efforts and single-handedly he'd been responsible for collecting the largest amount of money to go towards Kingsley's own Spitfire. Nobody used the expression DP when they mentioned George. He was no longer a displaced person. He was a respected member of the close-knit community who worked hard to support his adopted nation and care for his family and sick wife. They knew he'd tried to enter the Armed Forces long before the time came when he would have been conscripted, and they shared with him his sorrow at what was happening in his own homeland.

In 1944 the whole of the country felt the beginning of a sea-change in the progress of hostilities and on the sixth of June the Allied Forces landed in Normandy to begin the invasion and liberation of France. But one week later the first of Hitler's new secret weapon, the V1, landed in Britain and in September, the deadlier version, the V2 rocket found its target.

The Allies fought on and the end of the month saw the German surrender of Boulogne and Calais. One week before Christmas of that year Adolf Hitler launched his last ditch attempt to split the Allied Forces in their drive to advance towards Germany to destroy their supply lines. It was the beginning of what came to be known as The Battle of the Bulge.

◆

Godfrey had heard nothing from Richard Mancini. He didn't know whether he was alive or dead, and his efforts to remain hopeful and positive in his thinking became harder to uphold. Young Jean was a treasure, and he was grateful for all her help, but he'd reached the point when in his heart all hope had gone. He began to consider closing down Mancini Modes.

'Try to hang on a bit longer, Mr Jardeen,' Jean told him. 'I'll come in every night after work to help you. You know I will.'

'You are an angel, Jean Thompson. You know that? Coming to help with the sewing after you've done your shift at the factory. I don't know where you get the energy from.'

'From your dinners, Mr Jardeen. And the chance to use the shower. They're the only reason I come, really,' she joked. 'Whenever I have a place of my own I'm definitely going to have a shower installed.'

'Well, it's a pleasure to feed you,' he smiled. 'I only wish I could afford to pay you a little something for your time.'

'I don't need paying Mr Jardeen,' she said. 'I do it because I want to.'

Godfrey Jardeen was beginning to look his age. He had no reason to keep up with his usual cosmetic regime. He had no motivation to care about his appearance. The grey hair at his temples had spread around his ears and there was now a thinning patch at the back of his head where his scalp showed through. His once lively blue eyes had faded and sunk beneath fleshy dark pouches which lined his lower lids. He was lonely and isolated.

Apart from Jean and her family there was nobody he could call friend. If the worst were to happen and Richard was lost to him forever, he would be destitute. There would be no provision made for him. Whatever remained of Richard's family would have first call on the estate and he, Godfrey, would be out on his ear.

He had no alternative but to keep working. He rallied himself.

'Jean, you're a tonic,' he said. 'I don't know where I'd be without you. Go upstairs, will you my dear? In the bathroom cabinet you will find a dark brown bottle and a small paint brush. It's my hair conditioner. Would you help me to apply it? I think we might need to use the whole bottle.'

◆

Jean had found work in the factory across the street from Endura. Originally a carriage works producing single decker buses, Charles Cooper Ltd had switched to manufacturing various military utility vehicles ranging from mobile map printing wagons and articulated kitchen trailers to the accumulator trolleys used to start up aircraft engines. In the annexe to the main factory building the company converted the chassis of hundreds of private cars to ambulances and mobile canteens.

Jean was invaluable in this department. With Godfrey's permission to use contacts from Mancini Modes she'd acquired many large saloon cars, generously donated by their owners. She borrowed Godfrey's camera and took photographs of all the finished vehicles, pasting one copy on the factory wall, where an impressive gallery was building up, and sending another copy to the former owners so they could see how their generosity was helping the war effort.

By the time she'd exhausted her telephone contacts she found that the proud car owners had passed on her name to their wealthy friends and the situation became reversed. Now people were telephoning Charles Cooper Ltd and asking for Jean Thompson to come and collect.

She became an accomplished driver. She used public transport to go collect the donated private cars, drove them back to Kingsley, and in some cases delivered the finished utility vehicle to its destination where she'd have to wait outside the compound gates until she'd been cleared by the sentry on guard.

There were airfields and military bases in parts of the country she'd never heard of, let alone seen before. With winter frosts decorating hedgerows and carpeting the fields, their beauty filled her with longing. After the war, those were the kinds of places Hilda would like. Now that Jean could drive she would be able to take her sister to see some of those pretty country towns and villages. It would help Hilda grow stronger and get back to how she used to be.

◆

When Jean returned home from her shower and sewing session with Godfrey Jardeen two days before Christmas 1944, George was pacing the kitchen. Hilda was sitting quietly by the fire wearing a strange expression.

'What?' Jean asked immediately. 'What's happened?'

'Sit down, love,' Hilda told her. 'Come and sit by the fire with me. We've got something to tell you. Haven't we, George?'

Her pulse racing, Jean took a chair by the fire and sat, waiting. George stopped his pacing about but he was still agitated and his voice came in rapid shallow bursts.

'We're having a baby, Jean,' he gasped. 'It's happened. We're going to have a baby.'

He began his striding about the room again.

'George,' Hilda called to him. 'For goodness sake will you sit down. You're making me feel tired.'

George was bursting with happiness. He could barely contain himself; it was more than he could do to sit still, even for a moment. He jumped to his feet again and went to kiss his wife.

'Isn't she wonderful?' he said to nobody in particular. 'Isn't she just my beautiful Hilda?'

'Get out of the way, George, and let me give my sister a big hug,' Jean said good-naturedly. 'When?' she asked. 'When's the baby due?'

'We think it might be next June. We can't be absolutely sure,' Hilda said. 'I'm going to see a specialist doctor next week. Nothing to worry about, Jean. It's just because I've always been so irregular. You know.'

'And because they think thirty-five is old lady to have first baby,' George added.

Jean said she was so pleased for them. She said how thrilled she was to be an aunty to a new little person in the family. She kept her face bright, her mouth in a smile and her eyes full of joy and pleasure. She congratulated them, laughed and made all the right noises, but all she could see were the dark shadows under Hilda's eyes and the pale thin hands sticking out from the sleeves of her cardigan.

✦

Next morning Mr Cooper junior came into the annexe building looking for Jean.

'Jean,' he said. 'There's a visitor for you in reception. You can go early, if you like. We're finishing at twelve today anyway.'

Jean saw the smart uniform and jaunty hat and knew who was waiting before the wearer turned around to greet her.

'Sandra,' she called out. 'Look at you. You look terrific.'

Sandra eyed Jean's dirty overalls and her grease-smeared face.

'Pity I can't say the same for you,' she laughed. 'Come on, get your coat. We're going out.'

'Where are we going?' Jean asked.

'Wait and see. First we've got to get you cleaned up. Godfrey's waiting with the back-scrub and a nail brush and a big bar of carbolic.'

'Cheeky,' Jean chuckled, and linking arms they stepped out together.

True to Sandra's words, Godfrey was waiting for them.

'Don't look so surprised,' he told Jean. 'We know what we're doing. We've planned a little surprise for you, that's all. Sandra telephoned me last night when she got home on leave. Off you go, Jean. The shower's waiting for you. And there's a pair of Katherine Hepburn's hanging behind the door.'

They went to the grandest tea rooms in Harrogate. Sandra had borrowed her dad's old Vauxhall 20 and Jean whisked them over the tops, the countryside way, cutting across steep Pennine hillsides, snaking around river valleys and into the Spa town. They ate home-made scones with strawberry jam, followed by wedges of Victoria sponge filled with a buttercream made from margarine. They talked of cars and engines instead of fashion and make-up and surprised each other at how much they'd changed and learned during the course of the war.

Godfrey enjoyed every minute. There wasn't much he could add to the conversation on engine performance but he was thrilled they'd included him on their outing. He sat, beaming like a benevolent uncle, listening to their lively chatter and feeling he had people of his own after all.

On the way back he looked out at the Yorkshire countryside and remembered when he'd been worried about leaving the south of England. Since then he'd grown to love the hills and moors of his adopted county. He only hoped that by some miracle, Richard would return to him, safe and well, and they would be able to see more of it together.

As daylight faded, they reached the top of the last hill before the road made its final steep descent into the valley. Kingsley stood below them. Many of the mills and factories were still at work on this Christmas Eve afternoon and spirals of smoke and steam curled upwards from the chimneys. Where once he would have rejected out of hand the notion that there could be found anything beautiful in such a sight, he now rejoiced in the knowledge that there were people who knew better than that. They were down there now, giving their all, men and women working together to keep the machines running. They were to be admired. More, they were to be thanked for their efforts. He felt a surge of well-being and realised he was glad to be alive and living in a world where he was among people like them.

The girls were determined that Godfrey should accompany them that night too.

'It's Christmas Eve,' Jean insisted.

'Come on, Mr Jardeen,' Sandra coaxed. 'Think of it as a favour to us. Two young ladies like us out on the town? We need an escort. We don't want the town thinking we're out on the pull.'

He didn't need much persuading. He took them both back to the apartment above Mancini Modes after Sandra had dropped off her father's car at the foundry. He gave them luncheon meat sandwiches with some pickle he'd made himself from cauliflower stalks and green tomatoes which had never ripened on his window-sill. Then he brought out Richard's vanity case and helped the girls give one another a makeover before they set out again for the evening.

There was no dance at the Institute that year. A genteel pub-crawl was all the excitement the town had to offer. Sandra's uniform attracted attention everywhere they went and when the regulars learned that part of Sandra's job was the loading of ammunition into the rapid-fire armaments of fighter aircraft, the girls barely needed to buy a drink themselves.

In The Black Horse they joined in with a game of darts; in the Market Tavern they gathered around the pianist who was thumping out *Bless 'Em All*, *Roll out the Barrel* and other favourites, interspersed with Good King Wenceslas and *White Christmas* which had been recorded a few years earlier for the film *Holiday Inn*.

Godfrey had a passable tenor, and his rendition of *Silent Night* brought more than a few lumps in throats and tears in eyes. Sitting sandwiched between Godfrey and Sandra, Jean made her announcement.

'Our Hilda's having a baby.'

Godfrey began his congratulations, but Sandra had heard the tone of Jean's voice.

'I know I should be happy for her,' Jean continued. 'But I'm not. She's not well. I don't think she's well enough to be having a baby. And she won't say anything to George. He's like a dog with two tails bouncing all over the place. He can't see she hasn't got the strength to have a baby. She didn't have the strength to go back to work after the accident so how is she going to see this through?'

Jean waited for a response but both Godfrey and Sandra sat in silence.

'Oh, I'm sorry,' Jean apologised. 'I shouldn't have just come out with it like that. It's Christmas Eve and we're supposed to be out enjoying ourselves. Forget I ever said anything.'

Sandra shook her head. 'You don't have to apologise, Jean. We understand you're worried about your sister. But she'll see the doctor, won't she? They know how to look after her. Having a baby's not like it used to be, is it? We're not in the Dark Ages.'

Sandra caught a glimpse of Godfrey's horrified expression at what she was saying.

'Oh, shit,' she said. 'I've gone and opened my big mouth again without thinking. My turn to apologise, Jean.'

'Look,' Godfrey advised. 'Now is not the time to worry about things we can't change. We're all still here, and we're all still all right. Just look around us. The pub is full of people who've all got plenty to worry about, but who are doing their best to have a good time tonight. It's been a lovely day today, so I say let's keep it going.'

They drew their coats around them and went out into dark night streets to cross town for their next port of call. Other groups of Christmas revellers called out to them in the pitch black and they responded with their own best wishes:

'We don't know who you are. Can't see you. But, Merry Christmas, anyway.'

They were seated with a small group from Charles Cooper Ltd in The Cavendish just before closing when Sandra looked up to see her father staring down at her.

'I've parked the car round the back of the offices, Dad,' she said. 'It's all locked up. Don't worry, it's all right. Only, I thought it best not to drive it home tonight after we'd been drinking.'

'It's not about the car,' he said solemnly.

'Well, I said I'd come to Midnight Mass with you, Dad. But I'm not quite ready yet. I'll see you there.'

'It's not about Mass, Sandra.'

Sandra looked at him properly. She saw the knitted brow and the strain in his face.

'It's Ronnie,' he said. 'They're sending him home. He's not well.'

'When?' she asked.

'As soon as he can be moved. Your mother's gone hysterical.'

He turned to Jean and Godfrey: 'I'm sorry to break up the party,' he continued. 'My wife is asking for Sandra. I thought I might find you in here for last orders. I've put one in for you at the bar; the barman assumed you'd be having the same. I am sorry,' he apologised again.

'Jean, will you be at home tomorrow?' Sandra asked, throwing on her coat.

'Yes. Godfrey's coming round for Christmas dinner. We've pooled our coupons.'

'I'll try to pop in, then. Got to go back on Boxing Day, first thing.'

She pulled a face at them. 'Sorry about this,' she said, and hurried out of the bar with her father. Godfrey took hold of Jean's hands.

'Don't do it,' he said.

'I won't. Definitely not,' she replied.

'Good,' he said with a smile.

'I won't let that no-good Ronnie Logan spoil our Christmas, Mr Jardeen. I don't care what's happened to him. It's got nothing to do with me any more. I'm more concerned about our Hilda.'

'Right,' he said. 'Let's keep it that way, Jean. And don't you think it's time you called me Godfrey, my dear?'

'Absolutely,' she grinned. 'From now on you shall be *Godfreymydear*. Godfreymydear, shall we have that drink that's waiting for us?'

He brought back the two glasses paid for by Thomas Logan.

'Here we are, then,' he said. 'Bottoms up.'

'Thank you, Godfreymydear,' she answered. 'Up yours!'

He screwed up his face in a grimace.

'Did I say something wrong, Godfreymydear?' she asked in fake innocence.

'Absolutely,' he replied. 'Who cares? Merry Christmas!'

PART THREE

TWENTY NINE

DECEMBER 2009

Everything has been moving so quickly. There was I, planning a leisurely preparation for Deborah's visit and I've been rushed off my feet. After John Starling had been to see his old friend Gordon at the Craft Barns, he came back with a real bee in his bonnet. One of the units was about to become vacant and John had decided to take it on. Immediately.

We've had five days of madness. Working with John's existing designs we've bought in supplies of a selection of yarns, and using his colour plot Madeleine and I counted out quantities of each colour needed to complete each picture. We've had yarn everywhere. In the kitchen, on the table and over the backs of chairs we arranged strands of earth colours; blues and greens were spread out on the dining table; reds and purples over the backs of dining chairs, and so on through the whole house. We wound yarn around pieces of slotted card. Madeleine printed out instruction leaflets and header cards from her computer and we stapled the finished kits together using cellophane packs we'd ordered on the internet.

Madeleine discovered there are professional companies who specialise in this sort of assembly work and John worked out the cost per unit of using the service. He explained how to calculate costs and taxes and it's been quite an eye-opener learning the ins and outs of the retail trade.

John went through the procedure with us, clarifying details about wholesale prices, profit margins and VAT. He told us you need to be aware of what the market will stand, as he put it. If similar needlework kits sell for ten pounds, for example, it's no good putting yours out at twenty to cover the costs of your overheads, materials, printing and assembly work, your mark up and the added taxes. Your product would not be viable.

'But what if your needlework kit is simply so much better than the ones at ten pounds?' I asked.

'Ah, then you have a good reason for charging more,' he said. 'But you've still got to take into consideration who your customers are. And we have to remember that times are hard just now for a good many. But I know from experience when people cut back on their spending, they still like to have a small treat once in a while. Instead of going out to the pub or the restaurant, they stay in with a DVD and a big bar of chocolate. And they take up hobbies.'

'Lots of new businesses start up on the kitchen table,' Madeleine said. 'I used to think that was just a saying. Now I know it can mean literally on the kitchen table.'

'Yes,' John said. 'I know these last few days have been a bit hectic but it's only because there was so much to do at once. I think once we're in the unit there'll be enough space at the back to do some of this assembly work. Remember, it'll only be one or two at a time. We might not have to pay to have it done at all. That way we can keep our costs down.'

It pleased me that he used *we* instead of *I*. He really wanted to keep us included in his new business plan and both Madeleine and I felt the excitement of our new venture. It's fair to say we thoroughly enjoyed the challenge of those few days. Even little Christopher helped in his own small way and learned a lot about the names of different colours.

Gordon loaned some display racks to help us get started and gave us the name of the company he uses for displays in the main store at The Barns. John's sister, Margaret made some ruffled curtaining to run around the display counters. I hadn't realised until we went to look at the unit that all you got was the bare walls.

We stood, looking at the bare concrete floor and whitewashed walls. I couldn't help feeling dismayed at the holes left behind where previous occupants had removed their shelving and lights. It was Alex who came up with the idea of running a counter round three sides. He had it made and in position in no time at all. There was plenty of space underneath for storage shelves and we bought some plastic crates to hide underneath the counters, behind Margaret's curtaining. With a fresh coat of paint the unit began to look very pleasing, like a proper little shop. It certainly complemented the country shopping experience, the logo with which the Barns advertised itself.

John arranged for a card reader with his bank manager so our customers could pay by debit or credit card and he set up a simple sales tracking system so we could see as soon as any pattern of best-sellers began to emerge. As for manning the shop once it's open, there's a pool of part-time workers who staff the various units at the Barns, but to begin with John has three volunteers all willing to lend a hand until he's established. Madeleine offered to work in the shop when Luke is home and if she could have a lift in. I'll help out anytime. Then there's Alison, Alex's wife.

We met for the first time when we all went to have a look at the empty unit. I liked her immediately. She has kind eyes, and when she smiles her eyes smile too. We didn't have much time to talk and get to know each other better as we were all so involved in setting up the shop, but where I had felt that Alex had been cool and uncomfortable with me at our first meeting, Alison exuded the warmth of her friendliness. Together, they make a lovely couple. That's probably a most old-fashioned thing to say nowadays, but they look right together. You can tell they are solid; they fit each other and it's very obvious John thinks the world of both of them.

When Alex had finished the shelving and spotlights, Alison and I ferried over the stock and began to dress the displays and the window next to the door. Gordon had told John he didn't mind if the unit wasn't open for Christmas shoppers, as long as we made the place look ready and put up a sign to give visitors our opening date. But we were all keen to make a start once the meter readings had been taken and the telephone line installed. We set about making John Starling Designs look as professional as we possibly could.

We picked up some inexpensive fabric from a discount store on the outskirts of Norwich, and because we were all getting into the Christmas spirit, added some voile drapes with integral twinkling lights which looked superb draped across the glass panel in the door. I couldn't resist a few Christmas baubles as well.

I was getting swept along with the excitement of the season and the thrill of John's new enterprise. The finishing touch was the wall display. Alex had framed some of mother's finished needlework. We toasted the hanging of the last one with glasses of bubbly and took photographs of the completed shop.

'I wish your Mum could have seen this,' Alison whispered to Alex. 'Wouldn't she have been proud?'

Alex just looked at her and said nothing. It had slipped my mind that John's sister, Margaret had told me John had lost his wife fairly recently. Of course Alex's mother would be proud of her husband's new venture. I turned my head aside. It was their private moment; I didn't want to intrude. We locked up the new shop and after making further arrangements to meet again, went our separate ways home.

Then, quite by chance, I saw an advert in one of my magazines for a national needlecraft exhibition being held in one of the main exhibition centres in Birmingham. John, Alison and I discussed it over a cup of coffee next morning at the cottage. Madeleine couldn't get away to join us.

'I didn't know they had exhibitions for that sort of thing,' Alison said.

'Oh, yes,' John said. 'There are Trade Shows for just about anything you might care to mention.'

'What do you think will be on show?'

'What does it say in the advert, Audrey?' John asked me.

I read from the pages of the magazine: over five hundred stands, demonstrations, new products, agents required, accessories, shop fittings, display racks, merchandising, paper bags.

'How do you fancy a branded carrier-bag, Dad?' Alison laughed. 'I can see it now. John Starling Designs in racing green print on a gold foil bag.'

'Away with you,' he joked. 'You've got to walk before you can run. We'll manage very well with the ones we've got.'

'But it would be very interesting to go and see the show for ourselves, wouldn't it?' I suggested.

'I'll think about it,' John said.

'Don't think too long, Dad,' Alison told him. 'We'd need to make up our minds soon.'

◆

The car park at the Birmingham Exhibition Centre is enormous. There are acres of lettered and numbered areas. We rode up to the Halls on a shuttle coach packed with exhibitors in their smart suits and armed with laptops and briefcases. They all looked alike to me, like so many black beetles alighting from the coaches, streaming off in the direction of the coffee counters before making their way to their stands.

We'd had a very early start that morning, rising at three am to allow enough time for the journey on busy motorways, and we were all ready for breakfast once we'd arrived inside. We perused the catalogues over croissants and frothy coffee, then John sprang another surprise on us.

He'd already telephoned one or two major exhibitors and set up appointments with them to show his designs. Both Alison and I had wondered what he was carrying in the pilot's bag he had brought with him. I'd thought maybe medication, maybe sandwiches and a flask. But no, he'd come thoroughly prepared to show his work and seek orders.

'There's a few ways this could go,' he told us. Alison and I sat munching our breakfast, hanging on his every word. He was thoroughly enjoying himself. It didn't matter, of course, whether his new endeavour was a success or not. His livelihood didn't depend on it and for that reason, because we were all involved out of pure enjoyment, there was no need to feel nervous or anxious about the outcome. John was completely relaxed and in a great mood to drive a hard bargain.

'First of all,' he said, 'there may be no interest in what we have at all. Our timing could be poor now that people are cutting back on their spending. No matter. We'll still have our small retail outlet at the Craft barns to enjoy. In that case we would concentrate today on having a good look around and picking up tips. We'll be able to see at a glance which are the most popular styles. New and different ideas are not so easy to sell. It takes time to establish new products, not to mention a great deal of money. The retailers who've come here today to place their orders will most likely want to stick to what's known to be a good seller. So, there'll be more best-sellers on display. Take note ladies. We need to know what the hobbyists out there prefer.'

I glanced across the table at Alison and saw she was as mesmerised by John as I was. He was in his element. He delved into his bag and brought out two small notepads.

'Here you are,' he said. 'I want you to make a note about anything that strikes you and we'll get round the table with it afterwards.'

We took our notepads and pens from him and waited for our next instructions.

'Well now,' he continued. 'We might find some interest in our designs. I've done the calculations and I'm prepared to consider several options. There's enough margin to think about supplying wholesale on a limited range of designs. If we went that way there'd be home assembly work to do for anybody in the village who would be interested. Obviously, we would pay the going rate plus a bit extra. There is the possibility, however, that the wholesale suppliers may pay a one-off fee for the design and take on the printing and packaging themselves. What do you think?'

'It's your business, Dad,' Alison said. 'It's up to you to decide.'

'What do you think, Audrey?' he asked me.

'I think you can do both, John,' I remarked. 'But, I also think it would be sensible if you kept back some designs especially for the customers in Norfolk. They're the people who would be more interested in your local scenes. Those kits wouldn't sell in Leeds or here in Birmingham, for example.'

'Agreed,' he stated simply. 'Got your watches on, girls?'

He had us synchronise our watches as if we were embarking on a military manoeuvre, arranged to meet us for lunch and went to his first appointment.

Alison leaned across the table. 'That's John Starling, for you,' she said with a wry smile.

'I've never seen him like this,' I told her. 'I've usually had trouble getting him to tell me anything.'

She laughed. 'Norfolk people usually like to take their time to get to know new folks,' she said.

'But I haven't found that, Alison. In the village everybody speaks to me,' I said.

'Ah, that's because you're Walsingham Matilda.' she replied. 'Everybody wants to know you.'

'Why?' I asked. 'What's so special about me?'

She pursed her lips and looked thoughtful for a moment.

'I can't answer that,' she said.

We gathered up our things and agreed on a route through the exhibition halls. It took much longer than I'd imagined to cover the aisles. There was so much to see and we soon discovered if we showed interest in anything in particular we would attract the attention of one of the sales beetles who would approach us with a hand-held electronic device for taking orders.

I was impressed by the lighting on many stands and how products on display were enhanced by carefully positioned uplighting. I made a picture in my mind's eye of how I would like to see my own work lighted if ever I was lucky enough to have an exhibition. I made a note on my pad: *correct lighting- very important.*

We'd covered about half the Hall by the time our rumbling tummies motivated us to check the time. We made our way to the designated meeting place and secured a table. John arrived a few minutes later and we placed our orders. He had little to say over lunch: he was waiting for the outcome of his afternoon meeting with another company.

During the afternoon Alison spotted some unusual display stands. We collected a few brochures and price lists to take back with us. I took note of the floor coverings some had used. I thought sea grass matting was effective and would complement our country theme in the unit. More jottings on the notepad. I looked at the colours exhibitors had used as background for their products and remarked that too much neutral was bland and boring. I made another scribbling to remind us to look again at our dressing of the shop once the Christmas season was over.

By the end of the day we were exhausted. We met John in the reception area after his meeting and made our way to the shuttle bus for the car park.

Alison offered to drive us back and John accepted thankfully. He said he'd had good meetings and was very pleased with the results. He wanted to wait until our round the table meeting before giving us all the details and we were happy to defer. The long day had taken its toll on all of us.

Matilda honked when she heard me come back into the house and I went outside to talk to her.

'Now look here,' I said to her. 'You're not supposed to be a garden goose. You've got to be brave and fly away.'

She turned her back on me and scuttled into the outhouse. I went indoors to make a hot drink.

'Nearly Christmas,' I said to the Shrek head as I waited for the kettle to boil. 'And I still haven't made you a friend, have I? I must do something about that soon.'

THIRTY

Madeleine called round next day to see how the visit had gone. It was a shame she'd missed the opportunity but it would have been a dreary day for Christopher, down at push chair level with nothing but the backs of people's legs to look at. I suggested she come to the meeting John had planned and when I mentioned the possibility of working from home she said that would be a better way for her to help.

'I'd like to have a bit of money of my own,' she told me. 'I wouldn't have to account for what I'd spent it on if I'd earned it myself.'

I didn't pursue her comment. We took Christopher out into the garden to have a look at Matilda. She did her usual fluffing herself out, stamping her feet and honking and running up and down the garden.

'You'll miss her when she goes,' Madeleine said.

'I know,' I replied.

The telephone rang and I went indoors to answer.

'Malcolm! How lovely. I'm so pleased to hear from you. How are you?' I was thrilled to hear his voice.

'Okay,' he answered. 'Ma, will you send a Marks and Spencer Christmas pudding to Angela's parents? They're having a traditional dinner this year and Angela thinks they'd like to have one with a very English name. You'll have to use a specialist carrier to get it here on time because it's now too late for Royal Mail. There's Fed-Ex, DHL, TNT . . . . .'

He continued with his list of parcel carriers and explained how I would need to package the pudding carefully and what I should use for wrapping materials. He'd made an evaluation of the cost-effectiveness of bubble-wrap versus tissue paper, and had examples on a sliding scale to prove his figures. I couldn't concentrate. His words swam around my brain and my eyes were brimming with tears.

'..... so if you check online you'll see which company offers the best rate. Send me an email when you've posted it off. Okay?'

'Okay,' I said. 'Is that all?'

'Yes, that's all,' he answered. 'Goodbye, Ma.'

'Goodbye, Malcolm. Merry . . . . . .'

He'd already hung up. He hadn't asked anything. It never entered his head to enquire about his mother's well-being. I replaced the receiver and doubled up in physical pain. I pressed my arm firmly against my stomach to hold myself in. I felt sick. Madeleine rushed to my side.

'Audrey, what's happened?' she asked me.

I told her. In between holding my stomach and sobbing till my chest hurt, I told her how I felt.

'He has no idea how much he hurts me, Madeleine,' I told her. 'He has no feelings at all for other people. He only cares about himself.'

'Come and sit down,' she said. 'There's something I want to tell you.'

I followed her through into the living room. 'Christopher will be all right in the garden for a little while. Come on, Audrey.'

I stopped my snivelling and apologised to her.

'I'm sorry, Madeleine. I shouldn't have done that in front of you and the little one.'

'Don't be silly,' she said. 'We're friends, aren't we?'

'I thought I was an honorary Grandma,' I said with an attempt at a smile.

'That too,' she smiled back. 'Look, Audrey, you've been so good to me. There's something I want to tell you, but I don't want to upset you.'

'What is it? Go ahead.'

'There was a boy at my high school who was like your Malcolm. You know, the way you described what he was like when he was younger. When you told me about some of the things he used to do it reminded me of him.

His name was Ray and we were in the same year group all the way through school, so by the time we got into high school I knew him very well. I was one of the few people who understood him. I don't mean he couldn't speak properly or anything like that, but at times it was difficult to understand what he meant. It was as if he couldn't remember the right words to use, so he'd put together sentences that didn't make sense. Sometimes he'd get so frustrated that people didn't understand him and he'd get angry when we had to ask him to repeat what he'd said. Then he'd switch the subject of the conversation to something he was more comfortable with. Often, it would be the same subject and the same few sentences.'

'Like a recording that got stuck?' I prompted.

'Yes, that's right,' she said. 'As he grew older he spent more and more time by himself. The others had lost patience with him. He wanted to be included but he didn't know how to do it. He developed his own ways of coping with his frustration.'

'What did he do?' I wanted to know.

'He danced. He did a kind of robot dancing. It helped him to sort his head out, he told me, but it didn't help him with the rest of the class. They just thought he was weird.

'One day, our teacher explained to us. Ray had asked him to speak to the class and so we had this session, all of us, with Ray present as well. Afterwards, I decided to look it up on the internet and found a lot of websites dedicated to people just like Ray. It's called Asperger Syndrome and it's linked to Autism.'

I blinked back my surprise.

'Are you telling me you think Malcolm has had some kind of condition all his life?'

'I think you should look it up and decide for yourself, Audrey. I hope I haven't done the wrong thing.'

'No, dear. Of course you haven't done the wrong thing. I'm grateful to you for caring enough to try to help.'

Christopher came hurrying back inside looking for his mother.

'Mama,' he shouted at full volume.

'In here, Christopher,' she answered.

He stood in the doorway and grinned at us both then ran back outside.

'He was just checking,' I said. 'Now he can be brave again.'

The front door bell sounded.

'What now?' I said, standing up to check my face in the mirror wondering if I was presentable enough to open the door. Madeleine understood immediately.

'Would you like me to get that for you, Audrey?' she suggested.

'Yes please. I think I'd better go upstairs and tidy myself up. I look a sight.'

My box of personal belongings had arrived out of storage. Madeleine signed for it on my behalf and the delivery man left it in the hall.

'I'd better be off, now,' Madeleine said. 'It looks like you've got your evening planned for you, sorting through that lot. Audrey, don't forget to do a search on the internet. Here, I've written down a good place for you to start.'

She handed me a slip of paper with a couple of web site addresses. 'I think it might put your mind at rest. Give me a call to let me know when John wants to meet. Is he planning to open up the shop before Christmas, do you know?'

'I don't think he's made up his mind yet, Madeleine. Maybe he'll tell us at the meeting. I'll call you to let you know when and where.'

She bundled up her rosy-cheeked boy against the cold and I waved her off. I turned and looked at the carton of my things. At any other time I would have torn it open and dived straight in, but there was something more pressing. I switched on my new laptop.

After the first hour of reading my head was swimming. I needed a break. The descriptions I'd seen of typical behaviours of children with this condition astounded me. It was as if I had been reading about Malcolm, as though they were my own words. It was incredible; it was all there: the difficult baby with feeding problems; the wondering if your child was deaf; the strange speech; the awkward gait. They actually used the phrase *little professor*, words I'd used myself. I read about cluttered speech and immediately I remembered how if Malcolm had stopped in the middle of a sentence he would have to go back to the beginning and start it again.

I finished my coffee and went back to the computer to read more. I think I was looking for some exceptions to the usual rule; some excuse I could engineer to justify Malcolm's issues, but the more I discovered, the more obvious it became. My stomach lurched and my pulse raced. How could I have not known? How could I have let my son suffer through all these difficulties and done little to help him? Why had I never heard of this Asperger Syndrome?

When I clicked on the Australian Paediatric web site with its checklist for parents and teachers to help make their own informal diagnosis, I threw up my hands in despair.

'No,' I shouted. 'No. This can't be true!'

Malcolm had been born in the very country where there was so much help available, and I knew nothing about it. How could I have let this happen?

I went through the Australian checklist and answered all the questions. Malcolm ticked every box, every single one of them. My only son had a condition which explained all the strange behaviours of his childhood. He was still like it. It would never go away. He'd learned how to cope with it by himself without any help from anybody, including Jim and me. I felt terrible. What if I could have made his life so much better if I'd known the truth? If he'd been diagnosed with this condition would it have helped to make his childhood easier for him?

I couldn't take in any more but I bookmarked several websites so I could come back to them again. I made myself a hot chocolate to take up to bed and interrogated the Shrek head, blaming it for its annoying green silence as I stood at the kitchen hob.

'I'm as stupid as you are,' I told it. 'I talk to a green head every day and I don't get any answers. All I get is more questions. Why didn't I follow up on Malcolm's differences? Why didn't I insist on getting to the bottom of it?'

The magical green head of the all-powerful wizard stared at me in silence and I knew I already had the answer to my own questions. I didn't want to find out the truth. I was afraid the truth would cause trouble so I shied away from it. I should have forced Jim to face up to reality as well. I should have made him realise neither of us was helping our son by pretending there was nothing amiss.

We cheated our own boy out of the help he might otherwise have had because we were too cowardly to go through with it. Jim pretended it wasn't an issue and I let him. All those years we were living a lie, creating an illusion we were the average ordinary family and all the time our boy was confused and anxious about the very world we were creating for him. Growing up must have been torture for him. It was a miracle he'd found his own way through the maze, found his career path and found Angela too. Maybe I'd never given the girl the credit she deserved. I had been blinkered.

I stirred my hot chocolate fiercely. I was angry with myself and knew I needed to calm down before I'd be able to sleep. I opened the parcel in the hall. I found Christmas souvenirs and Malcolm's old school photographs. I put out a framed photograph I took of Jim and Malcolm when we were on holiday the year Malcolm was twelve.

Malcolm looks tall and gangly and too old to be hanging onto his father the way he is in the picture. We were at a Water Park, the kind with twisting spiralling slides, and high chutes. I remember Malcolm was afraid of the slides and wouldn't attempt them. He could see much younger children than himself having a whale of a time but he wouldn't be persuaded to give it a go. He hung back from all the rides and wouldn't even try the family slides where everybody sits together in a large rubber dinghy.

He grew anxious and started pacing and flapping his hands. Jim tried everything to coax Malcolm out of his fear but when Malcolm began to cry, Jim lost patience and walked off. Malcolm cried louder because Dad had left him and wasn't the least bit embarrassed people were staring at him. He really didn't know his behaviour was inappropriate for his age. All he knew was he'd been upset and frightened.

Jim couldn't cope with Malcolm's child-like behaviour. He expected more from his son and the more he distanced himself from him, the more clingy and wheedling Malcolm would be. It was as if he wanted to regress to his infancy. Now he *wanted* to be held and cuddled. Jim couldn't accept that his son was so emotionally insecure. It offended him Malcolm still wanted to be treated like a baby.

That night in our hotel room I explained to Malcolm that twelve year old boys don't usually cry in public about little things that upset them. I said that was why people were staring at him and that was why dad had felt uncomfortable.

Malcolm didn't get it. He didn't see what was wrong with what he did and perhaps he was right. I only wanted to help him see and understand the ways of the world but I didn't know then that the way most of us see the world is not the same as the way people like Malcolm see it. He could no more understand my world than I could understand his. We were like different species.

I thought about the boy Madeleine had told me about when she was at school. She'd made a better job of accepting Ray and his differences than I had with my own son. Where Madeleine had accepted Ray and adapted her own ways of thinking, I had tried to adapt Malcolm's way of thinking, tried to make him fit into the world around him.

I looked at the clock. Time for bed.

'Come on, Audrey,' I said out loud. 'You know you can't do any more today. Go to bed.'

There was nothing I could do to change the past. Armed with this new information, though, I might make a better job of the future.

THIRTY ONE

The ringing telephone wakes me. I glance at my bedside clock and I'm shocked to realise I've overslept. Quickly, I throw on my dressing gown and hurry downstairs.

'Hello?' my voice is thick and croaky.

'Hello, Audrey. It's Deborah. I'm just calling to let you know what time my train gets in. Are you all right? You sound different.'

'Hello,' I reply. 'I'm fine. To tell you the truth I've only just woken up.'

'Had a late night, did you?'

'Something like that,' I answer. 'I'm really looking forward to our weekend. You okay?'

'Yes, yes. I'm looking forward to it too. I get into Norwich at five past four. Is that all right with you? Got to dash. See you later.'

I tidy up the photographs and other things left out from the night before and slide the box behind one of the settees, out of sight. The Shrek head stares at me as I enter the kitchen.

'You're beginning to get on my nerves,' I tell it. 'You sit there with that half smile on your face as if you are in possession of some superior knowledge. One of these days I'm going to wipe that smug smile right off your face.'

I pick up some supplies at one of the larger supermarkets on the road to Norwich. It's a horrible experience. The aisles are crowded with Christmas shoppers and the checkout queues are too long. I find a parking spot in the short stay area outside the station and arrive just in time to see Deborah making her way along the platform.

She wears a scarf, tied turban-style around her head, so that at first I don't recognise her. Then it sinks in. She has lost her hair. I walk up the platform to greet her and she reads the unspoken question in my eyes.

'I'll tell you later, Audrey. For now, it's just so lovely to see you.'

I embrace her warmly and lead her to my car where we pack away her weekend luggage. Soon we're driving along Norfolk lanes.

'I had no idea how pretty it is here,' she tells me. 'No wonder you decided to stay. I can see why you've been bewitched.'

'Is that what's happened to me?'

'Of course. You've fallen in love, Audrey. It's like falling in love with a person except the object of your desire is a location.'

I laugh. 'You're right, Deborah. That's exactly how I feel. Wait till you see the cottage. You'll fall in love too.'

I show her to the guest room and after I've put away the shopping, wait for her in the kitchen. I glance at the Shrek head. My own head is full of questions again. Deborah finds me and I smile at her as she comes into the room.

'Welcome to my home,' I say. 'I put fresh towels out on your bed. Just let me know if you need anything else.'

'Thank you, Audrey. What a beautiful cottage this is. I had a jigsaw once, when I was a girl, with a picture just like this place. How fantastic.'

She moves across to the kitchen window and looks out into the garden.

'Audrey,' she cries. 'There's a . . . '

'I know,' I interrupt. 'There's a goose in the garden. Meet Matilda.'

'I thought *you* were Matilda.'

'I was for a short time. The people in the village still think of me as Walsingham Matilda but I gave it up. Matilda suits the name better than me, don't you think? She won't be here for much longer, I think.'

'What happened?'

I tell Deborah the history and she sits smiling as I explain the antics we endured to set up the enclosure and how we expected Matilda to fly away once she was fully recovered.

'I've heard of people keeping a goose as a pet, Audrey. In fact, there's an old saying that some witches kept a goose as their familiar instead of a cat.'

'Well, there you are then,' I reply. 'You said I was bewitched.'

Deborah is in fine form. She laughs and jokes along with me. This is not the same Deborah who telephoned me only two weeks ago when she sounded tired and low. Her eyes are sparkling and there is a buoyant energy about her which belies the turban and the pencilled in eyebrows.

'Is there anything you don't like to eat?' I ask her, thinking ahead to preparing dinner.

'No, I eat everything. But don't think about cooking tonight, Audrey. Let's go out to eat. I'd like to go somewhere where there are lots of people and a good atmosphere, especially if there's a log fire and jolly Christmas decorations. Would you mind?'

'I know just the place,' I tell her.

◆

The Inn in the Wood has a top class reputation. With its genuine thatched roof and ancient timbers, leaded, mullioned windows and stone-flagged floors, it welcomes its visitors into a haven of warmth and conviviality on a grand scale. The fireplace is enormous and on this December night a huge log fire licks at the chimney, illuminating surrounding garlands and wreaths of Christmas foliage.

There's a happy buzz of conversation: a choir of uplifted voices filled with anticipation of the holiday season. Laughter mixes with sounds of cutlery on crockery; the fire crackles in its hearth; wine corks pop and glasses chink. I begin to understand why this is what Deborah wanted. She wants to be in the midst of happiness. She doesn't want to talk yet about the nature of her illness.

'We were lucky to get a table,' she says. 'The place is nearly full already. Have you been here before, Audrey?'

'No, I'd only heard about it. I've never been, but I've wanted to for ages.'

'Why didn't you then?'

'On my own?'

'Yes, of course on your own. Why not? You travelled all the way from Australia on your own, Audrey. Are you telling me you couldn't walk into a lovely old pub like this on your own?'

'Well, yes, I suppose I am telling you that. It's different, isn't it, coming into a pub?'

'Not any more. I don't think so. Why should you miss out on a lovely experience? You mustn't let being on your own stop you from doing things you want to do.'

This is definitely not the same Deborah I remember. Something has happened to make her change. When I stayed with her last summer she was afraid of change. Now she's charging at it at full gallop. We order our drinks and sit at a table in the bar area, studying the menu and the various chalk boards advertising special dishes of the day. We both opt for one of their specials and are shown to our table, where decorated candles cast their cheerful glow over table linens.

'Perfect.' Deborah settles back in her seat and looks around the room. 'This is just what I wanted.'

We're on the dessert before she tells me.

'I was going to wait until we were back at the cottage,' she says, 'but now is as good a time as any. I've made a huge decision. Don't say anything until I've finished, Audrey, please.'

She puts down her dessert spoon and I watch as she takes in a deep breath and steadies herself.

'I've decided to leave him. I've thought long and hard about all that's happened between us over the last years and even before that. I've come to realise he's done nothing to help me mend our relationship. On the contrary, he's found a succession of ways to drive the wedge in deeper. I don't want to be with him any more and so, I'm going to leave.'

I'd thought she was going to tell me about her illness. I'd prepared myself to be ready to console her in her time of distress. It stuns me that the most important thing on her mind is her decision to leave Philip. I was expecting to hear about diagnoses, treatments, hospitals, specialists.

'You haven't said anything,' she tells me.

'I don't know what to say. Where will you go?'

'I haven't decided yet. It's too soon. But I'm not worried about it. When I'm ready to make that decision, I will.'

She sounds so positive, so assertive.

'You're thinking I've chosen a strange time in my life to make this move,' she says. 'Don't worry. This is absolutely the right thing for me to do at this time.'

'Are you strong enough for this, Deborah?'

'Do I look ill?'

'Actually, no you don't. But it's obvious you've been having treatment of some . . .'

'Radiotherapy. I've been having radiotherapy. I've had surgery and the prognosis is as good as one might expect. I feel well and strong and powerful.'

'Powerful?'

'Yes. It's a most peculiar state, to feel this powerful. You see, I've already faced the most terrifying thing there is. Nothing scares me now.'

✦

We sit in my armchairs with a nightcap and continue the conversation from where we left it at the end of the meal.

'When did you first find out you needed treatment?' I ask her.

'When I got back from Singapore. I'd had a routine scan before I went and the results came back positive. Breast cancer.'

'Oh, Deborah.' I sigh.

'But I was lucky, Audrey. If you're going to get breast cancer, the type I had is most easily treated and it was discovered in the very early stages. I had some ultra-sound tests and a lumpectomy. Lucky again, you see?'

'Why didn't you tell me?'

'I deliberately didn't tell you,' she says, 'for a good reason. Once you tell people you've got cancer, that's all you ever talk about. Ordinary conversations fly out the window. People ask you about your treatment and how you're coping. Of course they mean well. I know that, but it's lovely to have someone talk to you about other things, ordinary, everyday things. You were my special, ordinary, everyday person.'

'I hope I didn't disappoint you,' I say.

'No, you didn't. My biggest disappointment was Philip.'

'Why? What did he do?'

'You won't believe it. First of all he didn't come with me to the hospital for the results of my tests.'

'What?' I ask. 'He let you go on your own?'

'That's right. I don't know how I drove myself home. I was trembling with fear. Nothing could ever prepare you for hearing those words, *I'm sorry Mrs Wallace, your tests came back positive. You have a malignant tumour.*'

'Oh, Deborah,' I say. 'How awful.'

'That's not all. When I went in the house he just looked up from what he was doing. I said *I've got breast cancer*, and I stood there waiting for his reaction.'

'What did he say?'

'He said, *I'm sorry to hear that, but there's nothing I can do about it, so you don't mind if I just carry on with my emails.*'

'What?'

'Exactly. I couldn't believe what I was hearing. He was so cold, so distant.'

'Then what happened?'

'He carried on with his life as usual, as if nothing had happened. His main concern was how my illness was going to affect *him*. He told me he didn't see himself as nursemaid and that I wasn't to expect him to wait on me hand and foot.'

'No.'

'I told you it was hard to believe.'

'I take it you haven't told Philip about your decision yet?' I ask.

'That's right. Not yet. He knows I'm unhappy with the way things are but he won't expect this news. I can't tell him until I have all my own plans in place.'

'How do you mean? Wouldn't it be better to have it all out in the open?'

'No, it wouldn't. Not in our case. You don't know Philip like I do. I know what his reaction will be, and it'll be better for me if I'm ready to go quickly. I need to be able to go straight away. I don't want to listen to him. I don't want to hear all his *poor me* scripts.'

I gulp away my surprise. She is so forceful. I didn't know she could be so determined.

'Does that sound cruel?' she says. 'I suppose it might sound cruel to people who don't understand the nature of our relationship. I've had enough of him. The way he treated me after my diagnosis was the last straw. Audrey, what you saw last summer was an act. He's very good at it. He had me fooled for years.'

I don't want to judge. I let her go on.

'I know this must be difficult for you, and I'm so grateful you've offered to have me this weekend when you probably knew I was bringing my problems with me.'

'Deborah, don't . . .'

'No, hang on, please,' she interrupts. 'The thing is, you see, they don't feel like problems any more to me. I've made my decision and I feel good about it. In fact, for the first time in so long I'm actually looking forward to the rest of my life. I don't know how long or how short that's going to be, but then, none of us do, do we?'

They say there's a very fine line between bravery and stupidity. Deborah is not a silly woman. She's shown fortitude and loyalty to her husband through some difficult times. She hasn't made her decision lightly. She's carefully weighed her options. Yet at a time when one would think she might need all the support she could get she's going to cut herself off from everything in her life that is familiar to her. She's going to launch herself into the unknown with a relish that would seem to border on insanity.

'I think you're being very brave,' I tell her.

'I don't think so,' she says. 'I think I'm being sensible. I'm putting myself and my own needs first. I don't need the stress of the life I have with Philip. Stress is the last thing I need now. I have to concentrate on myself to keep well.'

'And being with Philip would prevent that from happening?' I ask.

'God, yes. I have enough to cope with just now without having to cope with him as well.'

'Do you want to tell me more about that?' I ask her.

'Eventually. Not now. I think I'd like to go up to bed if you don't mind. Have you any plans for tomorrow?'

'Possibly. I'm waiting to hear from a friend about a meeting that's upcoming. It won't be a problem. I'll tell you all about it over breakfast. Good night then, Deborah. Sleep well.'

I pour myself another nightcap and check outside on Matilda. She's gone into the outhouse for shelter against plummeting temperatures and has nestled into the fresh straw bedding I put down for her.

The night is clear and still. There is perfect silence in the surrounding countryside and the silhouette of an elm tree at the bottom of the garden stands like a skeleton against a starry sky. I remark the brilliance of the stars in their winter heaven and I gaze up at them, searching for the familiar Northern Hemisphere constellations of my youth.

I'm a teenager again, hanging out my bedroom window on the council estate, listening to late night shows on radio Luxembourg and looking forward to Mum's Christmas dinner. I blow out my breath to watch it disperse into the chill of night and I feel glad to be home, in England, with Christmas just around the corner and a new year full of the promise of new and exciting things.

THIRTY TWO

There are problems connecting our new telephone line in the unit at the Barns. John thinks it won't be possible to open the shop until after Christmas.

'Couldn't we manage with just a cash box?' I ask him.

'We wouldn't be able to take cards,' he says.

'But we could still take cheques,' I suggest.

'Hardly anybody uses cheques these days,' Deborah adds. 'Where's the nearest cash machine to your shop?' she asks us.

We don't know the answer. John sits at the kitchen table at my offer of a late breakfast cup of tea and mulls it over.

'Well,' he says. 'You've got me thinking about it again. I've just told Alison to forget about it until after the holidays. I'm waiting for some replies from the Needlecraft Exhibition before we hold the meeting we discussed before.'

I can see him thinking his thoughts out loud.

'Madeleine would like to be at the meeting,' I remind him.

'Yes, of course,' he says. 'I want to see her anyway about doing some home assembly work. I suppose we could open up the shop before all the rest of it is sorted out. We don't have to hold the meeting first, do we?'

'No,' I agree. 'Shall we look at a work rota?'

'Good idea,' he beams. 'How about you, Deborah? See yourself as a shop assistant for a few days?'

'I would love it,' she says. 'What will we be selling?'

'Good gracious, girl,' John scolds me. 'Haven't you told your friend what we've been getting up to?'

I leave John to explain to Deborah while I fetch a carton of *John Starling Cross Stitch Design Kits* for her to look at. Deborah claps her hands in delight.

'Fantastic,' she says. 'I can't wait to see the shop.'

We agree I'll take Deborah with me to the shop and John will meet us there after he's paid a visit to Madeleine.

Early customers, curious about the new shop at The Barns come right in with us as we open up. By the time John arrives we've already made a few sales using our own cash as a float to start us off.'

'I could get quite used to this,' Deborah laughs.

'There you are, John,' I say. 'I knew people would like your designs.'

'Blust me,' he answers, scratching his head. 'Which designs did you sell?'

'The local scenes,' Deborah tells him. 'I think the framed examples on the wall are a good selling point, aren't they? They give people an idea of the finished picture. Oh, I'm really enjoying this,' she continues.

John and I watch as she greets the next customer to come through the door. She has just the right touch, not too pushy. She tells her prospective purchaser about the new and exclusive range and two more *John Starling Cross Stitch Design Kits* change hands and the money goes into our cash box.

John takes over to allow Deborah and me time for a break and a hot drink at the Barns café.

'I'm glad I brought my woolly scarf,' Deborah says. 'You're going to need some heating in the shop.'

'You're right,' I agree. 'We've all forgotten about keeping warm.'

'Are you going to work in the shop on a permanent basis?' she asks me.

'No. I've offered to help out to get things started, but to be honest, there are other things I want to do.'

'Something exciting?'

'Yes, I think it's exciting.'

We talk about the Shrek head and my drawings and clay sculptures. I tell her my plans to rent an exhibition space in the gallery attached to the art shop where I bought my first sketch pad and pencils.

'You haven't shown me your work yet,' she says. 'Do you have a favourite subject?'

'Yes and no,' I answer. 'It used to be Christopher, the baby son of my young friend Madeleine. Then it became Matilda when she arrived. Now, I feel I want to move on again.'

'A goose and a baby,' she says. 'How comforting. Do you know what I mean? There's something really moving about it, like Mother Goose. Well, it's Christmas, why not? Why not put them together?'

I feel a flush of heat from somewhere deep inside me. The sensation courses through my body until I can feel my fingertips tingling. Immediately, images of a goose and a baby together flood my imagination and my face is so hot it must be glowing.

'Good heavens. What have I said?' Deborah says. 'Have I said something wrong?'

I take her hand across the table.

'Deborah,' I say to her, 'that's it. That's what I'm going to work on next.'

'What? Mother Goose?'

'No. I'm going to put Matilda and Christopher together. It's perfect. It sums up everything I want to say. Thank you. Thank you.'

'Steady on,' she chuckles. 'You're like a kid with a new toy.'

'Exactly. Look at me. I'm on fire with ideas. I'm burning up with it. I can't wait to get started.'

The rest of the day passes quickly. We make more sales and enjoy replenishing the display from our under-counter stocks. Deborah comes up with some ideas for rearranging the way we have set out John's designs and happily busies herself organising the stands and baskets. By closing time we have a list ready for Madeleine's home assembly, and call in to see her on our way home.

She comes to the door, but doesn't invite us in. She takes the list from us and hurriedly puts it into her pocket.

'I haven't told Luke about it yet,' she says, 'and he's come home unexpectedly today. I don't know if I'm going to be able to work on them tonight. Will that be all right with you and John? You're not in a terrible hurry for them are you?'

'No, Madeleine. There's no rush,' I say. 'Is everything all right?'

'Yes, thank you. He's in a bit of a mood, that's all. There's been some trouble offshore and because he's been sent home early, he'll lose some of his bonus. Look, I don't mean to be rude, but I have to go in now. I'll call you. Okay?'

'Remember what I told you. I'll come if you need me. Don't forget.'

'Thank you, I won't.'

'So that's Madeleine,' Deborah says as we climb back into my car. 'She's a bit wound up, isn't she?'

I don't want to say too much. Madeleine shared her problems with me in confidence.

'She's very young,' I say.

'She reminds me of myself when I was a young woman,' Deborah admits. 'I could see it straight away. I bet she blames herself for all his black moods. Poor thing.'

My telephone is ringing as we enter the hallway. It's Philip for Deborah. He doesn't greet me when I answer. He just asks for his wife.

I go to hang up my coat but I can clearly hear Deborah's half of the conversation.

I've had my mobile switched off.
Because I didn't want to be disturbed.
I sent you a text to let you know I'd arrived safely.
Philip, I've only been here for twenty four hours.
Stop it. You're being very unreasonable.

There's a long pause during which I can see Deborah shifting her weight from foot to foot and becoming agitated.

If you raise your voice to me, Philip, I will put down the phone. I don't have to listen to this.
No. I won't do that. You'll have to deal with it yourself.
I said no, Philip. Goodbye.

She replaces the receiver and I can tell she has hung up on him.

'Cup of tea?' I offer.

'Yes please, and I'd like to see some of your work, Audrey, if it's not too much trouble.'

◆

Deborah looks at my sketch books and I take her out to my makeshift studio in the garden. Matilda fluffs up her feathers and honks at us.

'Out of the way, Matilda,' I say to her. 'This is my studio. It's not yours, although you are the leading lady.'

Deborah inspects my workspace and I explain my working methods and show her the kiln. She's very quiet; she makes no comment until we're back inside.

'You simply must keep up with your work,' she says. 'Don't spend too much time in the needlework shop. You need to be in here everyday.'

'Yes, well, I'll get around to it eventually, especially now you've given me my next ideas.'

'No. You mustn't put it off,' she insists. 'Let me do your rota at the shop. You stay here and get on with your work.'

'There's no rush,' I tell her.

'Oh, but there is. You shouldn't put it off. Who knows what may happen tomorrow? Pardon me for saying so, but we're not getting any younger. You must keep on.'

She brings the subject up again over dinner.

'Please, Audrey. Let me do your rota for you at the shop. I could stay on a while longer till John sorts out his staff.'

'And Philip?' I remind her.

'What about him?'

'I couldn't help overhearing your telephone conversation with him earlier today. I know he was getting at you.'

'Audrey, you're always taking on other people's problems. Just look at you with young Madeleine. And how you are with me. I've honestly never had a friend like you before. Let me do something for you this time. Besides, I'd love every minute of it.'

'And Philip?' I repeat.

'I'm only talking about a few days extra. I wouldn't leave him on his own at Christmas, even though he probably deserves it. What dates are available for some exhibition space at the gallery?'

I go to pull out the brochure and check the dates. She takes it from me and insists I set myself a deadline.

'You must do this. Your work is amazing. I don't think you realise just how good it is. It doesn't matter that you haven't studied with the right people at the right art college and you haven't got the right connections. Anybody with an eye for beauty can see you have something unique. Those clay studies of yours are so inspiring, Audrey. They're full of feeling. They do something to your insides. Am I making sense?'

'For the third time, what about Philip? You haven't given me a straight answer.'

'Let's make a plan then,' she finally agrees.

♦

Deborah takes my car and drives herself to the shop next morning. It's Sunday, and the busiest day of the week at the Craft units when people flock to the Barns for their country shopping experience and enjoy a day out with either Sunday lunch at the restaurant or tea and cakes at the café during the afternoon.

'Enjoy your day,' she tells me as she pulls away. 'I shall. See you later.'

'Don't forget to give me a call if you need anything,' I remind her.

'Don't worry. I've got your number in my mobile. I know where everything is. I'll be able to do some assembly work during the quiet spells and I've got the electric heater I can plug in if it gets too cold.'

She disappears around the corner and I go back inside. I take down my reference books from the shelf and go over my ideas for glazing my first finished pieces. Some were lost in the first firing and had never made it to the biscuit stage. I'd been dismayed at the results of my earlier mistakes but I'd learned where I'd gone wrong and improved my technique. I want the subjects of my work to speak for themselves so I need a simple finish. No fancy high gloss glazes for me.

I throw on an extra warm fleece and a hat and scarf and go out into the workshop to prepare my space for the day's work. Standing at the old sink, I mix the glaze and dip the pieces to be fired. I organise the firing set up so I can make best use of the space inside my small kiln and carefully position my glazed pieces on the shelves. I set the automatic controls and close the outhouse door to keep Matilda out of harm's way. I look at my watch: the morning has gone. It's time for something to eat.

Matilda follows me as far as the kitchen door and stands solidly on her large pink feet, twisting her neck from side to side and trying to see inside. I grab my camera and let it run off a host of pictures, capturing the different expressions of her features. I replenish her water and sugar beet and again I set the camera on rapid fire as Matilda wriggles and fluffs herself out, stamping her large webbed feet and rocking from side to side. I know in my heart she has to leave soon and if she doesn't do so of her own accord, I must see she is taken back to where she belongs. It will hurt me to see her go but I have to do what's right for her.

I go inside and take off my outdoor clothing. I make a hasty sandwich and hot drink and decide to check my laptop for messages. There's nothing new in my email folder.

I pick up my camera and look at my digital images of Matilda, then I go back through the photographs I've taken of Christopher. I want to find a way of putting the two together and I'm at that pre-creative stage of being only vaguely aware of where I want to go with it. I'm looking for inspiration and I know it can't be forced. Will power is not enough to stimulate the creative process. Something has to break through the blank page in my mind and begin to create itself: at least, that's how it works for me.

I flick backwards and forwards through images stored in my camera: Christopher sucking his banana fingers; Matilda twisting her neck around so her head is almost upside down; Christopher laughing; Matilda honking. I look again at the last two pictures. Christopher is laughing with his head thrown back and his mouth wide open. He is helpless with the depth of his enjoyment and I recall when he was amazed by Matilda's antics and how she had allowed him to touch her back.

Now I know what I am going to do. But first I need to sketch out my ideas. Then, I'm going to need some more clay.

◆

Deborah returns from the shop in high spirits. She's carrying one of the under-counter storage crates loaded with materials for packing up replacement kits.

'How did it go?' I ask, catching her excitement.

'Great,' she says. 'I've enjoyed myself so much. You can't imagine.' She hangs up her coat and we go through into the kitchen. 'Hello,' she says to the Shrek head. 'Wait till you hear this.'

'You need to be careful about talking to that thing,' I tell her. 'It's addictive.'

'Have you had a good day too?' she says. 'I shall expect you to show me what you've done.'

'Yes, Miss Wallace.'

'Well, it's been busy in the shop,' she tells me. 'I've hardly had a minute to myself. Lots of browsers, you know. There's quite a bit of curiosity as John's designs are such a new concept. Most people are interested in local scenes but the garden designs are popular too. I didn't get chance to assemble any replacements but I've stocked up the displays from what was already made. I've kept a tally, so we should be able to cross-check, but I think we'll have to spend some time tonight making up some more stock or the whole place will soon start to look quite sparse.'

'You've sold so many?'

'You said Sunday was the busiest day and I've seen it for myself now. Do you know, they are lovely people, all of them. The staff in the other units all popped in to say hello. The customers are a joy to talk to. Even senior management from the main store came across to introduce themselves. Gordon, is it?'

'Really?' I ask.

'Oh, yes. He seems very affable. I told him I was just helping out for a little while and he seemed quite pleased that John had managed to get up and running in time for Christmas. I don't suppose it presents the right image if they've got closed units at this time of year.'

'Were you warm enough?'

'Yes. The little fan heater works very well. It's only a relatively small space to heat, after all.'

'Looks like we've got work to do tonight then. Shall we do it after dinner?'

'I think it might be an idea to let John know what's happening. I half expected to see him at some point today, actually.'

'He had arrangements today. Maybe he'll telephone later.'

Dinner is roast lamb with all the trimmings and the time we have both spent on our feet and away from the comfort of central heating has given us hearty appetites. We stack up the dishwasher and clear the kitchen table in preparation for our evening's work.

'Before we begin, let's have a look at what you've been doing today,' Deborah says.

'I have some figures in the kiln, but I can't show you them until tomorrow when they've cooled down enough. I've done some sketches of my next ideas, though. I'd be grateful for some feedback.'

I hand her my sketch pad and she settles back into her chair. She spends a long time looking at them and when she looks up there are tears in her eyes.

'That bad, eh?' I joke.

'Oh, Audrey,' she says. 'They are beautiful. What wonderful bronzes they would make.'

A fire sparks again in my belly.

'What did you say?' I ask. 'Bronzes?'

'Yes, bronzes. You put so much work into making your sculptures, and they are lovely, it's true. But you only get the one don't you? All that work to produce one finished piece. It seems such a waste that only one person ever gets to enjoy it.'

'I don't know the first thing about casting metals, Deborah,' I tell her.

'So, find out,' she advises in a matter of fact way.

◆

We're working on replacement needlework kits when Alex Starling telephones.

'Audrey? It's about the goose. Dad tells me she hasn't left.'

'That's right,' I say. 'What did you have in mind?'

'Thought we'd bring her over to the sanctuary as a sort of half-way house, you know?'

'Are there others of her own kind there?' I ask him.

'Yes, a few,' he tells me. 'She'd be better there amongst the others than on her own in the garden. I thought you might like to be present when we release her.'

'Oh, Alex, thank you. Yes, I'd love that. Is that where you are now?'

'No, no,' he says. 'I'm at home. The girls arrived home today for Christmas. Dad's here as well. We've been catching up with family news, you know, and the subject of the goose came up. The thing is, the girls would like to come as well. You haven't met my daughters yet, have you?'

'I'd love to meet them,' I say. 'Christina and . . . . '

'Laura,' he reminds me.

'Both home from university. How lovely. Your aunt Margaret showed me a photograph of them.'

'How about tomorrow?' he asks.

'I'd better have a word with John first. I'm supposed to be in the shop tomorrow. Deborah's had a very busy day there today.'

Deborah signals frantically to let me know she'll be happy to man the shop again. I tell John we're making up new kits to refill the stock baskets and he says he's been speaking to Gordon about the pool of part-time workers. He's set up a trial working rota. He telephoned Madeleine but hadn't managed to speak to her. Luke told him she wasn't very well.

My mind is on Madeleine as I staple together needlework kits and stack them in the storage crate.

'Is something wrong?' Deborah asks me.

'I hope not. John says Madeleine isn't feeling well.'

'She's probably got a cold or something,' she suggests.

'Yes, probably,' I agree.

I hope that's all it is, but I feel on edge.

THIRTY THREE

'Come on, Audrey. Cheer up.' Deborah encourages me. 'You know it was the right thing to do.'

'I'll miss her. It's not the same without Matilda,' I say. 'I'll miss her funny way of walking.'

'You've still got Shrek.' she says. 'Look, I've made him a Christmas hat.'

I look up. Deborah has arranged a tinsel crown around the Shrek head.

'Look,' she says. 'He looks like me now, with his head all wrapped up.'

What a good friend I have in Deborah. There she stands with her turban covering her poor bare head and her first thought is for my sadness at saying goodbye to Matilda. I get up from my chair and hug her.

◆

Matilda was very happy to leave me. Alex picked me up in the morning and between us we managed to manoeuvre Matilda into a transport crate and into the back of his *Scenic*. Christina and Laura were there to help as well. Christina is in her final year studying dramatic arts and Laura's at one of the country's most prestigious higher education colleges studying Sports Science.

We drove to the bird sanctuary and the four of us stood by the lakeside and watched as Matilda waddled out of the crate and headed for the water's edge. She did a bit of fluffing and stamping, then went to test the water. She never looked back. She stretched out her neck and went to meet her future. I strained my eyes to keep sight of her until she had become no more than a white blur in the distance. I needed to blow my nose, and as I reached into my pocket to find a tissue, I noticed that both girls were staring at me.

'Does it make you feel a bit sad?' Laura asked me.

'Yes, dear. It does,' I admitted.

'It's awful when you lose a pet. We had a dog once, when we were little and when he died we swore we'd never have another one ever again,' Christina added.

They both continued watching me, almost as if I was being inspected. They had their father's eyes, large and soft and dark. Alex noticed and intervened.

'Come on, everybody,' he said. 'Let's go inside and get a hot drink. It's cold out here.'

There was a small cafeteria serving toasted teacakes and hot chocolate. We sat by a window overlooking the lake and enjoyed our buttery treat.

'Dad says you're an artist,' Laura said.

'Oh, I don't know about that,' I replied.

'We'd like to see what you do, wouldn't we Christina?' she went on. 'Could we, do you think?'

'Don't be pushy, Laura,' her sister interceded.

'Of course you can,' I said. 'When would you like to come?'

'It's up to you.'

'Anytime,' I said, 'but remember I'll be working in your grandfather's shop at times. '

'Dad, what about tonight?' she suggested.

'Audrey has a friend staying with her at the moment, Laura. It might not be convenient,' he told her.

'Tomorrow, then,' she persevered.

'Come for lunch tomorrow, girls,' I said.

'Can we borrow Mum's car?' Christina asked. She turned to her younger sister. 'I'll drive,' she added quickly.

On the way back to the cottage I barely heard the girls' lively chatter or seasonal favourites on the car radio. I was imagining the glassy lake which was now Matilda's new home.

I saw again the grey winter trees surrounding the water, like misty feathers against the sky, and I watched her familiar shape growing smaller as she disappeared into the distance.

♦

'We really must do something about this place,' I say to Deborah, shaking myself out of my daydream and giving her an extra hug. 'We've got Christina and Laura coming for lunch tomorrow and apart from your efforts with the Shrek head I've no decorations up in the cottage at all. It feels more like Christmas in the shop than it does here.'

'Sounds like we're on a mission,' Deborah jokes.

We find a discount department store in the heart of the Norfolk countryside. Deborah buys a new outfit and I fill the car boot with festive decorations, fairy lights for indoors and chasing LED's for the trees and bushes outside the cottage.

'I know John has got his rota all worked out now,' Deborah says. 'But I'd really like to visit the shop again before I go home.'

'That won't be a problem,' I say. 'You can go whenever you want to.'

'Good,' she says.

'Do you know what I fancy to eat tonight?' I announce as the idea makes my mouth begin to water.

'What?'

'Fish and chips.'

'Fish and chips.' Deborah moans with exaggerated yearning. 'Oh, yes. Fish and chips.'

Later we sit with our meals on our laps, watching television and admiring our handiwork of the afternoon. The early sales have provided us with an abundance of Christmas cheer. Lights twinkle in the tree in the window; branches of holly adorn the walls in the hall; ivy twists around the banister.

Outside, in the real world, beyond our seasonal adornments, the credit crunch bites harder than winter frosts into people's pensions and savings. News headlines of negative equity and house repossessions compete with thousands of lost jobs and billions of lost pounds and dollars in the markets. High street names tumble into the dust of what seems to be the apocalypse of generations of capitalism. All around us, out there in the cities and towns, calamity after calamity explodes and mushrooms in a great billowing disaster, the inevitable after shocks of which we can only wait for, and know we must endure.

Yet here in my rented cottage Deborah and I sit in contentment with our fish and chips and our Christmas baubles. Deborah, with her turbaned head and frightening prognosis, planning the greatest upheaval of her life, anticipates with passion the next stage of her life. I too share in the enjoyment of new ventures and the expectation of yet more new pleasures. Our old lives are gone. We are both letting go. We are both moving into the excitement of the unknown and I begin to understand what she meant when she told me she felt powerful, untouchable. Our memories of Christmas 2009 will be happy ones.

Deborah rouses me.

'I think my hair is beginning to grow back,' she says. 'Do you want to have a look?'

She takes off her scarf and I can see bristles of greyish white. Her hair used to be a beautiful glossy brown.

'It makes me look like a convict, doesn't it?' she says. 'I'd forgotten how grey I really was before. I always coloured it, you know. I shall have to decide what to do with it once it's grown back in properly. What do you think?'

'I think it's time you had a change. You're planning to change everything else in your life, so why not your hair? How about waiting till it's a bit longer, then going for streaks of colour here and there instead of an all-over shade?'

'Brilliant,' she says. 'I shall have streaks of pink and purple, maybe a bit of hot red. I'll get a whole new wardrobe too. I need to. I've lost so much weight. Everything is hanging on me now. Come and help me choose, Audrey. I'd enjoy that.'

◆

Deborah is wearing her new outfit, a heavy cotton skirt and jacket from yesterday's early sales in Norwich. There are sales everywhere. The retail world is falling apart as the recession takes hold of people's fears for the future. Yet Deborah is not afraid. She's determined to enjoy each and every day. She's wearing a contrasting patterned scarf. She has her make-up on and looks ready to face anything.

We've put together a pleasing lunch including some vegetarian options with couscous and chick peas. I'm expecting a phone call from Alison to say the girls are on their way, but when I pick up the receiver, it's John.

'Audrey,' he says. 'Have you heard from Madeleine? I keep trying to get hold of her, but that man of hers keeps putting me off.'

My stomach lurches and I fear the worst.

'I'll go round there now,' I tell him.

'He won't let you see her, Audrey. He's acting very oddly. Anyway, I've taken over some materials to the shop to get the girls there to do some assembly work. Only, I don't want to deprive Madeleine of it if she still wants to do it.'

'Leave it with me, John. I'll see what's happening. I won't let Luke put me off seeing her. I can be very insistent when I want to be.'

'I know,' he says.

'Deborah,' I say as I reach for my coat, 'I need to find out what's happening with Madeleine. Will you stand in for me if the girls arrive while I'm out? I don't expect to be long. You can show them the figures I took out of the kiln this morning, and you know where I keep my sketches.'

I race out into the street, anxious and nervous, angry with myself for not getting in touch with Madeleine, letting it slide. When I pull up outside her house I can see the curtains are still drawn. My heart sinks. I rap on the door; no answer. I knock again.

Luke eventually opens the door, bleary-eyed and unshaven.

'She's not here,' he grunts and I catch him unawares by pushing straight past him, and before he realises what I'm doing, I'm through the hall and into their living room.

'Where is she?' I demand.

'I told you. She's not here.'

'Where's Christopher?' I demand again.

He slumps onto the sofa and lights a cigarette.

'She's taken him with her.'

'Where?'

'I don't know. If you must know, I don't care either. Satisfied?'

'No. What did you do to her? She wouldn't just go without saying anything to any of us. You must have done something.'

'It's none of your bloody business, woman. Why don't you just piss off?'

He takes another drag of his cigarette and I turn away from him and dash upstairs as quickly as I can. He doesn't bother to chase after me.

There's no sign of either Madeleine or Christopher in the bedrooms. I check the bathroom; no sign of them there either. Luke remains on the sofa, smoking his cigarette, surrounded by the detritus of several days' worth of slovenly living, sullenly ignoring the fact that I'm inspecting his home. Christopher's push chair has gone from its place in the hall and I can't see any of his or his mother's outdoor clothes that I would recognise.

'I told you. They've gone. Now piss off!'

This is the man Madeleine described to me as a fastidious type who insisted she keep the house in immaculate order and his son's baby things well out of his way. This is the man who punched her in the face because he couldn't have what he wanted for his lunch.

I want to spit at him. I want to hurt him. I want to take revenge on him for Christopher's sake. I want to tell him what a pathetic, useless piece of shit he is.

I do none of those things. I wait. I stand still and wait. I wait until he looks me in the eye.

'I'm glad she's left you,' I say when I have his full attention. Then I leave him to his self-pity.

On the short drive back to the cottage I go over everything again in my mind. Madeleine must have left suddenly, in a hurry. She must have been desperate to get away from him, not to have time to give me a call. She'll call when she can, I tell myself. She'll be all right. She'll be all right.

Alison's car is parked outside the cottage, John Starling's car is further along the street and they're all waiting for me in the kitchen. Deborah has brought in my fired figures and they're discussing them.

'Here you are,' John greets me with his arm around Alison's shoulder. 'We hope you don't mind all four of us being here, but we were as curious as the girls to view your finished work. Did you manage to see Madeleine?'

'No, I didn't. She's gone away for a while. She'll be in touch soon.'

Laura is staring at me; her sister gives her a nudge.

'We love them,' Alison says to me, holding up one of the figures. 'We all love them. Deborah has shown us your sketches too, and told us about your new ideas.'

Laura is still staring at me and again I notice the depth in her eyes, her lovely dark warm eyes. I feel as if I want to take hold of the girl and wrap my arms around her and hold her close. Her eyes want to tell me something but Christina moves to stand between us.

'I'm really impressed,' Christina tells me. 'Your work is sincerely stirring. I want you to know I feel quite moved by its honesty.'

'Oh, blimey,' I say. 'Thank you, Christina, but it's only a hobby, you know.'

'It shouldn't be only a hobby,' Laura says. 'You have to pursue this properly.'

'Told you so.' Deborah joins in.

I invite them to help themselves to lunch and we crowd around the small kitchen table, eating buffet style.

'I hear the shop is doing well,' Alison says. 'Sorry I haven't been across there yet, but Dad told me he wasn't going to open till after Christmas. And Deborah,' she continues, 'I hear you're the star saleswoman.'

'I absolutely love it,' she says.

'Bit much though isn't it,' I interject, 'coming to spend a short break with your friend and being put out to work?'

Deborah laughs. 'No, really, I mean what I say. It's not like work at all. It's like playing at shop, you know? When I was little I always loved those cardboard sweet shop toys I used to get for Christmas.'

'I remember those,' I say. 'There was always a little plastic weighing scale and a scoop to bag up the sweeties.'

'Oh, and a toy post office,' Deborah remembers. 'Do you remember those too?'

We happily reminisce about preferred Christmas presents of the past: the first baby doll; the popular Christmas annuals; the toy clarinet; the shiny red plastic telephone. Christina and Laura join in with their own favourites and argue good-naturedly about roller-blades versus computer games.

'When I was a lad, we were lucky to get an orange and a few nuts in one of our dad's old socks,' John adds.

'Oh, Granddad,' Christina wails. 'You come out with that old dinosaur every Christmas.'

'Well, it wouldn't be Christmas if I didn't, would it?' he laughs.

'I imagine you miss having the goose in the garden,' Alison says to me.

'Yes. I do,' I say. 'But I have lots of lovely photographs to remind me.'

Laura has wandered down the hall into the sitting room, looking at our decorations. I follow her.

'It's lovely,' she says. 'You've done it just like Grandma used to.'

She spins around and swiftly adds,' Do *hers*. Used to do hers.'

Her head goes down and she looks at the floor as she slips past me, back into the kitchen, where she quickly snatches up a pastry and nibbles at it self-consciously.

Christina throws her a quizzical look. I see Alison's worried expression as she glances quickly at John.

'What?' I ask. 'What is it?'

'Laura misses her grandmother,' John says to me. 'They were very close and a lot alike, in fact. We all miss her.'

I understand their grief. Christmas always heightens emotions and makes us feel everything more deeply. We remember happy times we spent together with our loved ones and we feel the bitter-sweet nostalgic yearning for times gone by.

After lunch Alison excuses herself and the girls.

'We've a bit of shopping still to do, Audrey,' she tells me. 'Thank you so much for the lovely lunch.'

'Yes, thank you,' echo Christina and Laura.

'Audrey, have you got plans for Christmas Day? We'd love you to join us. Dad will pick you up, won't you, Dad?'

John is momentarily taken by surprise.

'Erm, yes. Can do.' He swallows hard. 'Alex?' he begins.

'It's time, Dad. Please say yes. Deborah? Are you planning to be here for Christmas?'

'How kind of you to think of me,' she says. 'But, no thank you. I shall be going home soon.'

I wave them off and turn around to find John hovering behind me. He is flicking his fingers and chewing the inside of his cheek.

'John, are you all right?' I ask him. 'You've gone a bit pale. Come and sit down.'

He sits heavily in one of the armchairs and puffs out a sigh.

'John?' I ask him again.

'It's time,' he says, repeating Alison's enigmatic phrase, nodding his head. 'She's right. It's time.'

'Time for what, John?'

A car door slams, footsteps march up the path and the bell rings loudly, insistently. I leave John to his mysterious thoughts and go to open the door. Deborah stands behind me.

'Philip,' she cries out as I pull the door open wide and there on the doorstep stands her scowling husband. I invite him in and he strides through into the hall and straight on into the kitchen.

'Deborah, get your things,' he demands.

'I beg your pardon?' she says.

'You heard me. I won't wait long. Get your things. I'm taking you home.'

He stands with his arms behind his back, one hand clasping the other, like a headmaster addressing a miscreant school child.

'I don't appreciate being spoken to like that, Philip,' Deborah says quietly.

'And that's your trouble, isn't it? You don't appreciate anything I do for you.'

'Philip,' she says, keeping remarkable control, 'please remember where you are.'

'I don't care where we are,' he says, his voice growing louder.

'Then you will embarrass yourself,' she replies.

I move into the hall to join John in the sitting room, but Deborah calls me back.

'Don't go please, Audrey. I think I'm going to need you here.'

'You care more about someone you've known for two minutes than you do about me,' he says.

'Now you're being silly,' she replies.

'Well that's nice,' he says. 'I drive all the way up here and can you be pleased to see me? No! I'm being silly. *I'm* being silly.'

His face is turning red and his eyes grow wide in anger. Deborah sits at the table.

'Sit down, Philip,' she says, 'and let's talk about this sensibly.'

'Don't patronise me,' he snarls.

I remember Deborah told me that Philip never argued, that he'd walk away before getting into a confrontation. She'd wanted him to argue then. She'd felt, then, he needed to talk openly about his feelings. But this is not an adult exchange of differences: this is a man behaving like a spoilt child. I glance at Deborah to ascertain her expression. She's still calm.

He begins to pace the room.

'I don't know how you can do this to me,' he grumbles. 'I've done everything for you.'

'What is it you think I've done?' she asks him.

'Leaving me on my own at Christmas. How could you? What must people think? Poor old Philip. Left on his own at Christmas.'

'You know very well I always intended to be back at home in time for Christmas. All I've done is spend a few extra days in a friend's company. Days, I might add, that I've enjoyed more than any I can remember in years with you.'

Philip is not listening to her. He has wound himself up into such a state he cannot act rationally. He screams a foul tirade of grievances at her. He tries to make it sound as if every small upset between them has been her fault. He drags up examples from the very beginning of their marriage, peppering his invective with details of his own long-suffering support of her. He points out how she and their son have held him back, prevented him from doing what he really wanted to do. He discloses private intimacies between them in his attempt to show what a patient, generous husband he is.

'This all started ten years ago when she rejected all my advances,' he complains, directing his comments at me. 'It didn't matter to her that I needed some loving attention.'

'I wasn't feeling too good about myself at that time, Philip,' Deborah retaliates. 'If you remember, I'd just had a hysterectomy. Having sex with a demanding husband was not top of my priority list.'

'Get your things,' he demands.

Deborah looks directly at me and I read her unspoken question to me. Her eyelids are heavy and I can see she is close to tears.

'I think you should stay here, Deborah,' I tell her.

'And I think you should mind your own business,' he snaps at me.

'You've made it my business by attacking my friend here, in front of me, in my own home. Deborah doesn't need this now. What she needs is some comfort and happiness, not an irate, selfish husband haranguing her for not being at his beck and call.'

John appears in the doorway.

'You're not welcome in this house, sir,' he says simply. 'We don't have any aggressive behaviour here in this house. You must leave now.'

Philip is shocked. I can see it in his face. He wasn't aware there was anybody else in the cottage. His face contorts with rage and he trembles. He takes a moment to gain control of himself.

'My wife is not well,' he says to John. 'She has more treatment to undergo and she needs to be at home where she can be looked after properly. It wouldn't be a good idea for her to struggle home on the train by herself. She'll be more comfortable riding in the car with me.'

The rapid switch from outright fury to wheedling humility is astounding. The man is unbelievable. He should have been on the stage with that performance. He has exposed himself for the tyrant that he is, malicious and conniving. I take Deborah upstairs and leave John to show Philip the door.

◆

Deborah is taking a rest and I join John in the sitting room.

'How is she?' he asks me.

'She suddenly looks very tired. I think that took a lot out of her.'

'What will she do?'

'I'm not sure. I'd like her to stay with me until she decides.'

'Unforgivable piece of nastiness, that,' he says. 'Poor woman, as if she hasn't got enough on her plate at the moment.'

'I know,' I agree. 'And she had been doing so well. You know, optimistic, energetic. She's loved every minute in the shop.'

My insides are cramped and tense, my own tears not far away.

'What a strange day it's been,' I tell him. 'That's twice in one day I've been told to mind my own business. It looks like Madeleine has left Luke and taken Christopher with her.'

John gives an understanding nod. 'Where has she gone?'

'I don't know. Probably back to her parents. I hope so. Then there's Philip. How could I have been so taken in by him? He completely deceived me. I thought he was a charming man. I thought I was helping Deborah by telling her they could find a way to sort things out between them. How could I get it so wrong? I feel such a fool.'

John shifts in his seat and looks uncomfortable. His complexion pales again.

'How can people be like that?' I say, not expecting an answer. 'How can anybody be so false? I thought I was a reasonably good judge of character. I thought I'd reached an age where I'd experienced enough to know when I was being tricked. I can't believe I've been so gullible.'

John raises himself up in the armchair, straightens his back and sets his jaw.

'Audrey, I've waited too long and I know that now is not a good time for this, but if I leave it any longer you'll never forgive me.'

He takes a deep breath.

'I haven't the faintest idea what you're talking about,' I say.

'There are things I have to tell you. All this trouble today with your friend and her husband has made me realise.'

'Go on,' I say.

'I want to set a date for a meeting. A family meeting. I want to get it done before Christmas.'

'You sound so serious.'

'It is serious,' he replies.

'Why can't you tell me now?' I ask him.

'I'd like Alex to be present and there are some things I need to have with me. I'm sorry if it sounds odd. All I can say is I hope you'll understand my motives. Shall we say tomorrow?'

'Where?'

'Here is best. In this house. We'll come in the morning, after breakfast.'

I watch him as he gets up to leave. There is a weight on his shoulders and his face is drawn. He looks around at the Christmas decorations and a faint smile plays upon his lips.

'Till tomorrow,' he says and I walk to the door with him.

◆

Deborah is asleep, curled up on top of her duvet with her dressing gown wrapped around her. Quietly, I close her bedroom door and steal back downstairs. There are butterflies as big as eagles flapping around inside my stomach and I need to get out in fresh air.

I scribble a quick note for Deborah and leave it propped up against the Shrek head on the kitchen window sill, pull on my jacket and step out into the street. A thin sun lights the late afternoon and I breathe in deeply as I stride out. I'm tired. The day's events have been stressful and I can't even begin to imagine what it is John is about to reveal to me. I know it's going to be about my mother. I can sense it; I can feel it, but I can't explain how I know.

I find myself walking into the Priory gardens and I stroll among rose beds looking at the neatly pruned shrubs and hybrids. I decide to sit for a while at the top of one of the avenues where a brand new bench commands a view over the whole garden. I should have brought gloves; my hands are cold and I stuff them into my pockets. I sit till the light begins to fade. I watch, in semi-darkness as street lights come on, one by one, and Christmas stars hanging from lamp posts begin their nightly display.

A figure approaches me in the gloom. Her habit flows around her. She looks as if she's floating over the ground.

'Come inside,' she tells me. 'You've been sitting in the cold for long enough.'

I follow her into the room where first I met her and experienced the comfort of her words,

All in good time.

They are ringing inside my head now, those words. Inside my thoughts, they're dancing around with the words of Alison and John Starling,

It's time.

It's here now. The time is here. We've reached what Maria Theresa encouraged me to expect, the thing I've been waiting for. Tomorrow I will learn about my mother.

'John is going to tell me tomorrow,' I say to Maria Theresa.

'Good,' she replies. 'There is nothing to be afraid of.'

She pours two glasses of *Norfolk Punch* and hands one to me.

'This will warm you,' she says. 'Merry Christmas, Audrey.'

I raise my glass and my eyes are drawn by a framed sampler hanging on the wall. I walk up to it and recognise the fine stitch work.

'Is this . . . ?'

'Yes, it is,' she tells me. 'It's very fine work. We have more of her beautiful needlework in the chapel. Come to the Carol Service on Christmas Eve, Audrey. We hold an inter-denominational service every Christmas for the village.'

'Thank you, I will. And thank you for the winter warmer,' I say handing back my sherry glass. She walks with me to the Priory gate.

'Take a closer look at the bench you were sitting on before you go home,' she says. 'I think there's still just enough daylight to read the plaque.'

The butterflies have gone from my stomach. I am calm and I surrender to the moment of serenity as I read the words on the brass plaque. I'm not surprised by what I see there. It's as if there's been a secret place inside me where a seed of an idea has burst and reached out for the light. Maria Theresa has told me there is nothing I need to fear and so I placidly take in the words of the inscription:

In memory of Jean Starling who loved this place.

Poor John, I think to myself. He has nothing to fear from me either. I think it's rather wonderful that he and my mother found companionship in their later years.

THIRTY FOUR

SNAPSHOTS 1944-1945

Godfrey Jardeen arrived as agreed at George and Hilda's house for his Christmas dinner in 1944. George was in an ebullient mood. He'd insisted Hilda leave all the preparation and cooking to himself and Jean. He wouldn't hear of his wife raising a finger.

'If you see us doing something wrong you can tell us,' he said to her. 'I want you to relax today, my Hilda. We want to do this for you, don't we Jean?'

Jean would have done anything for her sister. She'd have given all she possessed to bring back some colour into Hilda's complexion and have her buoyant and energetic as she used to be. As she regarded Hilda's thin limbs and pale skin it seemed to Jean the fire had gone out of her. Hilda was always so quiet. She didn't join in with conversations in the lively way she used to. She'd lost interest in all talk of the progress of the war in Europe and beyond.

George would read aloud the newspaper headlines and say how he was sure the end was in sight. Since the liberation of Paris the previous August, he'd grow excited at the latest news of the German retreat and his eyes would sparkle at the anticipation of an Allied victory. He counted the names on his fingers, as town by town, city by city, Europe was freed from German control: Brussels, Antwerp, Ghent, Boulogne, Calais. Hilda only nodded and smiled at him. He didn't appear to notice how tired she looked.

Hilda sat in one of the fireside chairs, overseeing dinner preparations and reminding George how to make sure everything was ready at the same time. She'd made no objection to George's request she should sit by the fire and take it easy. It was out of character for her; she was happiest taking charge in her kitchen and enjoyed providing tasty, filling meals for her family, especially at Christmas when it was a real challenge to compose a celebration meal out of the meagre ingredients rationing afforded.

Turkeys were in short supply in Kingsley that year and the meal consisted of roast pork and stuffing made from breadcrumbs and sage. Godfrey had made the pudding himself and the *Indian Brandy* purchased from Cyril Hall, the pharmacist, usually taken as a tonic to combat the chills of winter, made a passable substitute for the real thing in the brandy sauce they cobbled together to accompany the pudding.

At three in the afternoon they listened to the King's speech on the radio and raised their glasses of sherry to remember those who could not be with their families. Conversation turned to the coming year and the happy event expected in the household.

George was suffused with pride.

'We don't care whether it's a boy or girl, do we Hilda? As long as everything's all right, that's all that matters.'

He launched into a well-rehearsed account of how he planned to decorate the new baby's room and Godfrey listened politely, offering to run up curtains for the new nursery as soon as they could decide whether they wanted pink or blue gingham.

Sandra Logan arrived just as the kettle went on for a cup of tea.

'Perfect timing,' she grinned as she took a seat. 'Are you all well and truly stuffed? I know I am. Hello everybody. Come on then, Jean. Give us a cup of tea. How are you, Hilda?'

'She's doing really well,' George answered. 'She's just got to make sure she gets enough rest.'

'I don't get the chance to do anything but rest,' Hilda said. 'I have to do as I'm told and sit with my feet up. I didn't know George could be this broody,' she added with a laugh.

'She enjoys all the attention, really,' George said and kissed her on the top of her head.

'Did you say you have to report back tomorrow, Sandra?' Godfrey asked.

'Yes, I do, and to tell you the truth I shall be glad to get away from the house.'

'Why? I thought you were happy to be home for Christmas,' he said.

'It's mother,' Sandra said. 'Honestly, she's running round like a headless chicken ever since we heard Ronnie's coming home.'

'Is he?' George queried. 'Why's that?'

'Picked up some tropical illness, apparently. They say he won't be fit again for some time. In any case, he's not fit to fight. He's not even well enough to travel at the moment, so we're not sure when he'll be back.'

Jean handed Sandra her cup of tea and went to sit in the vacant fireside chair, leaving the two men talking with her friend around the table. She was waiting for the subject of conversation to change. She had no intention of making enquiries about Ronnie's health or showing any interest in him whatsoever, and it annoyed her that George was finding it so easy to be affable.

Sandra was still holding the floor.

'Yes, it'll be good to get back to work and out of the way. I think Dad would come with me if he could,' she joked.

'And how is your father?' George asked. 'Busy at the foundry, is it?'

'It's been crazy. Dad says it was a good thing his predecessors had held on to a lot of the old machinery they'd used during the First War. They've been able to bring it out of mothballs and put it to good use. It's a madhouse down there. Mother's working in the office. Your Mam's at Endura as well, Jean. Did you know? Funny that, isn't it? Your Mam and mine working in the same place? Do you see much of her?'

'No.' Jean answered from her place next to Hilda. 'We choose not to.' Her face grew hot and she wished Sandra would stop.

Jean always felt uncomfortable whenever the subject of Mary and Charlie came up. She knew Hilda had good reasons for wanting to get right away from them. Jean had also witnessed too much of their scrapping when she was just a girl. She'd hated their drinking and arguing constantly about everything. She felt as though her childhood had been swallowed up by their selfish behaviour, that her existence hadn't mattered to them. Whenever thoughts of her parents sprang to mind, they were always bad memories that made her feel nervous, so she tried not to think about them.

All the same, it was difficult to cut herself off completely. As much as she loved George and her sister, Hilda, she sometimes wondered what life would have been like if they'd all got on well together. How grand it might have been to have a family that was loving and complete.

'So they've got your brother in hospital then,' Godfrey said. 'In England?'

'Not yet. He's still in India. They'll transfer him as soon as they can move him, and he'll have to spend more time in hospital here. I don't know for how long.'

'And this disease he's suffering from?' Godfrey went on. Jean knew Godfrey was thinking about Richard Mancini and wondering what had become of him, 'have they said what it is?'

'No. We don't know. We thought maybe malaria, but we're only guessing. We'll have to wait. Jean, if you hear from him, would you let me know? I only ask because I know he used to keep in touch with you, and you might be the first to find out what's happening.'

Hilda stared at Sandra in disbelief.

'How can you expect Jean to be concerned about your brother after what he did?'

'I'm sorry if I've offended you, Hilda,' Sandra said, 'But all that seems such a long time ago now. At least that's how it feels to me. I thought we'd all moved on from then.'

'It's all right,' Jean interceded. 'Sandra's right. It is a long time ago.' She forced herself to sound bright. 'I'll do what you ask. *If* I hear from him, I'll let you know.'

◆

On Boxing Day Jean went with Sandra for the ten-thirty-five train from Kingsley to Leeds in time for Sandra's London connection. In the ladies' waiting room someone had placed a bowl of early-flowering crocus corms on the mantel above the empty iron fire grate. The little flowers thrust determinedly out of the soil in their bright purple, like rows of sentinels on parade, standing to attention in a message of hope.

'Thanks for coming to see me off,' Sandra said.

'You're welcome,' Jean smiled at her friend. 'I know you'd have hated having your mother here, fussing and fretting all over you.'

'Take care of yourself, Jean. I hope your sister is going to be all right. Let me know as soon as the baby arrives.'

'I will,' Jean called out as Sandra alighted the train and pulled on the leather strap to let down the window in the carriage door. 'And you be careful,' Jean added as the train began to pull away from the platform.'

'Yes, I know. *If you can't be good, be careful*,' Sandra quoted as she settled into her seat and reached for her packet of cigarettes.

Jean turned and walked up the ramp to the exit and as she stepped out from the station forecourt into the street she looked up at a grey winter sky and bare branches on the trees. She had a sudden yearning for spring. She wanted more than anything at that moment to be rid of the grey and cold and to feel the warmth of the returning sun on her back, warming her bones. She wanted to see flowers and colours and people with happy faces, glowing with health and happiness instead of ashen with fatigue and nausea like Hilda's.

On her way home she called in to see Godfrey. He welcomed her in and she saw he'd been looking through his design books. One of them was open at the page he'd just been reading.

'Styles of the 1920s,' he said. 'One of Richard's favourite eras. If he comes back, sorry, *when* he comes back we must have such a party. What do you think?'

Jean saw the tears in his eyes.

'Of course we will. I should think everybody will have a party when it's all over. Oh, just think of it, Godfrey, the end of the war. It can't go on much longer, can it?'

'Who knows?' was all he could say.

'I saw some crocuses today,' she said wistfully.

'It's too early for crocuses.'

'I know. Somebody must have brought them on early. They were in the waiting room at the station. They were, I don't know, perky, cheeky. They made me smile. I'd forgotten how much I like flowers. One day, I'm going to have flowers all the time. One day, when all this is finished, I'm going to have a garden with flowers everywhere so I can cut them and bring them into the house. I miss them.'

'Do you know one of the things I miss?' he said. 'The sea. I used to love living near the sea. Richard and I used to live on the south coast. I love living here in Kingsley now, but I do miss the sea. Is it still there?'

'Well, I don't know if you're allowed to go on the beaches where you used to live. Most of it's been sectioned off. There's barbed wire everywhere. But I do know about the North Sea coast. You know I've been delivering converted vehicles to different parts of the country?'

Godfrey nodded.

'I've seen a lot of places. Some of them, I'm not supposed to talk about, but I know they're clearing land mines in Norfolk.'

'Already?'

'Yes. They started earlier this year. You can actually go and have a day at the seaside.'

His eyes filled with wonder and longing.

'I'm planning to take Hilda there when she's better. I can borrow a car from work, I've already asked about it. But there's nothing to stop us doing a reccy first, is there? How about it? It's a long way to drive but that's okay. I've done it before.'

His smile started at the corners of his mouth and grew until he resembled the Cheshire cat in Alice.

'Oh, a day at the seaside,' he said. 'Oh, Jean, how utterly super-dooper.'

They both had something to look forward to, something to take their minds away from worries about people dearest to them. It gave them something to plan, something to organise, something that didn't involve the war effort. Petrol coupons wouldn't be a problem: Jean could call in a few favours. They would work on it, and when the weather improved in spring they'd take a trip to see the sea.

◆

By the end of 1944 the Allies were ready to advance on to the central plains of Burma. Earlier campaigns had failed in their daunting task, fraught with supply and communication problems. During the previous year, fresh troops trained and acclimatised to jungle fighting and using pack mules had begun the building of all-weather roads to aid supply lines, only to be beaten back by the Japanese, still glorying in their victories in China, Hong Kong and the Philippines.

But the Japanese had supply problems of their own, and as the Allied Forces advanced southwards, they discovered evidence of their enemies' plight. Shortage of rations and sickness had resulted in the skeletal remains of hundreds of Japanese soldiers left rotting in the jungle. The Allies were gaining the upper hand. Using tanks and infantry, and supplied by frequent air drops, they advanced long columns, destroying Japanese resistance.

In his hospital bed in India, Ronnie Logan was catching up with news of his regiment. The West Yorkshires were going into Burma again and he wished he'd been fit enough to go with them. Each night he prayed for their success and safe return. Each day he focused on regaining his strength. Although he was lucky to be alive, and he thanked God for it, he had nevertheless contracted a myriad of debilitating conditions, such that the Medical officer had ordered him home on the next transport.

Not being needed was an unpleasant feeling. He was anxious to be away from the hospital where others were being patched up and sent back into the fighting. Nobody ever said as much to his face but he felt he was in the way. He was a burden on their limited resources and it would be better for everybody if they could ship him out and leave it to somebody else to look after him.

He couldn't stand without feeling dizzy let alone attempt to walk. At times, it was impossible to get his legs to move. He had to concentrate fiercely to get the message down from his brain that he wanted to put one foot in front of the other. His limbs were nothing more than skin and bone and his protruding joints and lower legs ached whether he was sitting or lying down.

Worst of all, after the fever had subsided, was the itching rash developing on his skin. It drove him crazy, night and day. It was constant. It never let up. He felt as if he wanted to scratch his skin away. Weeping ulcerated sores were tolerable compared with the persistent itching and his blurred eyesight was just something else to put up with. He wasn't going anywhere under his own steam.

◆

Richard Mancini would never tell a soul about his experiences when he returned home. When the Burma-Thailand railway work was nearing completion in October 1943, he couldn't believe his luck he'd survived the conditions and still had enough strength to withstand the journey in the back of a cattle truck, back to imprisonment again in Changi jail.

Thirteen thousand prisoners had died during the work on the railway, their malnourished, abused and tortured bodies unable to overcome the ravages of dysentery, typhoid and cholera. He'd seen unspeakable acts of inhumanity. Daily, he'd witnessed beatings and torture and daily, to preserve his sanity, he'd had to look away from corpses left lying where they fell.

Work began at six in the morning and they were expected to keep going until nine or ten at night, through heat and humidity, through hordes of biting insects and when the Monsoons came, through torrential downpours that had them standing up to their waists in mud.

They were fed rice and cucumber; one bowl a day. If they fell ill and couldn't do a full day's work, they were put on half rations. They must bow to their captors and ingratiate themselves for their meagre fare, and they must be sure to bow low enough or there would be another severe beating.

But there were favours to be won. Richard Mancini had long known how to recognise when he'd excited interest in another. He taught himself to ignore the degradation. He kept his thoughts on his own survival as he gave sexual relief to his enemies. And when he was rewarded with a cigar he took it back to the lads in the billet where it would be passed around while he made jokes and disparaging comparisons between the size of the cigar and the size of the Japanese erection.

His camp humour kept up morale. When they knew he had an assignation with one of the prison guards, the lads waited eagerly for his next account of the session of intercourse conducted out of sight of the commanding officer, in the bush or out in the mangrove swamp. Richard Mancini continued to entertain the troops with a reconstruction in mime and they slapped their emaciated hands together in applause at his antics.

He never let on he provided the same service for Allied troops as well. Some of them were straight men with wives and children waiting for them at home. He allowed them their moment of fantasy. He knew behind their closed eyes they were imagining a female form as they gripped his buttocks and pulled him onto them. He stayed silent as they used his body and watched them sidle away afterwards and slip back, unseen into their huts. Theirs were the only gifts he kept for himself. He wouldn't be able to explain to the lads who had given them to him.

When he earned an extra bowl of rice, it was shared out amongst the sick to help build up their resistance. Once, when he'd been given a pair of rough sandals by one of his frequent Japanese tricks, at the risk of a blow in the head from the guard's rifle butt, he begged another pair for a young lad whose feet were torn and bleeding.

Rather than the jeering homophobia he'd expected in the beginning, he earned the respect of his fellow prisoners. They protected him wherever they could. He became important to them. They didn't want to lose him. He was the only source of light in their grim lives of imprisonment. And when he was rounded up with a few other prisoners and shoved into the back of a cattle truck in preparation for the journey back to prison, some of them wept to see him go.

He spent the following year in a cramped cell in Changi. At first, he fully expected to be singled out to perform the usual services. One of the guards who'd supplied him with cigars for favours rendered had been instrumental in selecting him for transportation to the prison. It had been made obvious to Richard and the others who'd been chosen to make the journey what their purpose was to be. Rough hands grabbed them between their legs as they were pushed up into the back of the truck and the youngest of them was made to drop his trousers and bend over, with his legs spread while one of the Japanese soldiers prodded at his scrotum with the end of his shotgun.

But something had changed. The Japanese guard who had used him most often was absent. Richard silently rejoiced he'd lost favour. He apprenticed himself to an Australian prisoner with whom he shared the overcrowded cell making false limbs and crutches for amputees.

Bob the Oz never questioned Richard about the time he'd spent labouring on the railway. Everybody had been through some kind of hell anyway. There was nothing to be gained by reliving the experience. Richard was grateful; he wanted to put the memories of it behind him. They were both lucky to survive. They kept their heads down and ensured they stayed busy. They didn't know the end of the war with the Japanese was in sight.

THIRTY FIVE

Hilda's appointment with the consultant was set for late January 1945. She'd stopped feeling nauseous except for first thing in the mornings but rather than experiencing the bloom of pregnancy, her complexion was still pale. Her hair hung dull and lacklustre. A small bump was beginning to show but only because she was so thin. Her everyday clothes hung from her shoulders and instead of needing to let out the seams in her dresses, she'd secretly taken them in and moved the buttons on her skirts so they fit more snugly.

She had lost her appetite. Each evening George and Jean encouraged her to try to eat a little more.

'Come on, my Hilda,' George would say to her. 'For baby, my love. You know you must eat for the baby.'

'I'm doing my best,' she'd say. But nothing tasted as it used to. It was an effort to chew food that tasted of nothing.

◆

Jean knew Hilda was getting weaker every day.

'If only it was spring,' she said to George after Hilda had gone to her bed early again. 'I'm sure she'd feel better if only we could get her out in the fresh air.'

'She tires very easily, Jean. Even if sun was shining she can't walk far,' he said.

'It's not supposed to be like this,' Jean said. 'She shouldn't feel so ill. Why haven't you gone to see the doctor about it?'

'She won't go. She doesn't even want to see the special doctor next week.'

'We must make her go. How can we help her if we don't know what's wrong?'

'Maybe she is little bit afraid,' George suggested.

'Why would she be afraid? What is there to be afraid of?'

'It is first baby,' he said. 'Excuse me, Jean, I don't like to remind you, but you had much pain, yes? When you had operation, there was much pain.'

'Hilda's not afraid of pain. Hilda's not afraid of anything. I've seen her putting people in their place.'

'Well I will ask her,' he said. 'I will ask outright if there is something that she worries about.'

◆

On the twenty-eighth of January, the German army was pushed back into Germany itself, news Jean thought would have George whooping for joy. But for the first time ever in Jean's experience, George and Hilda were having an argument.

They were almost shouting at each other as soon as they came through the door after Hilda's appointment. Jean sat in the kitchen and stared in disbelief as their bickering grew into angry voices.

'I don't understand why you won't tell me,' George was saying. 'I am your husband. You should tell me everything.'

'Not in front of Jean, please George,' Hilda said.

'We are family,' George said. 'Why not in front of Jean? We deal with everything like family,' he insisted.

'Please don't shout at each other,' Jean interrupted. 'You never shout at each other. What's happened?'

'We see special doctor today,' George began.

'I don't want to talk about this in front of Jean,' Hilda insisted.

'We see special doctor today,' George said again. 'He examines Hilda. Special examination. Examination for women, you know?'

Hilda threw her coat back on and quickly buttoned it up.

'Will you come with me, Jean?' she asked.

'Where are you going?'

'Just out. Please come with me.'

Hilda looked at her husband.

'Calm down,' she said. 'I promise you I'll explain later, when you're not so cross. I'll be all right if Jean's with me. Don't worry.'

They left George looking perplexed, drumming his fingers on the table and gazing into space.

Jean helped Hilda walk across the road to Old Man's Park and they sat by the memorial.

'Are you going to tell me what happened today?' Jean asked.

'It's complicated.'

Jean smiled her encouragement. 'You know you can tell me anything. You know that, don't you?'

Hilda nodded. 'I was examined today, as George said. The doctor told me he's concerned about my pregnancy. I'm not as strong as I should be and I might have to go into hospital to wait for the baby. I'm sure there's nothing to worry about, Jean.'

'And that's what George was shouting about? It doesn't make sense. Why would he get mad about that?'

'He's angry with himself for not noticing I was not very well,' she said. 'Now you mustn't worry about anything. George will calm down and everything will be fine. Just you wait and see. We'll go back in a few minutes and it will be all settled.'

◆

Hilda's fabrication had the desired effect. Jean relaxed and was satisfied with the story Hilda had composed. The truth had been very different and Hilda knew she was going to need all her powers of persuasion to convince George it was better they leave Jean out of it. Hilda would need to summon all her strength and determination to protect Jean from learning things Hilda didn't want her to know.

The doctors *were* worried about Hilda's pregnancy. The midwife had taken her weight and noted the loss. They'd listened in to the growing baby's heartbeat and they'd taken her blood pressure. They had checked her own heart rate and listened to her chest.

After the internal examination, and while Hilda was dressing, Mr Carlisle, the consultant, had spoken with George who was waiting in the side office. They sat facing each other across the desk while Mr Carlisle flicked through Hilda's file.

'We are a little concerned about your wife,' he said. 'We think she may be further on than her dates led us to believe. However, of more importance is the fact that the baby must be given every opportunity to thrive, and for that reason we are considering admitting your wife to the hospital for complete bed rest for a time. I have gone carefully through your wife's medical notes but there seems to be an omission which is a bit puzzling. How was she through her previous pregnancies, Mr Pozyzcka?'

George smiled and shook his head.

'No sir,' he said. 'There are no other children. This is first baby.'

Mr Carlisle looked up from his papers. He leaned back in his chair and cleared his throat.

'I have examined Mrs Pozyzcka. It is clear to me this is not her first pregnancy. It will help us care for her and your child if we have full details of her medical history.'

He leaned forward, his hands clasped on the desk waiting for George's response.

'No sir,' George repeated. 'This is our first child. We have waited so long, and now it is happening. I can see my Hilda is not as well as she should be and I am grateful that you will keep her safe and well. Of course she must come to hospital if you say it is so.'

'Mr Pozyzcka,' the consultant persisted. 'I don't think you quite understand me. My internal examination of your wife tells me there has been a previous pregnancy. Was she married before?'

'There must be a mistake,' George mumbled.

'No mistake, I'm afraid,' Mr Carlisle said, shaking his head.

George drew out his handkerchief from his pocket, removed his spectacles and began mopping his brow.

'I don't know nothing about this,' he admitted, and when Hilda entered the room and sat beside him he didn't know how to look at her.

'Mrs Pozyzcka, we need to know the details of your full medical history,' Mr Carlisle said. 'I shall need to ask you a few questions about your earlier pregnancy.'

There had been no way out of it. Hilda had been forced to admit the truth. She apologised for not realising her doctor would need to know everything about her and she hastily concocted a tale of teenage romance and adoption.

She avoided George's gaze while she spun a yarn of her problem-free first pregnancy, the daughter she had given birth to and once she had begun the lie there was no way back out of it. The story snowballed, lie upon lie, until she wished she'd never started. It would have been simpler to tell the whole of the real truth, but at the heart of all of her deceptions lay the one thing most important of all: protecting her daughter. Jean must be sheltered from the nightmare of discovering she'd been the product of a crime so vile Hilda couldn't speak its name.

As long as Jean never knew who her real parents were, never experienced the crawling shame that had crept into her own soul and threatened to damage her for ever, it didn't matter how many lies she told. She would have to find a way, now, to make things right with her husband. She would think of something.

✦

It was weeks before George could bring himself to question his wife about the revelations he'd recently discovered. Even then, he was careful to keep his emotions firmly under his control.

He had gone along with Hilda's request not to discuss the subject in front of Jean. He'd agreed, in the end, it would have been too upsetting for his young sister-in-law to be involved after what she'd experienced herself. Jean was managing to deal with her older sister's pregnancy and that was enough to be going on with.

So he'd listened to his wife when she told him the explanation she'd given to Jean. He accepted he should keep up his own part in the story Hilda had fabricated.

In private, though, he couldn't let it rest. Whenever the chance arose to ask his wife again for the full, true story he took it. Each time, Hilda stuck to her guns and refused to tell him more. She insisted the adoption of her first child had taken place. She was very young, she said, too young to realise what she was doing.

It was nonsense. He knew his wife. He knew for certain she wasn't the type who could have given away her own child and then done nothing to try to find out about what had happened to her little girl. In any case, there must have been papers to do with the formality of the adoption. Somewhere there must be documents to prove Hilda's story. He wanted to know where they were but Hilda told him the system didn't work like that. She said such documents were kept within the local authority offices so the adoption was complete and final and there could be no going back. Mothers who gave away their children were never allowed to see them again, never allowed to know their whereabouts.

But George couldn't let it stop there. It had come as a bodily shock to him to grasp that his wife, his Hilda had kept this from him. Why would she do that? It would not have changed the way he felt about her. He would not have said to her that he could not marry her because of it. He would have understood; he would have accepted the child. But this, deliberately deceiving him, was beyond his comprehension. It began to eat away at him. He could not let it go.

◆

On the seventh of March British and American troops crossed the Rhine and at seven-thirty that same morning Godfrey Jardeen and Jean Thompson were half way down the Great North Road, recently renamed the A1, on their way to Norfolk in a borrowed BSMC Standard 8. At Newark they turned onto the A17 and climbed a steep escarpment that seemed to come at them out of nowhere. On the top of the hill they stopped for a break and took in the view.

'This is about halfway,' Jean said.

'I'd no idea it was so far. Look at it all,' he said, pointing out the countryside around them. 'Isn't this a country worth fighting for?'

At eleven they rolled to a crunching stop on a gravel car park overlooking the sea and they stepped out into bracing sea air to gaze at grey waves below them. Godfrey breathed in deeply and closed his eyes.

'Thank you,' he said, after a moment. 'You can't imagine how much this means to me.'

'It's my pleasure, Godfrey. I have my own reasons for finding this spot.'

'Next time you come, the war will be over and you'll have your sister and a new niece or nephew.' He sighed.

'Yes,' she said. 'I hope so.'

Godfrey had booked rooms at an inn on one of the Norfolk Broads. It was such a long way for Jean to drive all in one day and besides, he felt it was an opportunity to visit a part of England he'd never seen. They spent the rest of the morning walking along a safe section of beach and they had lunch in a pub near Sheringham.

During the afternoon they visited other resorts on the north Norfolk coast and headed back inland towards Horning as light began to fade and a cold mist rolled in from the sea.

The landlord of the Ferry Inn gave them the keys to their rooms and surreptitiously passed to them a hand-written menu for evening dinner.

'Don't know if you be staying with us for dinner,' he said. 'Only I thought I'd let you know that we 'ave sump'm a bit special on tonight. Can't let on to all and sundry, if you see what I mean, but as you be special guests I thought I'd write it down for you. Keep it hush-hush,' and he raised his forefinger to his closed lips.

They scanned the piece of paper he'd given them and ordered two places for evening dinner.

'We 'ave other guests this evenin',' he told them. 'We'll be fourteen in all. Should be a good do. The missus'll be serving drinks in the bar from about seven 'o clock. Ain't no point in startin' sooner than that out here. That be all right for you?'

They nodded their agreement and went upstairs to their rooms where they were delighted to find sumptuous carpets covering polished floorboards and soft eiderdowns on their beds. They had a bathroom all to themselves on their landing and thick towels had been laid out neatly for them on their bedside chairs.

'This is luxury,' Jean said. 'Oh, Godfrey. What a good choice you made.'

'It's time we had a bit of good fortune, isn't it? Let's make the most of it.'

'Do you think it will be all right if I have a bath?' she asked him. 'Would that be a bit cheeky?'

'That's what it's there for. You have a nice warm soak. I fancy a look around. Take your time and enjoy. Shall we meet up later in the bar?'

Gleefully Jean gathered her things and locked herself in the bathroom, humming to herself with the anticipation of the sheer pleasure of immersing her whole body in relaxing warm water.

Godfrey went outside and strolled along the bank of the Broad, looking out over the water and watching evening clouds racing across the wide Norfolk sky. He'd been gently strolling for about forty minutes and was on his way back to the lodgings when he heard the sound of a motor in the distance and saw a small craft coming towards him over the water.

Two lads manoeuvred a small boat against the bank nearest the Ferry Inn where there was a small wooden jetty. Six men in uniform climbed out. One of them stood waiting by the water's edge while the oldest boy handed a newspaper parcel up to him.

'Pick you up later,' the lad shouted as they pulled away from the jetty, made off across the water and disappeared into the distance.

'Thanks,' the man replied, giving a wave and jogging along the path to catch up with his friends. The six of them went into the Inn.

At seven-thirty they met again. Jean had put on her rust-red Joan Crawford and had added a small brooch at an angle across one side of the sweetheart neckline. She'd rolled her hair and Godfrey smiled to himself at the way she knew how to make the best of herself. She'd learned well from Richard, but he told himself he mustn't think about that now. He would only get upset and he didn't want to spoil what promised to be an exciting evening. They went downstairs together to find all the other guests had arrived and were taking drinks at the bar.

◆

George had Hilda to himself. With Jean away for the night he planned to bring up the subject of Hilda's first pregnancy again and get to the bottom of what she was hiding from him. He'd made up his mind he wasn't going to allow her to give him vague answers. He would pester until he was certain she'd told him everything.

'How old were you?' he asked her suddenly, his question taking her by surprise as she was clearing away the dishes after their evening meal.

'How old was I when? What do you mean?' she said.

'When you were pregnant first time, Hilda. I want you to tell me how old you were.'

'I was very young. I already told you.'

'No, Hilda. I want to know exactly how old you were.'

She wouldn't look at him. She filled the sink with hot water and began scrubbing at the cooking pots.

'Very young,' she reiterated.

'Very young is not enough. I want you to tell me *exactly*.'

She spun around to face him.

'Why? What difference does it make?'

'It makes a lot of difference to me. Was it just before I met you, or was it long time before that?'

Her face flushed, she looked away from him.

'I was just eighteen when we met. You were twenty three. You keep this secret from me for a long time now. When was it?'

'Why can't you just leave it alone, George? Look, I'm sorry I didn't tell you. I should have told you. I should have trusted you. I know that now.'

'But still you don't trust me enough to tell me now.'

'It's not like that. You don't understand. It's been awful for me keeping this secret all these years. Do you think it's been easy for me?'

'How would I know whether it's been easy or no? You tell me nothing, so how could I know how difficult it is?'

The blood drained from her face and she began to feel light-headed.

'You must stop now, George.' She left the rest of the dishes in the sink and took a chair by the fender.

'No,' he told her. 'I am not going to stop. I am not going to stop until you tell me everything.'

Her breath came fast and shallow and she put her head into her hands.

'Please, George. Please leave me be.'

'No,' he repeated. 'I am your husband. I have always been proud to be your husband. But now you make me feel not so proud. What kind of man is it whose wife will not tell him the truth?'

She raised her head.

'Hilda,' he said. 'Tell me now.'

'I was fourteen!'

He slumped into one of the dining chairs and stared at her.

'You were a child,' he said. 'It is like same as happened to Jean. How can I understand this? You were raped?'

'Yes, I was raped. I was attacked.'

'Who was it? Did you know him?'

'No.'

'But it was someone from Kingsley?'

'I don't know.'

'And the police could not find him?'

Her eyes flickered and her jaw fell slack. George caught her as she fell forwards out of the chair, her eyes filmy and her face deathly white.

◆

The party around the table at the Ferry Inn was in full swing. At the head of the dining table sat the landlord, Peter Baird, and filling the rest of the seats, besides Godfrey and Jean, were Mrs Christine Baird, Mr and Mrs Whitely, friends of the Bairds, the farmer, Josh Cantley and his wife Maureen, and six pilots from a nearby RAF base, who Godfrey had seen earlier.

'I saw you all as you arrived by private launch,' he joked.

'Good lads, those two,' one of them replied. 'Only, we have to keep it on the quiet.'

'Yes, of course. I understand,' Godfrey said. 'But aren't they rather young to be in charge of an armed vessel? Wasn't that a machine gun I saw fixed at the front?'

'There ain't no better boys than those two,' Peter Baird interjected. 'You could trust your life with either of them. Just kids, I know, but more common sense than most for their age.'

'Kids have to grow up quick these days,' another voice added. His voice sounded familiar and Jean twisted her head to look at where it was coming from. The man continued. Jean noticed his uniform was slightly different from the others and as he went on, she knew where she'd heard those sounds before.

'Are you Polish?' she asked him.

'That is me,' he answered.

'And you're a pilot too?'

'Was pilot, young lady. Not now. See this?' and he held up his empty sleeve. 'One arm short to be pilot now, and bad leg. Is my tough luck.' He grinned and his friends joined him in his self-deprecation.

'Never was any bloody good, if you ask me, sweet thing,' the one sitting next to him teased. 'Tells us tall stories but we don't believe him.'

They all laughed, and continued ribbing each other, but Christine Baird leaned across to Jean and whispered the truth.

Stannas was one of the most highly-respected pilots in the Polish 303 Squadron, flying Spitfires out of Kirton in Lindsey, Lincolnshire, till early '43. He'd achieved ace status, having shot down more than five enemy aircraft and it was ironic that a nasty road accident on winding country lanes had robbed him of his chance to double his score. He'd taken up tutoring at the training school and was visiting his old pal Freddy from RAF Coltishall, just down the river.

The five pound fresh water bream which had been delivered to the landlord in the newspaper parcel which Godfrey had seen being handed over earlier, was illegal, out of season and almost a prize specimen.

Peter Baird had baked it in a Mediterranean style sauce made from tinned tomatoes and dried herbs from his kitchen garden. Served as the entrée with his home-made elderflower wine, it ensured the success of his special evening. His guests couldn't wait to see the next course.

Josh Cantley knew exactly what was coming up next: his own hand-reared spring lamb which he'd butchered himself and donated to the dinner celebrating his and Maureen's wedding anniversary.

Freddy caught Jean's attention.

'How come you're free to go gallivanting around the country, young lady?'

'She's a spy, Freddy,' Christine said with a wink. 'This is her uncle Godfrey the famous sleuth from Casablanca.'

'Yes, and I'm Humphrey Bogart.' Freddy laughed.

'I work for Charles Cooper,' Jean told them. 'We convert cars for military use.'

'I knew I'd seen you before,' one of the other pilots said. 'You delivered an accumulator to us at Coltishall.'

'I've delivered more than one, actually,' she said. 'I've grown quite fond of Norfolk. I'd like to live here one day. I plan to bring my sister to visit after the war. She's not well at the moment.'

They drank a round of toasts to Jean and all the others like her who worked in the background to keep the flag flying. When she told them about her friend Sandra, they drank a toast to all the Sandras in the allied armed forces, and when the roast lamb was brought in and placed before them they sniffed at the air in reverence for a moment before drinking a toast to farmer Cantley and wishing him and his wife a happy anniversary.

After the dessert of fruit crumble and condensed milk the men fell into talking about the progress of the war. Jean heard them saying how they believed the worst of it was over, that Hitler had been beaten but he didn't acknowledge it yet. She listened with fascination at how they believed Hitler's plan in the beginning was to prosecute a quiet invasion of England, how he had never intended a full-scale head on charge across the English Channel. He'd wanted his troops to slip in quietly by the back door and take up positions being made ready for them by their secret agents and allies.

She heard about the day the countryside was crawling with agents from MI5 who swooped in across Norfolk and Lincolnshire the day after Stannas reported seeing unidentified airstrips and barn roofs painted bright red, pointing the way to safety for enemy aircraft.

The sound of a motor boat halted the banter and the men got up to leave. Godfrey promised to make each of them a pure silk cravat and after they'd said their goodbyes, they went out of the door arguing good-naturedly about which colour cravat they'd prefer. Jean watched from the doorway as two young lads who looked like brothers held the small craft steady for them to board and she waved as they disappeared into the darkness.

THIRTY SIX

When Jean returned from her trip to the Norfolk coast with Godfrey, she could hardly wait to tell Hilda and George about the places they'd seen and the people they'd met. She parked the car along the street by the Drill Hall and raced up the passageway to let herself into the house. The door had been left open but there was nobody in. When she looked around, Elsie was at the back doorstep.

'Jean,' Elsie said. 'Hilda's in the hospital, love. George has gone up there for visiting time.'

'Right. Okay,' Jean answered. 'They decided to take her in after all, then.'

Elsie muttered something under her breath.

'Has something happened?'

'I think she fainted, Jean love. She passed out. Yesterday, it was. The ambulance came for her and they carried her out. If you hurry, they might let you in to see her yourself.'

Jean didn't ask about the baby. There was no time for further questions. She flew out of the house and back along the street to the car. She slid into the driver's seat and sped along the route to the hospital.

She was just in time to catch the last few minutes of visiting time and was relieved to find Hilda sitting up in bed, talking to George. Hilda smiled and looked cheerful as Jean came into the ward.

'Jean,' Hilda called out to her. 'Come and sit down next to George. Here look, there's another chair. Did you have a nice time?'

'Never mind about me. I want to know about you. What happened?'

'She fainted,' George replied for his wife. 'Now she is here they will see that she eats properly and everything.'

Jean looked at him. He was worried; she could tell. She would ask him later, when they were at home. She didn't want to bring it up in front of Hilda.

'I'm all right,' Hilda told her. 'So you can both stop worrying. Look, I'm living the life of Riley in here. I don't have to do anything. All I have to bother about is if I've got enough magazines to read.'

'And have you?' Jean asked.

Hilda pointed to the stack of *Reveille* and *Woman* journals on one of the side tables and laughed. 'I hope I'm not in here long enough to get through that pile. I'd go bog-eyed reading that lot.'

A bell rang to signify that visitors must leave.

'Come again tomorrow, Jean and tell me all about your trip,' Hilda said. 'And George, would you bring me in my slippers, sweetheart? They do allow me out of bed sometimes.'

George kissed her and promised he wouldn't forget. Jean felt uneasy. On the face of it, her sister seemed cheerful and bright. She turned to give her a last wave as they reached the ward exit and Hilda raised her arm and waved back. The sleeve of her bed-jacket slipped down and Jean saw a bony length of Hilda's arm. She drove George back to the house in silence.

'I want you to tell me, George,' she demanded as soon as they returned.

'They think it's her heart,' he said. 'And then they think it's her breathing. They want to do some tests, but . . . '

'But what?' Jean insisted.

'Some tests are difficult to do because of baby. And Hilda is not strong. There are medicines Hilda could have now, but is not good for baby. So, we wait.'

◆

Jean watched George closely over the next few days. He spent a lot of time thinking and rubbing his chin, smoothing his moustache and generally fidgeting. He was like an animal in a cage; it was as though there was something about to erupt from inside. She tried to comfort him. She pointed out how cheerful Hilda had been each time they went to visit her, but nothing she said could help to soothe him.

George's discreet enquiries had come up with nothing: no record of the birth of Hilda's first child; no police report of an attack on a young girl. There was nothing. It was a dead end. But the thing that tore at him most of all was the way Hilda wanted to dismiss the whole affair. He couldn't understand why the wife he knew so well showed no regret at not knowing what had happened to her child. The only emotion she'd shown was her fierce determination to keep Jean out of it. She hadn't wept for the loss of her baby. That just wasn't like her.

He saw how Jean was doing her best to help him and could keep it to himself no longer.

'Jean,' he said to her. 'Come here and sit down. There is something maybe you can help.'

He began gently. 'Now then, my Jean. This is not going to be easy for me. I am going to tell you something Hilda did not want you to know. You know how she can be very strong woman, in her mind? She has used this way of thinking to look after us, yes?'

'I've only ever wanted to be just like her,' Jean said.

'But sometimes I think it is better to be not so fixed in your mind. You must let other people think for themselves.'

'I'm not following you,' Jean admitted.

'Hilda has kept something from you and from me for long time. Now that she has told me, I think you should know too. I think it will be better for Hilda to stop worrying about you finding out about it.'

'What is it?'

'When she was fourteen she had a baby.'

'Fourteen?' Jean gasped.

'Yes, only fourteen. She was attacked. The man was never found.'

◆

Jean felt the heat of her anger coursing through her body. She bombarded him with questions. She berated him for not knowing the answers.

'She collapsed,' he explained. 'The night you were away, she went into the hospital. There is no privacy there. I cannot talk about this now in front of other people.'

Jean knew immediately where she would get the rest of the story. She told George nothing of her intentions and next day, at lunch time, she slipped out of the gates at Charles Cooper and crossed over the street. She made herself known to the young girl in reception at Endura Iron and Steel Works and asked for directions to the canteen. Thomas Logan saw her at the reception office window.

'Jean,' he called out, coming out of his own office to stand with her in the corridor. 'What can I do for you?'

'I'm looking for me mam,' she said. 'Will she be in the canteen now?'

'In half an hour,' he replied. 'Would you come into my office for a moment?'

She was in no the mood for pleasantries.

'Why?' she asked him abruptly.

'Not out here in the passageway. In my office please.'

She followed him and he closed the door firmly behind them. He invited her to sit, and reluctantly, she took a chair by the desk. He spun his own chair around so he wasn't facing her when he began.

'Ronnie is at home now.'

'I know. I heard.'

'He wants to see you.'

'I've got other things to do with my time, Mr Logan,' she said in a flash, and got up to leave.

'Please hear me out,' he said. 'I don't think you understand what he has suffered.'

She stood over him and shrugged her shoulders.

'What makes you think I *care* what he's suffered?' she challenged.

'Please, just listen to me for a moment, Jean. If you will just sit down, I'll try to explain.'

She grudgingly complied.

'Ronnie is a devout young man,' he began.

'Huh! Don't make me laugh.'

'Regardless of what you may think of him,' he continued, 'he has always held dear to the ways of our church.'

'Mr Logan, you're wasting your breath,' she said flatly.

'It's his belief in our church that's causing him so much anguish. He is *ill,* Jean. And I don't mean only physically. If you only knew the half of what he's been through . . .'

'Let him go to your church, then. Let them sort him out. I don't see what this has got to do with me.'

'He needs *you* to forgive him. I don't think he will ever get better until you do.'

She felt her resolve weaken. She knew he'd seen the shift in her demeanour.

'Say that you will think about it, at least,' he asked her.

She lowered her eyes and nodded.

'I'll think about it,' she agreed.

◆

Mary Thompson was sitting with a group of workmates at one of the tables in the canteen when Jean came through the double doors. Jean braced herself for trouble.

'Mam,' she said as she came alongside. 'I want to talk to you.'

'I can hear you,' Mary said. 'Go on, then.'

'It's private,' Jean emphasised, staring at the group of women who were all eyes and ears. 'Will you meet me after work?'

'If you want,' Mary said without enthusiasm.

'I'll be waiting for you at the gates. What time do you get off?'

All afternoon Jean wrestled with her thoughts and feelings. She knew what she wanted to ask but she wanted to be sure she could do it in the right way. She wanted to be like Hilda; she wanted to let it be known she would stand for no nonsense. On the other hand, she didn't want to antagonise. She searched within herself for the best way to begin, the words to use which would give her what she wanted.

She met Mary at five thirty and took her to the lounge bar at the Victoria Hotel. She bought the drinks and they took a booth in the corner.

'What's this all about?' Mary asked. 'Bit posh in here, isn't it? This is where you come spending your money, is it?'

'No. I've never been in here before. I wanted to come somewhere different. Somewhere nice.'

Mary looked around at gilded mirrors and fancy wall lights.

'So, what do you want to talk about? I don't think you've brought me in here to talk about the weather.'

Jean thought she detected a softening in the tone of voice. She willed herself to keep control of the conversation.

'Hilda's not well. She's in hospital.'

'Why? What's the matter with her?' Mary asked.

'She's expecting a baby in June.'

'And nobody bothered to tell me, eh? So why is she in hospital now?'

'Because she's not well. There are complications.'

'What complications?'

Jean played the phrase she had been rehearsing.

'Something not right with her insides. They say that's why it took so long for her to get pregnant. There's been some damage to her insides.'

Mary emptied her glass quickly. Jean went to the bar to order more. Reflected in the mirror behind the counter, Jean could see Mary pulling nervously at her hair. Jean sauntered back casually with the refreshed glasses.

'Yes,' Jean went on, 'they seem to think Hilda isn't telling them everything. They're desperate to help her.'

'What do they want to know?' Mary asked, taking a large swig of her second drink.

Jean hoped she'd timed it right. She made her next play.

'They want to know what happened to the baby Hilda had before.'

Mary nearly choked.

'They know about that?' she cried out.

'Oh, yes,' Jean said. 'Hilda said it was when she was fourteen. That's right isn't it?'

Mary squirmed in her seat. Jean persevered. 'Yes. We all know now. Only, you see, to be able to help the new baby, they need to find the first one. Something about blood transfusions,' she lied.

She took a sip of her own drink and compelled herself to remain in control.

'We can't understand, you see, why Hilda would keep the information from her own doctors. If only we could find out what really happened . . .'

Mary Thompson's face paled. She looked as if she might throw up.

'That baby that she had, Jean . . .'

'Yes?' Jean prompted her.

'It's you. Hilda is your mother, not me. I'm your grandmother.'

Jean floundered. She hadn't expected this. Her resolve faltered and words wouldn't come. She sat, in stunned silence, as Mary rose from her seat and hurried away.

◆

George wanted to visit Hilda alone.

'Jean, would you mind if I have Hilda to myself tonight?' he asked when she came in.

'No, of course not,' Jean said. 'Tell her I'm thinking about her,' she added.

Hilda was all Jean was able to think about and she was glad to have the house to herself so she could concentrate on her ideas. She didn't know whether to laugh or cry and the more she went over the events of her life, the more it all fell into place.

Hilda was fourteen when she gave birth. Hilda was fourteen years older than herself. Hilda had been attacked; that's why she felt so angry and upset when the same thing had happened to her. Hilda had always hoped Jean would come to live with her. She had always cared for her as a mother would.

Hilda was struggling now because she didn't know how to tell George. But it was easy, wasn't it? George would understand. He would see straight away it would have been difficult for Hilda to tell him the truth in the beginning. Now that he knew half of it anyway it ought to be easier to present him with the rest of the information.

She started to feel better; she began to feel there was hope. She was able to see how Hilda, George and she could carry on with their lives and love each other in exactly the same way as they always had.

But that wasn't all of it, was it? Once George had accepted Jean was Hilda's daughter, there would be other questions to answer. Who was the father? Who was it who did this to a young girl? Where did it happen? How come nobody else knew about it?

A stabbing sensation of realisation chilled her as Hilda's words filtered into her mind and repeated themselves.

A girl's father is not the right person.

The room began to spin. The house closed in around her and sucked the breath from her. Her whole being turned in on itself and the world imploded around her. The awful truth ran cold in her veins.

Hilda *had* been attacked, but not by some stranger. Hilda had been raped, but not by some boy her own age. She'd been violated by the one man in the world a girl ought to be able to trust more than any other: her own father. *That* was why it had all been kept such a secret.

It suddenly became clear as crystal. It explained all the lies and bad feelings between them over the years. It was the real reason why Hilda had wanted to get away from Kingsley. It was why they could never be like an ordinary family; there had been such filth in their history they could never have a clean future.

And what did it make of her? What could she call herself? Mary was her grandmother. Charlie was her grandfather *and* her father. It was sickness beyond belief. The contents of her stomach came up into her throat and she dashed to the sink to vomit them away.

THIRTY SEVEN

Ronnie Logan's father helped him from the bathroom and across the landing to his room. Ronnie needed assistance with his clothes. His mother had offered to perform these intimate tasks for him but Ronnie didn't want her to see him undressed. He knew how his mother would react if she caught sight of his emaciated frame. He couldn't bear to listen to her. He knew God was punishing him and he knew he deserved it, but that didn't mean he had to listen to his mother's twisted version of whose fault it was he was in such a mess.

There was something the matter with his mother, Ronnie thought. He'd come to the conclusion she had a screw loose somewhere. She talked as if all the ills of the world were falling on only her doorstep, that her lot was much worse than anybody else's. He accepted his father's assistance, and only then because his father had enough sense to know when to talk and when to keep his mouth shut.

There was nothing more the doctors could do for Ronnie. They'd told him his recovery was in his own hands now. If he followed the eating programme devised for him, took the medication and used lotions prescribed for him, he should begin to see improvements soon. Nobody had told him how he was supposed to cope with the nightmares; nobody had explained to him how to deal with images that flashed before his eyes of half-eaten corpses, of screaming skulls and bloated bodies exploding and scattering their wormy contents.

Father Connolly had listened to his confession and tried to console him.

'You must be patient, my son,' he'd said. 'All in God's good time,' he'd assured him.

Ronnie had wanted to drag the priest from the confessional and beat the living daylights out of him. What did he know of children starving to death? How many times had he seen bereaved mothers carrying the maggot-ridden dead bodies of their infants for days till they themselves dropped dead in the mud? Did God Himself know about it? And if He did, why wasn't He doing something about it? Where was He?

His mother's pious attitude annoyed him. Her constant reassurances that God had helped him survive his torments irritated him beyond belief. She needed a slap, too. Dad should have seen to that years ago before she turned into this maudlin, simpering excuse for a female. She wasn't half the woman Jean Thompson had turned out to be.

His hands tightened into fists. He always found himself thinking about the same thing: Jean Thompson. She'd been at the start of all his problems and she was the only solution. There would be no place for him in the hereafter until he'd made it right with Jean Thompson. He swore his own private oath: a solemn agreement with God that if Jean Thompson would not come to visit him, he would concentrate all his efforts on building up his strength so he could get out of the house and go to see her.

◆

Jean discussed her dilemma with Godfrey Jardeen.

'I respect your opinion,' she told him. 'Begging your pardon, but you must be used to dealing with delicate situations. You know what I mean. I'm stuck. I don't know what to do for the best. I know half of the truth, and I think I'm right about the rest of it. How much should I say?'

'It's tricky. There's no doubt about that,' Godfrey agreed. 'But before we go into that, tell me how you feel about it yourself.'

Jean sighed and hoped she could find the words to explain to Godfrey how she felt.

'It's all mixed up,' she began. 'If it was just finding out that Hilda is my real mam, I think I'd be really happy. It's the rest of it that's hard to deal with. It makes me feel soiled, unnatural, not a proper person.'

'I can understand that feeling,' Godfrey told her. 'I used to feel like that myself. What you've got to remember, my dear, is that you haven't done anything wrong. It's not your fault, and it's not Hilda's fault. She must have been a frightened young thing, just like you were once.'

'It's hard to imagine Hilda ever being frightened of anything,' Jean said.

'I can see why Hilda has kept it from you all these years. She didn't want you to know because she wanted to protect you from those feelings.'

'Yes, I can see that,' Jean replied.

Godfrey suddenly bounced up out of his chair.

'I've got an idea!' he said.

♦

Godfrey's suggestion worked. The next time she and George went to visit Hilda in hospital, she put it into practice. She asked George to give her a few minutes alone with Hilda.

'Where's George tonight?' Hilda asked her.

'He's waiting outside. I wanted to have a word with you first. Please don't be upset. I think it's wonderful.'

'What is?'

'I know who my real mother is,' Jean whispered. 'Don't cry Hilda. It's all out in the open now, so you can stop worrying about it. It was a terrible thing that happened to you when you were so young, just like what happened to me. At least I knew who my attacker was. I can't imagine how awful it must have been for you, not knowing.'

Hilda stared at Jean, her eyes brimming with tears.

'I'm glad you're my mother. It doesn't matter that we don't know who my father is. And do you know what? I think George will be just as happy as I am when you tell him.'

Years of anxiety fell away from Hilda at Jean's words. She knew Jean had worked it all out for herself. She sensed Jean knew full well who her father was and had chosen to let it lie. Her beautiful, sensible daughter had put her own feelings aside and had given them the answer to all of their problems. At last, it could be over. Jean was right: George would be happy to hear this half-truth and they would have their lives back.

She blew her nose and wiped her eyes.

'Thank you, Jean,' she sobbed. 'I understand what you are doing for us. I'm so proud of you and I love you more than ever. I'll tell him now. Will you go and get him please?'

♦

George was walking on air as they left the hospital. He wanted to celebrate and suggested they buy some bottles from the brewery on their way home.

'Everything is going to be all right,' he grinned at Jean as they raised a toast together. 'Soon we will have new baby and we will be proper family.'

'We already were,' she agreed. 'We just didn't know it.'

'My poor Hilda has been ashamed of the thing that happened to her. She tried to hide it from us for good reasons, I think. But it has made her ill, all this worry. She will be better now.'

He put his arm around Jean's shoulder and hugged her hard. 'And we have you to thank for helping. You were brave to do what you did. Facing up to Mary like that. Just like Hilda. Brave and strong.'

He rubbed his hands together gleefully and threw back his head. 'Ha!' he cried loudly to the ceiling. 'Everything is going to be all right.'

♦

The month of April 1945 heralded rapid advances for the Allies, both in Europe and in the Far East. Hundreds of thousands of prisoners were taken as German resistance weakened further. Kingsley families tuned in to hear the latest radio broadcasts. A groundswell of optimism permeated through the people.

Jean Thompson acceded to Thomas Logan's request and visited Ronnie at his home. She left a written message for Thomas at his place of work so she was expected and they'd have time to do whatever they needed to do before she arrived. She knew Ronnie's mother, Sylvia would prefer it that way to give her the chance to absent herself and that suited Jean just fine. Feelings were mutual on that score.

Thomas Logan met her at the door and showed her through into the sitting room. Everything was the same as she remembered from her visits there when she was a girl: the armchairs identically arranged around the fireplace; the ornaments on display along the mantelpiece in exactly the same positions. That was a lifetime ago. It felt as though those times had all happened to someone else. So much had happened since.

She glanced around the room and caught sight of Ronnie sitting on an upright dining chair placed by the bay window. She swallowed hard and attempted not to let her astonishment show in her expression. She tried a smile.

'Come over here and let me look at you,' Ronnie said to her. 'I have a bit of a problem with my eyes at the moment. I'm waiting for glasses.'

Thomas discreetly removed himself.

'Give me a shout, Ronnie, if you need anything. I'll be in the kitchen,' he said as he left the room.

Jean moved a little closer and stood in front of Ronnie, trying not to stare at his shrunken size, his feeble legs with their protruding knee joints. His face had changed. His cheeks had sunk in on themselves, his eyes drawn back into their sockets. He looked like an old man.

◆

Jean Thompson had turned into the most beautiful woman Ronnie could remember. With her shining hair and long slim legs she waited there in front of him, her face the picture of poise and confidence. Her dark eyes drew him in and for a brief moment he recalled how he'd lusted after her in the days when his sexual prowess was the talk of the tap room. Now look at her. She could pick and choose with looks like that.

'What did you want to see me about?' she asked. 'Only, I can't stay too long.'

'You never answered any of my letters,' he said.

'What did you expect?'

'Did you read any of them?'

'Oh yes, I read them,' she replied. 'You never once asked me how *I* was feeling. You never mentioned the child I might have now.'

'Would it have made any difference if I had?'

'Yes, it would. If you'd asked me about myself, I would have replied,' she told him.

'And what would you have said?'

'I would have told you what I thought about you. I'd have told you straight.'

'I wish you had.'

'You didn't deserve my anger, Ronnie Logan. You made yourself less worthy than that. You were nothing to me. You were only fit to be ignored.'

He was amazed at her self-assurance. She was magnificent, like a big cat, a tigress. He knew then he'd lost the only woman who could excite him like that and he knew, also, he would stop at nothing to win her back again.

◆

Adolf Hitler committed suicide on the thirtieth of April. The news of his death arrived in England a few days later when newspapers screamed out the headlines and the whole of England awaited the German surrender. Kingsley buzzed with news. Shopkeepers came out onto the pavements to add to crowds who gathered there and join in with their deliberations. In the market hall, stallholders cried out the headlines along with the price per pound of their produce. Bus conductresses leaned out from the platforms of their buses and shouted the news at pedestrians they passed on their routes, and across the Town Hall square, where scores of people were gathering by the memorial to the fallen of the First World war, a lone figure on crutches limped past the throng on his way to the house on Larksholme Lane.

Elsie saw him waiting by George and Hilda's door.

'They're not in, love,' she called out to him. She saw immediately how unsteady he was and when she caught the pain in his eyes as he turned to look at her, she rushed to help him.

'Come in, love,' she said. 'Don't stand there waiting. You can come to me and wait for them. Come on. Look, that's my house just here.'

She took one of his crutches and he leaned on her as slowly they crossed the yard to her own back door. She helped him up the step and he sank, gratefully into one of Elsie's fireside chairs.

'You're young Ronnie Logan, aren't you?' she said. 'Used to work down the coal yards. I remember you. You delivered to me many a time.'

She said nothing about the changes in him. She remembered him as the good-looking young fellow who brightened her day with his silly remarks and good-natured flirting.

'You used to give me biscuits,' he gasped, fighting for breath after the effort of hobbling across the town. 'Damned crutches,' he went on. 'I'm not used to them yet. They're more of a hindrance than a help.'

'I think you're doing very well,' she encouraged. 'What does your doctor say?'

'Oh, I've just got to be patient. Look, thank you for helping me just now. Do you know when they'll be back?'

'I couldn't say, really. You know that Hilda's not well? She's in the hospital.'

'No, I didn't,' he replied. 'Jean never told me.'

'Ah, is it Jean you were waiting for?'

'Yes. I promised I'd call in to see her as soon as I was able to get about on these damned things,' he said, pointing at the crutches propped against the wall.

'Well you just sit there, love,' she said, 'and I'll make you a drink while you're waiting. Sorry I can't offer you a biscuit this time. Come back when the war's over and I'll give you a bag full.'

'It might not be long before it's finished in Europe. The Germans are bound to capitulate without a leader. I don't know about the rest of the world, though. The bloody Japs will never give in.'

Again, he fought for his breath. Elsie realised how much it was taking out of him. He must care very much for Jean Thompson, she thought, to make this kind of effort just to see her. She knew nothing of the events of the night of George and Hilda's party.

'Don't you worry yourself,' she told him. 'I can talk enough for the pair of us. You make yourself comfortable and I'll keep an eye out for when Jean comes back.'

Elsie kept going for an hour. He listened as she related all the tales she knew about the people of Kingsley and the things that had happened during the course of the war. She told him about

Jean and how she'd travelled around the country, collecting private cars and then delivering the converted vehicles to their destinations.

He closed his eyes and imagined Jean, confident and determined, rebuilding her life and forgetting all about him, not giving him a single thought. He visualised how she would look at the wheel of a car, her hair blowing in the wind from the open window, her skin fresh and clean and sweet-smelling. He fell into a dream of the two of them together where he was fit and strong again, where they laughed and loved each other and promised to stay together forever.

Elsie gently placed a blanket over him as he slept in her kitchen and when she saw that Jean had arrived home she slipped out quietly.

'Jean, love, there's a young man to see you. He doesn't look too good. I've taken him into mine.'

Jean lifted her head and Elsie saw the tears brimming in Jean's eyes.

'What is it?' she asked. 'Is it Hilda?'

'Oh, Elsie,' Jean sobbed. 'She's getting worse. They're going to have to bring the baby. She's not strong enough to do it herself. George is staying there with her.'

'There now,' Elsie comforted. 'It might not be as bad as you fear. She's in good hands, love. They know what's best. Leave it to them, eh? Why don't you come and see your visitor?'

In a daze, Jean followed Elsie across the yard and into her house and when she saw Ronnie, wrapped in Elsie's grey woollen blanket, asleep with his head twisted to one side so that the bones of his brow, cheek and jaw line showed clearly through the skin of his face, she cried out in anguish.

He awoke with a start and tried to get to his feet. She saw him struggling and a painful sensation of pity for him overwhelmed her. She could cope with no more. Her emotions in shreds, she turned to go.

'Wait!' he called after her. 'Marry me, Jean. I've come to ask you to marry me. I'll never be whole again without you.'

He collapsed back into the chair, his chest heaving as once more he fought for his breath, and he crumpled before her, dissolving into deep racking sobs. His eyes pleaded with her; those eyes that used to glitter for the girls and send them weak-kneed, now half-closed in pain. He sucked in a gasp of air.

'If I have to die soon,' he whispered, 'I'll go to Hell for what I've done. Marry me, Jean. Save me.'

THIRTY EIGHT

Berlin surrendered on the second of May. Since the assassination attempt on him, Hitler had not trusted his generals enough to appoint one of them his successor. Admiral Doenitz, chosen by the Fuhrer himself, was ridiculed in the British press who made much of the fact that the best the Germans could do was appoint an ex-pilot who was afraid of heights, a man who had been incarcerated, in Manchester, in the lunatic asylum before he was sent back to his homeland in 1919.

When the death of Goebbels was announced a day later and news reached the public of the thousands of German soldiers surrendering piecemeal, to the Allies, the people of Kingsley, as in many other towns and cities all over the country, waited on tenterhooks for confirmation of the full and final surrender. The unconditional surrender of the German forces came on the seventh of May, and Victory in Europe was announced the day after.

Bunting appeared along the High Street and all around Old Man's Park for the party being planned for May ninth. Trestle tables and benches covered the walkways around the centre of the town and throughout the streets. Every window and doorway of every shop and house boasted the red white and blue of the Union Jack. Trolleys and motor buses festooned with fluttering flags paraded the streets displaying their joyful message and everywhere people greeted each other with smiles and jokes and happy congratulations that they'd come through the worst time in history and would live to see their families back together again.

Hilda Pozyzcka never saw the celebrations for the end of the war in Europe. At half past six on the morning of May ninth she was delivered of a baby girl but did not live to see her.

◆

It didn't matter to crowds partying all over Kingsley, that it was raining. Nothing could dampen their exuberance as they danced the conga around the memorial in Old Man's Park. No amount of drizzle could spoil their enthusiasm for the day of celebration, paper hats and high spirits. It was of no consequence there were not enough male dance partners to go around. The women shared old men and boys between them: their own menfolk would be home soon. The war in Europe was over and it could not be long, surely, before the rest of the world was at peace.

Music played loudly on wireless sets fixed outside and everywhere joyful hordes joined in with their own accompaniments: beating pots and pans and clicking spoons together. Linking arms and high-kicking along the streets in time to the music, waves of people surged forward in an ocean of goodwill and happiness.

Behind closed doors and curtained windows George Pozyzcka sat in the dark of the shaded rooms of his empty house with his hands over his ears attempting to block out the noise of street parties outside. He'd sent Jean away from him. He couldn't bear to look at her tear-stained face or listen to her racking sobs. He sat, stock-still, in the kitchen, staring at the empty fire grate and going over in his head all that had happened.

There was loathing in his heart. Try as he might to quench the flames of smouldering hatred that burned into him, all his attempts at rational thought were consumed by the heat of the revulsion he felt for the Thompson family. They were all liars. All of them had treated him like a fool. He'd loved and supported his wife and Jean, provided for them, talked with pride about them, boasted of their successes, shared their joys and sadnesses, but this is how they'd repaid him. They did not respect him enough to tell him the truth.

He would never have learned the whole truth if Hilda had lived. She would have continued to keep it from him and Jean would have helped her do it. There was a sickness in their family, he decided, and the vile mouthings of Mary and Charlie Thompson outside the hospital, were proof of it. They did not know how to behave. They did not know how to treat people properly. They could not see he needed time to mourn his wife, that he should have been treated with the respect due to the head of his own small family.

Outside on the hospital pavement they tore at each other in front of him and Jean. They snarled and spat like animals. At first he thought it was regret at their estrangement of their own daughter, Hilda, which brought about the savagery between them. That, he could have understood. It was easier to see how they'd want to blame one another for cutting themselves off from their own flesh and blood. But it was when Jean, speaking with such ferocity it might have been his dead wife's voice he was hearing, demanded they remove themselves from her sight, that the full picture had been revealed to him.

Mary and Charlie Thompson turned on her. They shifted the target of their malice away from one another to Jean: Jean who he'd only recently accepted as Hilda's daughter, not her younger sister as the Thompsons had always led him to believe; Jean who he'd cared for; Jean who had made him proud; Jean who'd made him weep with sorrow when she'd been abused; Jean who had just lost her real mother, his Hilda, lying dead and cold in the mortuary while those two inhuman monsters raved like wild beasts.

He'd tried to defend her from their ravings. He stood with her against them as they spewed their vicious attack and when it was all over Mary Thompson's departing words as she twisted her vile head to fix her stare on Jean, vibrated through his brain and he began to understand.

'She's bad luck, that one, you stupid Polack. How could she ever be anything else?' And pointing directly at her she had added, 'Go on then, Miss High and Mighty. Tell him who your father is.'

Jean had stood her ground and refused.

'You tell 'im then, Charlie. Fancied something a bit younger than your wife, didn't you, Charlie? Thought you'd 'ave yer daughter instead, eh? Should have gone to prison for what you did, Charlie Thompson, you dirty bastard.'

Charlie Thompson was in no fit state to retaliate against his wife. The news of Hilda's death had come when he was already inebriated. He raised his hand to bring down a blow on her loud mouth but he overbalanced and stumbled on the edge of the pavement. He sat in the gutter and began to sob like a child.

'Go on, cry your eyes out,' Mary jeered at him. 'You'll piss yerself less.'

In disgust, George turned his back on them and walked home.

His baby daughter lay in the intensive care unit, struggling for her own life. His wife lay dead in the mortuary. His life lay in tatters around him and he could see no future he would want to be part of.

◆

Jean was distraught. George had dismissed her from the house and had glared at her as though he never wanted to see her again.

'He's in great pain,' Godfrey consoled. 'He doesn't know what he's saying. He doesn't mean it. Just wait and see, dear. He just needs time to be by himself for a while.'

Jean took the drink Godfrey offered her but found she was unable to swallow. She felt as if her heart would burst with the weight of sorrow buried within her. A noisy crowd of revellers danced through the arcade below Godfrey's apartment and he held her close to him as her anguish erupted into a howling scream of pure misery.

◆

Mary Thompson attended Hilda's funeral by herself. Jean saw her standing at the back of the small chapel. Jean turned her head away. When she looked again, Mary had gone.

At the end of the service the coffin was wheeled to its final resting place on a windy hillside overlooking the river valley and town below. Beyond the churchyard the ground rose into the full swell of the Pennine landscape and, above the tree line, moors stretched into the distance where they met a bright spring sky.

'She always loved the countryside,' George muttered to himself. 'Always wanted to be outside. This is just the kind of day she liked best,' he said as clouds scudded across the sky.

Jean approached him. 'George, I want to come home now,' she said quietly.

He looked at her. There was no warmth in his eyes and she feared his reply.

'I can't do it,' he said to her.

'What can't you do, George?' she asked him.

'I can't go on.'

He started to move away from her, past the small gathering of friends toward the cemetery gates. She ran after him.

'George,' she called. 'Wait! Please!'

She caught up with him and held onto his arm.

'George, you've got to keep going. You've got a little girl now. She needs you.'

'I can't do it,' he said again. 'Not by myself.'

'I'll help you, George,' she told him. 'I'll be there to help. We'll manage.'

'I don't want your help,' he said flatly. 'I don't want anybody's help. I don't want you and I don't want the baby. I don't want any part of this life of lies.'

He pulled his arm away from her and increased his pace to get away. She let him go.

PART FOUR

THIRTY NINE

DECEMBER 2009

Deborah is waiting for me in the kitchen when I return to the cottage. She wears an apologetic smile and her fingers fiddle nervously with her collar.

'I don't know what to say,' she tells me. 'I am so sorry, Audrey.'

I tell her there's really no need to apologise for her husband's behaviour.

'He's shown himself for what he truly is,' I say.

'Yes,' she agrees. 'Maybe now you can understand how I feel.'

I hang up my coat and we sit together at the kitchen table wondering where to begin. We both sense there is much the other wants to say. I take out the brandy bottle and two glasses. It's going to be a long night.

♦

The year after we first met, Jim Freeman returned to England as assistant coach to his former team and came looking for me. I'd fallen out with the idea of going to university and had taken a job at one of the banks along High Street. I still saw Rita from time to time and we went to the concert venues we'd frequented as schoolgirls. Sometimes one or the other of us might have a boyfriend, but there was nobody I was serious about.

Yet everything was changing. Rita's brother, Paul, had left home and was playing rugby regularly in Castleford. Barry had married a pretty blonde girl. They had a baby and I'd catch sight of them occasionally doing their shopping together or driving through the town. He didn't look half so sexy behind the wheel of a Hillman Imp.

I met Rita by the bus station one day where we planned to buy tickets for Freddie and the Dreamers at the booking office.

'Don't stay out too late. It's not good for you,' a voice said behind me. I spun around to see Jim grinning at me.

'Bugger me,' Rita swore. 'If it isn't old *Best Legs*. Where are the rest of the lads?' she asked peering over his shoulder.

'Training,' he replied. 'Down at the field. So, what're you doing tonight, girls?' he asked with a wink.

When the team went home to Australia, Jim stayed behind, found lodgings, a clandestine job and courted me in earnest. My Christmas present was the engagement ring we chose together: a solitaire diamond on a plain gold band. We married shortly after my nineteenth birthday.

'You were very young,' Deborah says.

'I didn't feel very young, somehow. I felt ready for marriage. Girls did, then,' I say.

'Show me your wedding photos,' Deborah asks. 'Have you got them here with you?'

'They're in that box behind the sofa,' I tell her. 'I had a box of personal stuff delivered out of storage the other day. I haven't got around to putting them away properly yet.'

We take the brandy with us into the sitting room and make ourselves comfortable. Deborah settles in. She looks almost excited at the prospect of viewing pictures of me when I was nineteen.

'I know what you're up to,' I say. 'You just want to have a good laugh.'

We're both amused by the serious poses and dreadful fashions of the time. Most female guests sport hemlines far too short to be suitable for a wedding. Mum has got it right, though. I remember she made her outfit herself. She always liked to wear what she called *costumes*, skirt suits with fitted jackets.

'Look at the hairstyles,' Deborah smiles.

'And the earrings,' I add.

The photographs are all monochrome. I think the professional photographer hired for the day said black and white wedding pictures were more desirable than colour, more dignified.

Our honeymoon was delayed for a while. I wanted us to have a last holiday together in Mum's favourite place, so we spent a week at the holiday camp before leaving for Australia.

We sailed on the *Oriana*, the fastest ship of the Orient line which became P&O. It took twenty one days to reach Australia instead of the usual month; the voyage itself was the honeymoon.

There were parties and dances, games on the decks and as we were Pollywogs, never having sailed over the Equator before, we were subject to a fun initiation ceremony, presided over by King Neptune himself who gave us our certificates proclaiming our seamanship.

Jim had been patient about the first night. Sharing a holiday chalet with your new bride's parents is not the ideal place to discover each other as man and wife. Jim asked me if I'd mind waiting. I was grateful for that. The creaky beds and thin walls of chalet bedrooms would have been an embarrassment. So we waited for the first night of the journey from Southampton.

He was gentle and kind. He had the experience of an older man and I trusted him completely. I wasn't sure what I was supposed to do and it's possible I disappointed him. Although I loved him and wanted to be his wife there was no sensation of waves crashing on the beach or romantic violins in the background. I wasn't aware of what an orgasm was supposed to feel like and when Jim asked me if I'd enjoyed him, I told him I had. It was true. It was enjoyable. I liked the closeness and warmth. I felt safe with his big strong arms around me and his legs entwined with mine. But I didn't find myself gasping like he was, nor shuddering and shaking. His face went red, I remember, and he did something queer with his eyes. I wanted to laugh.

When we decided to start a family and there was purpose to our lovemaking, it seemed al the closeness and warmth had gone out of it. It became mechanical, as boring as reading a technical manual, and after Malcolm arrived, the frequency diminished. Jim said he didn't want any more children. By the time he was nearly fifty he'd pretty much lost interest altogether.

Deborah continues looking through the album.

'Who is this?' she asks, pointing out one of the men in the photographs.

I lean over her shoulder to get a better view.

'That's Uncle Godfrey,' I tell her. 'I don't think he was my real uncle, just a family friend. He lived with Mum for a while after she moved here to Norfolk.'

'Oh, yes?' Deborah is putting two and two together and coming up with the wrong answer.

'No. It wasn't anything like that,' I reply. 'They'd been friends all through the war and when he lost his other half he had nowhere to go. I don't remember as much about his partner. He was a kind man. Mother used to say he was the life and soul of the party but I never saw him like that. His name was Richard.'

'They were a gay couple?'

'Yes. Been together forever. Mother thought the world of both of them.'

'You see, my Stephen could have that same sort of relationship with his partner, couldn't he? I hope he does.'

'It must have been very difficult for homosexual men to live their lives as they wished in those days. It was actually illegal, wasn't it?' I say.

'Some things change and others stay the same,' Deborah sighs. 'You can change the law faster than you can change some people's attitudes.'

I can tell she's thinking about Philip.

'Have you decided what you're going to do next?' I ask.

'I've been thinking about it since you went out,' she tells me, shaking her head and sighing.

'Oh, did I disturb you? I thought you were asleep.'

'No you didn't disturb me, Audrey. I was awake. I was just lying there with my eyes closed trying to make my mind up what to do.'

'And?' I venture.

'I don't want to go back.'

'Don't then. You're welcome to stay here for as long as you need to.'

'But it's Christmas,' she says. 'Doesn't that make me a selfish horrible person?'

'What would happen if you went back tomorrow?'

'It would be ghastly. He'd pick up where he was made to leave off today, *and* pile on extra agonies for the further slights he believes he's suffered. He'd think he was back in control of the situation and I'd have to tell him that wasn't the case, that I intended to leave after Christmas. Can you imagine how impossible that would be, living together with that knowledge hanging over us? No, if I went back it would be cruel for both of us; I would only be delaying, drawing out the pain. There seems no point in putting off what I intend to do anyway.'

'I agree with you,' I tell her.

Deborah leans back in her chair and looks puzzled.

'Audrey?' she asks me. 'Why didn't you go back to Yorkshire? Didn't you want to see your old home again?'

'I did go back,' I tell her. 'My last trip to England to see my mother was in 1987. Mum flew out to us for visits after that year. Malcolm was twelve then and didn't want to come with me so stayed at home with his dad. Jim couldn't take time off work anyway. While I was here I made the trip back to my home town.'

'Had it changed much?'

'Oh, how it had changed. I didn't recognise the place.'

I tell Deborah about the sweeping changes which had removed almost all the old streets in the town. The bus station, which had been the cause of the tearing down of the old Hippodrome theatre, had itself made way for a glass and concrete covered shopping area. The bank where I used to work was now a wine bar and the hairdresser's where I had a Saturday job had been torn down completely. The old open market, where stallholders called out their wares from under their tarpaulins, standing amongst trodden in cabbage leaves and squashed tomatoes had been replaced by a sterile-looking purpose-built concrete block, and the whole of the town centre had been pedestrianised.

The old Girls' Grammar School, a beautiful old stone building in a classical style with an elegant portico, was now a much bigger comprehensive and had sprouted concrete wings at each side and in the playing fields there were rows of portakabins, to house extra classes I supposed, which looked no better than the tin houses of the 1950's.

Where once Kingsley had the ambience of a Northern market town surrounded by open countryside with views up to the moors over Ilkley, it had now grown so much that one town ran straight into another. Open spaces had disappeared and it was *so busy*. I was used to busy. I lived in Sydney, after all, but Kingsley couldn't cope with all that extra traffic. There was permanent gridlock. Pavements were crowded. Stores were choked. There were simply too many people for the size of the place.

I went to the cemetery to visit my father's grave. It was a forlorn place with vandalised headstones and an air of neglect. I walked the pathways looking for other names from my family, but found nothing. I was acutely aware of how little I really knew about my grandparents. Mother never had an easy relationship with her own parents. When I was a child I very rarely saw my grandmother.

My father's parents were very religious apparently and didn't approve of his marrying outside their faith. I didn't see much of them either. But I don't remember feeling lonely as a child, or that I was missing anything by not having contacts with a wider family.

The extended family experience came once Jim and I had arrived in Australia. I met his sister, Chloe and her children. I met Jim's parents for the first time, and his aunts and uncles, cousins and half-cousins. It was overwhelming at first. There were so many of them; I felt I was struggling to fit in with them. They had all the history of their family experience holding them together: shared knowledge of people and places I knew nothing about. I couldn't join in with many of their conversations. It was like being on the sidelines at a Rugby match watching the play but not being part of it.

I began to lose my identity then. That's when I first lost confidence. When Jim's family teased him about why there were no babies yet, making jokes about him needing a striker to score, it didn't help me feel any better about myself. It was ten years before we had Malcolm.

Deborah tells me about her own early married life and the arrival of her children and we compare notes, as it were, in the way women do when we share confidences about each other. We are comfortable in each other's company. I tell her about my meeting with Maria Theresa.

'I thought you said your mother wasn't particularly religious,' she says.

'She wasn't,' I reply. 'Dad came from a Catholic family, but Mum wouldn't have anything to do with it. I don't know why. She never told me but I can remember overhearing arguments between them about it.'

I notice Deborah's glass is empty and offer her more cognac.

'Go on, then,' she says. 'I need knocking out tonight.'

I pour out the brandies and turn on the radio, selecting a classical music channel. A beautiful voice is singing *Casta Diva*, the haunting aria from the opera *Norma*.

'Oh, turn that up, please,' Deborah asks me, and sits silently enraptured by the exquisite soprano. 'Isn't she fantastic?'

'Who?'

'She's absolutely my favourite,' Deborah continues, still in a trance.

'Who is?' I ask again.

'Sophia Polanski,' she tells me. 'I adore her voice. Just adore it.'

'I can see that,' I say with a smile. 'She's made you go quite peculiar.'

'I would *love* to go and see her perform. I've tried to get tickets but you've got to be quick off the mark. Wherever she's appearing is a sell-out in the first hour. Haven't you heard her before, Audrey?'

I have to admit I haven't heard Deborah's favourite soprano before, but I agree her voice is special.

'Came from Canada, I believe,' she says, 'when she was quite young. There was an article about her in one of the Sunday supplements some time ago. She lost her parents when she was sixteen and her grandfather brought her and her younger brother to England to study her music. When her career took off, she came to live in Norfolk, too. You live in a very desirable part of the country, Audrey. Didn't you know? It's become very popular with arty types. They call it the new Cornwall. Well, that's what it said in the article, anyway. Of course, I don't know *exactly* where she lives. If I did, I'd be hanging around street corners hoping to catch a glimpse.'

'I didn't know you were such a fan of opera,' I say.

'Oh, yes. It's one of those things that's been sitting on the back burner waiting for me to turn up the flame, you know?'

Yes, I do know. That's how I feel about my modelling. I am keen; I am enthusiastic. I joke about it being only a hobby, but I'd be delighted if it turned into more than that.

'I interrupted you,' Deborah says. 'You were telling me about the Priory.'

I tell her about my encounter with Maria Theresa and how I'd always felt there'd been some mystery connecting John Starling and my mother. I mention the bench in the garden.

'Go on,' she encourages me. 'What did it say on the plaque?'

'I think it solves the mystery,' I say.

In memory of Jean Starling.

'What else could it mean? Mum must have married John.'

'Or his wife could have been called Jean as well as your mum,' Deborah suggests.

'No, that would be too much of a coincidence. It's what he wants to tell me tomorrow.'

I outline what John said to me after Deborah had gone upstairs, how he was bringing Alex to a family meeting and I tell her the strange way Alison had said *it's time*.

'I think he's been trying to tell me before but couldn't find the right opportunity.'

'But why would it need to be kept secret?' Deborah asks me.

'I don't know. Maybe they were afraid I'd think they were being silly, marrying so late in life. Maybe they thought I wouldn't approve. I don't know. I'll find out tomorrow.'

We both feel hungry and move back into the kitchen to rustle up a snack. I check my emails. There's a message from Madeleine. She's back in Wales with her parents and just wants to let me know that she's fine. She says she'll keep in touch.

We watch television news: more High Street names are due to close their doors for the last time. Sales prices are slashed even further. More redundancies are announced as the economic plight of the country decimates the business sector. Interest rates are cut to levels never before imagined. Good news if you're in debt, but not so good if you're a saver.

The news washes over me. I can't connect with it. I'm out of kilter with the world. I don't feel part of what's happening and neither does Deborah. Even though the financial outcome of the weak pound is bound to affect us in the end, we both have other things at the forefront of our planning.

FORTY

I can't sleep. Quietly, I put on my dressing gown and creep downstairs. The cognac has worked for Deborah but not for me. I make myself a hot drink and after patting the top of the Shrek head, for which I receive the usual baleful stare in return, I take myself off into the sitting room and browse my photograph albums.

When you're a child, time seems to take forever. When you are waiting for something it can't come quickly enough. Adults tell you for them, time passes too quickly: there's never enough of it to do all that must be done. But if you're looking forward to Christmas, or your birthday, when you are very young, you're impatient and the days stretch out endlessly between you and your desired event. You wonder how you will be able to get through all that waiting.

The night before we set off on our annual holiday, Mum always pinned up an old piece of black cloth on my bedroom window. She told me it was left over from the blackout during the war and it would help me get to sleep on those nights in July and August when light lingers and children want to go on playing. I didn't much care for the black cloth: it smelled musty. But while I didn't like the cloth itself, I loved the excitement heralded by its retrieval from the cellar.

I'd been waiting for years, it seemed to me at that time, for the arrival of the holidays, but once the black cloth made its appearance I knew the big day was only one more sleep away. I counted my waiting in sleeps, then, rather than in days, and I would cross off the sleeps on the calendar with growing anticipation of the pleasure of the journey and the thrill of arrival at our destination.

As I gaze at old snaps of members of my family, I'm aware that I too have reached the place where time passes all too quickly. These photographs are evidence: brief snapshots of people, places and events, frozen forever like little islands in the great rushing river of life which sweeps us along in its current towards our journey's end to deposit us, finally, in an ocean of souls.

Each photograph takes me into the past and reminds me of so much more than it immediately portrays. I can see the black cloth in my mind's eye as clearly as if I had a photograph of that, too. I turn the page.

Here I am in a Snow White fancy dress costume, designed by Uncle Godfrey and sewn by my mother, for which I won the fancy dress competition for under tens that year on holiday. I remember sitting with Uncle Godfrey on his sofa while he showed me his design book. There were beautifully illustrated pages of exotic Flapper girls, draped in sweeping cloaks, holding out their long elegant arms like *Erté* fashion plates. Some wore ornamental headdresses with feathers or rows of beads hanging over their foreheads, stopping just short of immaculately shaped eyebrows. Their eyes were always downcast with heavy dark eye shadow and impossibly long lashes. I wish I had that book now.

Here's a bonfire night photo of me and mum and dad, sitting around the embers of the fire built in the middle of the courtyard which stood behind our old house before we moved up onto the council estate. I'm wearing an unusual knitted bonnet with a rigid hair-band threaded through the front of it so it sat upon my head like a horseshoe, and sprouting out of the back of the bonnet is a long woollen tassel like a pony's tail.

I remember how that yard used to be strung across with everybody's washing, and how, on wash days, I played a game I'd invented myself where I allowed myself to stand only on the wet patches below the dripping clothes and sheets. As the flagstones dried, the game became more difficult, so that I'd have to leap from wet patch to patch until there was nowhere left to jump to.

Mother worked in one of the wool mills in Kingsley and, once I'd started school, I used to walk down the hill to where she worked and wait for her to finish her shift. I sat on top of a huge basketwork skip or else on an upturned bobbin and watched her work at her machine. Fingers flying, she'd thread the yarn through the eyes and levers, wind it around hooks and tie the ends with an intricate knot, cutting it with the special ring on her finger which housed a murderous blade.

There was always loud music on the radio, and when one of the women's favourites came on they would all join in together, but you could hardly hear them. Their voices were drowned by the noise of machines, hammering and rattling against old, oil-soaked floorboards. It gives me a shiver down my back to this day whenever I hear *Oh, My Papa – to me he was so wonderful*, and the sound of Eddie Calvert's trumpet.

Those lanolin soaked floorboards contributed to the devastating fire in one of the Kingsley mills which killed thirty seven women. I was at primary school when word came that children were not to be released from school at the end of the day until someone arrived to take them home. We didn't know what was happening, or that for some of us there would be no mother to come for us ever again. The women who died were trapped on an upper floor with no means of escape. I had nightmares for weeks after that.

Here's one of a group of children on bicycles in the middle of the street. The tall girl's name was Irene and she had a younger sister, Susan. They lived in the next street in a house with gas lamps. Their landlord hadn't paid for the cost of converting to electricity so through the 1950s they still took a match to light the mantles of their wall fixtures. I can recall the smell and the pop they made as they were lit.

The chubby boy in the cowboy hat dared me to climb up onto the Drill Hall roof. I shinned up the drainpipe and then grew too frightened to get back down again. His father had to climb up after me. My dad was too frail.

Two of the kids on bikes were from the house at the end of the street. Their dad had been demobbed late after he'd stayed on in Germany to assist with reorganisation after the war. When he came home he bought them a television set and sometimes they invited other children from the street to watch *Andy Pandy*. We would gather around the shiny wooden box, patiently waiting for it to warm up and sit glued to the Interlude pictures of a potter's wheel or a white kitten playing on a chair, until the start of *Watch with Mother.* The whole street squeezed into their house, parents and all, to watch the Coronation.

There was a party in the street afterwards and we kids performed a concert for the parents. The girls who had the television did a sketch from Bill and Ben, pretending to be string puppets, chubby John sang *She wears red feathers* and I sang *How Much is that Doggie in the window?*

We were always organising concerts. The adults would bring out their dining chairs into the streets and we'd perform dances and songs or snippets from films we'd seen at the cinema on Saturday morning.

We were all *minors of the ABC* and we knew the song and shouted it out every Saturday morning. Then there'd be the customary line up of birthday boys and girls before the programme could begin: two feature films and an assortment of cartoons.

Many of our childhood games were played outside on the street. It was safe: there were no cars.

All in together girls, this fine weather girls . . .

I can feel the smooth edges of sandstone flags beneath the soles of my shoes. I can hear the droning whirr of skipping ropes as they whizz over my head. I can smell fish and chips on High Street at eleven every Saturday morning when the fryers were turned on and the smell of warming beef dripping coated my tongue. I can taste the sharp tang of malt vinegar on a bag of scraps.

I hear the tinkle of the bell on the sweet shop door down Larksholme Lane where I lived before we moved to the council estate. In my mind's eye I can see shelves stacked with heavy glass jars of *pear drops, Devon violets and cherry lips* and I can see myself running, always running, skipping, chasing, throwing flat stones for hopscotch and chalking designs on the flat top of a wooden spinning top and tying bits of string onto the end of the leather on the whip.

I feel blessed I had such a wonderful childhood: a time of innocent games and healthy outdoor play. I felt safe and secure; I felt loved. I was very happy.

I close the picture albums and put them away. I take out some writing paper and the brochure for booking exhibition space at the gallery in Holt and begin to plan. Deborah is right. I must get on with it; I'm not getting any younger.

Time is speeding up and if I don't make efforts it will be too late. I'm lucky only my hips ache. My general health is good: I can see perfectly well with my off- the- shelf reading glasses and I still have full use of my hands. And, apart from drifting off into my reminiscences, I still have my brain.

Tomorrow John Starling is going to come and tell me what I have already worked out for myself.

FORTY ONE

SNAPSHOTS 1945-1965

When one bright Friday morning in October, Godfrey Jardeen received a typewritten envelope postmarked Australia, he hardly dared hope the message it contained would be good news. He propped it up against the mantel clock and throughout the day kept glancing at it as the hours passed by and evening drew nearer.

He prepared the tea time meal for little Audrey. She loved mashed potato and carrot in tasty gravy. He popped his head around the door of the spare bedroom he'd converted into a nursery for the little girl. She was still asleep amid quilts and covers and frills of a bright array of pink florals and gingham. Jean would be arriving soon to take the child home and he planned to open the letter then, when he wouldn't feel so alone.

◆

Richard Mancini and Bob the Oz had wondered what was going to happen. Within days after the Japanese surrender following the atomic bombs on Hiroshima and Nagasaki in August 1945, thousands of leaflets addressed to *All Allied Prisoners of War* fluttered from the sky above Changi.

Like confetti, papers twirled and twisted, dancing through the air in a mesmerising silent swarm and fell at the feet of the dumbfounded soldiers. The message read:

The Japanese forces have surrendered unconditionally and the war is over.

Supplies would be delivered to them as soon as possible and arrangements were being made to get them out, but owing to the distances involved it may be some time before this could be achieved.

Stunned, the men eyed each other, at first suspecting some trick, some mischief. It was too much to hope for, wasn't it?

Could this really mean they were going to be saved? They waited for somebody to say something.

'Bloody Hell, Dicky boy,' Bob the Oz grinned, indicating their pile of wooden prosthetics. 'What are we going to do with all these spare legs?'

Richard grinned back. They had made it. They were sick but they'd made it. They looked like bloody skeletons, but they had made it. He couldn't speak. His mouth was dry with shock.

'Don't go all girly on me now, Dicky,' Bob said, taking the leaflet from him. 'Give it here, you big girl. I'll read it.'

A small crowd gathered around them, tense, suspicious, waiting for the rest of the information from the air drop.

'Are you ready boys?' Bob began. 'Here goes.

You will help us and yourselves if you act as follows:
(1) Stay in your camp until you get further orders from us.

Ah, and I was planning on a trip to Bermuda,' he joked, and the men shuffled and began to relax.

'Keep going, Bob,' one of them called out. 'We're all ears.'

Bob continued.

'Right then, next point.

(2) Start preparing nominal rolls of personnel giving fullest particulars.

That's easy, mate. Jimmy here likes two eggs with his rashers and Steve prefers redheads. I'm hung like a bull and . . .'

The men eased into their positions in the circle around Richard and Bob. Some dropped to the ground and sat cross-legged, looking up at Bob as he read from the heaven-sent paper of their salvation, hanging on his every word.

'You'll like this one.

(3) List your most urgent necessities. Are you kidding? A redhead for Steve. . .

'A bath and some soap,' a thin voice shouted from the back.
'A bed with proper sheets,' another hoarse voice added.
'Flea powder.'
'DDT'

The murmur grew steadily into a buzz of conversation. They fastened on each new suggestion, arguing, disputing, feverishly exchanging their own wish-lists of preferred needs, but they were all agreed on one main thing: they wanted food. They desperately needed real food, and for the first time in years they allowed themselves to talk openly about it. They permitted the forbidden words and dreams of man size portions of steak; chicken legs with crispy skin; pork chops; mashed potato piled high with sausages. Bob interrupted their day-dreaming.

'Fellas,' he shouted. 'Hang on a mo! You all better listen to this:

> *(4) If you have been starved or underfed for long periods DO NOT eat large quantities of solid food, fruit or vegetables at first. It is dangerous for you to do so. . .'*

'Just give me the chance!' one cried.

'Nah, listen,' Bob replied. 'We didn't get through this far to go and do ourselves in at the last minute. We have to be careful, it says here. We have to take it steady, mate, and have small quantities. If the locals bring in food gifts, we have to make sure we cook it thoroughly, otherwise we'll be back on the shitter again.'

Bob handed over the leaflet and it passed from man to man as each of them absorbed the full implications of the news.

'Jesus, Dicky boy,' Bob whistled through his teeth. 'We really made it!'

Two weeks later they were on a transport ship and Richard slept like a baby for most of the journey.

◆

Jean Thompson finished cleaning her machine. With a small hand brush she swept between sections of the metal monster that took thread from enormous cones at the base of each and passed it through eyes and catches that twisted the yarn and wound it into balls of knitting wool. She had to stand on tiptoe to reach the top of the machine and she worked her way along, sweeping in downward strokes across the length of it which covered almost the whole width of the room. Stray pieces of lint and fluff could clog the machine and would hold up next day's production. Wages were paid by piece work. Cleaning your own machine properly was an important task at the end of each day, if you wanted to earn above minimum rate.

The overlooker, Duncan Bradley, called after her as he saw her going out into the mill yard.

'Finished first again, Jean?' he commented.

'Yes, and it's all done properly,' she retaliated. 'Got any complaints?' she added.

'I didn't mean anything wrong,' he said. 'I was only saying ...'

'And?' she asked, standing with her hand on her hip.

She had him on the back foot. 'See you on Monday, then,' he said.

He watched her walk across the mill yard and cursed himself for his awkwardness. She was a prize, was Jean Thompson. He would have given anything for her to smile kindly at him and give him the chance with her he so desperately wanted. He knew she was fixed up, sort of. He realised she had a man at home, sort of. But why she would settle for what she'd got was beyond him. He would have given her so much more.

He wasn't planning on staying as an overlooker at the mill forever. He had qualifications; he had a brain. And as soon as he was able, he would snatch the first opportunity that came his way to use his experience in engineering to open doors to something better than Kingsley could afford him.

He'd be in a position to give a smart woman like Jean Thompson what she was made for: a proper house of her own with a garden; a husband who could take her out to dinner dances and the theatre; buy her nice clothes and jewellery; one day a car of her own maybe. He had the brains all right, but he didn't have the nous. His lack of social skills tied him in knots. He didn't know how to talk to her. He would even have been prepared to take on the child, her sister's child who she was caring for till the real father returned.

Maltese Maria watched enviously from behind her own machine. She saw how Duncan felt about Jean Thompson. She knew he wanted her and behind her jealous eyes she began to formulate a plan to catch him for herself.

◆

Jean called in at the pork butcher on her way through town. Rationing was still in place but Godfrey was coming round for Sunday lunch and they'd pooled their coupons again. He was making the dessert, a suet pudding with a base of bilberry jam he'd made himself.

She stuffed the pork chops into her shopping bag and set out toward the arcade where Godfrey would be waiting with little Audrey. She was five months old now and so cute. Her little dimpled cheeks grew rounder with her wide gummy grin and her bright blue eyes lit up with joy.

George was a fool. He didn't know what he was missing. His adorable daughter charmed everyone who saw her and Jean loved her fiercely. She dreaded the day that George might return to claim her and take Audrey away with him.

But she would put up a fight. She wouldn't let Audrey go easily. George would have to prove he was her father and she'd made certain he'd find that difficult. It had been an easy matter to register the child as her own. In the days immediately after the end of the war, everybody was in such high spirits. The whole town had partied for days. She'd counted on there being a relaxation of rules. Nobody checked what she and her accomplice told the registrar.

Ronnie Logan was available to make himself useful. She knew she'd be able to get him to do anything for her and she'd persuaded him to pose as Audrey's father. They presented themselves as a happy young married couple. The registrar watched, with pity, as Ronnie struggled on his crutches to manoeuvre himself through the doorway and wished the pair of them all the best wishes in the world for their future together. Audrey became Audrey Logan.

Godfrey was playing peek-a-boo with the baby when Jean let herself into the apartment over the shop. The child gurgled and held out her arms when she saw her mother.

'I see you,' Jean sang to her. ' Are you playing with Uncle Godfrey? You clever girl.' And she went to hold her and cover her with kisses.

'Everything all right?' she asked Godfrey. 'Did she eat all her dinner?'

'She's an angel, dear,' Godfrey replied. 'Just a perfect angel.'

He went to the mantelpiece and held up the letter.

'This came today, Jean. Would you do the honours, dear?'

Jean's stomach turned over. With shaking hands she tore open the envelope and began to read. Godfrey sat, with his head in his hands, fearing the worst and not daring to look up.

Jean screamed and frightened the baby. She hopped around the room with the child in her arms, trying to comfort the baby and relate the letter's message at the same time.

'Oh, baby,' she cooed, 'It's all right. There, there. Naughty mummy. It's going to be all right, Godfrey. He's coming home.'

Godfrey leapt up from the sofa and took the letter in his trembling fingers. He stood like a statue, reading with a dreamy expression, then flopped back onto the sofa and composed himself, while Jean calmed little Audrey and cuddled her closely. Godfrey took a deep breath and began to read aloud.

'He's been in Australia,' he said.

'Yes. In the hospital. Is he better now?'

'Better than he was, he says, and. . . . what's the date today? My God, Jean. He'll be on his way so soon. How long does it take to sail from there?'

. . . I can't tell you how much it means to me, to know that I will be with you soon, Richard wrote, *I am so lucky to have you to come home to. My heart is bursting with joy. Tell Jean I have missed her too and can't wait until we are all together again. You are my family; you are my life. . . .*

Godfrey wiped his eyes.

'Wait till he finds out he's an uncle as well,' Jean laughed.

'He'll love it,' Godfrey said. 'Just as much as I do.'

◆

Ronnie was waiting for her when she returned with baby Audrey in the borrowed Silver Cross pram. Jean wheeled the pram into the front room and parked it alongside George's gramophone. Audrey bounced up and down with her arms outstretched, hoping to be lifted out soon.

'Not yet, sweetheart,' Jean told her. 'Mummy's got some things to do first. Ronnie!' she called. 'Could you come and sit here with her for a minute. Can you manage?'

Stiffly, Ronnie got up from his seat and shuffled past the cellar head. Jean watched him negotiate the doorway and carefully lift his feet over the rug.

'You're walking better,' she complimented him.

He smiled. He hadn't been sitting, waiting all day for Jean. He'd been exercising in the yard.

'I did twenty laps this morning and another twenty this afternoon.'

'You mustn't do too much,' she answered. 'You know what the doctor told you.'

She handed him a couple of baby toys and went back into the kitchen. Ronnie perched himself on the upholstered arm of one of the chairs in the front room and leaned over the side of the high pram, jiggling the toys.

'She's got two babies, fat face,' he told the baby. 'You and me both. We're both her babies.'

Ronnie knew it was going to take some time before Jean would be able to see him as anything other than an invalid. He wasn't stupid; he knew the real reason why Jean had accepted him. But if his idea worked, and the doctors were right about the success of his treatment she would eventually see the change in him. He planned to exercise and build up his strength every day. When the day dawned that he felt like a real man again he would win her affection. He knew he didn't have it yet.

◆

Thomas and Sylvia Logan called at the house on the lane to see their son one day while Jean was out at work and little Audrey was with her uncle Godfrey. They'd tried the front door without success and attempted to find the right house from the back. Elsie saw the two strangers as they appeared at the top of the passageway and did the neighbourly thing.

'Can I help you?' she asked them.

Sylvia turned her head and saw the diminutive elderly woman stooping over forwards from her neck so that she had to roll her eyes upwards in order to see them. The strange creature's tattered, children's clothing was quite distasteful. Sylvia didn't know how to deal with such types. She deferred to her husband.

'Thomas?' she whispered in his ear.

He cleared his throat. 'Yes, thank you,' he said. 'We're looking for our son, Ronnie Logan.'

'Ronnie?' Elsie asked. 'You're in the right place then, love. That's it there, the green door.' She hovered on her own doorstep to see them gain admittance.

'All right, love?' she called out to Ronnie when she saw him appear in his doorway. She retreated inside at his nod.

His parents seated themselves at the dining table in the back kitchen and he noticed how embarrassed they both looked.

'Ronnie,' his father began. 'We haven't seen much of you since . .'

'I can't get about too well,' he replied quickly, indicating his legs and crutches.

'No, of course,' Thomas admitted. 'And I'm sorry we've not been here to see you before now. That's why we're here today, Ronnie, to put things right between us. We don't want to be kept out of your life, son.'

Ronnie looked at his mother. He knew she'd have something to add.

'You haven't been to church, Ronnie. Father Connolly has been asking about you,' she said.

'Like I said,' Ronnie reiterated. 'I don't get about too well.'

'Dad will come and fetch you in the car. Won't you Thomas? And it would be quite all right if you were to bring the baby as well.'

There, it was out. This is what they have come for, Ronnie thought. They wanted to quiz him about the baby. He looked at the clock and wondered how long it would take them to get down to the real things on their minds.

Before five more minutes had passed they'd reached the root of their enquiries.

'Ronnie,' his father ventured. 'I'm sure she's a bonny little baby and you may well have feelings for her by now.'

'She is and I do,' Ronnie interrupted.

'But what you and Jean have done is quite wrong, you know. You know that, don't you?'

Ronnie said nothing.

'You can't just take on another man's child,' his mother said. 'You have to think about your own position here, your own future.'

He glared at his mother.

'They *are* my future,' he said.

'Ronnie, listen to me,' his father implored. 'One day George will come back for his child. He isn't a bad man, and I can only think that he's been ill and troubled beyond what I could ever imagine, for him to do what he's done and abandon his daughter. He'll come to his senses one day and return for her.'

'We'll deal with that when we have to,' Ronnie said.

'At least come back to the church, Ronnie,' his mother begged.

'I don't know about that,' he told her. 'God has a lot of explaining to do to me and I don't think He can.'

'Ronnie!'

'Leave him, Sylvia,' Thomas warned. 'I know you've been through hell, son and it's going to take you some time to feel like your old self again. Your mother and I want you to know that we care about you. We want to help support you. And Jean and the baby.' He turned to face his wife. 'I think that's all for today,

Sylvia. I can see Ronnie's got enough to think about. We'll leave it with you then, son.'

He reached across to lay his hand on his son's shoulder.

'No need to get up, Ronnie,' he said. 'We'll see ourselves out.'

✦

Ronnie planned to wait until the following weekend before he mentioned their visit to Jean, but the decision was taken out of his hands the next Saturday morning when Jean opened the door to Father Connolly.

'Yes?' she asked him.

'I was wondering if I might have a word with Ronnie,' Father Connolly said.

'I'll ask him,' she replied and left the priest standing on the doorstep as she went for a word with Ronnie herself.

'Who invited him? What does he want?' she demanded.

'Tell him to come in, Jean, and I'll find out.'

Jean busied herself at the kitchen sink as Ronnie and Father Connolly sat at the table at the back of the room. Audrey was playing happily with her toes and fingers, lying on her back on the rug.

'She is a beautiful child,' the priest said.

'She is, Father,' Ronnie replied.

'And you are her legal guardian, I understand?'

'To all intents and purposes, Father. I'm her dad.'

'Well now, that's a remarkable thing to do. Surely, that's the most Christian attitude to take,' Father Connolly said and brought out his diary from his pocket.

'There'll be enough space in my diary,' he said nonchalantly, 'for a wedding in April. How does that suit?'

Ronnie's heart plummeted. The priest meant well, he knew that, but he had just gone and opened up the very subject with which Ronnie needed to bide his time. Jean wouldn't be rushed. This was the last thing Ronnie wanted to discuss.

'We haven't talked about that yet, Father,' he said respectfully, wishing that Connolly would shut up.

'No time like the present, Ronnie. There's this beautiful little girl's future to take care of. Don't you want to bring her into the eyes of God? Your mother and father are in agreement with me. We're all ready to welcome you into the family of the church.'

Jean had heard enough. She spun on the pair of them.

'This is *my* home,' she addressed the priest, 'and this is not a subject I'm prepared to discuss with you.' She drew on all her training at Mancini Modes to keep control of herself and the situation. She stood with her hands held at her waist, just like Richard Mancini had shown her and she called on the improved vocabulary he had taught her as she delivered her dismissal.

'I am not a member of your church, Father Connolly,' she informed him, 'and I do not recall ever having expressed a wish to be so. As this child's mother, *I* shall be the one to determine her future. That is all I have to say. Good day to you, sir.'

'There was no need to be so rude to him,' Ronnie said as Jean closed the door on the priest.

'You don't think so?' she flashed.

'It's what they do, Jean. They think of all their parishioners as part of their family.'

'Not me and Audrey. We are not in his bloody church family, and we never will be, Ronnie Logan, so you can get that right out of your head.'

She knew she should have stopped there. She was aware that angry words would open up an uncontrollable litany of grievances but she gave in to the rising resentment within her. She couldn't stop herself.

'And what right have your mother and father got to go talking about us and trying to fix things up their way? Planning to get us married off so they don't have to feel ashamed, eh? Got to be able to hold their heads up in front of the congregation?'

Ronnie tried to calm her.

'Jean, don't get upset. Look, the baby can tell something's not right. Look at her little face.'

Jean picked Audrey up from the rug and kissed her. She lowered her voice as she swayed gently with the child in her arms.

'You can go to your confessions Ronnie if you need to,' she whispered, 'and while you're there you can tell that priest to stay away from this door. There's no new church members here for him to join his stupid flock, and there'll be no wedding either.'

She turned her back on him and rocking Audrey gently in her arms began to croon to the child, touching her face and stroking the fine baby hair.

'Knock on the door,' and she tapped on the child's forehead.

'Peep in,' and carefully she lifted an eyelid.

'Lift the latch,' a playful tweak of the nose.

'And walk in,' a touch of the lips.

She touched each ear and said, 'Take a chair, and put it there.'

And taking hold of Audrey's chin she nodded the child's head to the words, 'And how do you do this morning?'

The little girl reached up and grabbed Jean's hair in her chubby fist in a baby attempt to copy the movements.

'Mmm-amma,' she burbled.

FORTY TWO

George woke shivering. He looked at the woman lying next to him, for a moment startled by the fair hair spilling across her pillow. In repose she looked little more than a child, her sweet mouth relaxed and slightly open, her pink tongue slightly visible between her teeth. She slept like a child, carefree, untroubled, her legs stretched out diagonally across the bed with her feet on top of his own, and her flexed arms held, elbows bent, above her head.

She was perfect. Physically and intellectually she was perfect for him. On every subject she had an opinion and enjoyed a hearty exchange of views. She was healthy and robust with a passion for life and living it to the full. She told him of her ambitions, her dreams of moving to Canada and earning her own pilot's licence.

He could hardly believe the way she'd entranced him and the speed it had all happened. There'd been no time to feel any guilt about falling in love so soon after his bereavement. She had accepted all that had gone before in his life. She'd listened to his story without judgement and then, when he'd asked her for her honest opinion of his actions she'd told him the truth as she saw it.

He was enchanted. She spoke, much as a child, without fear of recriminations. Her honesty fell upon him like quenching rain after drought. It nourished him. He fed on her words like the thirsty earth until he felt refreshed. She recharged him. She blew away the arid dust of his bitter thinking and showed him a different, fresh way of living, without lies, without secrets. He could be himself again.

It surprised him she found him exotic. His foreignness excited her. She called him her Polish prince and she begged for stories of his homeland, details of the places he used to know, and when he spoke in the few words of his own language he could remember, she clung to him and gazed, wide-eyed into his face. *She* was proud of *him*.

'We'll make everything all right,' she promised him. 'They'll understand you haven't been well, that you haven't been yourself. We have to do it soon, George, before the baby is much older.'

He knew what she said was true. He regretted his actions. He should never have walked away from his own child like that, but he'd needed time to himself. He needed time away from them, out of the reach of the Thompsons, and away from Jean, too. She had lied to him as much as any of the rest of them and he still couldn't understand why she needed to do that to him. Hadn't he proved himself trustworthy? Hadn't he treated her better than her own filthy excuse for a father?

He'd written to Jean several times. Right from the beginning, after he first left Kingsley, he'd kept in touch and sent money for the child. He hadn't abandoned them entirely. Jean had not replied.

He looked across at the sleeping form next to him in their marriage bed and knew he was the luckiest man alive. It was destiny. It was meant to be. How else could he explain why he'd taken himself to that particular town at that particular time and found her? Why else was there employment, similar to the position he'd held in Kingsley, sitting waiting for him?

Everything had fallen into place so easily because it was written in the stars. He was meant to meet her, fall in love and be married within the month. And now that he had a new wife, as she had so shrewdly pointed out to him, his case for claiming back his daughter was all the stronger now he could offer a proper family background for her.

He kissed his new wife as she began to stir into wakefulness. He smelled her hair and the perfume at the back of her neck, still lingering after last night's celebrations following their registry office marriage. Fleetingly, he thought about Hilda. Briefly, he considered the likelihood that Jean would never be able to accept his re-marriage within six months of Hilda's death.

But what difference did it make? Hilda wouldn't have expected him to continue in grief for the rest of his life. In any case, it was what Destiny had planned for him. He'd grabbed at his chance of happiness with a woman who knew and understood him.

As soon as they could possibly make the arrangements, they would journey to Kingsley to sort out the next step of their lives as man and wife and begin to build their own family.

◆

As each day passed, Ronnie Logan worked on his fitness. He increased the number of laps around the confined circle of the courtyard, first one way and then the other. He helped Jean with the filling and emptying of the wash-boiler in the cellar. He learned how to bring up coal for the fire by lifting the scuttle up to the step in front of him, one at a time, until he'd reached the top.

He hoped for better results, faster, but no matter how hard he tried, he still felt exhausted by the end of the afternoon. Then, before Jean came home with the baby, he sat in an upright position on one of the dining chairs lifting cans of corned beef above his head to strengthen his arms once he'd reached the point where his legs refused to obey him.

And then, there was the cough. He had good days and bad days. Sometimes he was able to get through his self-imposed exercise programme without triggering the barking wheeze but at other times it became almost impossible just to stand in fresh air. Simply breathing in brought on choking spasms that made him feel dizzy and he would be forced to rest.

More than anything he wanted Jean to trust him with the care of little Audrey. He thought if only she could see them together, was able to witness for herself the love and care he wished to give to both of them, she would open her heart to him. She would see they could be happy together and perhaps she'd grow to love him just a little.

◆

Jean had relented over his suggestion they should have a night out to celebrate his birthday. Godfrey came to the house on the Lane to sit in for them.

'It's no trouble at all,' he said. 'In fact, it will make a change. I should only sit at home thinking about you-know-who, now that it's getting so close. Oh, don't get me going. Look at me, Jean. I'm all of a dither just thinking about it.'

He flapped his hands and fingers like an excited child and checked his hair colour in the mirror.

'Why don't we invite Elsie across for a game of cards and supper afterwards? She doesn't have much company. I should think she'd jump at the chance of a bit of a change, too,' Jean suggested in an attempt to calm him down, get him thinking about something else.

Elsie was delighted to be invited in for cards and supper.

'It's very kind of you to think of me,' she said to Jean, and offered to bring her card table with the green baize top. Godfrey offered to cook a celebration birthday supper but Jean said they would bring home fish and chips for everybody. It was what Ronnie preferred. Since his time in Burma he wouldn't look at anything remotely fancy or foreign-looking. Godfrey settled for baking a birthday cake.

They went to the Cavendish. Ronnie managed the short walk across the Lane without his crutches and stepped into the Lounge Bar with his girl on his arm and a smile as wide as the Irish Sea on his face. A small gathering was waiting for his appearance.

'Happy Birthday,' sounded in chorus around him and he swivelled his head from side to side to see who was there.

'Sidecar,' he yelled. 'Bloody hell, mate. I thought you were dead.'

'Nah, not me, Ronnie. I'm still here. Look, here's Irish Mick and Joey and all the lads from the coal yard.'

Ronnie greeted them. 'And Steve?' he asked. 'Where's young Steve?'

'Didn't make it, Ronnie. Got caught at Dieppe.'

'Shit! He was only a kid. Who else?'

'Big Frank from the Black Horse went down at El Alamein. Manchester Johnny, the Flaherty brothers at the Normandy landings.'

'What? Both of them?'

'Aye, lad. A lot's happened since we saw you. But we're glad you're here now. Aren't we lads?'

'Come on over here, Ronnie,' one called out to him. 'We've a lot to catch up on.'

He turned to look at Jean. She smiled and nodded for him to leave her and be with his old pals. Had she arranged all this for him? Had she organised this welcome just for him? She was smiling at him. She wanted him to have a good time. Maybe she did care a little, after all.

Maria Meranti sipped her glass of port and lemon and smiled winsomely at Duncan Bradley. It was no coincidence she'd suggested a drink at the Cavendish. She'd overheard Jean's conversation at work with one of the other women whose son was invited to Ronnie Logan's birthday drink. She'd heard it on the church steps as well when Sylvia Logan was talking with Father Connolly.

She'd persuaded Duncan it would be a nice gesture for them to attend Ronnie's surprise birthday drink. She patted her hair and smiled again at him. When she saw Jean go into the ladies' toilet, she followed her in and waited for her.

'Jean,' she said, her voice sweet as honey. 'It's so nice to see you out and about. I see Ronnie's gone to sit with his friends. Don't be by yourself. Come and join us.'

'I'm not staying long,' Jean said.

Maria's smile broadened.

'Well, come and finish your drink with us, then, Jean. There's no point in being on your own.'

'Hello, Duncan,' Jean said as she took her place, shuffling along the upholstered bench.

'Evening, Jean,' he replied. 'So, it's Ronnie's birthday?'

'That's right.'

'Isn't it wonderful how well he's doing?' Maria said, addressing her comment to Duncan and patting his knee. 'It's amazing what love can do.' And she made a noise like she was cooing over a cute puppy.

'He's doing well, yes,' Jean said. 'He works hard at his exercising.'

'Does he?' Maria asked too loudly. 'I expect that's because he can't wait to walk you down the aisle, Jean. I heard it's sometime next April, isn't it?'

Duncan stared at Maria. His face reddened. He wished Jean his congratulations.

Jean saw Maria's game immediately. It was no secret Maria Meranti fancied Duncan Bradley. The whole of the twisting shed knew Maltese Maria had the hots for him. It was obvious, the way she flirted in front of him, boasting that her legs were as good as Cyd Charise's well-insured pins, and bleaching her hair platinum blonde.

Thank you, Maria, Jean thought, and played along. It was as good a way as any to get Duncan Bradley out of her hair, get him to leave her alone and stop gazing at her with those sorrowful eyes.

'Yes,' she said, 'it's strange the way things work out, isn't it? But we haven't fixed a date yet. We both want Ronnie to be properly better first.'

Maria's face was a picture of joy. She looked as if she couldn't have hoped for a better result. She began to rummage in her handbag and pulled out a leaflet for the Hippodrome theatre, advertising a Christmas pantomime, Jack and the Beanstalk.

'Look,' she said, her voice breathy and excited. 'Isn't it wonderful? Live theatre in the town again? Shall we all go together? We could make up a four and all be friends,' she gushed.

'I don't think so, thank you, Maria,' Jean said. 'Ronnie wouldn't be able to get comfortable in those theatre seats. There's not enough room for him to stretch out his legs, you know.'

'Oh, I'm sorry,' Maria said. 'I didn't think.'

Oh yes you did, Jean thought. *It's all worked out very nicely for you. Clever girl, and thank you again.*

Jean decided to help along Maria's efforts to snare Duncan Bradley.

'But there's nothing to stop you two going together, is there? Come on, Duncan, why don't you invite Maria? You'd have a lovely time.'

She told them it had been lovely talking to them. She thanked them for their company and for coming along to Ronnie's birthday gathering. She said it was terrific to have such lovely friends and excused herself to rejoin Ronnie and his mates at the bar.

On their way out of the Cavendish, later when Ronnie grew tired and was ready to leave, she paused in earshot of Duncan and Maria, who had sidled ever closer to her prey and had spent the rest of the evening posing and pouting for all she was worth, and smiled generously at them.

'Don't they make a lovely couple?' she said to Ronnie as they made for the exit. 'Isn't young love wonderful?'

FORTY THREE

Richard Mancini reached home in December. He was demobbed with a large group of other FEPOWs and ushered through Leeds City railway station with orders not to speak to any of the horde of reporters waiting there. They were marched, en masse, to the prison at Armley in Leeds for the de-briefing session.

Already, attitudes towards him had changed and he felt once more the alienation of his days at boarding school when the other boys had sensed he was different, odd, queer. Obediently, he waited in line for the hand-out parcel of clothes, shuffling along on his thin legs and sore feet with all the other stick-men, shadows of men, a macabre chorus line of barely human marionettes. They gathered up their de-mob suits and trilby hats and turned their faces to the exit where waited home and family and God only knew what kind of a future.

A bundle of rough fabric hacked into a shapeless sewn thing with wide lapels and out of proportion buttons on the double-breasted jacket was pushed in front of him. He looked up into cold eyes and grimaced.

'Come on, feller,' the voice belonging to the eyes urged. 'Pick up yer pack, mate and be on yer way.'

Richard's lip curled in distaste and with chicken-bone fingers indicated the navy blue serge.

'I wouldn't be seen dead in this,' he exclaimed. 'It's so not my colour, darling.'

He wasn't able to mince his way out of the room: he ached too much. But he fixed the cold eyes with a piercing stare of his own and limped away from the British army forever.

◆

Jean had planned to go with Godfrey to meet Richard at the station in Kingsley. She just wanted to welcome him home, she said, then she would beat a hasty retreat and leave them alone for their first night back together again. She'd organised Audrey's day so she'd be having her afternoon sleep when it was time to leave, and Ronnie would be able to manage for a short time by himself.

Ronnie was all smiles. At last he was getting an opportunity to show Jean he could be a good father to his little fat face.

'Now, are you sure?' Jean asked again with one foot out of the door.

'For the third time, yes. You'd better get going. You don't want to miss him.'

'Right then, I'm off.' And she hurried along the passageway between the houses, the sound of her best shoes ringing and echoing on the sandstone paving and walls.

Ronnie switched on the radio and settled back for a quiet half hour. He had slipped into a dose when knocking at the back door roused him. He moved slowly to open it. His legs almost gave way when he saw who was there.

George was at the door, asking for permission to come into the house where once it had been his own name on the rent book. Sandra was with him. Ronnie felt confused. He looked from one to the other. How come they were here together? He gathered himself enough to greet his sister warmly.

'Sandra,' he said. 'You look fabulous. Jesus, when did you get all so grown up and sophisticated? Where have you been? Dad never stops talking about you. How come you're with George? You've just missed Jean, but she won't be long. Come in, come in.'

'You and Jean?' Sandra said.

'It's a long story,' Ronnie told her. He turned his attention to George. 'I don't know what to say to you. I don't think Jean would like it if I let you in when she's not here.'

'I'd like to see my daughter,' George said.

'I can't let you do that. Not without Jean here. You'll have to come back later.'

'Ronnie,' Sandra said quietly. 'We'll come back later if you like.'

'No, I didn't mean you, Sandra. Sit yourself down.'

'Ronnie, I think it's you who should sit down. I've something to tell you.'

✦

Richard couldn't remember walking up the platform and out of the station into the streets of Kingsley. It had all been a blur, he said afterwards, a dizzying blur of people and noise, tears and laughter as families and friends surged forward to greet their loved ones and welcome them home. He had no recollection of the brass band playing ceremonial marches. He couldn't even remember linking arms with Godfrey and Jean and promenading up Cavendish Street. It was as if he had floated there. He'd drifted on a cushion of euphoria to find himself miraculously transported to his own home where, deliciously swathed by the familiarity and comfort of his own favourite things, he finally felt his feet touch the floor.

He couldn't wait to get out of the uniform. Godfrey had laid out Richard's best, paisley silk pyjamas and a new dressing gown he had run up himself from some left over contrasting raw silk saved from Archibald Cutler's daughter's ivory wedding gown.

Jean heard his delighted squeal and kissed Godfrey on the cheek.

'It's time I was off. I love you both,' she said.

'He looks worn out, poor thing,' Godfrey whispered.

'Yes, he does. Don't expect too much from him, too soon.'

'I know, Jean. I know. I shall be very happy just looking after him.'

'Jean!' Richard shouted from the bedroom.

'What?' she shouted back.

'When I'm up to it, we'll have a party. Got to have a ceremonial burning of this bloody scratchy khaki ensemble. See you soon.'

'I'll be off then, Godfrey,' she said and took her leave.

✦

Jean knew something was wrong as soon as she walked into the house. She could smell *Evening in Paris* by Bourgeois, an unmistakable fragrance. In a flash of suspicion she examined the room for signs of subterfuge and imagined Ronnie had arranged to receive his mother while she was out.

'I didn't know your mother wore *Evening in Paris*, Ronnie,' she said. 'Just left, has she?'

'It wasn't her. It was Sandra.'

'Sandra's been here?' she said. 'Why didn't she stay? Is she coming back?'

Ronnie nodded.

'Yes, she's coming back and she's bringing her husband with her.'

'Sandra got married? When?'

'Last week.'

'And she didn't tell anybody beforehand? Oh, that's just like her. Oh, that's Sandra, all over. She just ups and does what she wants. Oh, I can't wait to meet him. Is he nice, Ronnie? Was he in the Navy?'

'You already know him very well, Jean,' Ronnie said, and his eyes were down-turned, his lips stretched thin. She was struck with a shiver of anxiety.

'Who?'

'Sandra married George last week at the Registry Office.'

'What?' Jean howled. 'No, that can't be right. Hilda's been gone barely six months. He wouldn't do that. *She* wouldn't do that. Not Sandra. No, it's not right, Ronnie.'

'I know how you must feel, Jean. But listen . .'

'No, Ronnie,' she wailed, 'I don't . . .'

'Jean, stop it. They're coming back tonight and he wants to see Audrey.'

'*No*,' she screamed.

'Jean,' he yelled at her. 'Listen to me for once, will you? We've got to keep clear heads now. He's coming back tonight and once he sees her, you know as well as I do, he's going to want to take her away.'

'No,' she cried out. 'No, please. No!'

'Jean, if you can't calm down and deal with this properly, you'd be better going out of the way. Now, stop it. Listen to me. I know what to do.'

◆

As they sat in Jean and Ronnie's best room, Sandra tried to defend George.

'He didn't abandon you completely, Jean,' she said. 'He always sent money.'

'And we've been saving it for her,' Ronnie interrupted. 'We haven't touched any of it. One day, she'll need it.'

With a smile, on Ronnie's advice, Jean handed the baby over to George, and right on cue Audrey let out a pitiful wail and twisted her little body holding out her arms for her mother.

'Mmm-a-mma,' she sobbed.

Against her instincts, Jean told George that Audrey would settle in a moment. He only had to be patient a while and she would stop struggling to get away from him.

But the child was afraid of the strange man whose face was too close to hers. Audrey's wails grew louder and began to grow into a screech. She arched her back in her attempt to distance herself from him and screamed with fear. George quickly handed her back to Jean, where she snuggled into her mother's shoulder and gave little gasping shudders as her tears subsided.

'You see how it is, George,' Ronnie explained. 'Audrey is settled here with us. It would be a terrible thing to take her away now.'

He stole a quick glance at Jean.

George's face fell. 'I should not have come like this,' he said. 'Out of blue, out of nowhere. You are right. It is too late. She loves you.'

'George,' Sandra began. 'It doesn't have to end here, sweetheart. To be a part of your daughter's life you must keep coming back, again and again.'

'And get in the way of her happiness? No, Sandra. It is too late.'

He stood up to leave.

'Where will you go?' Jean asked.

'We live in Colchester at the moment,' Sandra told them. 'But, for the future, who knows?'

'Will you send me pictures, Jean?' George asked. 'I will write, always, and let you know where we are. One day, maybe, you will tell her. Tell her that I let her go because I love her.'

His eyes were full of sorrow as he looked around the kitchen where in another life he had been proud to call Hilda his wife.

'I wish that it could have been different,' he said.

'Don't you want any of the things you left behind?' Jean asked him. 'Your records?'

'No. Play them for the child. Teach her about beautiful music and art. Take her to see the theatre. These things are important.'

◆

Sandra comforted him on their return to their hotel room. Her heart was full of love for him, her tragic Polish prince, a man unafraid to show the depth of all his emotions. She wrapped her arms around him and covered him with her kisses, promising they would have a new life of their own, telling him he'd done the right thing. He sobbed and shook with regret. He cried for his little girl, his beautiful child who was afraid of him.

He said he was a failure. He was a terrible father. He had abandoned his only child and he didn't deserve to have her with him. Sandra held him closer. She whispered to him that he'd made a selfless sacrifice and done a wonderful thing for Jean and Ronnie.

'Look how little Audrey has brought them together,' she cajoled. 'Didn't you notice the change in both of them? They really are a partnership now, darling. Their love for the baby has done that for them.' She kissed him and made him look into her eyes.

'I love you, George,' she told him. 'And one day we will have a family of our own. We will never forget little Audrey. She will always be dear to our hearts, and I am so proud of you that you've made my brother so happy.'

He found that he could smile. He looked into her eyes and saw the love she felt for him. He stroked her hair.

'You are right, my love,' he said. 'It is as it should be. These things happen for a purpose.'

◆

In the house on Larksholme Lane, Ronnie held Jean to him.

'You were terrific,' he said. 'You were fantastic.'

'You weren't so bad yourself,' Jean added, and it was a genuine smile of appreciation and admiration she gave him.

Ronnie saw it wasn't the look of love; it was the look of friendship. It would do for now.

FORTY FOUR

Mancini Modes entered its revival throughout the 1950s. Clothes were still rationed and, unless the people of Kingsley were able to get across the Irish Sea to Eire where American imports were freely on sale, they were limited as to what was available.

Godfrey took in overcoats for ladies and gentlemen and unpicked all the seams, turning the fabric, laying out the pieces, and stitching them back together again with the worn side to the inside. He turned collars and cuffs on shirts and blouses. Richard kept fighting off the symptoms of his illness, abdominal pain and frequent visits to the toilet. He worked with hands and fingers so thin they were almost transparent.

They revived the film star status for some of their re-modelled dresses and a new bevy of beauties graced the display behind the curved glass frontage: Marilyn Monroe, Rita Hayworth, Jane Russell.

Jean bought a second-hand treadle sewing machine and, thanks to Godfrey's meticulous training was able to send Audrey out in beautifully made cotton dresses in summer and hard-wearing corduroy for the winter. She made her underwear too, flanelette or recycled silk depending on the season.

Audrey went to infant school when she was four years old. She waved goodbye to her mother on the first day and skipped off, smiling and happy, wondering why some of the other children were making a fuss and bursting into tears. She was a bright child and had already learned how to read even so far as to pick up new words from Ronnie's newspaper, or Uncle Godfrey's recipe books or Elsie's magazines. By the time she was seven years old she had read most of the classics in children's literature and had won prizes in school of more book tokens to add to her growing library: Treasure Island, Robinson Crusoe, The Count of Monte Cristo, Gulliver's Travels, Black Beauty which made her cry and Heidi which made her bored.

In 1953, after Jean had viewed the Queen's coronation on the neighbour's television set, she determined they should have one of their own and the following year the prized possession was delivered to the house on the Lane.

In winter the television lived in the back kitchen where there was a warm fire and the Logans watched *The Grove Family* and *Zoo Quest*, introduced by David Attenborough. Through summer it was removed to the front room where television viewing took place less often.

Ronnie's health and strength had improved such that he had bought himself a bicycle and rented a small allotment alongside the railway line. On fine summer evenings Audrey, balancing on the cross bar of her father's bike, free-wheeled with him down the Lane and over the railway bridge to the small patch of land where Ronnie grew vegetables and kept a few hens. The child thrived on home-made soups, stews and pies, fresh eggs from the allotment and the occasional fresh roast chicken.

Birthday cards and Christmas greetings arrived each year from Canada, from an uncle Audrey had never seen. The monies went straight into her own account at the Yorkshire Penny Bank for her *bottom drawer*. Sometimes there were photographs: the uncle and his pretty wife with a little boy, named Stuart, and pictures of the lady sitting at the cockpit of an airplane, wearing a funny hat with ears.

For Audrey's tenth birthday, in May 1955, Ronnie and Jean set up a party in the courtyard at the back of the houses. All the neighbours and all their children came and ate egg mayonnaise sandwiches, pork pies and jelly and custard. There was fizzy pop for the children and a barrel of beer for the adults and the neighbours talked about another party they remembered where everyone came in fancy dress. Elsie ran inside and brought out the costume she had worn and Audrey put it on. It fitted her perfectly. Her mother got upset and went into the house and her father went in after her, but they never told her what it was about, so she promptly forgot she had seen her mother in tears.

Uncle Godfrey and Uncle Richard stayed back, after the birthday party. She could hear them all talking long after she had gone to bed. The distorted sounds of their conversation lulled her into sleep.

◆

'I've seen a private physician, Jean dear,' Richard told them. 'And I have a name now for this blasted condition. Ronnie, have you ever been given a name for what you came back with?'

'Not that I remember,' he replied. 'I think they just told me it was a tropical disease and I should expect it to be a long time before I felt right again.'

'And you have noticed improvements, haven't you?' Richard asked.

'Yes. But I still have to use the lotion when my skin breaks out and every winter the cough comes back.'

'I think there are two kinds of what we've got Ronnie. By all accounts there are hundreds of us, mostly POWs like myself but others like you who picked it up in Burma. It's called strongyloidiasis. Yes, I know, a bit of a mouthful. The thing is, Ronnie, you have to get the right treatment or else the bloody thing can go on forever.'

'Well, I'm doing what my doctor tells me. What more can I do?' Ronnie asked.

'Pester, Ronnie. Make a nuisance of yourself.' Richard said. 'We've got the National Health Service now. That's what it's there for.'

'It's always the squeaky wheel that gets oiled first,' Godfrey added.

Ronnie laughed.

'I'll take Jean with me next time, then. She knows how to kick up a fuss, make herself heard.'

'Is that a complaint or a compliment?' she asked. Her mouth was puckered as though she was annoyed, but her eyes shone with amusement.

◆

The deep-seated pain in Charlie Thompson's back forced him to take to his bed. He couldn't pinpoint exactly where the pain began and where it ended. It burned all the way through him and made him feel sick. He was an irritable patient, cantankerous and ill-tempered and he roared insults at his wife Mary as she attempted to make him more comfortable.

'Would you like me to fetch the doctor?' she asked him.

'No, I bloody wouldn't,' he bellowed. 'I'll be right in a bit. Get to work, woman, and earn your keep.'

She could have reminded him who was keeping who. She would have enjoyed pointing out to him that since the war he'd brought nothing into the house and that if it hadn't been for her he would have starved to death long since. He had her to thank for keeping a roof over their heads and providing coal for the fire. There was much she could have said, years' worth of home-truths long overdue for an airing. She shrugged her shoulders and left him to bawl at the wall. She'd heard enough. It would be a relief to go out to work.

Employment for women in the factories had ended after the war, their positions taken by the returning men. Mary had found a place where nimble fingers were needed, assembling parts for light switches, pieces too small for a man's large hand and thicker fingers. The money she earned, added to the £2.10 shillings State Pension Charlie received each week for a married couple only just kept their heads above water.

When she returned from her shift, Charlie was worse. He had ceased bellowing and ranting. He lay still and quiet, his complexion sallow and his eyes sunken in their dark-rimmed sockets. The enamel bowl she'd left at the side of the bed contained his foul-smelling vomit and the room reeked of it and stale sweat.

She removed the basin and wiped the linoleum floor covering with a strong bleach solution. The smell of it roused him.

'That stinks, woman,' he complained. 'Are you trying to kill me?'

'I don't need to,' she replied carelessly. 'You've been doing that to yourself for long enough.'

She slept in the kitchen, away from his stink and his groaning, and in the morning asked again if he wanted the doctor. He refused. He wanted nothing from her.

'That's what you get then, Charlie,' she said as she left the house for work. 'Nothing.'

By evening he had worsened further and she sent for the doctor against his wishes, but he vomited the prescribed drugs, howling with the pain each retch brought upon him, sinking back onto the pillow, his eyes staring and hollow.

From her makeshift bed in the kitchen she heard him calling her.

'Mary, I'm dying.'

She went to him and knew immediately that it was true.

'I won't last the night out,' he said.

'I'd better tell you the truth then, before you go,' she said.

She waited until he'd finished wheezing so he could hear better what she had to say. She leaned over him and said plainly.

'Hilda was never your child, Charlie Thompson. Do you want to know who her father was?'

He tried to laugh, but all he could manage was a pale smirk.

'I know, you silly cow,' he rasped. 'I've always known.'

'Jack Bolton,' she said. 'If only he'd lived . . .'

He smirked again. 'Mary,' he whispered. 'You once saw my discharge papers.'

'And you beat me within an inch of my life for it.'

'I could have saved him. I could have got him out. I didn't. I left him, the bastard.'

He groaned as a searing pain tore through his body and left him drenched with sweat. He fought to continue.

'Do you really think I would have fucked my own daughter? I did it for revenge, Mary. I did him and I did her. Fucked her. Fuck Jack and fuck you.'

He collapsed into a fit of coughing. Blood trickled from the corner of his mouth and there was a gurgling sound at the back of his throat. She left him to get on with it. By next morning he had choked on his own vomit and lay with the smirk still in place on his lips, unseeing eyes staring at the ceiling.

◆

Most of the mourners on the day of Charlie Thompson's funeral were his old drinking buddies. Out of respect for the man they remembered in the good times, when there was work aplenty and wages to be spent, they stood on the pavement outside the Black Horse and as the hearse moved slowly by, they doffed their caps and raised their pints of ale.

Jean attended the funeral service. She couldn't explain why she felt she should be there. It wasn't out of a sense of love or duty, but it offered her a means of putting to rest all the years of bad feeling. She needed to be there at the end, at *his* end, so she could finalise that period in her own life.

Mary tried to attract her attention but Jean slipped out of the chapel, intending to go straight home. Jean had no desire to stand at the graveside.

Mary caught her in the church yard.

'Jean,' she called out. 'Wait!'

'I'm going home, Mam, I mean . . .' She sighed. 'I don't know what to call you any more.'

'I'm your grandma.'

'It doesn't seem right.'

'But that's what I am.'

Jean shook her head. 'Some grandma.'

'Call me Mary, then.'

Her voice was softer than Jean had ever heard it. She sounded like she cared. It was the voice of a mother, a grandmother, a woman who loved and nurtured. And her face matched the voice. There was sympathy in the eyes and the tilt of the head. Jean didn't know how to deal with it. It was a new experience.

'I'm glad he's dead,' Jean uttered.

'So am I.'

'Why didn't you just leave him?'

'I should have.'

Jean turned to leave.

'No, wait, Jean. This is my last chance to put things right. I've done a lot of stupid things in my time. I know that.'

'I think it's too late for apologies,' Jean said.

'Listen to me,' Mary begged. 'Just let me tell you this. I know you don't want to have anything to do with me.'

'You can say that again.'

'You've every right to feel as you do. I don't deserve better.'

Jean met Mary's eyes. 'If you're trying to get me to feel sorry for you, it won't work.'

'No. It's not about me. It's about you. You can stop feeling so bitter about who your dad was.'

'I don't want to talk about that filthy story,' Jean whispered.

Mary grabbed her arm. 'It wasn't as filthy as you think. Charlie wasn't Hilda's father.'

'What?' Jean cried out.

'No. Hilda's father was Jack Bolton. I loved him, Jean. If he'd lived through the Great War . . .'

'What are you telling me?'

'Charlie and Jack used to be best mates. He's the one I should have married.'

Jean could hardly believe what she was hearing. For just that brief moment, she'd thought Mary had been reaching out, wanting to build bridges between them, and for a moment, Jean had been prepared to moderate her own stance. But now this?

'You tell me this now, after he's dead? After Hilda is dead?'

Mary hung her head. 'I should have spoken up before.'

Jean screeched at the top of her voice.

'You let Hilda die, not knowing? You carried on the lie while she was lying dead in the hospital. All those years she thought she was raped by her own father. She thought she was dirty!'

'I'm telling you now, Jean, so *you* don't have to feel dirty any more.'

Jean opened her mouth wide and screamed at the sky. She screamed for Hilda and she screamed for herself. She turned on her heel and fixed Mary with an incredulous stare.

'I feel sorry for you,' she said, finally.

FORTY FIVE

Boys with barrows waited for the train carrying holiday makers.

'Here, sir. Let me help you, sir,' they cried in one voice, competing for the chance to earn a small tip. Whisking luggage along the platform and out onto the station forecourt, they deposited their loads in the bus queue, nodded their thanks for the few coins and dashed back to the train to earn a few pennies more.

Buses arrived in multiples: special services laid on for the arrival every Saturday of happy campers and their children, here for the annual holidays and looking forward to a week of outdoor activities and entertainment.

'Here we are again,' Jean sang to Audrey as they entered their chalet and began looking around for where to put all their things.

Audrey finished the song.

'Happy as can be. All good friends and jolly good companeee'. She ran through the small rooms, admiring the curtains and bed covers and darted back into the tiny kitchen area, looking behind cupboard doors and opening drawers. She dashed outside through the open door and began running around.

'Don't get in the way, sweetheart,' Jean called after her. 'Uncle Godfrey wants to get their bags inside.'

Richard and Godfrey's own chalet was just along the block. Audrey peered into the windows of the chalets in between to see if she could see signs of any more children.

'When are we going to the beach, Mam?'

'We'll go tomorrow, sweetheart if the sun's shining. Not today, love. While dad's having his rest we'll go for a walk and see if anything's changed since last time. We'll pop into the shop as well and buy what we need for breakfast. Can you find my shopping bag, Audrey? I don't know where it went.'

'And can we find out when the competitions are?' Audrey wanted to know, still buzzing with the wonderment of being away from home and right next to the sea.

'Audrey,' Godfrey called. 'Do you want to come with me? We'll go up to the office and see what's on, eh? Give your mum a few minutes to get straightened out.'

'Thanks, love,' Jean smiled. 'Off you go then, you two. Don't get into trouble.'

The juke box in the American style milk bar was pumping out Johnny Ray and Audrey craned her neck to look at the teenagers, a newly invented race of human beings who wore different clothes from their parents and talked a language all of their own. They were adults, she thought, but not the same as adults, but not children either. Some of them smoked cigarettes and said bad words. She liked the girls' shoes, pointy toes and thin high heels, much higher than her mother wore. Some of the boys had that queer hairstyle called a D.A. It was rude, she'd been told, to say its full name: duck's arse. It made her smile, though, just the same, and she hugged her thoughts and was glad that Uncle Godfrey didn't know what she was thinking.

'Do you want to go in?' he asked her.

'Can we?'

'I don't see why not,' he said. 'You'll be a teenager one day soon. We'd better go in and see how to do it.'

Audrey chose a strawberry milkshake and Godfrey had a Knickerbocker Glory. They sat on high stools at the bar and Audrey watched the fascinating procedures of frothing milk for coffee and mixing the ingredients for milkshakes. The man behind the bar realised he was being scrutinised.

'Hello,' he said.

'Hello, Mister,' she answered.

'It's young John,' Godfrey exclaimed. 'Don't you remember Audrey? John who used to help with the luggage?'

'No,' she replied, unabashed. 'I don't remember.'

She turned her attention away from the counter area to take in the atmosphere of the place. The record in the juke box changed and she recognised the soft tones of the American singer Pat Boone. He was something called a heart-throb. Some of the girls made a loud sighing noise and closed their eyes. She didn't know what that was about.

'I thought you'd have your own business by now, John,' Godfrey said.

'I do,' the young man replied. 'I'm here to earn a bit extra. I want to buy some land, maybe a house.'

'You're not getting married, yet, are you?' Godfrey quizzed.

The young man laughed. 'No, don't be daft. I just think it would be a good idea. It's something I was always going to do with my brother, buy some land. Well, they're not making any more of it are they?'

'Did he change his mind?' Godfrey asked.

'He was killed in Korea. No, don't apologise. You didn't know. Nearly three years now.'

'Well, good luck to you,' Godfrey said. 'I hope it all works out for you.'

'Thanks. Look, sorry, I've got a customer. Got to go. See you later, maybe.'

'Yes, of course,' Godfrey said.

'I'm in the dance hall tonight. Waiting behind the bar.'

'What will he be waiting for, Uncle Godfrey?' Audrey asked.

'He means he'll be a waiter, you know, taking orders for drinks,' Godfrey chuckled.

They left the milk bar to the strains of Doris Day singing *Que Sera*. Audrey thought it was a song about a girl called Kay Sarah who kept asking her mother questions. She hummed the tune on the way to the reception office.

◆

'Didn't you want to come with us, Uncle Richard?' Audrey asked. 'We went in the milk bar and everything.'

'I felt just a bit tired, darling,' he told her. 'I wanted to have a little rest and then I'll be able to stay up late tonight.'

'That's like me dad,' she said with the innocence of childhood. 'He has to take rests an' all.'

'So, what did you find out, Audrey?' Richard asked. 'Are they doing a fancy dress this year?'

She reeled off a list of all the competitions. Richard listened patiently and they decided between them which ones they should enter. He volunteered himself for the knobbly knees, and rolling up his trousers, exhibited his proposed entry.

'Oh, you'll definitely win with those, Uncle Richard,' she exclaimed gravely. 'They're even more knobbly than me dad's.'

◆

The dance hall was full. From their table at the side of the parquet floor, Audrey thrilled at the throng of people in their Saturday night best clothes. A huge glitter ball suspended from the ceiling revolved slowly, casting its sparkles around the room and onto faces and satin dance dresses. Footlights on the stage made multi-coloured reflections of sequins and spangles from the musicians' jackets. Audrey took in all the jewel colours, a feast for the eyes. Gilded columns rose from the floor to the elaborate ceiling. Plush deep red carpet surrounded the expensive oak flooring. Candles in glass holders graced the tables and cast an enticing warm glow over glasses of exotic drinks. She fluffed out the skirt of her salmon pink, flocked nylon party dress so that it spread in a lady-like fashion over the sides of her seat and she sneaked a quick glance at her sequinned dance shoes, worn for the first time and glittering majestically in the half-light under the table.

A beautiful lady, dressed in chiffon in a shade of blue so pale she looked like the Ice Queen from one of Audrey's story books appeared from the side of the stage and she heard Richard say,

'Here she is. Shush! Let's listen.'

The lady sang a Doris Day song Audrey knew: *Secret Love*. Audrey knew all the words. She'd heard it played often on the radio at the mill where her mother worked. She wanted to sing along but knew she mustn't. That would have been bad manners, so she sat on her hands to keep control of herself.

'She looks wonderful,' she heard her mother say. 'How old is she now?'

'A hundred and forty-five,' Richard replied. 'Who would have guessed?'

The room applauded politely and then the lady was joined by a man in a fancy suit. It was the kind of suit Audrey had seen in films, so that he looked like Fred Astaire, only fatter. Audrey thought the collar on his shirt was too tight for him. She could see folds of flesh hanging over and wobbling when he began to sing.

They sang something together that Audrey had never heard before, but it must have been something really famous, because everybody went *Aahh* and clapped furiously at the end.

'Dear David,' Uncle Richard sighed and looked a bit sad.

Audrey looked at her mother. It was the second time in her life she'd seen her mother in tears.

The music picked up the pace and the dance floor filled with swirling couples fox-trotting their way through *This Ole House, I see the Moon* and the couple called David and Yvonne came back on stage to sing the last piece of the set: *Mambo Italiano.*

When the band struck up with *Rock around the Clock* it was like the tide had turned. The fox-trotters left the floor, skirts swishing as they moved, rustling against each other in a multi-coloured exodus of flushed faces and happy chatter. They were replaced by the teenagers, the girls in swirling circular skirts that spun around their legs and showed their knickers as their partners twirled them and swung them over and through their legs. The whole dance floor was turned into a living thing: heads bobbing up and down, legs kicking out to the sides, pony tails bouncing and whipping around in time to the music.

Audrey watched, fascinated, as the stage turned around. The band disappeared, and as their music faded away, other sounds grew louder as the stage completed a full circle and another orchestra came into view.

They began with waltzes, and yet another group of dancers took to the floor. Then it was time for the part Audrey liked best: the Old Time dances. She knew them all and she danced with her mother to the Valeta, the St. Bernard's, the Gay Gordons. She stepped out in her sparkly new shoes and felt every inch a lady. Uncle Godfrey came up to do an excuse me and while Miss Yvonne Armitage sang an Anne Shelton song: *Lay Down Your Arms,* Audrey proudly did the Military Two Step, curtseying to her uncle in all the right places as he saluted and bowed to her. Audrey glowed like Tinkerbell as Godfrey led her back to their group. A waiter with a tray came to their table.

'Hello, again,' he said. 'Is there anything I can get for you?'

'Well, I'll be . .' Ronnie exclaimed. 'Look who it is, Jean. How are you doing, John?'

'Keeping busy,' came the reply. 'Can I take your order?'

John, the waiter looked after the group all evening and Ronnie invited him to join them at their table when he took a break.

✦

Audrey passed the eleven plus examination easily. She was an accomplished reader and found the questions easy. She was offered a place at the Girls' Grammar school and proudly took her place on the first day, wearing the smart school blazer and carrying a new leather satchel on her back.

They'd left the house on the Lane which was due for demolition to make way for the first of Kingsley's supermarkets. Ronnie had made enquiries about the possibility of buying their own house but he couldn't get insurance because of the state of his health. There were no mitigating circumstances because he had given his health in service of his country. Without insurance he couldn't get a mortgage.

The council house they moved into, on a hill overlooking the town, was bright and airy with a proper pantry and plenty of electricity sockets. The bathroom was part-tiled and had a toilet and a sink, and there was another toilet, outside in one of the outhouses. Audrey never used the outside toilet and neither did her mother. Only Ronnie, to avoid having to climb the stairs to the inside loo, made use of the outside privvy.

New furniture was delivered to the Logan's to replace the old worn out chairs and uncomfortable sofa, and for the first time there was fitted carpet in the living room, wall to wall luxury in a large swirling pattern of green and gold. Jean sewed the curtains for all the rooms: gold brocade for the living room, a cheerful patterned fabric for the kitchen window to match the wallpaper design of baskets of fruit and vegetables. Audrey chose the material for her own bedroom window: a trellis design, covered in climbing flowers in pale blue and lilac.

A new television aerial was needed so they could pick up the new channel, and the Logans watched advertisements with amusement. There was a multitude of new television programmes: variety shows, comedies, wildlife and sport. Ronnie watched *Grandstand* every Saturday and called for quiet when it was time to check his football pools. Richard and Godfrey came to watch the wedding of Prince Rainier of Monaco to the American actress, Grace Kelly. They brought chocolates and they scrutinised the bride's and bridesmaids' dresses.

In 1959 *Juke Box Jury* was broadcast for the first time, and a new English pop star rose to the top of the charts with *Living Doll,* to rival Elvis and Bobby Darin, Buddy Holly and the Everly Brothers. Audrey was as happy through her teenage years as she had been through her early childhood.

✦

Richard Mancini died that year, aged 47, of multiple organ failure. He had borne his condition stoically and often said if it hadn't been for Godfrey's loving care, he'd have expired long since. The end, when it came was mercifully swift. He collapsed into unconsciousness and slipped into a coma. Godfrey was grateful his life partner was in no pain. He ordered forty seven pink roses for the cortege and arranged the funeral as carefully as if it had been a celebration banquet.

Richard had known his condition was more acute than Ronnie's and had thoughtfully made provision for Godfrey. But fashions were changing rapidly. Business at Mancini Modes was failing. At 62, Godfrey had neither the heart nor the energy to begin again. He renegotiated a separate lease for the apartment and the shop premises was re-let and converted into a betting shop.

The sixties arrived. Audrey developed different tastes in music from her mother, and on the summer holiday that first year of the decade, learned how to do *The Twist*. Regular outings to the cinema with Uncle Godfrey included the big hits of the time *Spartacus, El Cid, A Taste of Honey.* Godfrey treated Jean and Audrey to a coach trip, over the Pennines to Manchester to see the stage show *Oliver*. He accompanied Ronnie, Jean and Audrey on the summer holidays each year. They were his family and Jean wouldn't dream of not inviting him along.

In 1963 Audrey wanted to go away with friends who were hiring a caravan in Devon. Godfrey made the familiar journey to the Norfolk coast that summer with the Logans, and saw their relationship was in trouble. As the days passed and the awkward silences between Jean and Ronnie grew more protracted, he attempted to help.

'What's the matter?' he asked Jean when Ronnie had taken himself off to the bar and they were alone.

'What do you mean?' Jean asked him.

'I think you know what I mean, dear,' he said. 'You and Ronnie. What's wrong?'

'Oh, Godfrey,' she sighed. 'Where do I begin?'

'At the beginning is usually the best place,' he encouraged.

'I'm forty!'

'I wish I was,' he teased.

'No, listen, Godfrey. Audrey's growing away from me . . .'

'As she should,' he interrupted.

'Yes, as she should,' Jean agreed. 'She'll leave home soon and then it'll be just me and Ronnie.'

'But you always knew that.'

'I never thought about it like that. You don't think about what life's going to be like twenty years down the line, do you? You just do what you have to do for today.'

'So you question now whether you did the right thing?' he asked.

She hung her head. 'A bit like that, yes.' She bit her lip and a deep, sorrowful sigh escaped her. ' I never loved Ronnie, you know.'

'He knows that,' Godfrey said.

'I should have set him free. I used him. I wasn't fair to him.'

'He didn't want to be set free, dear. He used the situation after Hilda and George just as much as you did.'

'Do you think so?'

'I'm sure so.'

'It's just that, sometimes . . .' she began.

'Yes, go on,' Godfrey said.

'Sometimes, I wonder what it would have been like to really love somebody. You know, to fall in love and get married and do everything properly.'

Godfrey stirred and prepared for a difficult question.

'How are things in the bedroom department?' he asked gingerly.

Jean spoke through clenched teeth.

'There's never been a bedroom department.'

'What? Never?'

Jean blushed. She turned her head to the side.

'No, never,' she repeated. 'Not since . . . that night, you know. And I don't remember any of that, anyway. I was just a child. I hated him for a long time after that. Then, after Audrey, things got better between us. He's been a wonderful father to her. He has, really.'

She fell silent for a moment and Godfrey allowed her to take the time.

'He's not a well, man, Godfrey. In many ways. I didn't want him at first. I didn't want him anywhere near me. And then, as time went by, I grew to care for him and I would have . . would have . . made love. But he couldn't. He tried a few times but he couldn't do it and I think he became afraid of trying again. It made him feel a failure, like he wasn't a real man any more. It shocked him. Do you know what I mean? He'd always been such a man about town, hadn't he? Before the war. I used to hear stories, you know, about all his women in the past. I don't suppose he ever thought that he'd lose the ability.

'It's been terrible for him, Godfrey. He cried in frustration. How awful is that? After everything he's been through? Well, I told myself it didn't matter. I had Audrey to love, and you and Richard. But now I'm losing all of you, and all I have to look forward to is life with Ronnie, and I don't know if that's enough.'

Godfrey let out a sigh.

'Oh dear. Why didn't you talk to me about it before? Richard and I used to think at last you two had found happiness together. There was never any sign that things were not all right between you. Oh, Jean. I wish I'd known.'

✦

In the bar crowded with holiday makers, Ronnie had found an old friend.

'So, what have you been doing, John? Bought up half of Norfolk yet?' Ronnie asked.

'No, not yet,' John laughed. 'But I'm working on it.'

'I couldn't believe my eyes when I saw you over there in the corner. Is that your girlfriend?' Ronnie indicated the young woman waiting for John at a table by the window.

'No,' John replied. 'That's my sister, Margaret. She's here for the week with her husband. I drove across to meet up with them. Where are the rest of you?'

Ronnie rolled his eyes. 'Audrey's too grown up to come on holiday with us this year. Jean and Godfrey will be across soon. Richard passed away.'

'Come and sit with us, Ronnie. Come and meet my sister.'

✦

When Jean walked into the room with Godfrey, John Starling had to catch his breath. She had dressed her hair and put on a simple sheath dress which showed off her figure and her legs. Her full mouth opened into a sparkling smile as, on Godfrey's arm, she crossed the room towards them and came to greet them. There was something about her eyes that drew him in and he was aware of a melting sensation somewhere deep inside him. When she turned her smile directly on him, his stomach flipped as it might on a roller coaster ride.

She sat next to his sister and was soon in conversation with her. Through the rest of the evening he couldn't resist glancing in her direction. He watched her teeth and her lips as she spoke; he noticed how her eyelashes curled outwards, even the sweep of her hair across her cheekbone demanded his attention. She was everything a man could desire and he knew before the night was over he had fallen in love.

When he heard his sister making arrangements with Jean to keep in touch, his heart leapt with the thrill of the possibility of seeing her again one day.

✦

Audrey Logan married Jim Freeman in July 1964. As she walked out of the church on the arm of her new husband Jean Thompson brushed away a tear and thought about their mother. Hilda had missed the most precious day in a daughter's life. In that sweet moment of Audrey's happiness, when her eyes sparkled with the joy of being in love and dreams of a new life, Jean Thompson watched her sister becoming a woman in the eyes of the world. She swallowed back the choking lump at the back of her throat. Audrey was about to accomplish what her mother never did, except in death. She was going away. She was going to achieve the new life, full of hope and promise that Hilda had so longed for. Audrey was going to fulfil the dream and live the life her mother had dreamed of.

Throughout the week of the holiday at the summer camp, Jean gazed wistfully at the young lovers, and a part of her wished for an adventure of her own. They took a picnic to the beach and Jean, try as she might, could not feel she was part of the happy group.

She had a sense of being apart, of being on the outside looking in. It seemed everywhere she looked she was confronted with reminders she was different from everybody else.

Jim seemed to be a good choice of husband for Audrey and Ronnie liked him a lot. There was always something the two of them could find to talk about. She'd often find the pair of them locked in a heated discussion, arguing good-naturedly and putting each other down, culminating in a bout of laughter and another round of drinks.

Ronnie was happy in Jim's company. He became more like his old self. He was able to forget for a short time about his aches and pains and the growing weakness in his limbs, the deteriorating shortness of breath.

But, more than ever, Jean felt alone. Audrey and Jim were blissfully happy, that was obvious. Ronnie, too, had found peace within himself. He'd settled into accepting his limitations and found pleasure in the simple enjoyments of daily life. Even Godfrey, in his own way, had come to terms with the altered circumstances of his life without Richard and had opted to spend some time travelling the world to see the places they'd have visited together had Richard lived. Jean recalled Godfrey's words as he left for the first leg of his journey.

'Jean, dear, if there's something you've always wanted to do, you have to do it. If you can afford it and it's not hurting anybody, you must get on and do it, dear. I think we may be allowed to put ourselves first sometimes, don't you think?'

Dear Godfrey, he would be half way across the Atlantic by now, looking forward to seeing the sights of New York. Of course he deserved this treat, and Richard, through his generous provision, had made it possible for him. Theirs was a story of true love. Richard had shown the depth of his caring so that even after his death, Godfrey would be taken care of.

Suddenly, a choking sensation took her by surprise. Now, at this time in her life, and more than ever before, she longed for love. Her body ached to be touched, to be held, kissed and loved. All around her there were other happy couples, happy families, playing in the sand and holding hands in the sea. Couples lay together in the sunshine, gazing into each other's eyes, stroking hair, kissing. She tried to shake off her loneliness.

'Anybody fancy a drive out?' she said.

Nobody did. Audrey, Jim and Ronnie were settled in their deck chairs on the sand.

'Take the car if you want to, Jean,' Jim suggested.

'Are you sure?' she asked.

'Yeh. No problem. That's why I put you on the insurance. I know what you're like, can't wait to get behind the wheel.'

She hurried to the chalet, showered and changed into a pair of Capri pants and cotton blouse. She quickly ran a brush through her hair, grabbed the car keys, dropped them into her handbag and strode toward the parking lot near the reception block where Jim had left the hire car. When she spotted the telephone box, an idea formed itself. She pulled out her diary and some coins and rang the number.

'Hello, Margaret? Is that you? It's Jean here.'

FORTY SIX

She never intended it to happen. When he'd suggested she go along with him to view the cottage she accepted out of curiosity. He was so pleased with his new acquisition, so proud to show her the house and to talk about his plans. She'd thought she would return to the others afterwards and tell them who she'd chanced to meet, and they'd be happy to hear his news and learn how well he was doing.

He gave her directions to the village in the Norfolk countryside and she drove them, looking across at him occasionally, catching his enthusiasm for his new project. As she changed gears, her hand brushed against his and a jolt raced through her abdomen into her pelvis in a shudder of surprise. She turned her head to look at him and saw, by the sudden slackness in his mouth and the darkening of his eyes, that he had felt the same piercing quickening.

I can't want him, she thought. *I mustn't think like this.*

They came to a halt outside the cottage and, as she pulled on the handbrake, he placed his hand on top of hers. Again, a fire rose in her belly and she heard him whisper to her.

'You feel it too, don't you?'

Look at him, she thought. *Why would he want me? I must be ten years older than him, at least.*

'This is my house,' he told her.

It was beautiful. She'd never seen a prettier cottage and she walked with him up to the door and went inside. He showed her the garden and told her his plans for a pond and a vegetable patch. He proudly explained his ideas for modernising the kitchen.

He talked and talked and she didn't listen. His mouth was moving and she knew words were coming out of it, but she didn't hear them. All she could hear was the drumming in her ears.

He took her hand in his.

'Don't you know how I feel about you?' he said.

'Yes,' she said.

'I wanted to show you this place,' he said. 'It will be waiting until you can come to me.'

'What?'

'I will be waiting. I have been waiting since I first knew I loved you. There'll be no other woman living in this house until you are here.'

'I can't leave Ronnie. He needs me.'

'I know that and I'm not asking you to leave him. All I want is for you to know and understand that I am here waiting for you. I love you, Jean. I think I loved you from the very first.'

His soft words caressed her hungry heart and she wanted to dissolve into his arms. Gently, he touched her face and she turned her head to kiss his hand. He lifted her face and when his mouth found hers she groaned at the warmth and touch of his lips.

This is what love is, she told herself. *This wanting, this need to have him inside me, to feel his body, to know that I please him as he pleasures me.*

He smiles as he loves me. He throws aside our clothes and kisses me, kisses me, as he takes me to his bed. He runs his hands across my back and shoulders, turning me so he can run his tongue against the back of my neck. His hands come up in front to caress my breasts, and the gentle pulling of my nipples sends spasms to my groin. My back arches. I want him, I want him.

Oh, let me remember this. Let me dream about this when he is gone. He turns me again and his mouth is at my breasts. I cry out. I hold his head to me and beg for more.

We are on the bed now. His fingers tease and caress between my legs as he kisses my mouth, my face, my eyes. He tongues between my breasts and down, down, slowly, tantalisingly, down, and flicks across my swollen sex.

I want him, I want him. Remember this, Jean. Remember this forever. This is what love is. Oh, let me always remember this.

He shows me the force of his desire. He displays himself to me. I take him in my mouth and taste him, suck him. He groans his pleasure and we know that we are close, so close. His eyes are soft and dreamy and he begins to whisper to me as I open to him and I take the length of him inside me.

Jean, oh my love, he says to me. I love you my darling.

This is what love is. This is how it is meant to be. Something bursts inside me and it's like the explosion of a firework: a Roman candle of shooting stars, wave after wave of glorious, delirious heights of ecstasy. We tumble and roll together, laughing, kissing, loving. Oh, I must remember this, every detail. Let me remember this. He will forget me; he is a young man; he will find love again. This is all there is for me.

◆

Margaret knew as soon as she saw her brother returning to collect his own car that something had happened. She called Jean into the house.

'What do you think of John's house?' she asked.

'It's wonderful,' Jean told her.

'He's told me all about it, Jean. I know what his plan is. I know who the house is for. No, let me finish. I'm not one to judge. No, I'm not going to do that. I know he loves you, and by the look on your face you love him too. If I can see it, so can everybody else.'

Abashed, Jean looked away.

'You can't go back with that look on your face, girl. They'll see it for themselves. Why don't you go upstairs and use my bathroom, and while you're there you can put your blouse back on the right way round.'

'Oh, Margaret,' Jean said. 'What must you think of me?'

'I think you've got to be careful. People can get hurt.'

Ronnie Logan saw for himself. Jean couldn't disguise the light that shone from her. It glowed from her skin, from her eyes. She told him she'd been to visit Margaret, John Starling's sister. She said she'd spent a lovely afternoon and that she'd so enjoyed being out in the car by herself.

She told him too much. She offered too much information about where she'd been and who she'd been with. He knew she was lying, covering up the whole truth, chattering too much and he chose to leave it be. Nothing could come of it. If she'd had a holiday flirtation, that's all it was. Somebody else had admired her, made her feel womanly, that's all. He didn't blame her.

On the last day of the holiday Jean took the car out again and returned with the same rejuvenated spirit, the same glow of health and happiness. She laughed and joked with Jim and Audrey, enthusiastically joining in with the talk of Australia and the honeymoon voyage.

Ronnie watched her closely, saw the sparkle in her eyes and knew then there was another man involved with the change in her. He'd heard it often enough from the women he'd bedded in his youth, how their husbands could tell they'd been playing away, the giveaway signs from women unused to hiding indiscretions. His heart sank with the depressing jolt of reality. He couldn't give Jean what women needed. But surely it couldn't be John Starling? Not young John.

As previously arranged, John visited them at the camp on their last evening. Audrey and Jim were taking a last walk along the beach and came into the bar to find Ronnie, Jean, John and Margaret waiting for them.

'I'm so glad you came.' Audrey said.

'Can't let you set off to the other side of the world without saying goodbye,' Margaret said. 'Anyway,' she added, 'it's been a tradition between us, hasn't it? Especially for John.'

'That's right,' John agreed. 'I was just a lad when we first met. Used to cart your luggage in for you.'

They all laughed and Ronnie caught Jean's discomfort. He saw as well the glance between her and John and knew, at that moment, what had happened between them.

It *was* John, after all. It was John who had put that smile on her face, had brought Jean back to vibrant life. He was the one who'd lifted her out of her resigned acceptance and turned her into the desirable woman she'd been before.

Well, it was all right. A holiday fling. A release. He swallowed back the tightening in his throat and thought about the years of selfless devotion she'd given to others. If anybody deserved a few days of romance, it was Jean. Why shouldn't she have what he himself had never been able to give her?

He stopped watching them. He knew they exchanged glances and smiles when they thought nobody was looking. This was the last night. Would she be upset at leaving him behind? Would she have regrets? She'd need to say goodbye to him properly. They wouldn't be able to do that in front of the others. When Audrey and Jim decided to take a last turn around the park he asked Margaret if she would help him across to the chalet.

'You finish your drink, Jean,' he said. 'Margaret doesn't mind, do you? I'll say goodnight to you now, John. We'll keep in touch for next year as usual. No, don't get up. I'm just a bit tired, that's all.'

Ronnie Logan never mentioned John Starling again. Not by name. As his condition worsened through the autumn of 1964 he began to feel the need to broach the subject of what Jean might do when he was no longer around.

'You could get in touch with George and Sandra again,' he suggested. 'George doesn't know Audrey is married now and in Australia.'

'I might,' is all she would say.

'Jean,' he began. 'I want you to know you have been so good for me.'

'Stop it, Ronnie,' she said.

'No, Jean. Let me tell you. You saved me. You know as well as I do that I'm not getting any better. Winters have always been hardest for me. I might not get through this one.'

A pang of intense sorrow rushed through her and she felt weak and suddenly tearful. She stood looking out of the kitchen window at the unkempt patch of overgrown garden, not wanting Ronnie to see the tears in her eyes.

'We never did do anything with that lot out there, did we?' he said to her.

'It doesn't matter, Ronnie,' she said.

'But you always wanted flowers, Jean.'

'You haven't been well enough, Ronnie.'

'I want you to make a new life when I'm gone,' he said.

'Stop it, Ronnie, please. I really don't want to talk about it.'

She walked through into the living room and sat by the fire. He followed her and gingerly lowered himself into his own chair facing her, and with his hands, lifted his legs into a more comfortable position.

'You deserve to make a new life for yourself, Jean. Find someone who loves you. Don't be afraid to be happy. There's someone out there just waiting for you.'

She burst into tears, could hold it back no longer.

♦

Ronnie died in November, one week before his birthday. On the certificate the cause of death was given as pneumonia but Jean knew the truth. For Ronnie, and for hundreds of other FEPOWs, brought down by diseases they had endured since the war, there was no justice. They died from their war wounds as surely as if they'd fallen on the field of battle.

She had done as he asked. She included his parents in the making of the funeral arrangements and stood with them at the service in St. Anne's, the Catholic church in the centre of Kingsley.

Thomas Logan, retired now and in his seventieth year, held her arm and treated her kindly. He guided her through the service, understanding she would find the Catholic ceremony an alien thing. Sylvia ignored her. She took comfort from the circle of female friends gathered around her, and walked to the graveside with them rather than her husband.

A hand reached out and touched Jean's arm.

'Jean.' A quiet voice, vaguely familiar. 'I'm so sorry.'

Jean turned to face an elegant woman with perfectly coiffed hair drawn back into a French pleat, the streaks of silver swept up from the sides and built into the bouffant crown. She wore a classic fine woollen suit of pale grey and carried a black patent clutch bag to match her expensive shoes.

'Don't you recognise me?' the woman asked in a mixed accent of clipped Northern vowel sounds and sing-song Canadian intonation.

'Sandra?'

'Hello, Jean.'

Jean felt lost for words. The limited, stilted language of their written correspondence over the years would not suffice. It could not come anywhere near describing the mixture of conflicting emotions threatening to overwhelm her. She was pleased to see her old friend yet horrified at the same time. It was how she imagined it would be like looking into a mirror for the first time after being in a coma for twenty years, the passage of time staring you in the face and catapulting you into reality.

This is where you are now, the mirror would say. *Twenty years have gone by. What have you done with them? Ah, yes, you have been asleep. You have done nothing.*

Sandra had obviously done well with her twenty years. Her make-up was immaculate, her outfit expensively well-cut. Jean knew from Sandra's letters that life in Canada had been good to her and George and that now they ran their own flying school. But Jean had always imagined something more Annie Get Your Gun about their enterprise: log cabins, ranch houses, checked shirts and cowboy boots; fresh prairie winds and cool, clean air; steak and fries for breakfast.

The stylish woman Sandra had become was more Diana Dors than Betty Hutton, more *Camay* than *Coal Tar*.

'Is George with you?' Jean stuttered.

'No. We couldn't both get away together, but he's well.' She reached into her handbag and took a photograph from her purse.

'Look, Jean. Here he is with Stuart on their last camping weekend. They came back with a freezer full of fish. We're still eating it.'

So, the checked shirts did have a place in their lives, after all. Jean studied the faces of father and son: relaxed and happy, George without glasses and moustache, his arm around the teenager standing as tall as his father and wearing a baseball cap with the peak to one side. Sandra pressed another picture into Jean's hand.

'And this is my daughter Eleanor. She's only three. She was a surprise.'

Jean didn't want to look. She didn't want to see the face of George's second little girl in case she looked like Audrey had at that age. But the child was the image of her mother with beautiful golden curls and the same cheeky smile.

'She's lovely,' Jean said, and handed back the photographs. Sandra smiled.

'How is Audrey?' she asked, finally. 'Isn't she here?'

'I was going to write to you soon, Sandra. I meant to tell you, but, what with Ronnie being so ill . . .'

'Why? What's happened? Is she all right?'

'Yes. She's very happy. She got married. Last July. She's gone with her husband to Australia.'

Sandra took in a deep breath and shifted uncomfortably.

'I couldn't tell her, Sandra. I just couldn't do it. She's so happy now. Isn't it best just left alone?'

The gathered mourners were waiting at the graveside. Thomas Logan came to offer an arm to the two women. They walked with him and when he left them together to rejoin his wife they stood, holding hands with heads bowed as the priest completed the ceremony.

'I understand,' Sandra whispered, and grasped Jean's hand more firmly. 'George is happy too. You're right. It was best left alone.'

Jean smiled her gratitude. 'Are you staying in England long? Maybe we could . .'

'I have to go straight back. Mum and Dad are taking me to the airport tonight. Come back to the house with us.'

Jean saw Sylvia Logan eyeing them as her husband approached them and knew what she must do.

'No thank you, I won't.'

'If there's anything we can do . . .' Thomas offered.

'Thank you, I'll be all right,' Jean said, wondering where the years had gone and whether she would indeed be all right. Her words had sounded confident but she questioned, in her heart, how she was going to manage on her own. She said her goodbyes and crossed the road to the bus station for her journey home, alone to the council house on the hill.

♦

Jean didn't feel well. Christmas was just around the corner and she had no enthusiasm for festivities. Godfrey was celebrating the coming season in Brazil. Jean had delayed sending him the news about Ronnie. She didn't want Godfrey to cut short his travel plans and come rushing home when there was nothing to be done. In any case, it was a pleasure to receive his postcards from the fabulous places he'd seen. There was a growing colourful collection on her pantry door: the Empire State building; Hula-Hula girls from the Hawaiian islands, other pictures of famous landmarks and national costumes. He sent letters too and recipes from far-flung places for her to try, some so exotic she could find the ingredients only in the burgeoning Asian quarter in Bradford, where dark-eyed children gazed at her curiously in her western dress and uncovered hair.

She didn't know if it was the stress of recent events or the onset of early menopause causing the discomfort in her abdomen and the general sickly feeling that had turned her stomach against the spicy meals she'd been trying from the recipes Godfrey sent. And work was a problem too. She'd returned to the mill immediately, the day after Ronnie's funeral, thinking it was by far the best thing to keep busy. The house was so empty now. There was nobody to feed apart from herself, nobody to look after, only her own bed to make each morning, her own clothes to wash and press. The companionship of the other women at the mill would help lift her spirits, she thought. They'd help her to keep going and get on with her life. But before the end of the afternoon she was ready to stop. She needed to sit and rest and she forced herself to continue so that by the time she returned home at the end of the day, she was exhausted.

Finally, she relented and admitted she needed time away from her work. Her GP advised two weeks' rest and told her it was the stress of her recent bereavement causing the headaches and nausea. Jean accepted the prescription medicine and put the bottle of anti-depressants on her bathroom window sill. She stood and stared at the bottle of bright pink and yellow capsules. She didn't want to have to rely on drugs for her recovery. It didn't seem natural to her. Human beings were supposed to cope with their emotions. They were designed for it, weren't they? Didn't everybody have to face some sort of personal tragedy in their lives? She would try to do without the pills.

She couldn't sleep. Each night she waited until the end of the television broadcast, until there was nothing left to watch, nothing left to take her mind away from her troubled thoughts, and then she'd flick through magazines, reading the same sentence over and over again until her eyelids began to feel heavy.

In her lonely bedroom she quickly fell asleep only to wake an hour or two later, fatigued and nauseous, wishing her head would stop its involuntary worrying and let her sleep.

She awoke one morning to a bright blue sky and an early frost glistening on the roofs. It had been a better night: she had slept without waking so frequently and she felt she had enough energy to attempt clearing out the house. There were some of Ronnie's old bits and pieces in the outhouse: hand tools and gardening equipment from the days when he was well enough to keep the allotment.

Wearing several layers of clothing and a woollen headscarf to guard against the December chill, she pulled out several large wooden trays and old enamel buckets full of odds and ends. She was sorting through them when she heard footsteps coming up the path toward the front of the house.

Seventy-five year old Mary Thompson stood there. Jean straightened up and waited for her to speak.

'I'm sorry to hear about Ronnie,' she said.

Jean did not respond. She didn't know how.

'It can't be easy for you,' Mary added.

Jean shrugged.

'Every time you show up, it's bad news, Mary. What is it this time?'

'I just came to say I'm sorry. Can I come in?'

'What for?'

'Me legs ache. It's a long walk up that hill,' she said, indicating the way she'd come.

'You've walked all the way?'

'From the tin houses. That's where I am now. But this last bit's a step too steep for me now.'

Jean had no stomach for a fight. She invited her grandmother into the house and made tea. They sat, facing each other like strangers in a waiting room. Jean put down her cup on the fire hearth. She didn't want the tea; it tasted as if the milk was curdled.

'Is your tea all right?' she asked.

'Yes, why?'

'Mine tastes funny, that's all.'

'Does it?' Mary nodded her head. 'I thought so.'

'What do you mean *you thought so*?' Jean snapped.

'Jean, I haven't come here to cause trouble. But I only had to take one look at you to know what condition you're in. It's written in your face.'

Mary put down her own cup and offered her granddaughter a consoling smile.

'I'm tired, that's all,' Jean said.

'You will be, Jean, if you don't look after yourself now. You're pregnant, love.'

Automatically, Jean's hand slipped to her belly. She tried to remember the date of her last period. She couldn't be certain.

'How can you tell?' she said. 'How can you know?'

'I've always been able to tell,' Mary answered with a little laugh. 'I've known before women know themselves. It's just in your face. You just get a certain look in your face.'

'I can't be. I'm too old now.' Jean dismissed the idea.

'Plenty get caught on the change, Jean. I think you should go and see your doctor.'

Mary got up from her chair.

'Look, I'm sorry. It looks like it's all gone bad again. Just as you said. Whenever I turn up it's got to mean bad news. All this time you waited for a baby of your own and now it's happened too late, eh? Too late for Ronnie to know. Poor bugger. I'll go now. I am sorry, Jean. It's bloody awful bad luck.'

◆

The child was due in May. Jean made her plans. Calmly she set about what she wanted to do. It came easily to her. She was going to leave all the dark days behind her. There was a bright clean future waiting for her.

She left a message for Godfrey at his apartment, told nobody else of her intentions and left Yorkshire to build a new life in Norfolk.

He'd said he would be waiting for her: the father of her unborn child, John Starling.

◆

When Godfrey returned from his travels and discovered the note from Audrey, he immediately wrote to the forwarding address she'd left for him. He was surprised she hadn't told him about Ronnie's death and was disappointed he hadn't been with her to comfort her and lend his support. She'd helped him through his own bereavement and he felt he should have been present to help her through the adjustment of being alone. Concerned for her, he travelled to see her.

Margaret opened the door to him and invited him in. He stepped into a lively scene of happy domesticity. There was Jean, sitting in a captain's chair, surrounded by cushions and with her feet supported on a cushioned stool. Her hair was shining the way he remembered when she wore her *Joan Crawford* that night at The Ferry Inn all those years ago. Her eyes were shining, too.

'Godfrey,' Jean said. 'Oh, I'm so happy to see you. But you shouldn't have come all this way.'

'Nonsense,' he said. 'To tell you the truth, Jean, I'm a bit offended you didn't tell me what was happening.'

Margaret intervened.

'Jean's having a baby, Godfrey. Can't you tell? Sit down and I'll make you a cup of tea.'

'What? When?'

'May,' Jean told him.

Godfrey tried to work it out.

Margaret said, 'Best you sit yerself down, Godfrey boy, before you fall down. Jean's having John's baby and then they're going to be married. You'll stay here with us of course. Just as long as you like.'

She bustled about the house like a mother hen. Godfrey watched her as she took charge of everybody and everything. He saw Jean's radiant smile, felt the happy atmosphere of the household and knew that everything was going to work out just fine.

FORTY SEVEN

DECEMBER 2009

Alison has come along with John and Alex. She's helping to carry what looks like photograph albums similar to my own. The atmosphere they bring with them is almost tangible. They walk into the cottage with funereal expressions, the polite fixed smiles of condolence on their faces. They walk slowly, quietly and with hushed voices.

Deborah helps me make coffee. There's an uncomfortable edginess as we take seats around the kitchen table. John places the albums and an old biscuit box in the middle of the table, straightening and re-straightening the pile and avoiding making eye contact with me. I decide to take the bull by the horns.

'I read the inscription on the bench in the Priory gardens,' I say. 'John, I think it's wonderful that you married my mother.'

I expect him to look relieved that I've worked out his secret but instead he wipes his forehead and is agitated. Alison looks at John, encouraging him to take up my opening.

He rubs at his chin and breathes deeply.

'Jean wouldn't marry me at first,' he says. 'Not when she first came to Norfolk. She wanted to wait until after Alex was born.'

'Sorry?' I ask him. 'Did you say when she *first* came to Norfolk? That was in the sixties, John, just after I left for Australia. Just after dad died.'

'Yes,' he confirms. He takes a deep breath. 'We were married in 1966. I have the photographs here.'

He passes me an open album and I recognise the face of my mother, smiling up at the young man by her side while he holds an infant boy on his shoulder. They all look so happy.

Aghast, I glance at Deborah, searching for some moral support of my own, some gentle reminder from a friendly face that this is reality; this is really happening. I'm not making this up. She can't disguise her shock. She looks as if she has stumbled upon something terrible and fascinating.

'Would you prefer me to leave the room?' she asks kindly.

'No. Stay, Deborah, please. This is a bit much to take in, John.'

Alison takes my hand across the table and smiles warmly.

'Dad has wanted to tell you for so long, Audrey. I hope you can understand how difficult it's all been for him.' Alison says quietly and goes to stand behind her father-in-law, where she gently touches his shoulder and smiles her encouragement to him.

'There's so much to tell you,' John says, shaking his head. 'I really don't know where to begin.'

He reaches into his box of photographs and selects one in particular. It's a copy of one I have in my album. He places the snapshot in front of me and, gingerly, he taps at it with a shaky finger. His arm shakes too; his whole body is unsteady and there is moisture in his eyes.

'This is the best place to begin,' he tells me, still tapping at the snapshot. 'These are your real parents. George and Hilda.'

My hand goes to my mouth. I sit, dumbstruck, glancing from face to face and recognising only pity in their eyes.

'My mother's sister and her husband,' I say, recognising the couple in the picture, sitting by a wall in a field with a picnic spread out before them.

'No. They're your parents,' John repeats. 'Your mother died when you were born. Jean and Ronnie brought you up.' He wipes his eyes with the back of his hand. 'Jean was your sister, Audrey. Hilda was mother to you both. After Ronnie died, Jean came to live here in Norfolk and we married a year later.'

'You both hid this from me for more than forty years?' My voice is cracked. It's incredible; I can't take this in. Again, I search the faces around the table. Again, I see pity in their expressions. 'Why?'

John tries to speak. He begins and stops, his voice faltering. Alex turns to me.

'Let me help, Dad,' he tells him.

I switch my gaze to stare into Alex's eyes and a rush of tingling cold runs through me. The eyes! Laura has them too, large and dark and warm. They are *her* eyes.

'Mum was always too embarrassed to tell you the truth about us, Audrey.'

'Why?' I ask him.

'You've got to remember she came from a different generation. They had a different way of thinking. She was ashamed of what she'd done.'

'I don't understand what you're saying, Alex. What had she done?'

'She couldn't bring herself to tell you about me and dad because you would have worked out that I was conceived before you went to Australia.'

John's head droops. He looks thoroughly miserable. I remember the day he told me he would like to be my friend but was afraid that one day things would come out about him.

'Is this the one bad thing, John?' I ask him.

He nods. When he raises his head I see the tears in his eyes.

'I loved her so much,' he says. 'From almost the first time I saw her. But I should have waited.'

'Tell me about the first time you saw her, John. Tell me how it all started, please.'

He brings out more photographs and shows me a group picture of people on holiday, standing outside a wooden chalet.

'That's me,' I say. 'Look, that's Uncle Godfrey, too.'

John indicates a smart young man in staff uniform.

'And that's me,' he adds. 'I knew your family way back then.'

I take hold of the snapshot and examine it closely. I inspect the image of the young John in the picture and lift my head to look at him now.

'You knew me when I was just a girl,' I say.

'Yes. You used to love the fancy dress competitions.'

'But I don't remember you. I don't remember you at all.'

'Why would you?' he says.

'But when I was older, you were there then?'

'I used to meet up with Ronnie and Jean each year. The last time, you were just married.'

He points to another photograph. There's Dad and John. And Jim. My Jim! There they are all together, smiling and relaxed. I stare at the photo, and at John, and back at the picture again.

'Why don't I remember you?'

'It's a long time ago, Audrey. You only had eyes for your husband, then, as I remember. And, well, I've changed a lot. You wouldn't have recognised me anyway, even if you did remember.'

I turn to Alex and indicate the snapshot.

'And it was then? It was during that last holiday?'

Alex nods. His father looks sheepish.

I try to swallow, but my mouth is dry. There is a peculiar fluttering in my stomach and I don't know whether to laugh or cry. I know that it's the sudden shock; I know that's what shock does to you. I can't focus properly; my thoughts are all over the place. I force myself to speak.

'So, when I came back to England, to the house in Wells?'

'That was always Margaret's house,' John tells me. 'Jean lived with my sister and her husband Lawrence until Alex was born. Then we married and came to live here in Walsingham. When you came to visit we used to do a bit of swapping about. Margaret came here to be with me and Alex and Jean went on her own to Wells.'

They swapped houses so that I wouldn't know about John and Alex?

They kept it a secret for over forty years?

And I thought they'd met and married in later life. They had loved each other for more than forty years and I knew nothing about it. The fluttering inside me has escaped and is running riot through my body, down my arms and into my fingers and my legs are trembling. They had a son together. Alex. They felt they had to hide him from me. She was *his* mother. Not mine. No, not my mother. Alex is not my brother; he's my . . what? What is he? He's my nephew. I'm his aunt! *She* was my sister; not my mother.

I pick up the photograph again of the couple with the picnic. *That's* my mother. The woman in the picture. She's the one. The photograph falls from my shaking fingers.

Deborah is beside me with a glass of water.

'Here,' she says. 'Take this, Audrey. You look a bit faint.'

I take a sip and they wait for me. My head begins to clear.

'It all seems very complicated, John. It doesn't make sense to me.'

'Jean had her reasons for wanting to hide the truth from you, Audrey,' he sighs. 'I went along with it for her sake. It was important to her that nothing spoiled your memories of her, but as she grew older she began to regret the deception.'

He reaches into the inside pocket of his jacket and hands me a letter.

'She still couldn't face up to you. So she asked me to give you this letter. I was to give it to you once you'd learned the truth and you were ready to go back home. But you decided to stay, and it just got harder and harder to tell you.'

Again, I search their faces. I read their kind and loving eyes, their caring expressions. My face is hot and I feel foolish. They have all known this secret for so many years and I am an outsider; I am apart from them, on the edge, marginalised.

'It would have been better for all of us if I'd never come,' I say.

'No,' John says. He gets up and moves around the table, taking the seat next to me. He makes me look into his eyes.

'It's better for it all to come out,' he says. 'I know it must be very difficult for you, and I blame myself for not persuading Jean to tell you before. But, well, we managed for so long pretending that Jean lived alone in Wells, and then later on, when you had started your own family, Jean came to visit you in Australia.'

'But I always wrote to the house in Wells. So your sister would bring the letters to you here in Walsingham,' I say, working things out as I speak,' and that's why mother always used to tell me she didn't like using the phone. It wasn't that she was nervous about it, was it? It was because she wasn't actually there. She was here. In this house. *This* house.'

I remember my first sight of the cottage and how I'd always felt that it was just the sort of home my mother would have loved. And the garden! It was *her* garden. The flowers that grew around the front door and the shrubs and bulbs in the borders were *her* choices. I find that I am smiling because she finally got the garden she wanted; at last, she had her choice of cut flowers to bring indoors.

I look at the furniture. *Her* furniture. It was she who had polished the walnut dining table to its beautiful warm glow. It was *her* china in the cupboards that I'd been using since I arrived. But what about John? It was his home too. He had lost his wife *and* his home.

'For goodness sake, John,' I say to him. 'You gave up your own home for me to stay in. Why did you do that? Where have you been staying?'

'At Margaret's,' he says simply. 'It seemed the right thing to do.'

An image of a man's overcoat hanging behind one of the bedroom doors at the house in Wells crosses my mind, and I understand. I gaze deeply into all their faces, their kindly smiling faces and I am amazed and delighted by the love I see there. Maria Theresa was right. There is nothing to be afraid of. I am not an outsider, after all. I am part of them.

'You must come home, John,' I say. 'There must be other places I could rent.'

'No,' he says adamantly. 'This is your home now. It's what Jean would have liked. In any case, I'm very settled at Margaret's and she likes having me there. It's not so strange, brother and sister living together in their old age. We get along with each other.'

'But it was Alex's home, too,' I add.

Alex laughs. 'If you're happy here that's all that matters, Audrey. We're not that much into polishing all these old bits of wood, are we Al?' he looks at his wife. She smiles back at him.

'I didn't know what to do about the rent money,' John tells me. 'I didn't want to take it, you see. It's not as if I need it or anything. Only, it would have made you very suspicious at the outset if I hadn't. I've opened up a special account for it and we can decide what to do with it later.'

'I don't expect to live rent free, John,' I say.

'We're all in this together,' he smiles. 'We'll decide together.'

Deborah catches my eye. 'Do you mind if I ask something?' she says.

'No, of course not,' I tell her. 'What did you want to know?'

'I'd just like to know who you really are, Audrey. I'm sorry to sound so ridiculous, but it's so fascinating, and I'm really curious about it. Who *were* Hilda and George?'

I pick up the photograph of them and realise that I can't answer Deborah's question.

'Is this the only picture of them, John?' I ask.

'There aren't many. That one was Jean's favourite, but there are others here.'

He slides one of the albums across the table. There are photographs of a party with people in fancy dress. My parents are dressed in Roman togas made from bed sheets. They look like old time movie stars, posing extravagantly for the camera. There's another of Hilda in her bus conductress' uniform, looking slightly stiff and proud.

'May I borrow these albums for a while, John?' I ask him and he nods his agreement.

'What happened to him, John? My father? You say that my real mother died when I was born, but what happened to my father?'

Again, John appears sheepish. He doesn't want to tell me and he grasps his hands together, rubbing his fingers, rocking in his seat.

'John?' I ask again.

'He was ill for a time. Jean told me it was all too much for him, just when the war had ended and everybody else was so happy, and he was so miserable because Hilda had just died. Jean and Ronnie looked after you and when George was better he wanted to take you with him.'

'And?' I press him.

'Jean couldn't give you up. You were her little girl. Ronnie felt the same. They loved you, Audrey. They all loved you.'

'It must have been a terrible time,' Deborah says. 'I can't imagine how awful it must have been for all of them.'

'Well anyway,' John continues, 'George got married again and went abroad with his new wife.'

I turn the pages of the albums, glancing briefly at the reminders of my past, promising myself to come back to them and study them more closely, make the images fit into the new pattern of my life, the real one, the true one. I have to look at these photographs again with different eyes.

'So I was never Audrey *Logan*, was I?' I exclaim. 'Who was I then? What was my real maiden name? Thompson? Yes. I must have been Audrey Thompson.'

There is silence around the table. We all look to John for the answer. He coughs and shakes his head.

'I don't know, Audrey,' he tells me. 'You had different fathers. Jean's maiden name was Thompson. But I don't know yours.'

'What?' I say in disbelief. 'You don't remember?'

'No.'

'Didn't mother tell you?' I can't say her name. I can't say didn't *Jean* tell you?'

'If she did, I've forgotten,' he replies. 'I'm sorry, Audrey, but you've got to remember that I never knew them. I never met either of them. It wasn't something important to me that I had to remember. They were a part of Jean's life long before the two of us. I'm sorry.'

I feel as if I'm on a fairground ride, being spun and twisted, thrown from side to side, turned upside down and knocked and buffeted by the morning's revelations. I hold my head in my hands and sigh.

'Don't you remember anything about him?' Deborah asks on my behalf.

'Only that he was from Poland originally. I do remember that it was an unusual name, but I honestly can't say what it was. I wouldn't even recognise it if I saw it written down,' he says.

'What name did you have on your birth certificate, Audrey?' Deborah asks me.

'Logan, of course. That's who I thought I was. Mother, *Jean* must have registered me as Logan.'

I get up from the table and stretch my back.

'Look,' I say. 'It doesn't matter. It's all so long since that it doesn't matter.' I rest my hand on John's shoulder. 'I'm glad you told me, John,' I tell him. 'It doesn't change anything. I love living here, and here is where I intend to stay. Maybe she put the rest of the story in the letter. You'll understand if I don't read it just yet. Anyway,' I add, 'I've got a whole new family now, haven't I?'

Alison joins me and takes my hand.

'I'm so glad you feel that way,' she says. 'We all are.'

Deborah still looks puzzled and I can see there's something else she's curious about.

'What is it?' I ask her.

She searches for the right words. 'It's about the rest home, Audrey. You know, the religious retreat. I'm sorry to be a nuisance, but don't you want to know about that?'

John nods his head. 'Yes,' he says. 'You might think that was an unusual arrangement. It couldn't be simpler, really. Jean did a lot of sewing for the Priory. She was very good at making women's undergarments. She met Mother Maria Theresa one day in the gardens and got talking about the roses. Maria Theresa snagged her habit on some thorns and Jean repaired it for her. One thing led to another. They trusted her to make all their repairs. It's a small group of women at the Priory and they didn't have anybody who could sew to Jean's standards. Then, when she took up her cross-stitching she made some decorative samplers for them.'

'So they became close friends?' I ask him.

'That's right, and religion didn't have anything to do with it. They just liked each other. Maria Theresa was delighted with the altar cloth Jean embroidered for them.'

'Ah,' I say. 'That's what she must have been referring to when she told me they had some of her beautiful work in the chapel. Maria Theresa invited me to the Christmas Eve service,' I explain.

'Good,' John says. 'We shall all go together then.'

Out of the corner of my eye I notice Alison and Deborah are having a private chat and the next thing I know, our visitors are putting on their coats and taking their leave. I hear them telling me goodbye and saying we'll meet again soon. I smile and wave them off and follow Deborah into the sitting room, where I flop onto one of the sofas.

'Put your feet up, Audrey,' Deborah is telling me, and I swing my legs up and lie back against the cushions with child-like obedience. She disappears and comes back with a throw from my bed which she arranges over me and I make no objections although I don't understand why she is doing it. I'm not tired.

'You're shivering,' she tells me. 'You've had a shock. Close your eyes, Audrey. Try to relax.'

I let my lids close, and feel my body sinking into the comfort of the cushions. Gradually, the twitching in my legs ceases and the warmth and softness of the cover lulls me into a doze.

I'm floating on a cloud of memories, sailing through the sky, riding along on the spine of a photograph album, bucking and dodging, leaping over grey clouds and heading towards a setting sun. All around me are faces from the album shining out from their own pink fluffy frames. There's my real father, Polish George with his moustache and thick spectacles, and there's Ronnie Logan, the man who wanted to be my father, with his thin face and legs.

Faces are smiling at me out of their candy floss clouds as I ride past them: Hilda, in her working uniform, blowing kisses at me as she falls asleep and Jean, the woman who could not give me up, holding out her arms to take me with her, vaulting over church spires and steeples, skipping past the dark places, leaping, running, flying together arm in arm, and waving at the geese and babies playing together on their own soft clouds.

We fly towards the setting sun and watch as it turns into a fire, the flames licking around the great green head of a magical all-powerful wizard.

FORTY EIGHT

Deborah is sitting opposite me, looking at me over the top of her magazine.

'Hello,' she says. 'You're awake, then. Do you feel better now?'

'Yes, thank you. How long have I been asleep?'

'About an hour or so,' she tells me. 'That's all.'

'What time is it? I'm hungry.'

'I'm not surprised,' she says. 'You missed lunch. It's four 'o clock. Would you like me to make you something?' She lays down the magazine she has been reading and gets up.

'No. Let's go out,' I say. 'I could do with some fresh air.'

'Are you sure, Audrey?' she asks. 'It's cold and dark outside.'

'Just what I need,' I say, swinging my legs off the sofa and reaching for my handbag. 'We'll walk down to the pub and see what's on their menu, shall we?'

The air is crisp and cold. The short walk revives me and I feel ready to face the world again. Christmas stars hanging from street lights swing in the breeze, twinkling over the pavement and cars parked outside the high street shops. The butcher waves to me as we pass, the postmistress mouths *Merry Christmas* through the window, and my spirits soar with the glow of well-being. I have found where I belong. Here, in this small corner of England, surrounded by friends and a newly-found family, I have discovered contentment. I've learned what it means to be at peace with oneself. I have been truly loved. I still am. What more is there to need?

There's a small group at the bar in the Dog and Gun. I recognise one or two faces and they send across their greetings as Deborah and I choose a table by the hearth. We sit in comfort, basking in the heat from the log fire and sipping a nicely warmed Shiraz.

'You look different,' Deborah says.

'Do I? How? In what way?' I ask her.

'Like the cat who got the cream,' she laughs.

I laugh with her. It's true. It's a wonderful feeling.

'Thank you for your support this morning,' I say to her.

'It was nothing. It's only what you would have done for me. *Have done* for me, Audrey.'

'Well, it means a lot. I'm glad you were there.'

'It was a lot to deal with, all at once like that,' she says.

'Mmm,' I agree. 'Audrey, the mystery woman. Half Yorkshire, half Polish, but we don't know exactly who the father was, thought her sister was her mother, married an Australian and finished up in Norfolk.'

'You couldn't make it up,' she says. 'Nobody would believe you. You should write it all down. It would make a cracking good story.'

'No, I don't think so, Deborah,' I reply. 'I'm no writer. In any case, there's so much of it that I shall never know. No, the truth of it all is lost in time, isn't it? I shall never really know what happened.'

Deborah shakes her head. 'It's such a shame John can't tell you George's surname. You can't begin to research into it without a name to go on.'

'I'm not going to, Deborah,' I tell her. 'I'm going to leave it alone. It's too late now. Besides, there are other things I want to do. I've found a small foundry specialising in casting artworks. I'm going to give it a go.'

'Brilliant!' she says. 'Will it be expensive?'

'Yes, if I never sell. But no, if people want to buy what I make.'

'Oh, go for it,' she says.

We choose from the menu and sit, like two old cronies revelling in the simple pleasures of friendship, food and conversation.

'When will you read Jean's letter?' Deborah asks me.

'Tonight,' I say. 'When we get back.'

'And you'll know that you're reading it in *her* house, Audrey, surrounded by *her* things. I should think that would be very comforting for you. It's so fitting, isn't it?'

I agree with her. I shall have a better picture of the woman who wanted to be my mother. It won't be the whole story, but then, none of us ever knows that. Maybe we're not meant to.

EPILOGUE

NOVEMBER 2010

When I think of my mother I find it so easy to remember her face. It's still the face of Jean Thompson that I see and it makes me proud she was really my sister. They were remarkable women, Hilda and Jean, mother and daughter, loving and strong, and they gave of themselves to the end to protect and care for those they loved.

Their story couldn't happen in today's moral and social climate, where we have television talk shows covering every subject under the sun, where we're expected to bring everything out into the open to reach that desirable state of closure. My real mother and my sister were bound by the expectations of a former age where honesty was not encouraged. It was simply too shameful to live with the reality of family problems.

Mother Maria Theresa's advice has helped me accept all of this and so it's easier to understand why Jean felt she must continue the illusion throughout the years. I read her last letter with tears in my eyes. It was full of love and regret. We all make mistakes; nobody is perfect and of course that includes me.

I'm still trying to patch things up with Malcolm. I understand now many of the misunderstandings between us came about as a result of his neurological differences. I saw the signs; I knew he wasn't like other children through his developing years and I didn't do enough to help his father come to terms with it. But, to use another current expression, I'm not going to beat myself up about it. Malcolm has found his soul-mate in Angela. They are alike.

As Madeleine once pointed out to me, we all need to be with our own kind. It doesn't matter that what makes them happy would drive me mad. I must allow them to be different in their own way. Malcolm is never going to be the man I wished him to be. He's never going to be the son I wished for, and that's not his fault. It's not mine either. It is what it is. I doubt he'll come to visit me in England. He wouldn't see the point. He doesn't feel emotional ties in the same way as the rest of us.

As for the others who have made this journey with me, I rejoice in my new found wider family. My nephew, Alex has accepted me with kindness and generosity. His wife Alison has become a lovely friend. I watch their children's budding careers with fascination: Christina has won her first role on the professional stage and Laura eagerly awaits London 2012. It's rather fine to be their great aunt Audrey.

Grandad John Starling continues to be the character he always was, keeping himself busy, loving his new business role. He is bemused by the success of his creative venture and shares his ideas for new designs with me.

Madeleine often emails me from Wales. She's gone back to college to study for a degree in Child Psychology while Christopher is in nursery. They have limited contact with Luke.

Deborah is still staying with me at the cottage and works at the Barns managing sales for John Starling. She looks better and is happier now she's no longer so emotionally drained. It still surprises me I was so taken in by Philip's false façade. It's a pity he couldn't find the strength to support Deborah when she needed him, but I think it's working out for the best. She's had more tests recently and all seems well.

Matilda the goose is with her own kind too, where she belongs, but her image, like the face of my mother, will stay with me forever. She was literally a flying visitor in my life who stayed for the briefest time, and in that short episode changed everything.

Who would have guessed the impact of my paintings and bronzes of a goose playing with a baby? Who could have foreseen the popularity of *Walsingham Matilda*? I didn't. Yet an exhibition of my work opens tonight at The Forum and I am to be wined and dined by city dignitaries.

Other Norfolk names are also celebrated, including the soprano, Sophia Polanski. It's a strange feeling to be included in such an illustrious gathering. Naturally, Deborah is thrilled to have the opportunity to hear her sing. We're having a party afterwards at the cottage. That should give old Shrek head on the kitchen window sill something to grin about. I've been so lucky.

As I enter the reception area at The Forum cameras flash. My agent hurries across the room to take me on one side before we take our places at table.

'Audrey,' she says, 'there's a gentleman would like a moment of your time before the formalities get under way. He's very old but very perky. Says he's ninety five and it's getting past his bedtime.'

I can see the old man sitting at the back with a young man by his side.

◆

Lost in his thoughts, the old man was considering his life and the strange turns of fate that had brought him to this place. He spent a lot of his time in nostalgic day-dreaming, and often, when he woke from an afternoon nap, he had to remind himself he was ninety-five years old and that during his lifetime he had much to be thankful for.

He'd made many good choices. He'd experienced much of the best things any man could hope for, and now his granddaughter, Sophia was reaping the benefits of some of those choices.

Look at her, he thought as he caught sight of her holding court amidst a clamouring rabble of photographers and media types. *Like a film star.* She knew how to handle them. She had her grandmother's charm, her confidence. She exuded glamour and they swarmed around her like moths flitting at a light.

She was a leading name in the heady world of prima donnas and grand opera houses. Her dressing rooms were sumptuously furnished and decorated with vast urns of roses. Invitations came from around the world. She sang at command performances in all the royal houses of Europe. She moved in a glittering circle of chauffeur-driven saloons, penthouse suites and private jets sent to whisk her elegantly to grace the opening of the next new hotel in Dubai, where her concert performances commanded fees the like of which would have seemed impossible when he was her age. Sophia's diamond necklaces, worlds removed from the paste imitations of the war years, symbolised for him the ultimate success of the poor Polish immigrant and his family.

He nodded wistfully and smiled quietly at his grandson sitting next to him. Andrew was doing well, not in the same superstar way as his sister, but he was a likeable young man with talents of his own and one day the world would recognise it.

The old man patted his chest. In the inside pocket of his jacket, next to his heart, he carried fading photographs of those who had not lived to see this day: the family he had loved and lost, his son and daughter-in-law, Sophia and Andrew's parents taken from him in the same flying accident as his own dear wife. Sophia grew more like her each year. Sandra would have been so proud.

◆

I approach the old man gently. It looks as if he has nodded off.

'Hello,' I say. 'How are you? You wanted to have a word?'

He stirs and shakes himself, but remains seated.

'This is my grandson, Mrs Freeman,' he says very formally, 'and we'd both like to say how much we admire your work.'

'Thank you. Are you staying for the reception?'

His young companion replies.

'Yes. My sister's singing.'

'Your sister is Sophia Polanski?'

'Yes, that's right.'

'From Canada?'

'Yes. Grandad here brought us to England when I was quite small. We live in Norfolk now. I'm teaching at the Art College. That's where I first read about you.'

'Well then, I'm sure you know more about the art world than I do,' I tell him.

'Ah, but knowing is not the same as doing, is it?' he says with a grin.

'And you are a doer?'

'One day. Hope so.'

He shrugs his shoulders and the old man pats his hand.

'I'll look out for your work then,' I tell him, 'and hope I'm still around for your first exhibition.'

'It's a deal,' he smiles.

'So who shall I look out for?'

'Andrew Pozyzcka. Don't worry about the spelling. Nobody can ever spell my name. That's why Sophia changed it to Polanski. It's easier to remember. Grandad here didn't like that at all. Says he'll disown me if I do the same.'

I raise my hand in goodbye and wish him luck as I turn to join the party and I can see the old man is still shaking his head in disapproval.

'Fliss,' I say to my agent Felicity as we make our way toward the stage and the top table. 'Have you any contacts at City Art College? I'd like to make some enquiries about that young man. There's something different about him.'

ABOUT THE AUTHOR

Celia Micklefield was born in Keighley, West Yorkshire. After a career in teaching she left England to live in France where she was inspired to write her second novel, Trobairitz the Storyteller. She returned to the UK and now lives in Norfolk where she continues writing novels and short stories.

Her website is www.celiamicklefield.com
You can find her
@CMicklefield on Twitter
Celia Micklefield FaceBook author page.

More books by Celia Micklefield

TROBAIRITZ the Storyteller
a contemporary female troubadour entertains a group of drivers at an overnight truck stop in southern France by telling them a fascinating story.

THE SANDMAN and MRS CARTER
A dark, pyschological drama narrated by five named characters and a mystery voice.

QUEER AS FOLK
A second collection of short stories full of people's quirks and foibles.

ARSE(D) ENDS
A first collection of short stories inspired by words ending in the letters a.r.s.e.

PEOPLE WHO HURT
Abusers and codependants - looking for answers.
A memoir.

A MEASURED MAN
to be published in spring 2021

We hope you've enjoyed Patterns of Our Lives. Your review would be most welcome.